D0993208

# DARK OBSESSION

Second Book in the

CELTIC MAGIC TRILOGY

BY KATHY MORGAN

This book is a work of fiction. Names, places, characters, and incidents are either a product of the author's imagination or are used fictitiously. Any resemblance to actual persons, living or dead, incidents, or locales is entirely coincidental.

Published in the United States by Dreamweaver Publishing, Atlanta, Georgia

Copyright 2016 by Kathy Morgan Rosenthal

ISBN 13: 978-0692764077 (Dreamweaver Publishing)
ISBN 10: 0692764070

All rights reserved/ This book, or any portion thereof, may not be reproduced or used in any manner whatsoever, without the express written permission of the publisher, except for the use of brief quotations in a book review.

Cover design by Diana Buidoso
Interior layout by Thomas White
Author photo by Paige Sweany

# *Dedications*

To Brad, my real-life romantic hero. Thanks for always being by my side, for making me laugh heartily, feel deeply, and learn things (like math) that I had never wanted to know. Most of all, thank you for your patience with my obsession, with all of my writing and endless re-writing, and all the times I've been 'in the zone', instead of present where you are. I love you!

To my esteemed Editor, who also happens to be my loving son, Eli Price. You, my darling, are a genius. Thanks for your almost OCD-attention to detail, and for knowing when to stand your ground and push me on an editorial change, and when to recognize the irrational creativity of an author and just let it go. I love you, honey.

And, as always, my endless love and appreciation goes out to you, Mom. A fellow lover of words, you instilled in my heart, as a young child, an insatiable love for reading and writing. I feel your encouragement in everything I do, and know that you're up there always rooting for me. I miss you, Mom, more than mere words can say.

# *Chapter One*

It was as it had been before the dawn of time, with eternal night hovering again above creation's horizon. It was a darkness comprised, not of nothingness as before, but of the impermeable blackness of a great demon-spawned iniquity, an entity so malignant that for countless millennia it had been forbidden the light of day. Hidden secrets were bound in the earth's molten core where, throughout endless ages, the ancient Evil had lain imprisoned in a pit of immeasurable darkness.

And as night descended across the land, Hades held its breath in wicked anticipation. As prophesied, there were wars and rumors of war, every thought of man evil continually. And yet, this juncture in time was only the commencement of troubles. In the beginning, humankind had been given dominion over the earth, but relinquished their leasehold in the early moments of creation. While there had been no redemption for the fallen angels cast out of heaven, full transfer of earth's title to the god of this world had been withheld, until weak and selfish man might consider an offer of atonement for their inequity.

Chance after chance, they had been given. The Great Flood. Deliverance from a tyrannical Egyptian ruler. A virgin birth. Even a divinely ordained death and resurrection offered for their deliverance. And still they continued to shun the light, self-propelled toward the very darkness they embraced.

If it was darkness they desired, then darkness they would surely have. For millennia, the Fallen Angel, Balthazar, next in line only to Lucifer himself, had stood guard over the Underworld while the

Prince of Demons slept. Since the casting of the *Geis,* evil spirits had roved, to and fro, throughout the earth. Seeking, watching, they awaited each appearance of the Woman of Promise, as surely as did those for whom she was prophesied to bring deliverance. Once, twice in millennia past, this Chosen One had been thwarted, as Balthazar sent forth his Minion to possess the soul of a willing mortal. Through this godless individual, easily manipulated by the powers of perdition, the Minion had used every weapon in his demonic arsenal against the Woman, bringing the One from the first millenium to madness, from the second millennium to death. And in this third measure of time, all hell was prepared to break loose in the endeavor to put a stop to this Redeemer, she whose role for this final season was to bring about the dissolution of the *Geis.*

For should she succeed in her quest, the Awakening of the great Beast and devil, known also as *An Garda Geis,* Guardian of the Enchantment, would be disavowed. Thus, he would continue to sleep, while the divine timeline would again be reset in man's favor.

Increasingly weary of his responsibility, Balthazar grew impatient now, looking forward to the glorious end of all life as the inhabitants of the earth had known it. And as the Awakening drew ever nearer, his master, the Beast, had at last begun to Dream. And, with the Dreaming, the Fallen Angel felt his burden grow exponentially lighter. Already humanity was straining, striking out one against the other, a sure sign of his master's loosening restraints.

Rules, rules. The meticulous Creator had established a law to govern everything in the cosmos. Gravity, physics, science. The *Geis.* With a great shuddering sigh, Lucifer's lieutenant ministered to the one whose name could not be mentioned upon the earth. *Anathema.* "Not long now, oh great and magnificent Angel of Light, and you will step into your rightful place, finally free to rule from your seat upon the mount of the congregation in the sides of the north."

His whisper echoed throughout the vacuous void that contained him. "Our plans are working well. Even now, all things pure and godly are a joke to most of humanity, laughed at or disdained as unpopular and politically incorrect. Time is short. The residents of earth are coming apart at the seams. They have violated every clause of their contract with the Alpha and Omega, with the One who has always been. At last we, the deserving ones, those first created and unjustly cast from our home in heaven, will take possession of that planet called earth and there secure our permanent home."

Michaela Daniels tapped her foot to the lively beat of a traditional Irish jig, surprised to see the place so packed on a Tuesday night. Taking another swig of her pint of Guinness, she glanced around Dublin's oldest pub, the Brazen Head, purported to date back to the early thirteenth century.

She had arrived in town earlier that day for the Royal Dublin Society Horse Show, an annual event scheduled to take place from August 5th through the 9th. Michaela had competed full-time on the international show jumping circuit for the past six or seven years, ever since she had bailed out of Brown University shortly before earning her degree—a stunt that had almost given her father a coronary. It wasn't so much that he was concerned about her future; no, it wasn't that at all. What had had the old boy slavering at the mouth was that his only child, the honor roll student he bragged about to all of his hoity-toity friends, had wasted all the money he had laid out for her 'keeping-up-with-the-Joneses' Ivy League education.

The next few days should prove interesting, she considered, a half-smile alighting on her lips. Yep, she would be competing against one of her parents' new bloodstock acquisitions in a show long recognized as one of the top equestrian events in the world. No worries. She had every confidence in her prize stallion, Wind Spirit, whom she had named in honor of her Native American heritage on her father's side. Which reminded her, her parents would be arriving in Dublin on their private jet later that night and she was expected to meet them for breakfast first thing in the morning.

*Oh, joy.*

Someone squeezing in beside her at the crowded bar jostled her arm. Dark liquid sloshed over the rim of her pint-sized glass.

"Sorry," a deep male voice apologized.

"No problem." Michaela glanced up with a forgiving smile. And froze.

*Oh. My. God.*

Eyes, an arctic blue so pale she could almost see herself reflected in them, gazed down at her. Perfect lips curved into a bad-boy grin. The man's hair, parted in the center, caressed his masculine jaw line in a scrunchy wave. It was the same dirty-blonde color as Brad Pitt's, and he was sporting the same smokin' *Achilles* body, too. Oh yeah, definitely a bad boy, she thought, checking out his black leather jacket and the worn studded jeans.

*Damn.*

"With the horse show starting tomorrow, the place is totally chock-a-block." The rusty voice with the sexy Irish accent went down smooth, but then finished with an unexpected jolt. Bailey's Irish Cream spiked with a double-shot of Jameson.

"Another Guinness?" He nodded at her glass. "Least I can do is replace what I spilt."

"Thanks."

He ordered two pints of Guinness and a G and T.

*Gin and tonic, a lady's drink.* Of course. Dude who looked like that wouldn't be here alone.

His fingers tapped impatiently on the bar. As he shifted his position, the movement stirred a subtle masculine scent that made her want to rub up against him like a cat. She breathed him in and purred.

He glanced down at her thoughtfully, and smiled. "You live in Dublin?"

"No, my first time in the city."

He fixed those fascinating eyes on her again. *Wow.* She felt the force of that gaze all the way to her core. Never—*ever*—had a man affected her like that.

"Ah, an American, is it?" He propped a worn leather boot on the brass footrest that extended from the front of the bar.

"Yep. In town for the horse show."

"As am I myself," he said. "An exhibitor, are you?"

She nodded. "Yeah, but I'm also jumping. My own horse. You?"

His expression darkened. "I'm with someone who owns several of the animals on the schedule this week." He deftly changed the subject. "You're here on your own, then?"

"Unfortunately. A friend of mine from County Clare was supposed to meet me here." She gave a rueful grin. "Except Arianna went and got herself preggers. And since she's due to pop any day now, her husband isn't letting her out of his sight."

The interest in his expression sharpened. "Arianna? From Clare? That wouldn't be the MacNamaras, would it?"

"That's them. Friends of yours?"

"We're…business associates," the Irishman hedged. "Name's Liam, by the way. Liam O'Neill. From County Kerry."

She checked his ring finger and, finding it bare, offered her best flirtatious smile. "Very pleased to meet you, Liam O'Neill from County Kerry. I'm Michaela Daniels from Biddeford, Maine."

The bartender set the drinks down. Liam moved a Guinness in front of Michaela, before paying with a colorful twenty-euro note. As she was raising her glass to take another sip of the first beer, her arm was jarred again. *Really?* Beer spilled down the front of her shirt.

"Sorry." The sultry-voiced female inserting herself between Michaela and the hot Irishman beside her sounded anything but.

"Is there a problem with the drinks?" The obvious remark directed at Liam made his lips thin. The guy looked seriously annoyed. "You've been delayed a wee while, pet."

Michaela grabbed a napkin off the bar and swiped at her shirt, which left pieces of white tissue embedded in the gold and black knit.

"Michaela, meet Aideen," Liam said abruptly. "She's the one owns the horses I'm just after mentioning. Aideen, Michaela's a show jumper riding her own entry this year."

Aideen's hair was a rich auburn color, cut short in a pixie style that dipped strategically over one eye. No doubt meant to draw attention to the strange, sparkling lavender of her irises.

Colored contacts?

Supermodel thin and tall—only slightly shorter than Liam's approximately six feet—she looked haughtily down her nose at Michaela, who didn't top five-two in three-inch heels.

Michaela stopped herself from sticking her tongue out at the woman. But only just.

*Very mature, Michaela.* Still, she couldn't help but feel stupidly pleased that she had taken time with her appearance before heading out for the evening. Caught at the crown of her head with a golden clip, her waist-length black hair streamed down her back, creating the effect of a long, shiny fall. Her dark brown eyes she had outlined in a black kohl pencil. Her top, the one now smelling like a brewery, was long and fitted snugly over a pair of calf-length, black leggings. Which—if she did say so herself—looked spectacular with the gold and black, spindly-heeled sandals she was wearing.

Liam handed Aideen the gin and tonic. "I'll meet you back at the table straight away." Clearly dismissed, the other woman sent a sneer in Michaela's direction before stomping away.

"I hope that won't leave a stain," Liam murmured as Michaela took one last swipe at her top.

"No biggie," she said, sliding off the barstool and hooking her purse over one arm. "Maybe I'll see you tomorrow at the horse show."

"I'll make it a point." His voice dropped an octave. "Sure, I'm looking forward to seeing you ride." A crooked smile accompanied the double-entendre, sending her stomach into a long loop-de-loop.

*Dude is definitely trouble*, she mused.

Not to be outdone, however, Michaela slipped on her light jacket and gave him the 'come hither' motion with her index finger. As he leaned his head down, she whispered in his ear, "You want to watch me ride? I can assure you, you won't be disappointed."

Feeling smug to have gotten the last word in the sexy exchange, she gathered her hair out of the collar of her jacket with one hand and, with a secret smile on her lips, left the pub without looking back.

✧

Liam collected Michaela's untouched drink, along with his own, and carried them to the table. "Bought her a pint, did you?" Aideen spoke in Gaelic, a pout in her husky voice.

He gave a long sigh of exasperation. *Shite.* He had been seeing the woman only a few short weeks and already she was clingy and demanding. "Considering that we took turns spilling her first drink all over her, I bought her another, aye. You've a problem with that?"

"Not a'tall. I'd not be wasting a thought on that little *mortal* slag." She said the word as if it were a venereal disease.

"I'm growing bored, Aideen."

"I can remedy that, *a ghrá*. Let's go back to our room. You know, if we were living together—"

"*Aideen....*"

But she was not to be deterred by the warning tone of his voice. "Wasn't I after recognizing you as my *anam cara* on our first meeting. And I've expressed my willingness to sacrifice my life for eight months, take on the shape of a rugby ball and go through countless hours of birthing torment to provide you an heir—"

Liam's eyes grew hard. "We've been together casually for three weeks. Any talk of an *heir* would be premature at this point. And don't be getting any bold ideas in that lovely head of yours, either." Women of his race controlled conception by the strength of their will alone. Liam knew he would be bleeding damned before being shackled with a responsibility to which he had not agreed. "Besides, you know yourself, we've less than three months remaining until the end of—"

"Sure, you're not after believing that bloody bollocks." Her tone dripped with contempt.

For a few seconds, magic crackled in the air between them, male ire pitted against feminine resentment. Still edgy and aroused from his encounter with the wee mortal vixen, Liam drove his fingers through his hair. As always, the tousled strands only fell forward again, framing his face.

He shoved his chair back and stood to his feet, fire burning in his eyes. He held his hand out to his companion. "We'll be retiring to our room now."

Anticipation shivered through Aideen's body as her eyes traversed Liam's form, stopping pointedly on the front of his trousers. A smug smile touched her plump, too-red lips. Apparently presuming that the aroused state of him had something to do with her, she slipped a manicured hand into his much larger one and slithered out of her chair.

Pillows stuffed behind her back, Michaela sat propped against the headboard of the bed in her hotel room, her cell phone to her ear. "Hey, girl, so what's the word? Got an ETA on my new little nephew?"

"You make it sound like he's being delivered via UPS."

"Well, that would make it a lot easier, wouldn't it, sweetie?"

"God, I feel like a freaking beached whale. I'm swollen all over and my back's killing me. He'll probably grow up to be a soccer player, if my abused kidneys are any indication."

"Oh, babe, I'm sorry you're feeling so miserable. I'll be there in a few days to take your mind off of it."

"With any luck the 'wee fella', as Caleb's taken to calling him, will be making an appearance before that."

"But you're only about eight months along. Shouldn't you have a few more weeks to go?"

"Watch your mouth, girl!" Arianna snapped. "Actually, the gestation period for *Tu*—uh, I mean, for babies in Caleb's family runs about a month short. Not to worry, though, because the doctor assures us the baby's already at his full birth weight and perfectly healthy."

"Well, good. I'm off the circuit for a few weeks, so you can put Auntie Michaela down for one of the midnight feedings."

"You're on. Now tell me, what kind of trouble have you been getting into all alone in our capital city?"

"Well, if Dublin men are anything like the one from Kerry I just met in the bar, I'm moving here permanently," Michaela declared.

"Do tell." There was a dry smile in Arianna's voice.

"God, Arianna, this dude was, like, seriously hot. I think I'm in love."

"Well, I'm glad to see you're behaving yourself at least. Back in your own room at a decent hour."

"No choice. He was with some high-fashion bimbo with legs that stretched all the way to her tonsils." Michaela paused, took a sip of the Sprite she had snagged from the mini-bar.

"A girlfriend, or just a date?"

"She was acting all possessive like, but the vibe I got off him was that she hadn't closed the deal." She tugged the clip from her hair. "Said he knew you guys."

"No kidding." Arianna got quiet. "Um, did you get his name?"

"Really? You think I'd let something like that get away without an introduction? Name's Liam O'Neill."

Arianna made a humming sound on the other end of the line.

"Why? The guy an ax murderer or something?"

"Nah, nothing like that. I've just heard he has issues."

"Yeah, don't we all?" Michaela crossed her ankle over her knee and picked at the lint attaching itself to her leggings.

"I guess. So, you still meeting your parents tomorrow for breakfast?"

"Just shoot me already and put me out of my misery," came the droll reply. "Anyway, in order to—*so graciously*—fit me into their busy schedule, we're going to be eating at the butt-crack of dawn. And you know me and early mornings."

Arianna grunted in the affirmative.

"So guess I'd better go now and get some shut-eye." She picked up the remote control and flicked on the television for company. "See you Sunday, sweetie."

❧

'Twas a new time, a new age. The thought came to the Chief Brehon as he sat at his desk in the castle solar connected to eight of the other members of the Council by means of a bloody *videoconference*. Though the Internet connection was secured, the group communicated only in their true native tongue, a language not of this world and known by none other than the Council members. A vital element, he considered, given the seriousness of the situation plaguing the planet at present.

For almost three thousand years, meetings of the Council of Brehons had been held annually in Scotland. They were purposely scheduled away from the members' Irish homeland so that their discussions wouldn't be intercepted and carried back to the lair of the sleeping Beast by his demons and imps. But with the deadline for fulfillment of the *Geis* now less than three months away, the dark Enchantment that had plagued his people for three millennia was at risk of becoming set in place and immutable. An event that would threaten the very existence of all human kind.

The unveiling of the Woman of Promise was imminent. At the end of each thousand-year period since the laying of the Enchantment, a mere mortal had been drawn by the Fates from across the sea, and propelled into an attempt to contravene the impossible terms of dissolution of the *Geis.* The requirements were stringent. She could not be aware of the existence of either his people, the *Túatha de Danann*, or the *Geis* that had kept them bound. Each time, it had been the woman's love for one of their leaders that led her blindly in search of the location of an ancient artifact. A single misstep on her part, or theirs, would disqualify her instantly from the quest.

Both times in the past the women had failed—and suffered greatly for their involvement. After the first thousand years, dating back to the time of Christ, ancient records reveal that the Chosen One had gone irrevocably mad. The next Woman, a thousand years later, had died a horrible death, torn apart by wild animals—or something more sinister. The culprit had never been identified.

And now the third, and final, thousand-year period was racing to an end.

If this millennium's Woman of Promise failed in her task, all life on earth that would not only end, it would end badly.

When he had met his new wife, Arianna, just under a year ago, Caleb MacNamara believed that she was a mere mortal, perhaps even the long-awaited Chosen One. But signals had been crossed because of her mixed parentage. Her mortal father, recently deceased when they had met, had raised her in the States, choosing to conceal from her all knowledge of the magic in her heritage. Poor man had been forever broken-hearted when his wife, a water sprite, had left himself and his daughter to return to the Land beneath the Waves. Understandably, he had feared losing his daughter in a similar fashion.

All members had now logged on, he noted. Except Liam, o'course. "Who's apparently after finding something more important to do with his time," Caleb grumbled under his breath before calling the meeting to order.

## *Chapter Two*

The private dining room in Dublin's Merrion Hotel was all ornate wood, crystal chandeliers, and Old World elegance. "Sit up in your chair, Michaela. You're slumping again," her mother scolded, then sighed. "This Irish weather is so damp, it makes such a mess of my hair."

Michaela shook her head. Her mother's bit part in her first motion picture in 1979 had brought Sarah Woods fame—and fortune, when she attracted the attention of now sixty-five-year-old movie mogul, Terrence Daniels, whose Native American dark good looks hadn't tarnished with age.

And, while her parents fought like the proverbial cat and dog, the man worshipped the very ground his shallow wife glided upon. Accrediting her success and opulent lifestyle to her fragile, blonde beauty, Sarah, at age fifty-five now, was battling time with every weapon in the plastic surgeon's arsenal.

"You're beautiful, sweetheart," Michaela's father cajoled, his hand covering his wife's on the white Irish linen tablecloth.

*Gag.* "If you'll excuse me for a minute, Sarah, Dad, I'm going to the powder room."

By any standard, Michaela's relationship with her mother had always been distant, weird. Requiring Michaela to address her by her first name, she had said it just wouldn't do for her fans to know she had a child. And certainly not now, when that child was twenty-eight years old.

Why in hell did she continue to put herself through the torment of their company? She grumbled inwardly as she stomped down the hall like a petulant child. Passing the public dining room to her left, she glanced inside. And smiled. Liam, the gorgeous guy from the previous evening was sitting at a table in the corner with his supermodel girlfriend. He looked up. Ice-blue eyes connected with hers.

And caught fire.

Michaela stopped and stared, mesmerized by the contact. Frozen to the spot, she could feel her heart pick up its pace. Knees weak, her breathing deepened. She had been attracted to men in the past, of course, but it had never been anything like this. The vibes radiating between them were so intense that the woman Liam was with turned in her seat and, frowning, followed the direction of Liam's gaze. Her lips tightened, strange lavender eyes sparked with fury.

A jolt that felt strangely like a massive charge of electricity zapped Michaela out of her mental fog. Stunned and confused for a moment, she gave her head a shake, and then continued down the hall to the restroom.

A cool, sunny breeze stirred the wonderful musky smell of horseflesh as Michaela walked the jumping course. Referring to the paper in her hand, she memorized the layout, pacing off the number of strides between each jump as she planned how to negotiate each twist and turn.

Brought over from the Simmonscourt Pavilion where he had been stabled, Wind Spirit was pawing the ground, prancing and snorting, as she mounted him. "What's wrong, boy? Calm, now." Michaela patted his withers, applying a steady pressure with her thighs to gentle the animal. An experienced Hunter, and usually rock steady, the stallion's uncharacteristic display of nerves was more than a little unsettling.

Even with her petite stature, Michaela sat tall in the saddle. Her Brindley jacket, in a slim-fitting French blue, embraced her curves and provided a clean contrast against her white low-rise, leg-hugging breeches. The soft black leather of her Spanish cut boots rose to her bent knees. When her name rang out over the loudspeaker, she adjusted the chinstrap on her black riding helmet.

As horse and rider flowed together over the soil and grass surface, Wind Spirit leaned into an effortless cantor, and then sailed smoothly over the initial twelve jumps, going clear. They completed the first round successfully, with neither time, nor jumping faults, the demerits assessed against a horse for knocking down an obstacle or disobeying his rider's commands. Since a Jumper competition judged on turnout and style in addition to skill, the course was colorful and creative. Michaela's adrenaline was stoked by the complex and technical obstacles, which included verticals, spreads, double and triple combinations, and a number of turns and changes of direction.

The stallion's movements were bold and powerful, yet fluid. Fast, yet accurate. And though he possessed the long, sweeping stride, the smooth discipline required to compete in the Hunter class, Michaela would never have considered clipping his wings by entering him in the quieter, more conservative competition.

The jump-off round began with a few of the original riders disqualified. Although there were fewer obstacles, the height and spread of the fences were far more difficult, the turns tighter, and the jumps set at unusual distances. Michaela knew she would have to adjust Wind Spirit's stride in order to successfully clear the obstacles.

She inhaled a deep breath and smiled to herself. God, how she thrived on the rush.

Again, Michaela heard her name announced. As she tapped Wind Spirit's flanks with her booted heels to begin the course, her eyes made a casual sweep of the stands. There, to the left of the arena, arms resting on the fence, Liam stood watching her.

Even as the woman he was with watched him.

It was in that split second of distraction that Michaela lost her concentration and faltered. Luckily, she and the magnificent animal beneath her had been a team for over five years and had grown accustomed to covering for one another's mistakes. Reading her invisible signals, the stallion cantered toward the first obstacle with a smooth, easy rhythm. Michaela recovered hastily from her momentary lapse and communicated the spot for the jump. His back up, head reaching forward, lower legs tucked under his forearms and bending at the forelocks, the stallion showed a great bascule, a dolphin-like form, as he flew effortlessly over the fence.

"Focus, Michaela," she muttered, as she reached down and gave the stallion an acknowledging pat. "Thanks for that, buddy. You're a star."

Another fence, and then they were approaching a three-obstacle combination. Wind Spirit took the first fence, then with one stride, two, he cleared the second. But as he was flying over the third and final obstacle, Michaela felt his flesh tremble and she heard a frightened whinny as if something had spooked him. The distraction caused his left foreleg to drop slightly, just enough to tangle with the top rung of the barrier. At that same moment, Michaela felt the saddle shift beneath her. Instinctively, she recognized the instant the leather strap beneath the horse's belly snapped. Suddenly weightless, she couldn't counteract the momentum that was flinging her forward over the stallion's broad head. She grunted as her body slammed into the grassy earth beneath the giant hooves. She rolled into a ball as the animal fought to avoid trampling her, even as he struggled to regain his footing.

There was a sickening crunch. A stunning pain slammed into her left temple.

And the world turned black.

⁂

When Michaela regained consciousness, the pounding in her head was keeping time with the waves of nausea assaulting her. The brightness of the sun was burning her eyes. No, not the sun, she thought confusedly, as she squinted upward at the fluorescent lights overhead. It took a moment or two for her to comprehend that she was on a stretcher in a hospital emergency room hooked up to a beeping monitor. An IV protruded out of one arm. An oxygen thingy was clipped onto her right forefinger. *What the hell?* A few seconds later, recollection of the recent events began to filter through her aching head.

Oh, my God. *Wind Spirit*.... Had he been injured while trying to avoid trampling her?

Michaela attempted to sit up, but the curtained cubicle whirled and spun around her. Vomit climbed its way up the back of her throat and she gagged. With a pained groan, she dropped her head back onto the thinly padded stretcher. "Hello," she called out weakly. "Anybody home?"

A nurse stuck her head around the curtain. "You're back with us, so," she said, in her crisp Irish accent. "You've been unconscious a good while."

Long enough, Michaela discovered, for them to have examined her, taken blood for tests and shot some x-rays. Apparently, she hadn't broken any bones in the fall. Although she had a nasty lump right below her left temple, and was diagnosed with a Grade 3 concussion, she felt fortunate to have escaped a skull fracture. Looked like her new LAS headgear had been a good investment after all.

"Your parents phoned," the nurse informed her. "They said to tell you they've appointments out of town, but will monitor your condition with the nurses' station."

*Nice.* Now, why should that bit of news surprise her? Or bother her, for that matter. "Do you know where my purse is? I need my cell phone to make a call."

A few minutes later, Arianna answered the phone.

"Hey, it's Mick."

"Hey, you. Thought you were jumping today. What's up?"

"Look…I'm fine, okay? So, don't get upset. I just didn't want you to hear about the accident on the news."

"An accident?" Arianna's voice was laced with panic. "My God! Where are you now?"

"Emergency room."

"You're at the hospital? Are you okay, really? What happened?"

"No biggie, I just got thrown is all. Caught a hoof in the head on the way down. I'm in one piece, though. No broken bones or anything. They're wanting to keep me here until tomorrow for observation, but I'm signing myself out. Just wanted you to know I'll be heading over your way when I make my escape."

"You're leaving against doctor's orders? You think that's wise, Michaela?"

"Look, I'm fine. I just want to get out of here."

"I thought your parents were in Dublin. Are they with you?"

"Yeah, right." Michaela gave a cynical huff. "They called while I was knocked out and left a message that they had appointments."

"Well, that's just great. Look, babe, I've been having Braxton Hicks contractions all day long, so it's probably not a good idea for me to come to Dublin. But, if you're determined to leave the hospital, I'll send Caleb over in the chopper to pick you up."

"No way, José. If you go into full-blown labor, you're going to need your husband there to help you."

"Yeah, what was I thinking? He wouldn't go, anyway. The man's not giving me a minute's peace. I can't even go to the freaking bathroom alone. Hmm, wait a minute. I have another idea. I'll call you right back."

About five minutes later, the phone rang. "Okay, here's the deal," Arianna said. "You know that guy you met? Caleb's friend, Liam? Well, he's a stunt pilot and has his own helicopter, so Caleb called to see if he flew it to Dublin for the horse show. He did and he's agreed to fly you over here to us."

"What? You gotta be kidding. I don't want to see him right now. With all this swelling and bruising, I gotta look like Frankenstein's bride."

"Oh, for God's sake, Michaela, you're in the hospital. He won't be expecting a beauty queen. He'll be waiting to hear from us, so just give me a call when you're being released. He'll be over to pick you up." As Michaela continued to protest, Arianna issued her final decree. "It's a done deal, so don't bother arguing."

Michaela knew when she had been beaten. Hanging up, she blew out a breath and dug into her purse for a hairbrush, makeup and a mirror. *Grief!* All swollen, and with her head wrapped in a bandage like this, she looked like a freaking abused mummy. Figuring there wasn't much she could do about her matted hair, she opened her makeup bag and began the arduous task of trying to repair some of the visible damage from being thrown off a horse.

His backpack slung over one shoulder, Liam scooped the electronic key off the chest of drawers in the hotel room.

"What do you mean, I've to book a commercial flight back to Kerry?" Aideen yanked another drawer open and continued slapping clothes into a suitcase.

Liam shrugged. "Told you, I've a friend needs a favor. An emergency."

She shot him a skeptical look. "Emergency, is it? Wouldn't have anything to do with the clumsy, black-haired mortal falling off her bloody horse, now would it?"

"Actually, it would," he replied unconcernedly. "She's being released from hospital today and a mutual friend needs for me to transport her to Clare."

"And I can't fly along, because...."

"Because I'm not invading these people's privacy by bringing someone there uninvited."

"I saw the way you were looking at her last night at the pub. And today at the hotel. At the competition, as well. You fancy the little slut. Best know, if you do this today, it's over between us."

The ultimatum hardened his expression, cemented his resolve. "I think that's best, Aideen. You know yourself, this hasn't been working for either of us."

Aideen's lavender eyes shot daggers. The water glasses on a tray on top of the dresser clacked together, before one glass lifted and flew across the room, smashing into the wall.

Liam rolled his eyes at the childish display as Aideen fired back. "You'll be sorry." She threatened him quietly, as she reached for the handle of her rolling suitcase. "*Very* sorry," she repeated. The door opened as she approached it, the force of her temper slamming it behind her as she exited the room.

The original plan was for Wind Spirit to be moved to the stables at Arianna's home at the end of the week, after the event had ended. But now, with Michaela unable to continue in the competition, she arranged for his immediate transport to Clare.

After completing the hospital's release forms, acknowledging she was leaving against medical advice, she found herself sitting in a wheelchair inside the emergency entrance, waiting for Liam. A sleek, black Jaguar XK pulled up in front of the sliding doors and Liam climbed out of the car. Tall and well built, he was wearing the same black motorcycle jacket from the night before. Again, a shock of unruly ash-blonde hair framed his angular face. He removed his aviator sunglasses, and ice-blue eyes met hers. A cocky grin settled on his lips. Damned if that look he was giving her wouldn't be all the foreplay a girl would ever need.

Michaela gave a nod toward the Jag. "Nice ride."

"A rental, to get around whilst here in Dublin."

After helping her into the car, he climbed into the driver's seat. Leaning over, he examined the lump on the side of her head. "Nasty piece of work," he muttered.

Cringing as his fingers moved over the raw and swollen area, Michaela was surprised to find his touch not only gentle, but strangely soothing as well. A warmth radiating from his fingertips seemed to ease the pain throbbing in time with every beat of her heart.

"They had my head all wrapped up in a turban, but I made them take it off. I think a wound heals faster if it's exposed to fresh air. So where'd you park the chopper?"

"Weston Airport, about eight miles out."

"Okay, but I have to go check out of the hotel first, get my luggage."

"We took care of all that. Arianna checked you out and I collected your bags on the way here. Everything's in the boot."

"The boot?" she grinned. "You mean the trunk."

"Right, the *trunk*." He smiled back at her and repeated the word with a pronounced southern drawl that made her giggle. *Giggle? Good grief.*

Liam's eyes met hers, considering. "Reckon they didn't feed you here, so we'll grab a bite before we take off. Hungry?"

"Starved." The engine roared as the car shot forward. The extra horsepower put a smile on her face as it pushed her back against the seat.

❧

It was dark, after nine o'clock by the time they landed at the helipad on the castle grounds. Michaela had gotten to feeling pretty rough during their last half-hour in the air and she found herself wishing Liam would touch her head again, make the pain go away. And that she was even thinking such a thing meant the knock on her head had to have been a lot more serious than she thought.

Now as they hiked toward the castle, Liam kept looking at her, frowning. Finally, he took her hand and pulled her close. With an arm around her shoulders, he supported her the last few hundred yards to the medieval fortress her friend called home.

Arianna flew down the thick, stone steps and wrapped her in a giant bear hug.

"Well, look at you, little mama." Michaela held her friend at arms' length, then patted her rotund belly. "I've missed you, girlfriend. Your old man been treating you right or do I have to kick his ass?" She sent a teasing wink at Caleb, who was conversing with Liam at the gargantuan front door.

Arianna laughed and slipped an arm around Michaela's shoulders. "Yeah, he's behaving himself for the most part," she said, shooting him a flirtatious look.

"Baby on the way and the honeymoon's still not over. Now that's what I'm talking about." Michaela slid an arm around Arianna's waist as they all entered the foyer.

"Can I get you guys something to eat? Drink?" Arianna asked. "Or should I show you upstairs to your rooms, so you can freshen up first?"

"We had a bite before we left Dublin. Besides, I feel like a herd of elephants are stampeding through my head, and I'm about to drop. Would it be totally rude to ask you to just show me to a bed, where I can collapse?"

"Course not," Arianna replied. "*Mi casa* and all that. Liam?"

Michaela followed the direction of Arianna's glance and found the men still speaking together softly in Irish.

"I'd fancy something to drink, actually," Liam answered.

"Well, why don't you guys go on up to the solar, while I take this one upstairs and put her to bed."

After making their way to the fourth floor, Arianna opened the door to the suite of rooms she had occupied during her first stay at the castle. It was the same room Michaela had stayed in during Caleb and Arianna's wedding.

Michaela followed her through the sitting room and on into the bedroom. "Gotta pee," she announced and disappeared into the adjoining bath.

When she returned to the bedroom, she found Arianna digging through her suitcase, which had been delivered to the room by one of the castle staff. "We'll unpack tomorrow," her friend announced. "For now, let's just get you into bed." She pulled one of Michaela's sheer nighties out of the suitcase and grinned. "Expecting company tonight?"

Michaela plopped into an overstuffed chair in the corner. "I wish. I have so many bumps and bruises, dude could walk in here bare-ass naked, and I wouldn't be able to do anything about it. And, speaking of Liam, what's up with him? What were you doing, hiding the hottest guy I've ever seen in my life?"

Arianna chewed on her lip. "You don't want to touch that. Believe me, Mick, the man's way out of your league." Her brows furrowed with concern. "Your eyes are all squinty."

"Yeah, got the mother of all headaches. I can finally empathize with your migraines."

"Let me see that bump on your head." Her friend's fingers moved deftly over the throbbing, aching lump. Just like with Liam, Michaela felt a surge of warmth, then a complete absence of pain.

"Damn, that feels better. What'd you do? Some kind of fairy magic?"

A guarded look came over Ariana's face. "Just get your nightgown on and get to bed."

"Geez, you've gotten bossy," Michaela teased as she stripped down. "Need a shower first."

"Not tonight. You need to lie down before you fall down. Right now."

After slipping on her nightclothes, Michaela climbed the three wooden bed steps to the large bed on a dais. With a contented sigh, she slid beneath the goose down duvet.

Arianna looked at her and took a deep breath. "I'll leave you to get some sleep now. Here's your mobile," she said, handing Michaela her cell phone. "Keep it handy and call me if you need anything during the night."

# Chapter Three

Pain, pain. She was drowning in a sea of agony. It hurt to move, even to open her eyes. Disoriented, Michaela squinted into the pitch-black darkness. It was cold as hell. It took a second or two before she remembered where she was. At her friend's *castle* in Ireland, she thought, as she rolled onto her other side. But the minute her head touched the pillow she groaned, her body jerking at the sharp jolt of pain.

The spot near her temple, where she was sure she sported the outline of a hoof-shaped lump, felt even worse now than it had when it first happened. On top of that, every muscle in her body—violently wrenched when she hit the ground—was screaming. Her arms and legs and torso were undoubtedly covered in purpling bruises, the result of being trampled beneath the stallion's giant hooves.

Every movement was pure torture. And, of course, she had to pee in the worst possible way. Gritting her teeth, she felt around for the lamp on the bedside table and turned it on. *God bless you, Arianna,* she thought, as she spotted the bottle of pain pills she had gotten from the hospital and a glass of water sitting within easy reach. Not a believer in prescription meds, she had to admit that this time was an exception. After swallowing a pill, she threw back the duvet, glad she hadn't tried to climb out of bed in the dark. She had forgotten it was perched up on a dais several feet above the floor and would have broken her fool neck.

Feeling for the wooden bed steps with her feet, she slid gingerly off the mattress. "Ow, ow, ow." She hobbled toward the bathroom like an arthritic old lady.

She flushed the commode, washed her hands, and opened the bathroom door.

*An explosion rocked the stone edifice and a blast of heat stole the breath from her lungs. Greedy flames licked up the curtains, devouring the fabric in gigantic bites. The fire gobbled up the heavy mahogany furniture, ate the Persian rugs stretched across the floor and consumed the bedclothes on the mattress where she had been sleeping.*

*A spark caught the end of her nightgown and raced up the silken fabric, leaping into her long hair. She slapped at the stinging flames, as the acrid smell of burning hair assaulted her nostrils. The odor of her own scorched flesh sickened her. She shrieked and sobbed as she slammed the bathroom door shut and dove into the shower. Spinning the faucets, she stood beneath the rush of cold water shooting down on her, dousing the inferno. As she sank to her knees, shivering from the icy flow, she could only pray that someone would hear her screams before the entire castle burned to the ground.*

As the stream of water suddenly ceased, she cried out. She batted at the strong, masculine arms reaching for her until she recognized a familiar voice that calmed her hysterics. She went limp in Liam's arms as he wrapped a towel around her and lifted her off the shower floor. Soaked and disheveled, she looked up at him. Usually cold as ice, his blue eyes blazed now with concern. "Michaela, what's wrong? I was in the next room and heard you screaming. Are you in pain? Do you need a doctor?"

"The fire," she gasped, unable to catch her breath. "The room… is on fire."

"Calm now. Sure, there's no fire, pet." He cradled her in his arms and gently carried her out of the bathroom. "Look around yourself, so. You've had a bad dream is all."

Her breath sobbed in her throat as he sat in the armchair with Michaela curled in his lap, her eyes squeezed tightly shut. Head on his shoulder, her long, black hair stuck to her face and neck in wet, tangled strands as she hesitantly opened her eyes and peeked at the room.

Everything looked the same as it had when she had first climbed out of bed. "But the fire…."

"Was a nightmare." Liam completed her sentence. "Only a nightmare, wee one."

Although she didn't have the strength to argue the point, Michaela knew better. She had been fully awake when she went in to use the toilet. Why she had suddenly been caught up in that fireball horror, she couldn't fathom. She guessed that being kicked in the head must have knocked something loose up there.

Embarrassed by the outburst, she extricated herself from Liam's embrace and slid to her feet. "I'm okay now," she said softly, holding the towel tightly around her. "But I'm soaked and…well, practically naked, so...I'm going to go put some clothes on. You should get on back to bed. I'm so sorry I disturbed you. And…thanks for coming to the rescue."

"No worries."

At the door, he hesitated for a long moment before speaking again. "I'm in the room right beside you, should you need anything."

"I'll be fine. *I hope*," she whispered to herself, as he pulled the door shut behind him.

❧

Just before daybreak, Michaela was jolted awake by the sound of a woman screaming. She switched on her lamp and stumbled down from the bed, every square inch of her body protesting each step. It took a moment before she realized that the horrifying screams were coming from the floor above. From Arianna's family suite.

A sick chill filled her with dread as she recognized the sound of her friend's voice.

She scrambled into her clothes as quickly as her bruised and crippled body would allow. Twisting her hopelessly tangled hair into a bun, she stuck a plastic stick through the mess. Moving gingerly, she left the room and headed toward the staircase down the hall. Despite the early hour, she noticed that every light in the castle was ablaze. As she wound her way up the stone steps leading to the fifth floor, she felt relieved that Arianna's agonized wails had subsided. She knocked on the door of the family's apartment.

Flanagan, the slight and stoic castle steward, greeted her, looking pinched and pale and yet somehow proud and pleased, all at the same time.

From somewhere inside, probably the bedroom, Michaela could hear Arianna cursing her husband out. Something about his being a son of the devil himself.

Michaela's lips quirked at Caleb's indulgent response. "I am indeed, my love."

"Eight months to the day." Arianna's voice rose on a shrewish screech. "You certainly didn't waste any time, now did you?"

"I did not." His agreement was an obvious attempt to placate his wife with the proper level of penitence.

"Except when it came to telling me about that magic birth control thing," Arianna verbally slapped at him. "I'd say you wasted *plenty* of time when it came to that."

"*A mhuirnín*," he answered softly, "'Twasn't a thing I was all too familiar with meself. If you recall, I did suggest you speak to Brian Rafferty's wife about women's issues."

Flanagan cleared his throat, apparently disturbed that a castle guest was overhearing the private exchange.

"I want to see her." At Michaela's demand, the little man, who had barely an inch or two on her own height, hesitated. "That's my *sister* in there."

"Yer sister?" He looked confused, as if a blood connection

between the two women changed something important. "Didn't know the two of ye were related."

Michaela let out a huge sigh. "Well, we're not…at least not by birth. But we grew up together and we're sisters in every other sense of the word."

Flanagan seemed to wilt, to lose inches off his already diminutive size. "I'll check with Himself," he replied and, turning on his heels, left Michaela to pace the floor in the sitting room.

A couple of minutes later, he returned to the door and motioned her to follow him down a small hall. As they entered a bedroom the size of a small arena, Michaela found her friend propped up on pillows like royalty, on a bed so high and large it could easily have slept six adults. Michaela slanted a raised-brow look at Caleb. Just what kind of debauchery would a single man have been up to in order to own a bed like that?

Up close now, Michaela examined her friend's appearance, and her heart clenched in her chest. Arianna looked exhausted, her naturally light complexion far too pale. Even with the early morning chill of a building made of cut stone, she was sweating profusely, her damp hair spread out, limp and tangled, across her pillow.

Brows furrowed with worry, Caleb glanced over his shoulder and offered a weak smile. It was hard to decide who looked the worse for wear—the mother-to-be or her loving husband.

Taking a fortifying breath, Caleb dipped a washcloth in cool water and wrung it out. He drew it down his wife's flushed cheeks, then wiped the perspiration beading her tired brow. He reached under her head and gathered her moist hair away from her neck.

"Michaela's here, love," he told her gently.

Arianna raised her head and forced a smile. "We're having a baby." Her voice sounded raspy from all the screaming.

She sounded so young and lost, so completely overwhelmed by

the violence of her body's demands, that Michaela's heart broke in two. She joined Caleb at the bedside. "I can see that."

Caleb's maternal grandmother, Táillte O'Clery, bustled into the room. She had been the midwife for Arianna's mother, as well as for her own daughter, who had died in childbirth bearing Caleb. "I've a cup of broth for you, luveen," she said to Arianna. "Help keep yer strength up."

But before her friend could take a sip of the fortifying liquid, she moaned and rolled onto her side in a miserable ball of agony. Caleb climbed onto the bed beside her and spooned her, wrapping her in his arms.

"The pain is so bad, I think I must be dying," Arianna moaned. As the cramping in her womb seemed to release her from its grip, she looked at Mrs. O'Clery. "Granny, there must be a mistake about… about my heritage. Are you sure? About my mother, I mean?"

Michaela felt like she was intruding on a private moment, like she was missing something. The old woman gave Arianna an indulgent smile and patted her hand. "This is completely normal, pet. To be expected, I'm afraid."

Arianna looked over her shoulder at her husband. "You heard your grandmother. I hope you know our son is going to be an only child. Because if I survive this, you, love of my life, are *never* going to touch me again."

"I wouldn't think of it, *mo chroí*," Caleb cooed.

Wise man, Michaela thought, as he concealed the smile tugging at his lips.

There was a knock on the door and the old woman went to answer it. Michaela heard Flanagan's voice. "I've refreshed the ice." Apparently, all who made their home in Castle MacNamara had fallen under the spell of the new lady of the manor. Michaela could almost feel the expectant hush in the air as everyone awaited the birth of the new heir. "Maeve's after preparing a celebration feast for after the wee babe is born," Flanagan went on. "She's wanting to know if our new mother would fancy anything heartier than the broth for now."

"A slice of fresh baked bread to go with the soup would be lovely," Granny answered.

"And a cup of coffee," Caleb called out from the bedroom.

"Now, she shouldn't be having caffeine," Granny scolded.

"The coffee's for me," Caleb shot back, his expression droll.

"You drink a cup of coffee in front of me right now, and I'll cut your heart out," his sweet wife threatened.

This time, Caleb couldn't hold back the chuckle. "Granny, how about a cup for the wee mother here? Just a few small sips?"

"Ah, go on then, Flanagan. Might as well make yerself useful, seeing as you're the likes of an old mother hen, running back and forth. Bring up a pot of coffee and three cups for the young people. And a cuppa tea for meself."

"I'll get some fresh towels out of the bathroom," Michaela offered, needing to make herself feel useful.

"Oh no, another one," Arianna whimpered. Clutching her husband's wrist, she rode out the wave of contraction as, helpless to ease her friend's pain, Michaela left the room.

As she returned to the bedroom a few minutes later, a stack of fresh towels piled in her arms, she could hear the expectant mother speaking to her husband, a grumpy pout in her voice.

"You know, when I first got pregnant, I thought you'd do that… that thing you do with your hands…so it wouldn't hurt so bad."

*That thing with his hands?* Instantly, Michaela pictured the way both Liam and Arianna had touched the lump on her head, and how it had seemed to ease the pain.

"*A stór,* I've done all can be done, letting the heat soothe the ache, smooth out the roughest bumps in the road, without affecting the contractions. But as Granny's after explaining to you, 'tis a fine balance between easing the discomfort and stopping the labor altogether. Now, you'd not fancy staying pregnant forever, would you, love?"

*What?*

"God forbid," Arianna growled.

On a step stool at Arianna's side, Granny tented the sheet over the laboring mother's knees and checked for progress. "Get in bed behind yer sweet wife, me boy," she announced. "You're about to meet yer new son."

As he positioned himself behind Arianna, Michaela murmured, "I'll leave you guys to your privacy."

"No, Mick, stay. Please," her friend pleaded. "I want you here when your nephew arrives."

Michaela glanced up at Caleb, who inclined his head, approving his wife's wishes. Standing by the wall to the left of Arianna's head, out of everyone's way, she watched the beautiful scene unfold before her. The husband nuzzled his wife's neck from behind, his hands gently molding her swollen belly. "See, my love? 'Tis almost over," he whispered in her ear.

And so it was. Minutes later, through a veil of happy tears, Michaela watched her dearest friend cradle her wriggling baby boy in her arms. Dubbed Patrick Kieran MacNamara after both his grandfathers, the infant was born with a shock of curly black hair and long, dark lashes that would, one day, drive all the girls wild. He cried lustily, and then began to root at his mother's breast.

"Just like his da," Arianna said softly, looking as if she were about to burst. She kissed her son's cute little button nose, while his father's long, protective arms enveloped them both.

Arianna's grin was so big her face could hardly contain it. "Hey, Godmother," she said to Michaela, after several minutes had passed. "Come meet our new baby."

Murmuring to the infant in words Michaela couldn't understand, Caleb placed him in her arms. And, just like that, she understood what maternal love was supposed to be. She kissed his forehead and cooed softly to the sleeping child, then looked at Arianna, her heart overflowing with the sweet wonder of it all. Here in an ancient Irish castle with her prince of a husband and precious newborn son, her best friend was living a real-life fairytale.

Finally, she allowed the proud papa to reclaim his son and bent over to kiss her friend on the cheek. "I think I'll go call Auntie Tara now."

"Good idea," Arianna agreed.

Tara Price was the third member of their sisterhood. She and Arianna first met Michaela at the age of twelve, when Michaela had joined the karate demonstration team the other two girls had belonged to.

As she went to get her cell phone, Michaela experienced that rare and wondrous sense that everything was in perfect balance, exactly as it should be. And that unhappiness had been banished permanently from the world.

❧

As she passed the room next to hers, Liam stepped through the door. His hair still damp from the shower, Michaela caught a whiff of soap and shampoo, intermingled with that underlying musky scent that was Liam's alone. If she lived with the man, she thought, she would do her part for water conservation. Two to a shower.

She greeted him with a cheery smile. "Hey you. We have a new baby."

His face went carefully blank. "We do?"

Michaela giggled. "Not *us*, you doof. Arianna just gave birth. And I'm the proud Auntie of a beautiful, black-haired baby boy."

He responded with that cocky half-grin that tipped one corner of his mouth. And curled her toes. "Oh, well, fair play to them. And yourself." He sounded genuinely pleased.

"I'm surprised you didn't hear all the goings on. She had a rough time of it. Woke me out of a sound sleep."

"Being awakened by a woman's blood-curdling screams once in a night is God's plenty." A twinkle in his eyes, he made the remark in a dry tone.

"Yeah. Sorry about that."

"You faring any better today?"

"Well, except for the goose egg on my head and hobbling around like a senior citizen, I'm spectacular."

"Aye, you are indeed."

Michaela smiled inwardly at the backhanded compliment.

"C'mere to me, so." Liam stepped closer and gently grasped her jaw, tipping her head so that he could examine the injury.

Michaela flinched and held her breath. She expected him to touch the sore spot the way he had done the day before, but this time, he only looked at it. "Bruise is spreading and turning dark purple. Looks worse today than when it happened."

"Pretty normal, I guess." Michaela's entire being was focused on that single point of contact, where his nimble fingers caressed her jaw.

As he released her and took a step back, she let her eyes feast. The gray tee shirt he wore revealed the lean cut of his muscular frame. In those scuffed black boots and faded jeans, damned if dude didn't look good enough to eat.

*And I'm positively ravenous.*

A wicked smile quirked one corner of his mouth. "Myself, as well," he murmured, his voice low, intimate.

*Did I say that aloud?*

"I'm going to the kitchen for some breakfast now," Liam announced. "Join me?"

"I, uh, no. Thanks, but I don't think so. I haven't even showered yet. Anyway, the kitchen sent scones up to the solar with a pot of coffee during the big event, so I'm good for now."

"Right. Well, I'll be off then. Sure, maybe I'll see you again before I leave for Kerry."

At the thought of him going away, Michaela felt suddenly stricken. She probably should have expected the strange rush of emotion. After all, the man had arrived on his white horse the day before and rescued her from the clutches of the medical authorities. And last night, sword and shield in hand, he had shown up to save her from the towering inferno. "Let's make a point of it. And Liam?"

He tipped his head to one side and raised his brows.

"Thanks again for bringing me here." She lowered her voice. "And for last night."

He looked at her, eyes intent. Watchful. His hand reached out, his thumb brushing across her lower lip. "My pleasure," he said softly, then dropped his hand and turned to go.

As she let herself into her room, she peeked first around the door checking for a firestorm, then sniffed the air. It had been only a bad dream, she told herself. Just a dream, that's all. But if that were true, she pondered, why then did the pungent smell of burning hair still linger in the room?

## *Chapter Four*

Tara didn't pick up the phone, so Michaela left a voice mail to share the happy news. Afterward, the tall bed looked so comfy and inviting that she climbed onto the mattress, telling herself she would stretch out for just a couple of minutes before jumping into the shower. But all the interrupted sleep the night before must have done her in, because she dozed off almost immediately.

When she woke up, she saw that an hour had passed. Moving carefully, she grabbed a quick shower, then made her way back upstairs to check on the new family. She knocked on the slightly open door leading into the apartment's sitting room and stuck her head inside. "Arianna?"

"In here, changing the baby." Her friend hollered at her. "Come on back."

Michaela located the nursery next to the master bedroom. "I've heard new mothers described as 'glowing', but until now, I didn't realize the remark was to be taken literally. You're beautiful, girlfriend."

Standing in front of a mahogany changing table, Arianna glanced over her shoulder, a huge smile on her face. "Yeah, I should write a book: How to Lose Twelve Pounds in Less than Eight Hours. After a shower and washing my hair, I'm actually starting to feel human again. Only thing is, I can't seem to wipe this stupid grin off my face. It's like I'm the only woman in the world who's ever accomplished such an amazing feat. There now, he's clean." Arianna gathered the bundle of joy into her arms. "Come over here, Auntie Michaela, and get a look at your new nephew sans all the blood and gore."

"Tell you the truth, I was so whacked out watching the miracle of it all, I didn't even notice the mess."

"Here, take him." Arianna held out the swaddled infant. "He spit up on me, so I have to go change."

Michaela's jaw unhinged. "You're leaving me alone with him? But I—I've never taken care of a baby before."

"Well, then, it's high time you did. I'll only be in the next room. Now, come on. Sit over there in the rocker. It's the one Granny used to rock Caleb in. And me, while Da was at work."

With all the relish of being ushered in front of a firing squad, Michaela allowed herself to be positioned in front of the antique wooden chair. Gingerly, she lowered her bruised and aching body onto the embroidered seat cushion.

Arianna fit the powdery smelling infant into the curve of her left arm…and Michaela fell in love. She didn't notice when Arianna left the room. Could see nothing but the perfect little face framed by a mass of black curls. A crescent of long dark lashes brushed his rosy cheeks. As she traced a finger down the side of his face, rosebud lips pursed and began a sucking motion. His head turned, rooting for Michaela's breast. When he couldn't locate the nourishment he was seeking, his little face turned red, tiny hands balled into fists of frustration.

Just as he was starting to mutter and grumble, mommy reappeared and Michaela looked up in relief. "I think he's hungry. And I can't help him there."

Arianna scooped him up in one arm and, with her other hand, unbuttoned her shirt as skillfully as if she had been performing the routine forever. She bit her lower lip, face scrunching up in pain as he latched onto her breast. "Ouch, the old nipples are raw already. I'm hoping they toughen up in a day or two."

Michaela laughed. "Now that's way too much information, my friend."

At a rap on the door leading to the hall, Arianna rolled her eyes. “Probably more of the castle staff wanting a peek at the new heir,” she said good-naturedly. “Caleb’s down at the stables, so would you mind inviting whoever it is into the sitting room? Tell them I’ll be out in a few minutes, as soon as the baby finishes nursing.”

“No prob.” Ducking out of the nursery, she headed to the solar and opened the door. *Liam.*

His blue eyes lit up. “Came to offer my congratulations to the new parents.”

“Caleb’s at the stables and Mama’s feeding the new edition,” Michaela explained. “If you wait a couple of minutes, she’ll be right out.”

“No worries. Just tell her I’ll call over and see Caleb. I’ll be back up with him in a wee while.”

As he was speaking, the room around them grew dark and threatening. It began to shift and move as if they were on a boat overtaken by a heavy swell. Her head swimming, she could feel a worm of dread burrowing beneath her skin. Catching herself on the edge of the open door, she barely managed to keep from toppling over.

“What’s the story? Michaela?” Liam’s voice sounded faint, as if it were coming from a great distance.

Before she could answer him, however, the floor began to buck and roll. She shrieked and tightened her grip on the door, as a surreal scene began to play out in front of her. The walls of the solar quaked and rippled. The flagstone floor cracked apart at the seams. Michaela found herself staring down, down, into the volcanic layers at the center of the earth. And beyond….

Huge fists of fear gripped Michaela’s heart, before grabbing her throat in a stranglehold.

*Gagging on the putrid vapors, she could identify the rancid smell of death, as if some large animal were slowly decomposing beneath the splitting stones. Unable to keep her balance, she slumped to what remained of the rippling floor. Her unbelieving gaze fixed on the jagged stone as the foundation broke away from around her. Gargoyle-like creatures, their lambent eyeballs bulging from bulbous-shaped heads, crawled through the rubble toward her, their thick, leathery skin tinged a sickening shade of green.*

"You're awake. *Awake.*" Michaela kept repeating the word like a mantra, hoping it would vanish the nightmare creatures clawing their way up from the molten netherworld with talons that were hooked and sharp.

It seemed she could hear somebody whimpering, short, high-pitched sounds coming from somewhere beyond the phantasm. It took a minute or two before she realized that the mewling sounds were coming from her own mouth.

As she drew her legs in close to her body to avoid the grasping, clawing limbs of the demons set on dragging her down into the pits of hell, she felt a warm, firm grasp on her upper arms. Liam's hands were strong and comforting, his voice commanding as he spoke to her softly, nonsensical words that talked her off the ledge of terror. Afraid to move, she teetered at the precipice of the great, dark pit until the soft-spoken words in a mixture of English and Irish compelled her finally to open her eyes.

Liam was crouched in front of her. A radiant blue glow seemed to emanate from his eyes, the heat in them melting the blocks of ice that encased her limbs.

Clearly unaware of the events of the past several minutes, Arianna came around the corner, the smile melting from her face as she rushed over to Michaela. "Mick? What's wrong?" She jerked her head toward Liam. "What happened to her?"

"I, um—I got dizzy," Michaela explained. "That damn knock on the head."

Liam's eyes narrowed; he wasn't buying that for a second.

"Jeez, Mick, that's not good. Let me get Caleb and we'll take you over to the hospital."

"No, no. I'm okay now."

Liam stood and stretched his hand down to her. She grasped it and he pulled her to her feet, while she muffled a painful groan. When he didn't release her hand, she looked up at him questioningly. His gaze locked on hers, his face without expression. In an instant, the entire event flashed again through her mind, only this time a protective presence encapsulated her, preventing her from experiencing the horror.

Liam dropped her hand and stepped back, his features bleak.

He glanced at Arianna, his semblance of a smile seeming contrived. "Fair play to yourselves on the wee one. Just wanted to stop in and congratulate you before heading to the stable to speak with Caleb." His next comment he directed toward Michaela. "I'll be back up to see you before leaving for home."

She nodded, relieved that he wouldn't be leaving forever without stopping to say goodbye. They had only just met. So, it made no sense that she should be feeling such abject sorrow over the thought of never seeing him again.

Arianna frowned. "What's up with him?"

Michaela's shoulders twitched. "Damned if I know. Probably just putting distance between himself and the American nut job."

"Yeah, okay. Now, suppose you tell me what's really going on here."

Not wanting to worry the brand new mother, who had just been through a physically draining and grueling ordeal, Michaela prevaricated. "It's like I said. Just some dizziness from the accident."

"Don't even." Arianna knew her far too well. Taking her by the hand, she pulled Michaela over to the sofa in front of the unlit fireplace, where she coerced a full confession about the weird meltdowns.

༺༻

Rounding a large oak tree on the winding path, Liam spotted Caleb leaving a log building to the left of the stables and called out to him. "Looks like congratulations are in order, my friend."

"Thanks, mate." Caleb paused, frowned. "And what else is on your mind, so?"

"There's something strange going on here with the little Yank."

Caleb motioned toward the door he had just exited. "Let's go into the office, so we can sit down."

Liam followed him into a sparsely furnished room with dark wood flooring, where the smell of leather and saddle soap mingled with the musty scent of horseflesh. Jackets were tossed over bridle racks on walls made of roughed-up planks of knotty pine. Leather riding boots stood in the corner beside a three-tier rack that held a couple of saddles. Although the crowded space contained a well-worn desk and leather chair, it was more tack room than office.

Caleb shut the door and dragged a straight-back chair up beside the desk for Liam, then settled into his own chair behind the desk. "So, what's the *craic*?"

"As I said, there's something not right with your wife's friend, Michaela."

Caleb's eyes sharpened. He tilted his head in a go-ahead gesture.

"Last night she woke me up, wailing like a bleeding banshee. Found her huddled in the shower, so I did, her eyes vacant, cold water pouring down on her. She was going on about a fire."

"A nightmare." Even as Caleb offered the suggestion, his tone made a lie of the words.

"That's what I was after thinking meself at the time. But a few minutes ago, something else happened that changed my mind. She slipped into some sort of vision, just melted onto the floor in front of me like a stick of butter in a hot cast iron skillet. Then she went to whimpering about hellfire and demons coming to get her like. She was refusing to speak of any of it afterwards, so I touched her, took a look for meself. Fecking desperate's what it was, with the flagstone floor cracking apart beneath her, monsters rising out of the abyss and grabbing for her legs."

Caleb scratched at his unshaved chin, his eyes drifting away for a second, before meeting Liam's again. "And both times 'twas you yerself who pulled her out of it?"

Liam gave a single nod.

The two men stared at one another, a silent message exchanged. Liam slumped, then hedged an alternate possibility. "Could be a result of the crack on the head."

"Perhaps. But you know yerself that the content of these… visions…is indicative of something else entirely."

Liam pushed to his feet and began to pace. He stopped to finger a bridle hanging in the corner. "Is there no other woman currently under consideration?"

Caleb frowned. "If you bothered yer arse to attend Council meetings," he scolded mildly, "you'd know that no one has yet been identified as a likely candidate."

"Bloody bollocks." Liam uttered the curse softly, his words almost a whisper.

"I'm thinking Michaela's relationship with my wife adds merit to the possibility as well."

"How so? After learning that Arianna wasn't a mere mortal, we realized we'd been mistaken in considering her last year a'tall." Liam sat again, his fingers loosely interlaced, hands hanging between his legs.

"All true, however, a waking dream she had the night we were married resembles the visions Michaela's having." Caleb's chair creaked as he shifted position, clearly uncomfortable to be sharing something so intimate. "My wife was sucked into the

Imaginal and dragged down into Hades, where she was forced into a confrontation with the Beast."

Liam's pupils narrowed to pinpoints. "What happened, so?"

"In the vision the creature spoke, threatened her. Ordered her to return to the States."

"But why? She's not a mere mortal, and therefore can't assume the role of the Woman of. . . ." Liam's voice trailed off as understanding crept into his eyes. He blew out a breath. "If she went back to the States, her friends would have no reason to come to Ireland. Or, if visiting, to stay for any length of time."

"Exactly. And I fear that may be the reason Michaela's being threatened with a similar vision. To frighten her enough that she'll leave. And never return."

"Brilliant," Liam muttered in sarcasm.

But Caleb didn't let it drop there. "O'course, there's the requirement that the Chosen One will develop an attachment to one of our leaders. Ah sure, anyone who's not after being stone cold blind can see the girl's attraction to yourself."

With a cocky half-grin, Liam tried to make light of the situation. "One of many."

Caleb rolled his eyes. "I suppose the question then is: do you return her regard? The sacred scrolls proclaim the attraction will be mutual."

Liam rejected the idea outright. "Course, I'm attracted to the woman. She's stunning, for God's sake. But aside from a perfectly natural desire to get the leg over with the little mortal, I've no feelings for her a'tall."

The vehement denial was met by a bland recitation of Shakespeare. "The gentleman doth protest too much, methinks."

Liam straightened in his seat, anger crackling in his eyes. "And what if you're mistaken, mate? Should I forfeit my freedom during these last three months on earth, before life as we know it may be changing forever? Besides, I'm under no compulsion to protect the woman. As I said before, I feel nothing for her a'tall."

Caleb's gaze didn't waiver. "According to the *Geis*, the one of us whom the Woman desires will be called by the Fates to be her champion. What exactly did you do when you found her cowering in the shower last night, my friend? Did you wake her? Leave her there? What?"

Liam licked his lips. "I turned off the shower, o'course. She was in a daze. She was cold and shivering, lips turning blue, so I wrapped her in a towel."

"And left her sitting on the floor?"

"I'm not an animal, for feck's sake. I picked her up. Held her. Warmed her until she came back to herself."

Caleb's brows went up in a knowing arch. "I wouldn't have considered you the likes of such a nurturing type."

As Liam opened his mouth to reply, Caleb interrupted. "Look, man, I'm well aware it's your opinion that there's no way for the Enchantment to resolve itself after three thousand years. But what if you're wrong? The fate of the whole world…that of your family and mine…rests heavily upon our shoulders. Do you not reckon, then, that we've an obligation to at least try and play this thing out?"

Liam could feel the noose tightening around his neck, roping him into a commitment of which he wanted no part.

"Are you willing to give it the benefit of the doubt, man?" Caleb went on. "Go along, at least for the present? Just in case you're wrong?"

Liam's lips twisted in bad humor, while cynicism darkened his tone. "I suppose I'll give it a go, at least for now. I'm willing to stay for a day, two at most. Just until we find that all of this is merely a result of the woman's concussion. That herself and meself have naught to do with one another in the cosmic sense. No responsibility for *saving mankind*."

"And if it appears ye do?"

Liam stretched his neck to the left, then rolled his shoulders. "If so, I'll take the Woman back to Kerry with me. Deal with the problem from there."

Caleb had begun to say something else, when a sharp look of panic cut across his face. He shoved to his feet. "The baby. I don't want her near my son. Torann, come." The man called to the giant Irish wolfhound, who lay curled up on the other side of the desk.

"Sure, you don't think she'd hurt the wee boy."

Caleb glanced back over his shoulder as he headed for the door. "Visions of hellfire and demons crawling out of the bloody abyss? What do *you* think?"

Trailing behind Caleb and his dog at a distance, Liam muttered under his breath. "That I may have just gotten myself totally bollixed."

## *Chapter Five*

Exhausted, both physically and emotionally, Michaela had said goodnight to everyone early the evening before. Thankfully, she had slept through the night without further incident. Although the Irish weather was dark and gloomy when she woke up, her spirits were soaring. At dinner the evening before, Liam had mentioned his plans to remain at the castle for another day or two.

Even more crippled this morning than she had been yesterday, if that were possible, she limped into the bathroom. Under the circumstances, she supposed she should have been grateful that she was, at least, able to manage a shower without the assistance of medical personnel. Drying off, she stood naked in front of the mirror and examined the angry black and yellow splotches marring her body.

She huffed. "Looks like I got run over by a train, instead of a horse."

While her hair was icky in the extreme, she decided to put off washing if for another day. Give the scab forming on the lump at her temple another day to heal. Carefully avoiding the tender spots on her scalp, she brushed and plaited her long, black locks into a single braid, the way she wore it during competitions.

In a western-style shirt and dark blue jeans, she shoved her feet into a pair of ankle boots. By the time she headed upstairs, looking to beg a cup of coffee, it was just shy of nine a.m. As she approached the door to the family's apartment, she could hear laughter spilling into the hall.

She peeked inside. Her eyebrows shot skyward, jaw dropped.

*Tara.*

"What in the world…? When did you get here?" Four sets of eyes shot in Michaela's direction.

Sprawled wearily in an armchair, Tara smiled up at Michaela, the new addition to their family tucked serenely in the crook of her arm. "Hey, you. Had to fly over here to see my new baby."

Through all the banter, Michaela could read the concern in Tara's pale green eyes. Sisters by another mother—and father—the three girls had always been more family than friends. And, just like with natural-born sisters, there existed a certain dynamic, a kind of sibling rivalry, that kept them at odds. While Arianna got along perfectly with each of them, Tara and Michaela had a long history of banging heads.

"So, how are you doing?" Tara asked. "I'm guessing your horse didn't manage to kick any sense into that stubborn head of yours."

"Nope. Hard head here." Michaela feigned knocking on her skull, then changed the subject. "Mmm, I smell caffeine. Somebody just hook me up to an IV and I'll take it straight into my veins."

"Table in the corner. Breakfast buffet." Eyes glazed with new mother exhaustion and utter contentment, Arianna looked radiant perched on her husband's lap in an overstuffed armchair. "Help yourself, sweetie."

Michaela poured herself a cup of coffee and doctored it up the way she liked it. As she buttered a slice of soda bread still warm from the oven, she looked out over the room. With the classic blonde features of a cover girl, Tara looked beautiful, even when exhausted from the red-eye flight the night before. It was an assessment Liam seemed to agree with, if the appreciative glint in his ice-blue eyes were any indication.

Coffee and bread in hand, Michaela sat in the only available seat, on the opposite end of the sofa from Liam. She was sensing a weird vibe from him this morning. He seemed to be avoiding eye contact, uncomfortable. The long-legged redhead he had been with in Dublin came to mind. Who knows, maybe the man preferred his women tall.

Like her friend, Tara, who was five foot eight in bare feet.

Her appetite now spoiled, Michaela set her plate on the piecrust table to her left. She quietly sipped her coffee, while the conversation spilled good-naturedly around her. Caleb nuzzled his wife's neck and whispered something in her ear that increased the smile on her face. He moved her gently off his lap and went to the buffet table to top off his cup of tea. But instead of bringing it back with him, he left the cup on the table and walked over to Tara. He reached down to check the baby's diaper, a macho excuse to touch his son.

"Nappy needs changing." Proud papa scooped the newborn onto his shoulder, patting his tiny back as he disappeared with him down the hall.

Michaela noted the dazed look on Liam's face, as if he couldn't believe his eyes.

"How long are you staying?" Although Michaela had directed the question at Tara, Liam answered as well.

"Until tomorrow," they replied in unison, then looked at each other and broke into identical grins. As if they had known each other forever.

Michaela's heart dropped to fill the sudden hole in her stomach.

"I'm heading straight from here to Pompeii in the morning," Tara explained.

"Pompeii? You're an archeologist, so?"

She nodded. "I've been lusting after a shot at this particular dig for quite some time."

"She's been invited to teach a field school there," Michaela offered. "Plus, she'll get to play around with those perfectly preserved bodies from the Vesuvius eruption."

Liam appeared properly impressed. Seemed like the man not only liked his women tall and beautiful, but successful and well educated as well.

*So, let him have her.*

"I have a meeting tomorrow afternoon with the Anglo-American Project, University of Bradford. They've been conducting investigations of a complete block of the city." Clearly in her element, Tara's eyes lit with excitement as she talked. "I'm stoked. Just think, I'll be digging around in a city buried under tons of molten lava over two thousand years ago."

"I've seen photos of the Pompeii remains set in plaster casts that preserved their postures at the time of death. Fascinating." Liam's eyes, focused on her friend's lovely face, reflected his admiration.

Michaela set her cup on the table next to her bread plate. The coffee she had just finished drinking soured in her belly. Stomach churning, she could feel the dull ache centered at the bump on her head begin to radiate outward. Afraid she was about to humiliate herself by throwing up on the floor, she pushed to her feet, planning to go lie down until the nausea passed.

"Oh, no. Not again." Just as she breathed the words, the room took one slow rotation around her.

And everything faded to black.

"She's sleeping peacefully." Arianna reported to the others as she returned from checking on Michaela again.

"Should she be sleeping, concussed like this?" Tara asked. "Are you sure she's not unconscious?"

"She's *sleeping,* Tara."

"So, what about these hallucinations she's having?"

Caleb gave an almost imperceptible nod to Liam and stood up.

"I've some work to attend out on the property, so I'll leave you ladies to sort this out. Liam, join me?"

As if he had just been granted a stay of execution, Liam jumped to his feet.

As soon as the two women were alone, Tara began to dig. "So, what's up with Michaela and Liam? Don't tell me she's already gotten herself involved with the guy."

"She does like him."

"Like him?" Tara blew out a short puff of air. "You'd need a CO2 laser to cut the sexual tension between the two of them. Damned if I didn't feel like a voyeur just being in the same room."

Arianna lifted a shoulder. "You have to admit the guy really is hot as hell."

"Shame on you," Tara scolded affectionately. "A married woman, and with a brand new baby no less."

"Yeah, and my husband's way hotter. But just because you own a Rembrandt doesn't mean you can't appreciate the beauty of a Picasso."

Tara chuckled. "Good point. At any rate, I'm far more concerned about the hallucinations she's having than I am the state of her love life. I'm afraid this kind of thing could indicate a brain hemorrhage."

"I know. But the hospital did a full battery of tests—MRIs, CT scans, x-rays. They found nothing to be concerned about."

"Still, they wanted to keep her overnight for observation." Tara gave her head a shake. "I swear if I didn't have to go to Pompeii, I'd pack her butt up and take her home with me tomorrow. Get her to a neurologist in the States."

Arianna grabbed Tara's coffee mug and went over to the breakfast table, which had been cleared except for the coffeepot. She topped up both their cups. "I know you're not going to want to hear this, babe, but there may be another explanation for all this."

Tara stirred cream into her coffee, then dug a packet of stevia out of her purse. "So, shoot."

"It's been said that a blow to the head can awaken latent psychic abilities."

"Oh, for God's sake." Tara looked at her as if she had just lost her mind. "I can't believe you'd even suggest that horse manure to me."

"I just think we should be open to all possibilities."

"Agreed. And there are two. One, that, as we speak, our dear friend's brain is slowly bleeding into her cranium, causing irreversible brain damage. Or two, she's had some kind of psychotic breakdown and she's seeing things that aren't there."

"As usual, I so appreciate your open-mindedness." Arianna let the sarcasm rip as she exhaled a slow, exasperated breath. "But just in case the hospital in Dublin missed something, Caleb and I will take her for another round of tests when she wakes up. If they still don't find anything, we'll have her speak to a psychologist." She leaned forward, her right hand wrapped around her coffee mug. "But if the shrink doesn't find anything either, I strongly suggest you consider the concept of a *third* possibility."

❧

Michaela felt much better after waking from her nap. She was probably pushing herself too hard, given the jolt her body had taken only a couple of days before. As she was about to leave her room, she heard a rap on the door, so light it wouldn't have disturbed her had she still been sleeping.

*Liam.* "Thought I'd check on you. See how you're getting on."

She gave him a sheepish grin. "Aside from being totally embarrassed, I'm feeling much better, thanks."

"That's grand. I…em…I'll be leaving for Clare first thing in the morning." At the announcement, Michaela's heart sank like an anvil in a rushing river. "Was wondering if you're up for a walk this afternoon."

She smiled. "You know, I think that's just what the doctor ordered. Some fresh air and exercise. I was about to trek over to the stables to visit Wind Spirit, bring him an apple to apologize for abandoning him the past couple of days. Let him know that the accident in Dublin wasn't his fault."

"Brilliant. Are you ready now, or do you need some time?"

"Actually, I was just on my way up to the solar to let everyone know I'd returned to the land of the living."

"They've been checking on you whilst you slept, so they know you're well. Still, we'll leave word with Flanagan on our way out."

When they got to the winding stone staircase, Liam stepped ahead. Michaela recognized the maneuver for what it was: a way to prevent her from falling down the stairs, if she were to black out again. *Please, God, don't let that happen.* She liked Liam—*like* being a totally inadequate word to describe the depth of feelings she had for a man she'd only recently met. Accustomed to being a strong, independent woman, she wasn't comfortable playing the role of a damsel in distress.

After speaking to Flanagan on the way out the front door, they walked down the giant stone steps into the courtyard. Michaela inhaled a deep breath of the salt-scented air. "This place really is awesome."

"Aye, 'tis. And with just a wee glimmer of sunlight shining through the clouds today for our benefit." Wrapping his hand around hers, he led her down a scraggly path into a wooded area. "Shortcut to the stables," he announced, plucking an apple from his jacket. "For your horse."

"How did…?"

"I always take one with me after breakfast, for a snack later in the day."

Rounding a curve in the trail, they spilled out onto a clearing. Michaela's best equine friend stood in a paddock in front of a vine-covered stable. "Come on. I'll introduce you to the love of my life."

Wind Spirit nickered and moved toward them. The red-haired groom, who looked to be about sixteen years old, glanced their way and grinned. "He's all warmed up and ready for a trot."

Michaela climbed through the railing and took the reins. "He looks great. Thanks for taking such good care of him."

Patting the stallion's withers, she took the apple Liam had given her and held it out. The horse bared his huge teeth and gently plucked it from her hand. "Come on, boy. Let's go for a stroll," she said and nimbly mounted the massive animal bareback.

Liam reached up and put his hand on her thigh. "What are you at, woman? With the spells you've been having, your friends'll eat the head off me if I let you ride."

Michaela looked at him sideways, a defiant grin showing a lot of white teeth. "Did you just say *let* me ride?" With an in-your-face cluck of her tongue, she tapped the stallion's flanks with her heels and Liam stepped back out of the way.

After a trot around the paddock in a combination of circles and figure eights, she leaned into a canter for a few seconds, before slowing the animal down. She dismounted and walked the horse out until his heartbeat returned to normal. Eyeing Liam, who was standing silently, arms resting on top of a fence made of rough-hewn logs, she led Wind Spirit into the stables. She had almost finished brushing him down before Liam appeared at the stall.

"I'm after going back to the castle now." Tone gruff, his body rigid, the man didn't look very happy with her. "Are you coming along or will you make your way back later?"

Michaela bit her bottom lip. "I'll come with you now, if you don't mind waiting for me. I just want to find the stable boy and let him know I'm leaving."

"I'll meet you outside."

A few minutes later, Michaela joined him at the paddock. "Hey, thanks for waiting."

"No worries." Arctic blue eyes, as cold and distant as their color, glanced down at her.

As they started down the path toward the castle, Michaela had to skip along to keep up with his long strides. Finally, she grabbed his arm and tugged him to a halt. "You're not pissed off because I wanted to ride my horse, are you?"

He looked away from her, sighed, then turned back. "You're a big girl. If you want to chance your neck, sure it's yours to do with as you please."

As he began to walk again, she hurried alongside him. "You don't understand, Liam. Wind Spirit's very sensitive. If I hadn't ridden him, he'd have believed I didn't trust him anymore."

Liam stopped short in his tracks. Long fingers wrapped around her upper arms as he pulled her onto her toes and leaned down. "'Twas plain foolhardy, is what it was. You, a professional, and yourself not even wearing a helmet. If you'd had another vision, you'd like to have fallen off your horse and finished the job on that pretty little head of yours."

Maybe he was frustrated with her. Maybe it was the flash of anger. But, just like that, his mouth was on hers in a punishing kiss. Searing, electrical. Earth-shattering. Michaela heard herself moan and she moved in closer, her body molded to his, arms twining around his neck. His hands moved from her arms to down her back. To her butt. Cupping her backside, he lifted her and her legs encircled his waist. Covered from head to toe in bruises, she felt not a single twinge of discomfort. She knew only the heat of his mouth on hers, the exquisite feel of his hands on her body. The blazing heat of him warmed all of the cold, empty places that had always lived inside her.

Time lost all meaning. Days, weeks…an eternity…passed before he tore his mouth from hers. His burning gaze locked on hers, he let her slide down the front of his body over the impressive lump in his jeans. Michaela's eyes were unfocused, her breath heaving.

"I've to leave for Kerry first thing in the morning."

Why was he telling her that now? Did he want to make it clear that his interest in her was only physical? Again the thought of his leaving, of never seeing him again devastated her. Suddenly she was nine again and standing over the inert form of her first pony, who had just died of colic.

"And you'll be coming with me."

*What? What did he say?* "But…but I can't…."

"You've to recover somewhere anyways. Maybe being here at the castle, with its history of war and mayhem, is somehow propagating the visions you're having. My home in Sneem has no such history of violence. 'Tis set back in the woods, quite lovely and serene. May be just the thing to turn off the nightmares."

"No, Liam. Absolutely not. I'm here to help Arianna with the new baby. And, besides, you and I hardly know each other." As she gazed into the blue depths of a sea of polar ice, a drugging sensation began to creep up her arms and legs. Sharp-edged panic knifed through her at the thought that she was going down again into that burning pit. But almost immediately, a sense of peace settled over her, smoothing out the serrated edges of hysteria. A euphoric high began to build in the center of her being, and then it spilled over, saturating every cell, every molecule in her body with unspeakable joy.

He bent and kissed the tip of her nose. "You'll pack directly when we get back to the castle. We'll be after leaving in the morning at first light."

And a suggestion that had sounded completely absurd not five seconds earlier seemed now to be perfectly sane. "I haven't unpacked, so it won't take me very long to get ready."

As they were climbing the concrete steps to the front entrance,

Liam's cell phone rang. As he slipped it out of his jacket pocket, Michaela glanced at the display: *Aideen*. His mouth set in a grim line, he pushed a key, rejecting the call.

"Problem?" Michaela asked.

"Not a'tall." With a don't-give-a-damn attitude, he slid the silenced phone back in his pocket.

# *Chapter Six*

By the time Michaela got up the following morning, Tara had already left for her early morning flight to Pompeii. Just as well, she thought, figuring she would be catching enough flack from Arianna about going away today with a man she had only just met. The fact that her friend seemed supportive, even encouraging, at the news struck her as very odd.

Kisses all around, and then they were boarding Liam's helicopter for the flight to County Kerry. Thankfully, she hadn't gone into a mental meltdown since the day before, so maybe the rough patch was over.

*Fingers crossed.*

Headset in place, Liam locked in his flight plan and the chopper lifted smoothly from the helipad outside the castle. Michaela could feel the drone of the engine in her bones as she watched the new man in her life manipulate the aircraft's controls.

She focused on his hands. Strong, masculine. Long fingers covered in a light sprinkling of sandy blonde hair. She relived the heat of those hands on her back, his fingers massaging her buttocks as his mouth coaxed a passion from her that had before existed only in her deepest, darkest fantasies. The thought of spending a few more days with him got her heart to doing funny little twirls in sync with the dance of the chopper.

As they meandered down the coast, Liam dropped in altitude from time to time to give her a better view of a heritage site, an island, or the craggy cliffs edging the shoreline. His voice distorted in her headset, he pointed out the Cliffs of Moher where she and

Tara had accompanied Arianna to scatter her father's ashes during their Thanksgiving visit last year. Further south, they dipped over the Blasket Islands. All self-confident male, that cocky grin he flashed her way from time to time stirred her deepest yearnings. She couldn't imagine the thrill of soaring through life with an extraordinary man like this at her side.

As they dipped again and moved from the coast out over the ocean, Michaela looked down onto the twin peaks of a rock jutting up out of the water. "Skellig Michael," the metallic voice in her ears informed her. "Rises a couple of hundred meters out of the Atlantic. Druids inhabited the island about fifteen hundred years ago, drawn by its freshwater spring. Over time, first one monk and then another found his way onto the island, eventually leading to the founding of a hermitage there."

Michaela looked down at the World Heritage Site. "Are those steps?"

Liam nodded as he flew over the summit. "The monks built a warren of Spartan huts to live in, carved directly into the rock. If you're in Kerry a while, we'll take my boat and do a day trip out to Skellig for a bit of exploring."

Just the thought of boating out to a deserted island evoked a soul-deep shudder. "Unless there's a way to land the chopper on that small piece of rock, this is as close as I'm likely ever to get." At her companion's questioning look, she explained. "You might have heard about what happened to me and my friends on our boat trip to Inishmore last November."

Liam's light-hearted expression grew solemn. "When Arianna was abducted and nearly burned at the stake."

"She *was* burned at the stake," Michaela corrected. "Her heart actually stopped beating from smoke inhalation. Thank God Caleb got there in time to do CPR and bring her back."

"Right," Liam murmured, returning the copter to flying altitude.

"I don't know if you're aware that Tara and I were on the boat with Arianna. We were drugged almost to the point of overdose."

"I heard she'd her friends with her that day. Didn't realize 'twas yourself. Hmm, that does add another dimension to the question." He spoke the last words thoughtfully—as if to himself.

"What question?"

"Em.... Ah, look. You can see the estate down below." They were circling above a heavily wooded area, a veritable Garden of Eden lush with tall trees, bushes and verdant greenery. On a landing pad several hundred feet behind a sprawling mansion, Liam set the chopper down.

Ducking beneath the spinning rotor blades, he rounded the front of the aircraft. "I've an appointment in town in a wee while." He spoke to her as he helped her climb down from the passenger side. "A meeting in Killarney about the purchase of an island." She glanced at him sideways, figuring he was kidding.

He wasn't.

"Would you fancy coming along? Do some shopping? Sightseeing? We'll have supper in town, then drive through the Gap on our way back."

"Sounds like fun. Umm, are we going to the house first? I need to bring my luggage in."

"The servants will collect it. We'll get the car and leave straight away."

⁂

The *car* was a Bugatti, which made what would have been a leisurely trip to Killarney a thrill-ride. Sinking into the Veyron's plush leather seats, Michaela waited outside for the few minutes Liam was in his attorney's office. The sleek, black automobile with the two-million-dollar price tag would have been a rare sight in most U.S. communities. Not surprisingly, it drew more than its fair share of attention in this mid-sized Irish town.

As they were about to pull back onto the road, Michaela's stomach growled. Liam looked over and gave her a crooked grin. "Better get you fed."

He headed straight to Kate's Cottage, where they shared a traditional Irish meal of shepherd's pie. While they were eating, a group of school children stopped in, passing through on their way to a step-dancing competition and the other diners managed to cajole them into a couple of dances. By the time the two of them left the restaurant, her stomach was full and the small muscles around her mouth were aching from all the smiling.

Kate Kearney's restaurant sat at the foot of the Gap of Dunloe, which separated the MacGillycuddy Reeks—Ireland's highest peaks, according to Liam—from Purple Mountain.

As they traveled the gravelly mountain pass that wound through the rough terrain, Michaela held her breath through the hairpin twists and turns on a single-lane road more suitable for horse-carts than for motor vehicles. The picture-postcard beauty of Ireland was evident all around them, the purple heather and yellow gorse bushes standing vibrantly against splotches of lush green grass. Ferns, mosses and varieties of wild flowers blanketed the scraggly dark earth. In sloppy disarray, massive boulders cluttered the towering hillside dotted with white-fleeced sheep.

As they were crossing a narrow bridge that skirted a rushing stream, Michaela cried out. "Stop, Liam. *Stop*!"

He stomped down on the brakes and the car skidded on the loose shale lining the pavement. "What? Michaela, what is it?"

"Look." She pointed toward the right of a small bridge they were about to cross. A lamb was trapped on the fencing, the heavy fleece on his hind leg tangled on a strip of barbed wire. "He must have been trying to jump the barrier to get to the stream for a drink."

"For feck's sake, woman." His tone testy, Liam pulled the car to the side of the road and killed the engine. "The way you shouted out, sure I thought I'd run over a child."

Michaela bit her lip to conceal a grin at the scolding. Climbing out of the car, she sat on the concrete abutment and swung her legs over the side, sliding down the damp green grass toward the unfortunate creature. Still miffed about the scare she had given him, Liam followed thin-lipped. He took hold of the animal's trapped back leg and examined it. "No abrasions or other injuries," he reported. "Hold his leg steady now, whilst I cut him loose." Pulling a Swiss army knife out of his back pocket, he proceeded to slice through the hopeless tangle.

Liam cooed to the agitated creature in a language Michaela didn't recognize and the lamb stopped fidgeting, becoming as docile as a family pet.

"Mission accomplished." She and Liam watched as the fortunate animal bounded away, then stopped, turned his head, and looked back at them. Michaela touched Liam's arm. "Aww…, look. He's saying 'thank you'."

"Animals are smarter than most people realize. He knows we helped him." Liam closed the blade and slipped the knife back into his pocket. "No telling how long he'd been trapped there. Sure, he'd have died eventually if we hadn't happened along."

Pleased, Michaela smiled to herself as they continued their journey south without further mishap. About five miles or so up the road, they turned onto the route that would take them to Sneem via the Black Valley. "I don't think I've ever seen anything quite so glorious as this." Michaela played with the end of her braid, absently searching for split ends. "And all the wildlife. So far, I've seen a deer, a fox. Even an owl. This place is simply magical."

Liam glanced at her, his gaze inscrutable.

"Are we going back to your home now?"

"Unless you fancy stopping in town for a pint on the way."

"I'd like that."

As soon as they arrived at Dan Murphy's Pub in Sneem, Michaela excused herself for a bathroom break. Signs on the doors read *MNA* and *FIR,* respectively. Figuring MNA was probably the Irish derivative for 'MAN', she pushed the other door open—and found a guy standing at a urinal, fortunately with his back to her. *Oops.* Backing out of the door, she let it swing silently shut.

After using the facility, she tidied her makeup and returned to the bar, where she found Liam sitting at a table beside a tiny platinum blonde. Her hair was short and spiked; silver piercings decorated the side of one nostril and her lower lip, while several other earrings cascaded down the sides of both ears. Her blue eyes were outlined in kohl, face white, lips black. In black leather pants, boots and a studded jacket, she reminded Michaela of a Goth sugarplum fairy.

Another girlfriend, Michaela presumed, the delight she had been feeling earlier turning to disappointment.

From their body language, the two of them appeared to be having a heated discussion. As Michaela approached, she could hear the woman's low, plaintive tone. "She's after bringing Mam a piece of pottery she burned at her shop. Trying to insinuate herself into the family, so she is. I can't tolerate that woman, but now that Da's passed, Mam fancies a grandchild to keep the family name from dyin' out."

"Like that matters at this point," Liam muttered. As he spotted Michaela, he stood and pulled out the chair beside him. "Michaela, I'd like you to meet my sister, Catriona."

*Sister?*

"Michaela's here from the States, visiting a mutual friend."

The two women exchanged pleasantries.

"So, how d'ya like Ireland?"

"Love it. It's absolutely charming."

Apparently pleased by the response, Catriona's gaze shifted toward the front of the pub and her eyes lit up. "Cian, over here," she called out to a large, blonde man dressed as if he were her identical twin. Eyebrows raised, he pointed toward the bar, then made a drinking motion with his hand.

Catriona shot an inquiring look at Liam. "Guinness," he said, then turned to Michaela. "And yourself?"

"Same."

Catriona raised two fingers toward the beautiful blonde man. "My husband," she told Michaela, blue eyes, like her brother's, twinkling. "Liam introduced us."

"Do you live near your brother?"

"Not far. Most of the family live within a few kilometers of one another."

As Cian headed toward the table with two pints of the rich, dark brew, Liam went to the bar to fetch the other two. Liam's sister and brother-in-law were funny, easy-going, and clearly devoted to one another. Michaela couldn't help but like them instantly. After a visit that was pleasant, but far too short, the four of them left the pub, promising to meet up again soon.

"I'll come kidnap you one day for lunch." Catriona's promise came with a flash of her brother's crooked grin.

Hoping to get to know Liam's sister a little better during her stay in Sneem, Michaela accepted the invitation. As she was going around to climb into the Bugatti, she saw Catriona give her brother a hug. "She's lovely. A keeper." Those words offered in a stage whisper, she sent Michaela a wink. Her next comment to her brother was offered so softly, it was hard to hear what she was saying. "Doesn't really matter anymore whether she's one of us, now does it?"

Liam's face went carefully blank and, with a slight shrug, he climbed into the cockpit of the Grand Sport Vitesse.

The sun had set by the time they arrived back at Liam's place, the house nestled in an enchanted woodland of oak and beech trees. They proceeded up a long and winding driveway, crossed an ancient bridge and passed several grassy islands and prehistoric monuments, before pulling up in front of a two-story manor house. With a slate gabled roof, pale gray stucco and pristine white doors and trim, the home's understated elegance seemed a contradiction to the wild and reckless man at her side.

"This is beautiful, Liam. How big is the property?"

"Not too. About twenty hectares. There's a bike trail through the woods, a tennis court behind the house, and an exercise room upstairs, should you feel up to a work out whilst you're here."

"Excellent."

A grandfather clock, antique buffet and a couple of comfortable chairs graced the hallway as they entered the house. A white, square post banister with a top rail matching the deep mahogany floors curved left to the second floor.

"Kitchen's down the hall to your right should you get a craving for a midnight snack."

"Thanks. I'm good, long as I have my coffee in the morning."

"Grand. Now, the servants will have delivered your bags to your room upstairs. If you fancy unpacking and freshening up a bit, I'll take you up there. We'll meet for drinks in the drawing room, second door past the kitchen in, say, forty-five minutes?"

"Great. See you in a few." Michaela was pleased for the chance to touch base with Arianna and let her know all was well. Not to mention that she could use a little private time with her friend to gossip about this man, who had so quickly captured her attention.

"I feel so much better." Having changed into a pair of jeggings and a comfy tee shirt, Michaela took a nice sip of her chamomile tea.

She and Liam were relaxing on a plush leather sofa in front of an impressive black stone fireplace that remained unlit. His arm around her shoulders, he absently massaged the back of her neck as they talked. "I really appreciate your bringing me here to chill for a couple of days. I hated bringing all that head-trauma drama into Arianna's home, what with the new baby and all."

Liam smiled. "I've to confess I fancy havin' you here to meself for a wee while. Give us a chance to get better acquainted, without all the distractions." He leaned down and kissed her, a light brush of his lips, once, twice.

Michaela grinned up at him. God, the man was simply adorable, the way all that ash blonde hair fell stubbornly to either side of his face every time he pushed it back. His fair complexion, bronzed by the sun, provided a striking contrast to the clear blue of his eyes, eyes so deep, so soulful, she felt like she might get lost in them and never find her way back. "I'm glad we have this chance, too. Living in two different countries, we would have probably never seen each other again otherwise. Can I ask you something personal?"

He raised a brow.

"That girl I saw you with in Dublin. Had you been dating for long?"

He shook his head unconcernedly. "We'd been seeing one another casually for a few weeks. Nothing exclusive. Not on my part, at any rate."

She pressed her lips together. "So, you're not involved with anyone."

"I'm not, no. And since I first capped eyes on you at the pub that night, I've been drawn to you, Michaela. I invited you here so we'd have some privacy to explore this attraction between us."

Direct. No game playing. She liked that in a man. And, God

knows she had never felt this way about anyone before. This serious fascination, the fulfillment of her every sexual fantasy. Silly, but he reminded her of the heroes in the vampire romances she liked to read. There was something secretive about him, something dark and alluring that drew her to him like a moth to a flame. Oh, yeah, she definitely had to be careful with this one, or risk getting burned.

It was crazy. She was totally infatuated. Just sitting beside him like this had set her heart to beating like a tom-tom. She inhaled, blew it out, trying to mask the breathless excitement in her voice before she spoke again. "I feel the same way, Liam. But we hardly know each other. I…don't know anything about you. Who you are. What you do."

He smiled that lop-sided grin again. *Damn.* "I'm a stunt pilot, an investor. An entrepreneur. I dabble in real estate and various businesses. As for my family, I have one sibling, a sister whom you've already met. My father passed away a couple of years ago. We weren't close, so no need to offer condolences. My mother's strong-willed and we rarely see eye-to-eye on anything, so, needless to say, I avoid contact with her as much as possible."

Michaela snorted. "Sounds like my family. Except my dad is still living. And I'm an only child." She grinned. "My mother, whom I must call by her first name, mind you, blames me for her stretch marks. She's a *movie star*, you see, so my birth was a terrible inconvenience."

"Movie star, you say?"

"Well…according to her. In actuality, she's a B-grade actress who manages to work regularly due to the fact that my father is a famous Hollywood producer."

"Ah, I see."

Michaela took another sip of her tea. It had gotten cold, so she set the cup aside.

"Shall I heat that up for you?"

He rested a hand on her knee. She went all soft and mushy inside. "Heat what, exactly?" Michaela knew she was coming on strong. Probably too much, too soon. But she could never remember wanting anything more in her life than just to be held in this man's arms, to feel that sexy mouth of his possessing hers again.

Oh, yeah. There it was again. That grin that set her body on fire every time he flashed it her way. And, as if he had snatched that thought right from her mind, he bent his head and granted her fondest wish in the world. He took her mouth in a kiss that was so commanding, so devastating, so downright molten that she melted in his arms. His lips nibbled, coaxed hers to open. And he was inside…her heart. Her soul.

His hands on the bruised and aching parts of her body were gentle. As before, each touch, each caress, seemed to lessen the pain of her injuries. He moved over her on the sofa, supporting himself on both arms as he pressed her gently against the throw pillows, one knee inserted between her thighs. The weight of his body, the masculine hardness of him pressing against her core, warmed up all the dark and empty places she kept buried inside.

She wrapped her arms around him and was raising her head to fit her mouth more securely against his, when the sofa pillow pressed against the hoof-shaped lump near her temple. She cried into his mouth, and the delicious weight on top of her was instantly gone.

Liam was sitting on the edge of the sofa, a concerned look on his face. "Sorry, wee one, I wasn't thinking…should have waited."

Michaela bit her bottom lip. "No, don't be sorry. I want you as much as you want me. But, as much as I regret it, stopping is probably for the best. I never move this fast, Liam. Never. We'll be even better together once we've gotten to know each other a little more."

"We will, indeed."

Michaela stifled a yawn.

"It's after nine o'clock and you're not long out of hospital. Not to mention that you were up early this morning and we traveled all day. What d'you reckon we say goodnight for now?"

As much as she wanted to spend more time with him, Michaela was exhausted—and aching from parts of her body that she hadn't even known she had. "Much as I hate to admit defeat, I think you're right. I've had it for one day." Then she remembered the terrifying dreams…visions…whatever the hell they were. She wondered how close the master bedroom was to the room where she would be staying.

"No worries. I'm right down the hall from you. I'll know if you have any further problems."

*What the…?* Again, he seemed to have plucked the thought right out of her mind—which was, of course, a totally irrational notion. Another disturbing symptom of possible brain damage resulting from the kick to the head.

Liam stood and held out his hand. She accepted it and he pulled her off the sofa. Leaning down, he kissed her neck below her right ear. "Sleep well, luveen. I'll see you in the morning."

As Michaela floated up the stairs to her room, she smiled to herself. Was this what it felt like to be falling in love?

## *Chapter Seven*

The room was dark, the weather dreary, when Michaela woke up the following morning. While it was early—only seven a.m. Irish time—her body clock deducted the five-hour time difference, making it feel, to her, like the middle of the night. Excited by thoughts of Liam, she was unable to get back to sleep, so she lay in bed testing various muscles for soreness. Hmm.... Other than the bump on her head—which still hurt like a mother—the wrenched muscles and other bruises on her body were actually beginning to feel a little better. More importantly, however, she had made it through the entire night without turning into a raving lunatic. Not that she hadn't had troubling dreams, because she did. But, for some reason, she had seemed to possess a kind of kill switch on the monsters starring in her nightmares. She could recall the terror of an evil force chasing her down the halls of an ancient mausoleum. But instead of freaking out and going into a psychotic breakdown, she turned to the phantom pursuing her and commanded him to halt. "Or I'll wake myself up!" she had threatened. The entity didn't obey her command, of course, but just kept coming toward her, trailing her, stalking. Her consciousness somehow awake and aware outside her sleeping mind, she told herself to wake up.

Lo and behold, her eyes had flown open, heart racing, pulse pounding in her ears, as she lay in the bed staring up at the ceiling.

As she mulled over the events of the previous evening, it occurred to her how strange Arianna's behavior had been during their telephone call the evening before. Maybe it was the stress of a new baby, or the fact that she was married now, but all the poking fun and teasing warnings Michaela had expected about the new man in her life just hadn't happened. Arianna had been uncharacteristically quiet, subdued. More than once, she had bemoaned the fact that she hadn't tried harder to convince Michaela to stay at the castle. *Under her and Caleb's protection.* When asked what she had meant by that strange allusion, she hemmed and hawed, then blew Michaela off. And forget gathering any intel on Liam either. It would have been easier to extract launch codes to a nuclear missile silo from the president.

The sound of raised voices downstairs interrupted Michaela's musings. Though she could make out only snippets of the conversation, it was clear that someone down there was *not* in a happy place. Her first thought was that it was the crazy redhead that Liam had been dating. But surely not. The woman couldn't possibly have the audacity to show up at a man's home uninvited at this early hour of the morning.

Well, hell. In dire need of her morning caffeine infusion, Michaela had been just about to get up and raid the kitchen for a cup of coffee. But as wisdom dictated staying out of the crossfire of whatever battle was going on down there, she wrapped her hair in a towel and jumped into the shower in the large *ensuite* bathroom instead.

After the hot water had soothed all her sore and aching parts, she slipped on a long-sleeve blue pullover hoody and a comfortable pair of faded jeans. It was the middle of August, and would have been blistering hot in the States. But here in Ireland, the mornings and evenings were cool, the afternoons pleasant.

Padding over to the door in her socks, she listened. No more angry voices. Good, everyone must have cleared out while she had been in the shower. Slipping out into the hall, she pulled the door quietly shut behind her. She was in the kitchen, poking around in the cabinets for a bag of coffee, when she heard the hum of conversation from the vicinity of the drawing room.

"Sure, 'tis a stubborn one you are, Liam O'Neill," a cultured female voice lamented. "Always have been."

"Mother, I told you not to concern yourself with this." *Liam.*

"And how is it I'm not to concern myself, when it's the fate of my future grandchild that we're speaking of."

*Grandchild?*

"Grandchild?" Liam's usually even tone rose several octaves. "With Aideen? Oh, no, there's no grandchild. Nor will there ever be one. Not with that woman. Not ever! And, speaking of Aideen, when did she call and wind you up about all this? And how the bloody hell does she know I've a houseguest? Is she stalking me now?"

*Awkward.* Heart beating rapidly in her chest, Michaela wished she could wiggle her nose and disappear through the ceiling, back up to her room. She was tempted to beat a hasty retreat now, but risked almost certain discovery. And the last thing she wanted was to get caught eavesdropping.

That was so *not* the way she wanted to meet Liam's mother for the first time.

"Ah, sure, you're being overly dramatic, boyo. Aideen's prepared to give you an heir, to continue the family name. Not many of our women would even consider such a thing, given the current situation with the curse. Not to mention the pain involved."

"You did it twice," Liam pointed out evenly.

"For your father's sake." There was a petulant sigh in the woman's voice that Michaela imagined was always there. "You know yourself, son, getting involved with a mere mortal's a bad idea. Best keep to one of our own kind, so."

*Mere mortal? Their own kind?* Michaela was flabbergasted. If Liam and his family weren't mortal, then exactly what the hell were they? And what was this thing about a curse?

"So, I've said me piece." After making the declaration, Liam's mother started making noises about it being time to leave.

Now or never, Michaela told herself and tiptoed out of the kitchen, making a mad dash for the staircase.

*Whew!* Just in the knick of time. The sound of footsteps and quiet voices traveled down the hall on the floor below, and then the front door opened and shut. Totally freaked by all the weird stuff she had overheard, Michaela really, *really* needed to talk to her best friend right now. Grabbing her cell, she punched in the contact for Arianna. And got voicemail. Probably busy with the baby, she thought, blowing out a frustrated breath.

Her voice just above a whisper, Michaela left a desperate message. "Hey, it's me. Listen, Arianna, you gotta call me as soon as you get this. Something very strange is going on here and I need to talk to you."

❧

After hiding out in the bedroom for about fifteen minutes, Michaela heard a light knock on her door. She put down the book she had been reading. "Come in."

Liam peeked around the door. "Hiya. Thought you might like to join me for some breakfast." He didn't sound upset or concerned that Michaela may have heard the private goings on down there, so she figured she wouldn't mention it either.

"Sounds good. What are we having?"

"Eggs, rashers, tomatoes. Whatever you fancy."

"I don't eat meat, but eggs and tomatoes sound great. And coffee," she added with a growl. "I need coffee *now*."

The solid oak table in the eat-in kitchen seated eight. Michaela sat in the chair closest to the island that dominated the center of the space, while Liam chopped and diced, sliced and sautéed, masterfully preparing their meal. Early morning sunlight struggled through the clouds and spilled through a large window overlooking an organic garden. "We have it enclosed to protect the produce from the deer roaming the property," he explained.

"I love a man who cooks." Although Michaela was teasing him, the talent really did ring up a *huge* plus on the new relationship scorecard she had been keeping. *Check, check.*

"I amuse myself in the kitchen is all. Look out the window. See? There's a doe with her fawn. We prohibit them from the garden, but we've salt licks and other delicacies set out for them to enjoy."

Michaela joined him at the counter, where a clear view of the back yard extended into the acres of lush greenery she had witnessed from the helicopter. "Aww…that's so sweet. I'm glad you don't hunt them."

"No, this is their home. A sanctuary, so it is. We all need a bit of that from time to time, do we not?" He stirred the contents of the pan in front of him, then glanced at her. "I failed to mention last night that I've to leave for Paris this afternoon."

Michaela's stomach sank at the news. "You're going away?"

"Mmm. An air show." He seated her at the table and placed a plate of scrambled eggs, a grilled tomato, some baked beans and a slice of toast in front of her. Hoping he hadn't cooked the eggs in sausage drippings, she prodded them gingerly with her fork. "No, I used butter only," he clarified, again seeming to make direct reference to her thoughts. He set his own plate on the table and took the seat beside her. "The air show alternates annually, held one year in June, the next in August. I was hoping you'd accompany me today. More coffee?"

"Yes, please. Half-cup." She chewed and swallowed the bite of egg in her mouth. "Umm…I would love to go to Paris."

"Brilliant. After we've eaten, I've a few errands to run. I'll be a couple of hours at least. 'Twill give you time to pack."

"I haven't really unpacked yet, so I'll be ready whenever you are."

Liam's cell phone rang. He looked at the display and frowned. "Sorry," he murmured. Excusing himself from the table, he left the kitchen. Michaela could hear him in the hall.

"Yes, I rang you. You've to stop this, Aideen. I'll not have you winding up me mother. And how did you know I've someone staying here with me, so?" A pause. "There's nothing between yourself and myself. We'd a few laughs, so we did. A wee bit of fun, getting the leg over. Nothing more." Another pause. "No. I didn't invite you along to the air show. You're daft, woman. I don't know what you're on about. We're finished, full stop. Now, please don't contact me again."

Michaela stuffed down the last bite of her breakfast, which stuck in her throat. It was weird, but she knew that if he ever spoke to her like that she would be heartsick. Devastated. And she had only known him for a few days. *You'd better think this thing through, girlfriend.* Always before, she had been the one to love 'em and leave 'em, so to speak. But that wouldn't be the case this time. Not with this man.

A few seconds later he turned the corner into the kitchen. "Sorry, I had to take that call."

"No problem."

While they tidied up together, he seemed preoccupied. Finishing up, he hung the dish towel on a rack to dry. "Now that that's done, I'm off to town. Is there anything you're needing?"

She smiled and shook her head.

"Make yourself at home then, luveen. If you're after getting bored, we've a well-stocked library across from the drawing room. You might find a book you fancy there."

"Thanks, I'll check it out."

Not much in a reading mood, Michaela took a leisurely stroll around the property, then she showered again, this time washing her hair. Taking a few extra minutes with her makeup—I mean, she was going to Paris, after all—she chose her wardrobe carefully, selecting a pair of black leggings and a form-fitting burgundy top that contrasted beautifully with the ebony black of her long hair. Figuring they wouldn't be away for more than a day or two, she unpacked everything she wouldn't need, leaving in her carryon only the items she would use for the trip.

Remarkably, with all the traveling she had done, this was to be Michaela's first time in Paris. Not to mention, of course, her first flight in a fighter jet.

"What kind of plane is this?"

"MiG 29." Liam's deep, sexy voice sounded tinny coming through their headsets. "A Russian fighter."

"Mmm. So how about a practice run? You know, a stunt or two?"

Liam gave his head a shake. "I'd have thought you'd had enough of being jostled about already."

"Nope. In fact, I'm starting to get a little bored." Eyes alight with excitement, she patted her mouth to simulate a yawn.

Liam grinned, a mischievous glint in his gaze. "Bored, is it? Well, we can't have that."

In the next instant, to Michaela's squeal of delight, he sent the plane into a nose-dive of at least a couple of thousand feet. When her stomach settled, she punched him lightly in the arm. "Is that the best you can do?"

"Not a'tall." His lips curved into a wicked, wicked grin.

For the next few minutes, Michaela held her breath as Liam piloted the aircraft into a series of aerobatic maneuvers, including a death-defying spin.

She couldn't wipe the stupid smile off her face. "Now, that's what I'm talking about."

For the next hour or so, they chatted, teased and laughed as if they had known one another forever. And then the jet began to drop in altitude. "Look down below," Liam said. "We're approaching Paris now."

ஃ

It was a thirty-minute ride into the city from Le Bourget Airport, where the air show was scheduled to take place the following morning. It took several hours to complete the preparation, inspections, and required paperwork, so it was early evening before they made their way to the hotel.

Michaela stared out the taxi window, in proper awe of her first visit to The City of Lights.

Liam reached over and lifted Michaela's gaping chin. "I'll have the driver take us on a quick tour of the city before heading to the hotel, will I?"

"Yes, please. I know it's too late to get into any of the attractions, but I'd love to see some of the places I've heard so much about."

Passing the Arc de Triomphe at the western end of the Champs-Elysees, Liam pointed out the Louvre to the east and the Seine River to the south. The driver continued around the city, pointing out several other historical monuments. There was the Pantheon, Les Invalides, the Sorbonne, the Hotel de Ville, and Notre Dame.

Finally, they were arriving at their destination. "The *Ritz*?" Michaela shot the Irishman an incredulous look as they pulled up in front of the masterpiece in eighteenth century architecture.

He shrugged. "'Twas closed for renovations from 2012 until mid-2014. Thought we'd be after checking out the new and improved facilities."

Now Michaela was no stranger to opulence. She had been raised with great wealth. But this place…this was extravagance unchecked. A structure immersed in history, the Hotel Ritz was where Diana, Princess of Wales, had dined with her lover shortly before her death in the fatal car crash. A home away from home for royalty, politicians, film stars, writers, and the like, even Ernest Hemmingway had made his headquarters here for a time.

Refusing the assistance of a bellhop, Liam proceeded to their accommodation, the Windsor Suite, furnished with Louis XIV antiques, tapestries, and fine rugs. Even the walls themselves were colored in decorator shades, including almond green, pearl gray and salmon.

"This is beautiful, Liam." Michaela eyed the massive bed, every nerve ending in her body hyper-aware of the fact that she would be sharing it with him.

"Do you fancy changing for dinner now?" Liam asked. "The food's gorgeous, the restaurant's two Michelin starred."

Lingering over a candlelit dinner of Japanese Kobe steaks for Liam, a vegetarian medley for Michaela, it was heavenly to just relax and get to know one another better.

"How's the lump on your head, so?" Liam inquired. "You've not had a bad dream or hallucination since leaving Clare, have you now?"

"Last night, at your place, I had a nightmare, but it was weird."

"Weird, how?"

"Well, as it was starting to get really scary, to seem very real, I suddenly realized that I was dreaming…*while I was dreaming.* And I was able to consciously wake myself up."

Liam's brows drew together thoughtfully. "Hmm…. A waking dream."

"I've heard of that, but I've never experienced anything like it before. It made me feel safe, like I was in control."

"And so you were." Liam emptied the last of the bottle of some French red wine Michaela couldn't pronounce into her glass. "I've made reservations for the Moulin Rouge tonight. But you're still recovering from that nasty knock on the head, and starting to look a bit peaked. Since we've to be up early in the morning for the air show, what d'ya reckon we do the town another time?"

Just the sound of Liam's deep and accented voice, the touch of his hand as it brushed hers on top of the table, had Michaela so seduced at this moment that she would have agreed to anything he proposed. She was a little tipsy from the alcohol, still a little wired from the thrill of the flight, from being here in Paris, at the Ritz, no less, with the most incredibly awesome man she had ever met. Every touch, every word they spoke became foreplay for the night to come. But the attraction wasn't purely physical. No, far from it, Michaela thought. There was something about this man that called to Michaela. Something raw and wild, almost magical. It was something that made her believe, as ridiculously old-fashioned—as scary—as it sounded, that he was *the* one, the man she was meant to spend the rest of her life with.

Plain and simple, Liam suited her.

"I'm good with staying in tonight." The silent message exchanged between them was fraught with meaning.

"Are you…sure?" Liam asked.

"Like I told you before, Liam, this is…well, moving really fast for me. But it seems like there's something different…something special between us. Like we're in sync somehow." The flickering flame of the candle reflected off the polar blue of his eyes, making it appear for a moment that he had flinched at her words. "I'd like to be able to take our time to explore…whatever this is. But we live an ocean apart. So it's pretty much now or never for us."

After that conversation, things seemed to change. The seductive daredevil, take-life-as-it-comes, male he had been until then became suddenly subdued. Withdrawn. Commitment phobic, Michaela surmised, accepting that she had read far more into the connection between them than was actually there. A man with his outrageous sexual appeal, his amazing good looks and incredible wealth, could have any woman he wanted. Silly how she had convinced herself that she had seen a spark of something real.

Back in their room, he begged off going to bed. "I've a few calls to make about the air show in the morning." He gave her a chaste kiss on the forehead. "Go and lie down, get some rest. I'll join you in a wee while."

Lying in bed, Michaela listened to the quiet hum of his voice in the next room until she drifted off to sleep.

# *Chapter Eight*

When Liam awoke the following morning, he was wrapped around a little pixie with long black hair and petite athletic limbs. 'Twas disturbing, how good it felt just holding her this way, especially when he'd not a habit of actually *sleeping* with a woman. Truth be told, very little 'sleeping' ever took place between himself and his bedmates. Once the activities of the evening were over, they were over. He got up and went home to his own bed.

As he breathed in the sweet scent of the wee woman curled up in front of him, she murmured and snuggled against him, pressing her fine bottom against that aching part of him that he rarely denied. Why had he reacted so strongly to her sentiments of something special between them? Why had he allowed her mere mortal illusions of some grand romance interfere with what would have otherwise been an incredibly satisfying sexual encounter for the both of them?

'Twas complicated, sure. She'd have undoubtedly become with child, as the seed of a *Túatha de Danann* male was exceptionally fertile. No mortal birth control method would have been sufficient to prevent conception and, unlike their own women, Michaela would have no control over her body's reproductive process. Still, with only three months until all would be fulfilled, one way or the other, there was no longer any danger to her of the birthing death from the *Geis*-induced blood poisoning. With the way things appeared at the present, the whole world would be the likes of a bloody pile of rubble before she could come to term.

Unless, o'course, the Woman of Promise should appear and resolve the *Geis*. Oh, aye, he scoffed, after three millennia *that* was about to happen. And yet, if he were to be totally honest with himself, 'twas just that possibility that was after cooling his loins the evening before. Her talk of a *connection* had forced him to admit to himself that he actually fancied the little Yank. *Fancied.* 'Twas the only word that fit these ridiculous, bizarre feelings he'd been experiencing for her since she'd come into his life. Oh, he'd had plenty of women before her, sure. Had fun with them, enjoyed their company and shared their bodies, their sexuality. But never before had he felt…possessive. Or protective. Or, whatever the feck else he'd been feeling since he met the little minx. He recalled his conversation with Caleb about that very topic: the possibility that Michaela may be the Chosen One, and Liam, himself, with some divinely ordained responsibility for keeping her safe, blah, blah, blah.

All he knew right now is that he wanted inside of her in the worst possible way. Considering that her almost certain pregnancy would be a complication neither of them needed now, he regretfully untangled his limbs from hers and slid quietly out of the bed.

As he stood to his feet, he heard a slight intake of breath. The woman was awake and had noted the nude, erect state of him. His eyes connected with hers. "Good morning, luv. I've to be at the airport by six a.m., so we'd best be up and about."

"Oh." Shyly, she bit on her lip, that juicy morsel Liam wanted more than anything to nibble on himself. Still, her disappointment that he hadn't attempted a sexual liaison the evening before was evident in the hurt and embarrassed look on her face.

He tipped his head. "You were sleeping when I came to bed. You've been through a lot the past few days. Thought it best that we postpone our first time together until you're up to the sexual acrobatics I've in mind."

She gave a slight smile and looked away.

Liam knew she hadn't bought his explanation. 'Twas simple. *Too* simple, so it was. And he strongly doubted that anything between them would ever be quite that elementary.

After the show, they had flown straight back to the airport in Ireland, where they dropped off the MiG and picked up Liam's helicopter. Now, alone in her room at his place, Michaela found herself dealing with a bunch of unanswered questions. Feeling the need to talk to her best friend, she tried to call Arianna, but there was no answer. *Again.* She had to admit that she was beginning to get more than just a little bit miffed by her friend's lack of communication. Oh, she understood that Arianna had a family now—was a new wife and mother and all that went with those roles—but for her not to return a single call, especially when her supposed good friend was recovering from a scary head injury.... Well, suffice it to say, that Michaela's inner child was stomping her feet and throwing a full-blown temper tantrum as she relived a similar neglect, that of her parents when she was growing up.

Stretched out on the bed, she went over the events of the past couple of days. Like most air shows, this one had been amazing—the roar of the jets, the death-defying stunts of the pilots, the reaction of the crowds—but, unlike all the other shows she had been to, this was the first time she had felt like she really had a stake in the game. She had been choking on her heart during Liam's entire demonstration. And, given the newness of their relationship, the sheer and utter terror she had felt for him defied explanation. Not an experience she was looking forward to repeating any time soon.

Too close too soon, she warned herself. She had known him for less than a week and, *go ahead, admit it,* she was already half in love with the guy. Not smart, she knew. Not when he kept his phone on vibrate and she could hear it going off every little while. A variety of different women calling, no doubt. Or maybe just that one crazy, jealous bitch. Either way, it didn't matter. Because she didn't do drama. And she sure as hell didn't share.

*Share? Yeah, right.* They would have to be *doing* something for her to share him. And that just wasn't happening. I mean, the two of them had slept together in the world famous Hotel Ritz, in the most romantic city in the world, the freaking City of Love, for God's sake, and Liam hadn't touched her. Blamed it on her injuries, of course, but she was no dumb broad. She knew something else had been going on in his head.

Something she intended to get to the bottom of.

But what she needed right now was a good, hard workout. Sweat out some of the confusion she was feeling from the unanswered questions, the frustration from her disappointment of the evening before.

Michaela hopped off the bed and the room began to spin around her. *Oh God, no. Not this again.* But, while the vertigo caused by the blood rushing from her head ended almost immediately, it left her shaken. Luckily, she hadn't had any uncontrollable nightmares, or visions, or whatever the hell they were, since she had left Arianna's place a couple of days earlier. So, maybe Liam had been right. Getting away from any lingering ghosts attaching themselves to the medieval castle must have helped. Either that, or it was just a sign that the knot on her head was healing. In either event, she was grateful to be back in control of her mind.

The thought lifted her spirits. *Now off to find that workout room.*

With sweat dripping into her eyes, Michaela pushed past the pain, working her weakened muscles to the limit of their endurance.

Beginning with some stretches and a little weight training to ease out the kinks, she was now moving through a series of advanced karate forms. As she snapped a sidekick, she saw Liam pop into the room wearing shorts and a muscle shirt, a towel slung casually around his shoulders. *Damn.*

A saucy grin on her face, Michaela approached him, throwing out a challenge with a two-handed shove. "You up for a sparring match?"

"I think the question is, are *you* up for one?" He snapped his towel at her, then tossed it aside and began to circle her. He advanced with a series of chops, kicks and sweeps, all skillfully pulled.

Although she was a black belt in Tang Soo Do karate, the guy proved to be way out of her league as they moved, hot and heavy, into a skilled martial arts exchange. As he allowed the occasional blow to glance off her body, it was clear he was taking it easy on her. "That the best you got?" she taunted.

Sweat dripping down one cheek, Liam swept her feet out from under her, then caught her to break her fall onto the mat. "Not a'tall. I've more for you, sure." Rolling her over, he pinned her beneath him and took her mouth in a tempestuous kiss.

*God.*

His lips moved down her cheek, her neck, and then his hand found one breast. Her breath caught in her throat. "Oh...."

He looked down at her. "Don't think for an instant that I didn't desire you last night, wee one. I've fancied getting my hands on you since the moment we met. Tell me now if you want me to stop, and I will. Otherwise...."

No freaking way that was going to happen, Michaela thought, every cell in her body like a military guard standing at attention, focused on those skillful hands, that practiced mouth. But then she heard his cell phone begin to rumble from a table by the door.

*Nothing like a call from another woman to spoil the mood.*

"Better get that." She glanced pointedly toward the table, then looked back up at him again.

"No." Clearly pissed by the interruption, his eyes reflected an ice storm at the polar caps.

"I insist. I think we're done here for the moment."

He heaved an irritated sigh and rolled off her. Stalking to the table, he swiped up the phone and glanced down at the display. It was fascinating, watching the way those dark thunderclouds cleared from his face. "Hiya." A pause. "Aye, she is." A perplexed look on his face, he walked back over to the mat and offered the phone to Michaela. "It's for you."

Sitting cross-legged on the floor, it was Michaela's turn to look confused. "Hello? Oh, hey. Yeah, um, feeling much better, thanks." A long pause. "Sure, that sounds like fun."

She got to her feet and grabbed her towel, wiping the sweat from her face. "Your sister's heading into town this afternoon to do some shopping and invited me to come along. I think I'll run upstairs now and take a shower. You need me to pick up anything while I'm out later?"

Liam shook his head. "No. I'll just finish my workout, and then I've some business calls to make. I'll see you girls when you get back."

Saved by the bell, Michaela thought as she left the room. As much as she wanted Liam, she couldn't help but feel anxious about taking things so quickly to the next level. She was already experiencing emotions, the depths of which she couldn't understand. With the increased oxytocin levels brought on by such intimacy, she feared their lovemaking would only bind her to him more irrevocably. From the beginning, things had moved too fast between them. And now, sharing his home like this was feeling far too domestic for her own good.

Catriona called out to her brother from the window of her silver Porsche Spyder. "I'll be taking your woman out to lunch before I bring her home, so you'd best be finding yourself something to eat on your own."

"No worries."

It didn't take long for Michaela to confirm her initial impression of the woman. Smart, funny, outgoing, just generally a nice person, she and Michaela clicked like a perfectly tooled lock and key. As they wandered through shop after shop, they laughed and teased like they had known each other forever. Catriona helped her pick out a shirt for Liam—a thank you gift for inviting her to stay in his home. In addition, she purchased a Celtic cross key chain for herself and a few other trinkets, souvenirs for some friends back home.

When they were finished shopping, the two women stopped at an Indian restaurant for a bite to eat. Michaela chose the palak paneer, a vegetarian dish consisting of spinach and a mild, Indian cheese. "Wow, this is outstanding." Michaela scooped up another big bite. "I didn't expect an ethnic restaurant here in Ireland to be so on par with the ones in the States."

"Yer man who owns this place is originally from New Delhi. Sure, this country's become a melting pot in the past decade or so, a regular League of Nations." While raising another bite of chicken korma to her lips, Catriona shifted her gaze to somewhere over Michaela's left shoulder. She frowned and put her fork down.

All at once, Michaela's head began to feel swimmy, her stomach queasy. Fearing an embarrassing episode, she excused herself from the table and retreated to the ladies room. A splash of cool water on her face helped to shake off the sickening sensations. After repairing her damaged makeup, she headed back to the dining room.

As she turned the corner, she spotted Catriona speaking with another woman. *Crap.... Aideen.*

"Are you well?" Catriona asked as she approached the table. "You'd grown a bit pale."

"I'm fine. Still a little dizzy from the accident is all."

"Em, this is Aideen." Visibly uncomfortable with the situation, Catriona continued with the introduction. "She…em…."

"Is Liam's girlfriend." As Aideen finished Catriona's sentence, her even, white teeth were revealed in a sneer.

Michaela squared her shoulders. "Funny, that's not how I hear it."

"Is that so?" Eyes that sparked an eerie lavender color peered into hers.

"Look, lady, I don't know what your problem is, but you really need to back off. Believe me when I tell you, you don't want trouble with me." Michaela could feel her temper crowning at the woman's intrusion on their private meal. "Besides, I have to admit I'm surprised at you. I would think that stalking a man who has no interest in you would be beneath you, demeaning. You're only embarrassing yourself."

"Oh, am I now?" A cold, cruel smile crawled over the woman's classic features as she accepted the gauntlet Michaela had thrown down in front of her.

"Aideen, this isn't appropriate," Catriona protested in a stage whisper. "We're having our dinner now. If you've any grievances to air, you should be taking them up with Liam."

The woman shook her head. "The grand cheek of him, bringing the little mortal back to stay with him in his home." She turned her angry eyes toward Michaela. "And yourself," she spit out. "If he'd any care for you a'tall, he'd not have done such a foolish, foolish thing."

Michaela felt trapped in the woman's odd-colored eyes. Unable to look away, she could feel the room around her take one slow spin.

"*Stop!*" At Catriona's sharp tone, the woman snapped her eyes in her direction.

Michaela felt like a fish yanking free of a hook.

"You'd best mind yourself, Aideen, lest you allow this mischief to go too far." Sweet Catriona's lethal tone seemed at odds with the woman's usual demeanor.

The admonition must have worked, however, because Liam's ex seemed to reconsider whatever she had had in mind. With another cold stare in Michaela's direction, she turned on her heels and stomped away.

Michaela gave her luncheon companion a raised-brow look. "Awkward."

"Indeed. And, sure, Liam will be none too pleased to be hearing of it."

The two women finished their meal quietly, the confrontation putting a damper on the lovely time they had been having together. As Liam's sister dropped her back off at his house, she touched Michaela's hand. "I've so enjoyed our visit. Please, don't let what happened today affect your feelings for my brother negatively."

Michaela smiled and nodded.

"I've already told him that Aideen was after showing up and causing problems."

When could she have contacted him? Michaela wondered idly. They had been together since the conflict and Catriona hadn't touched her phone.

But as Liam opened the front door, the fury in his eyes seemed to emanate from every pore. "Are you well?"

"Of course." With a wave, she called out to Catriona. "Thanks again. I really enjoyed myself."

As the silver roadster roared out of the circular drive, Liam closed the front door. "You're sure you're fine."

Michaela set her purse down on the hall table. "Yes, Liam."

*Good grief! Why was everybody freaking out over the antics of one stupid, jealous woman?*

"Not having any other…problems?"

"Not really. Got a little dizzy a couple of times, but nothing major."

"Hmm." He paused, took a considering breath. "Bringing you here has proved to be a bad idea, I fear. Best if I return you to your friend in Clare. We'll leave first thing in the morning."

Michaela stared at him for a moment, blind-sided by the abrupt about-face. Then, with a short nod, she excused herself and retreated upstairs to her room.

❧

After the wee sprite had gone off to the bedroom, Liam rang Caleb. "There's trouble brewing here, I'm afraid."

"With Michaela? What's the *craic*, man?"

"Nothing to do with the visions. The protection charm I placed around the property seems to have kept any of that at bay."

"What's the trouble, so?"

"I'd been seeing a woman, one of our kind, o'course. Had her with me in Dublin, when I met Michaela. 'Twasn't working out, so I ended things. I've a notion she has it in her head that the wee Yank's the cause."

"Shite."

"Aye. She ran into my sister and Michaela whilst they were in town today, and there was a full on row between herself and the mere mortal."

"Not good."

Liam could feel the tension radiating from the other end of the line. "'Tisn't, no. My sister said that Aideen started to conjure up some faerie magic, but Catriona put a stop to it."

Silence greeted the remark.

"I fear that's not the worst of it, though. She's a bit of a wild card, is Aideen. Tends to skip back and forth across the line separating the *sidhe* and the mortal world."

It was one of the most dangerous things a member of their race could do. The lure of the faerie kingdom experienced by the transformation to a purely magical being often seduced a person to remain in that state, to voluntarily give up his or her mortal soul.

"What about yourself? After spending this time with Michaela, do you sense a connection? One that may be *Geis*-based?"

Liam blew out a breath. "There's an attraction, to be sure. But she's an intelligent, outgoing, exotically beautiful woman. So, who's to say it's not merely chemistry and nothing to do with the Enchantment a'tall?"

"True, true." Caleb's concession sounded insincere. "So, what's the story, mate? Are you considering bringing her back here, whilst we get this sorted? My wife's regretting letting her go without a fight. She wants her friend here with us, under our protection. Just in case."

For some unknown reason, the suggestion that she be safeguarded by anyone other than himself made Liam's ire rise. "If all this is anything to do with the *Geis,* it's *my* protection she's required to be under."

"What do you suggest, so?"

"I want Michaela away from Aideen's influence. I've already told her I'll be bringing her back to Clare in the morning. I reckon I'll have to remain there with her for the present."

"You're very welcome, o'course. Whatever her issues, it's best that the four of us be dealing with them together. I'll contact the Council members, update them on the situation. Since you'll be here tomorrow, I'll call another online meeting for Wednesday morning. 'Twill give yourself and myself a day to get things sorted before meeting with the others."

# *Chapter Nine*

Michaela was beginning to feel like a freaking yo-yo. Confused by Liam's rejection of her, evidenced by his desire to dump her off with her friend, Michaela was up, packed and ready to leave his home first thing on Tuesday morning. What would normally have been a three-hour drive, the Bugatti accomplished in less than two.

Arianna greeted them at the front door. "Hey guys. So how's the hard head."

Still nursing hurt feelings over the way her friend had gone incommunicado, Michaela produced a slight smile. "Much better, I think."

"So…no more weird dreams and stuff?"

"Not since I left. So, how's my sweet little nephew?"

"Sleeping." Arianna beamed. "I swear, he gets more beautiful everyday. Looks just like his da."

Fidgeting through all the girl-talk, Liam finally spoke up. "Speaking of Caleb, where is he?"

"At the stables, as usual," Arianna replied. "One of the mare's is about to foal."

Excusing himself, Liam went off to find Caleb.

"*Men.*" Arianna snickered as she led the way upstairs to the family solar. "They'll do anything to avoid hanging out with a newborn."

In the kitchen of Caleb and Arianna's apartments, Michaela sat at the table while her best friend poured two cups of coffee.

"So, little mama. How are you getting along? Haven't talked to you since I left."

The two women knew each other far too well for either of them to engage in circle talk. While it was clear that her friend recognized the strain between them, Michaela had noticed something as well. Arianna was sporting those bruised dark circles under her eyes that she always got whenever something was stressing her out. Michaela only hoped it was the result of a lack of sleep and the responsibility of caring for a newborn, and not indicative of something more serious. Like the newlyweds having marital problems.

"I'm sorry I didn't call you back like I should have." Arianna set Michaela's coffee cup down on the table and took the seat beside her. "There's been a lot of…adjustment. First, well, the pregnancy happened so fast, and now a brand new baby. Kieran's less than a week old, but, thankfully, he's already sleeping through the night."

So, whatever issues Michaela was sensing weren't arising from midnight-feedings exhaustion. And the dark circles under her friend's eyes weren't the only red flags that something had changed. Arianna seemed different somehow, as if she had blossomed, gained a certain maturity. And not necessarily in a positive way. Michaela couldn't quite put her finger on it, but there was something else going on here, something her friend clearly didn't want to discuss.

Arianna stopped talking. "Don't look at me like that, Mick. I'm happier than I've ever been. Truly. It's just that it's a whole new life. A new world…."

"Okay, if that's all it is. I was worried, just couldn't understand why I hadn't heard back from you. Tara called a couple of times from Italy to check on me, but you didn't return any of my calls, even after I'd left several messages. It really hurt my feelings, especially under the circumstances."

"I know, sweetie, and I'm so very sorry. It seemed like every time I sat down to call you, something popped up to distract me. The guys have some…business together, and Liam let us know you weren't having any more hallucinations."

"Yeah, it's Liam I wanted to discuss."

"Me, too."

"Well, then? Talk to me already. I'm afraid I'm totally getting in deep here, like way over my head. I really, *really* like this guy, Arianna, and that worries me. I get the distinct impression that there's something going on with him that I'm not being told. Some deep, dark secret that you and Caleb and Liam are all privy to, but that's being withheld from me."

Arianna took a deep breath and got to her feet. She was refilling their coffee mugs, when baby Kieran began to cry in the next room. The smile that lit Arianna's face removed all doubt about her happiness. "He's in the study. What do you say we continue this in there."

Arianna bent over the hand-made wooden cradle resting in a corner alcove beneath an open window. Standing beside her friend, Michaela breathed in the salty air as she gazed at the breathtaking view five stories below. The surf rolled rhythmically onto a dark-sand stretch of beach cluttered with huge gray boulders. The perfect spot to sit and meditate while she healed.

Arianna scooped the infant into the crook of one arm. "Just like a pro," Michaela teased. "You're getting pretty darn good at that."

His little face scrunched up and he began to cry. "Oops. Hungry again? Here, you take him, while I go warm up a fresh bottle. Nipples are all cracked and sore, so I have to alternate between bottle and breast."

Michaela settled into the antique wooden rocker with the sweet smelling little boy all snuggled in her arms. She felt her heart melt. She would have so loved to have children. But the riding accident she had had as a young teenager had damaged her uterus and the doctors told her she would never conceive. Holding Arianna's baby felt good. Too good. It was bittersweet.

After he had settled down, Michaela walked back to the

cradle, tucked him in and squatted down beside him. "You are so beautiful." As she whispered the words, sea-green eyes stared up at her. Then he broke into a wide smile and cooed. Now, she didn't know much about babies, but was a newborn really supposed to be this communicative? Just as she was pondering the question, the little guy with the thick, black curls so like his father's looked pointedly over her shoulder. Thinking he had recognized his mother approaching, Michaela's gaze followed his. That was when she discovered that his eyes were focused on a half-finished bottle sitting on a table behind her.

Suddenly, the bottle lifted off the table and began to float in the air. In horrified fascination, she watched it fly past her and into one tiny, outstretched hand. "I did *not* just see that." Michaela stumbled to her feet and backed away from the cradle, trying not to hyperventilate. "What is this? A freaking episode of *Bewitched?*"

As the periphery of the room darkened to gray around her, she let out an unbelieving cry and crumpled into a heap on the floor.

When she came to, she was stretched out on the chesterfield sofa surrounded by Arianna, Caleb, and Liam. How long had she been out? "Are you okay, sweetie?" Arianna was applying a cool, damp cloth to her forehead. "What happened?"

Good question, Michaela thought. What *had* happened? Then, it all began to come back to her. The baby, the bottle....

She sat up and jerked a glance toward the cradle. Baby Kieran was sleeping peacefully, his bottle back on the table, right where it had been when she had first entered the room. "Another hallucination," she explained morosely. "And here I thought I was done with that crap."

"What did you see?" Caleb asked, a worried look on his face.

At first, Michaela refused to tell them what had happened. They would think she had lost the plot and needed to be put away. But when they wouldn't let it go, she described the episode with the floating bottle. The three of them exchanged troubled glances. When Tara was here, she had advised her to see a neurologist. Michaela had a very bad feeling that she might just need a psychiatrist instead. "I feel like I'm suffocating," she said, sitting back up. "If you'll all excuse me, I need some time to myself. I'm going to take a walk over to visit Wind Spirit."

She didn't plan to go riding. At this point, she didn't trust herself even to take her precious stallion out of the paddock. She wouldn't risk him being injured by riding him on unfamiliar terrain with her head in this condition. About forty-five minutes later, she saw Liam approaching from the direction of the castle. She led the horse into the stable and was brushing him down when he joined her.

"Dinner's being served in the Great Hall." His tone was abrupt as he stepped outside to wait for her to finish her chores.

A little while later, as they were returning to the keep, Michaela found she had to skip to keep up with his long strides. Finally, she stopped, hands planted on her hips. "What's up with you, anyway?"

"What do you mean?" Liam hedged, seeming taken aback by the pointblank question.

"I guess I'm just a little confused here, so I'm kind of hoping you can straighten something out for me. I believed there was a strong sexual attraction between us. But, while that's been going nowhere, you have hardly left my side since the day you brought me back from Dublin. What gives?"

His mood dark and brooding, he said nothing. But the look on his face communicated clearly that he would rather be doing anything else in the world than having this conversation.

"Look, Liam, I'm not trying to pressure you here. The reason I'm being so direct is that I really would have liked to get to know you better. But, after what happened today, I think it's best if I return to Maine. I just can't keep being a burden on my friends."

"You're no burden." And that gruff comment was all she managed to get out of the man.

ঌ৵

"She's planning to leave for the States."

Liam and Caleb were in the study, sipping a glass of Jameson before dinner. "Not good," Caleb said.

"No."

"My wife needs to be included in this conversation." Caleb closed his eyes and a few seconds later Arianna joined them in the study, holding the sleeping Kieran in her arms.

She smiled. "You called?"

Caleb didn't return her smile. "Your friend is talking about leaving, going back home."

"That's probably the safest place for her," Arianna muttered darkly, as she lay the sleeping baby gently in his cradle in the corner.

"You know yerself, she can't be leaving until this *craic* is sorted."

"I don't like this, Caleb. All the subterfuge. The potential danger she's in. She's my family—my *sister*, for God's sake. I cannot countenance continuing to keep her in the dark."

"I know, *mo chroí,* but what choice do we have?"

"I'm tempted to just sit her down and tell her everything."

"And, if you do, what then? If she is the Woman of Promise, the only one who can resolve the *Geis,* your actions would disqualify her from the role. 'Twould curse your own child—doom the whole bloody human race to destruction."

"I know, I *know*."

"Anyways, you know the law. Anyone who discloses the existence of our people to someone fitting the profile of the Chosen One will be tried for treason. And if convicted by the Council of Brehons, he or she would be sentenced to permanent exile, at the very least. Which would mean being forced to transform, banned forever from this physical plane."

Arianna took a shuddering breath.

Liam, who had been sitting quietly, spoke up. "I believe the wee woman cares enough for me to remain here, if I ask her."

Arianna looked stricken. "So, you'll use her *mere* mortal feelings of romantic attachment to manipulate her into staying?"

"At least until we can get this figured out, until we determine whether or not, she *is* this significant person."

Arianna looked him square in the face. "*Don't.*" She stressed the word like a royal decree. "Do *not* take advantage of her physically. I mean it, Liam. If you don't share her feelings, then don't touch her. Don't you dare break her heart."

With her edict firmly established, Arianna retrieved her child from the cradle and fled the room, leaving the two men sitting in silence.

# *Chapter Ten*

Becoming more and more computer savvy of late, the members of the Council of Brehons logged in for their online meeting. During roll call, the scribe, Seamus O'Donnell, noted that both Caleb and Liam were together at the castle. "So, Liam, what's the *craic*, man? Is it some sort of conjuring spell you're under, forcing your attendance here today?"

Taking the good-natured wind-up as 'twas intended, Liam commented dryly. "Ah, you're a stitch, mate. Should have been a comedian instead of a short-order cook."

The redheaded giant, owner of a critically acclaimed fine-dining establishment in County Galway, laughed out loud. "*Touché*, my friend."

After assuring that everyone was properly accounted for, Caleb called up the first—the *only*—order of business for the day, the fast-approaching deadline for resolution of the *Geis*. "Have any of you knowledge of anyone—other than my wife's friend, Michaela—who might fit the prerequisites of the Chosen One." He paused, stressing the urgency of the situation. "We've but three months remaining, gentlemen. Three months until all will be lost."

When no one could offer any possible alternatives, members began to discuss the increasing political and societal problems facing the world today. MacDara Darmody spoke up. "We've increasing problems with the global economy, o'course, with recent health concerns like the Ebola and Zika virus outbreaks. And, as always, there's the powder keg of unrest in the Middle East." A clinical psychologist and adjunct professor of early prehistoric anthropological studies at NUIG, National University of Ireland Galway, he was well equipped to address how those issues might tie in to the Awakening of the Beast. "We've to keep our eyes fixed on Israel, gentlemen. As I'm sure James will agree, anything connected with that tiny nation is after being fodder for the evil one."

Father James Conneely inclined his head. "Throughout history, Israel's always been the barometer by which the hand of God was measured. 'Twas always the same, Lucifer trying to wipe out the redemption of mankind by destroying the olive branch from which the seed of David would come. That failed, so now he's after trying to prevent His return by destroying the human race before the appointed time of fulfillment of all things."

"According to the ancient scrolls, The Woman *will* appear before the deadline." This from Thomas O'Dhea. "'Tis our responsibility first to recognize and then to protect her."

Until this point, Liam had sat quietly listening. "In millennia past, the Chosen One didn't survive 'the calling' despite our protection. My understanding is that the responsibility for her safety belongs to the one of us appointed by the Fates to champion her."

Caleb nodded. "This is true."

"In that case, I'd like to discuss the situation with Michaela. I've become involved with the woman, and would like to know how to ascertain whether she's any connection to the dissolution of the *Geis*."

"Caleb's told us a bit about the situation," Father Conneely asserted. "You've spent time with her, so?"

Liam accepted the challenge. "Time, yes. But we've shared no intimacies."

"My concern here is that we're grasping at straws," Seamus said. "The woman had a knock on the head, resulting in some hallucinations. Is there anything more concrete, more definitive than that for us to consider here?"

"As ye recall, last year we thought it possible that the One we're awaiting may have been my wife," Caleb began. "'Twas a suspicion later proved moot by virtue of her *Túatha* heritage. Still, I believe Arianna may be connected to the Woman of Promise in some fashion. In a vision forced upon her by *An Garda Geis* the night we were wed, the Beast threatened her, ordering her to return to the States. At that time, she expressed concern that the Chosen One may be one of her friends. Now, considering that possibility, and the fact that this individual must be a mere mortal kept unaware of the truth about our people, including the existence of the *Geis*, we've been very keen to keep those details a secret from her friend."

"Until now, Liam, you've been reticent about getting involved with the search for this woman." Eighty-two-year-old Brian Rafferty brought forth the topic that was on everyone's mind. "What's changed, in yer opinion?"

Liam cleared his throat. "As ye all know, I've considered it unlikely that the *Geis* will be resolved after all this time. It's been three millennia, for feck's sake. So, to answer your question, do I believe that Michaela is this 'Chosen One'? Not a'tall. However, given the dire circumstances in which the world finds itself, 'twould be irresponsible for me to ignore the possibility, however remote."

Caleb spoke up. "The major concern at the moment, I believe, is that she's considering returning to the States straight away. Because of the dreams and visions, she feels 'tis the best place for her to seek medical and psychological intervention."

In one accord, council members decreed that this not be allowed to happen until the question of her possible involvement in the dissolution of the *Geis* could be resolved.

"What, besides compelling her magically to remain here, can be done to prevent her leaving?" Brian asked.

"If she *is* the one," Caleb replied, "it's Liam himself who would be her champion, as he's the one of us to whom she's been drawn."

"As there's not enough time remaining for concern about a birthing death, the prohibition against mating with a mere mortal has become a non-issue," Seamus put forth. "Given that her attachment is to yourself, Liam, 'twould be no hardship on your part to seduce her into staying."

"Aye," Liam agreed quietly.

"Better yet, if she desires to seek medical help or counseling, why not offer to set it up for her here?" MacDara asked. "Would your wife be willing to intervene?"

Caleb gave a slight shrug. "If she believes that doing so is in her friend's best interest. She's very torn about all of this, as you might imagine. The two of them grew up together, like family."

"I'm happy to travel down from Donegal tomorrow," MacDara continued. "Since I'm a licensed psychologist, 'twouldn't hurt her friend if your wife were to arrange an evaluation for her. Not only would that answer the question of whether the woman's after having a psychotic episode, but with access to delve into her psyche I'll be able to search for clues that may help us determine the matter before the Council as well."

With the tentative plan set in place, the meeting ended.

While the men were tied up on business, the girls drove into Ennistymon and stopped at the Falls Hotel for lunch. A delicate sun shined over the Georgian manor house nestled on fifty acres of wooded vale. Deciding to take advantage of the perfect weather, they ambled through the gardens and along the riverside walk.

"I feel like I'm missing an appendage." Arianna laughed. "First time I've been away from Kieran since he was born."

"You know Caleb's grandmother is taking good care of him."

"I know. Anyway, we needed some alone time, just you and me. So much has happened since you've been here."

"Yeah. I don't know what's going on with me. I feel…unsettled. A little panicky. Like something terrible's about to happen."

Her friend looked worried. "I wish…there was something I could do to help you."

"I'm going have to go back home, Arianna. I can't keep hanging around here causing drama. You have too much on your plate right now, as it is. Anyway, all that weird crap seemed to stop while I was at Liam's. I really thought it was over."

"Me too."

"Maybe it's the castle. You know, being medieval. With all that ancient history, there's gotta be a few ghosts hanging around." She waved her hands. "Who knows, maybe I'm just picking up vibes."

A strange look crossed Arianna's face. "Maybe. I wouldn't be surprised."

Michaela stopped walking and turned to her friend. "No? Have you ever seen anything spooky there? Anything you can't explain?"

"A couple of times."

"Seriously? Tell me."

Arianna's arm looped through her friend's as they continued along the woodland walk beside the River Inagh. A gentle breeze stirred the scent of flowers and fresh-cut grass. The rolling green hills and manicured gardens bathed the senses in delight. "Well, when Caleb first brought me to the castle, I had a…a vision, I guess you'd say. I was suddenly back in ancient times, watching a battle. There were knights and horses and everything."

"No way. Why didn't you tell me this before? Maybe all the craziness happening with me really is connected with something supernatural at the castle. You said it happened a couple of times?"

A dismal look came over Arianna's face. "Yeah, but my first… uh…visitation wasn't at the castle. It was back in Maine."

As they passed a chestnut tree, a couple of old donkeys in a connecting field followed along the fence beside them. "You're kidding."

"Nope. It was my father, the night he died."

"Your dad appeared to you? And you kept this to yourself? Now, I can get why you wouldn't admit that to Tara, but why didn't you say anything to me?"

"You were worried enough about me dropping everything to leave for Ireland. How would you have felt if I'd told you Da had told me to come back here?"

Michaela gave a slight shrug. "Point taken. Still, you should have told me about this before now. With me seeing things that aren't there, I really thought I was losing it. Hey, what do you say we turn around and head back to the hotel? All this fresh air and exercise has my stomach growling."

"Yeah, me too."

As they reversed their direction, Michaela continued digging for information. "Okay, so back to your dad. What makes you think it was really a…a ghostly visitation. That you weren't just dreaming?"

"Because he handed me a key."

Michaela stopped again. "A physical key? To what?"

"The front door of my cottage here."

"Whoa. That's some heavy stuff, Arianna. Damn, I can't believe you're only telling me this now." They climbed the eighteen or so stone steps leading to the hotel entrance. "Oh, wow. This is striking."

"Yep. An eighteenth century mansion kind of built around an old medieval castle."

"I love Ireland. I swear, I don't think there's any other place on earth quite like this."

Arianna beamed. "Let's eat at the Cascades restaurant. It's quieter than the bar."

Floor-to-ceiling windows gave the dining room an expansive

feel, while the chandeliers, burgundy window treatments, and high-back tufted chairs added just the right touch of opulence. Seated at a table overlooking the falls, for which the hotel was named, they scanned the menu. "Okay, so tell me what's going on with you and Liam."

"Dude's absolutely yummy."

"Know that. I got eyes." Arianna chuckled. "But there's more going on with you than a physical attraction."

"Yeah. Scary."

An older woman with salt-n-pepper hair tied back in a bun appeared at their table to take their order. "Have you decided?"

"I'll have a salad with balsamic vinegar and oil," Michaela said.

"Me too, only with blue cheese dressing."

"And to drink?"

Michaela looked at her friend and shrugged. "Hey, it's five o'clock somewhere. What do you say we get a bottle of wine."

"You sure you should be drinking alcohol, what with your head injury and all?"

"Yeah, no problem. Besides, I think I could really use a drink about now."

"Okay, then, let's do some mead," Arianna suggested. "It's a wine fermented with honey, instead of sugar. Dates back to about 7000 BC."

"Sounds good."

As the server bustled away, Arianna settled back in her chair. "So, how'd you like Paris?"

"It's Paris. What's not to like?" Michaela grinned. "We weren't there long enough to really take anything in, but still it was amazing. The old buildings, being immersed in all that history."

"I'll have to admit I was worried when I heard you guys were going there. You hardly know Liam, Mick. You sure this thing isn't moving too fast?"

"Yeah, pot, kettle, etc.," Michaela shot back, brows raised. "Look how fast you and Caleb hooked up."

Arianna started to open her mouth.

"I know, I know, he was your dream dude and all that. Which is *really* weird."

The bottle of mead arrived at the table and the server poured them each a glass. "Salads will be out soon," she announced with an efficient smile, before hurrying away.

"*Slàinte.*" Arianna raised her glass in a toast.

Michaela clinked her friend's glass and took a sip. "Anyway, you don't have to worry about Liam dragging me into bed, because nothing's going on in that department. *Nothing.* Not even when we spent the night in the world's most romantic city. It's like he's holding back for some reason, keeps blaming it on my injuries. Tell you the truth, it's starting to make me doubt my womanly charms."

"I respect the fact that he's moving slowly, Mick. After all, the two of you only just met. It's a little soon to be getting physically involved, don't you think?"

"Normally, yeah. But we live in different countries, so if there's anything between us, we have to figure it out now. And, I know I joke all the time about jumping the guy's bones." Michaela took a deep breath. "But there's something I've never told you, told anyone."

Arianna's brows drew together in a frown. "What?"

"Well, I've never.... I mean...I've done some heavy petting, of course. I'm not a child. Still, I've never actually given myself to anyone before, not all the way."

"You've got to be kidding me. And after you gave me all that grief about being a virgin myself?"

Michaela gave a lopsided grin. "It's not like a religious guilt thing, the way it was with you. And I haven't built a monument to my hymen, or anything crazy like that. It's just that I've never met anyone who did it for me that way. At least not until now."

"Yeah, I get that." Arianna bit her lip.

"This really is different, babe. I mean, *God*, all that man has to do is look at me and my knees turn to jelly."

Michaela didn't miss the shadow of concern that fell across her friend's face. "Don't worry, kiddo, it's not just a physical attraction. Granted, on the outside, dude's a rebel, all chains and black leather, take-my-clothes-off-and-do-me-now, crazy sexy. But, on the inside, I sense a man who's good and honorable, something deep about him that he hides from everyone else."

Arianna nodded as she took another sip of her wine. "I know just what you're saying."

"Did I tell you I met Liam's sister? She picked me up for lunch and shopping, so we got to spend a little time together. I really like her. The only fly in the ointment is Liam's ex-girlfriend. The whole time I was in Sneem, she was stalking him. And me too, I guess. She showed up at the restaurant where Catriona and I were having dinner."

Arianna frowned. "That is so not cool."

"Tell me about it. There's something eerie about her too. About her eyes. I think she must wear those crazy colored contacts."

"Did you get to meet Liam's parents?"

"Well, his dad's dead." At the flicker of pain in Arianna's eyes, Michaela reached across the table and touched her hand. "I'm sorry, honey. I didn't even ask how you're doing with that."

"I'm fine, usually. Too busy to dwell, know what I mean? Anyway, you were telling me about Liam's family," she said, abruptly changing the subject.

"His mom showed up at the house while I was there, but luckily, I was able to avoid her."

The salads were served and Michaela placed her napkin in her lap. "Mmm. This looks good."

"Yeah, the food's amazing here." Arianna took a bite, chewing thoughtfully. "So, what's this about avoiding Liam's mom?"

Michaela dug in and spoke between bites, explaining the uncomfortable situation at the manor house. "Everything he told me about her reminds me of my own flaky mother."

"So, his mom likes this…ex of Liam's?"

"I wouldn't say 'like' exactly. His sister clearly detests her, which is good for me, of course. But the snippets of conversation that I overheard sounded like his mom was encouraging him to be with her." Michaela swallowed her last sip of mead. She picked up the bottle and topped off Arianna's glass, before refilling her own. "I don't know what to do. I feel like I should just pack up and go back home. But the thought of leaving Liam, of not giving this thing between us a chance to develop, to see where it might go…."

"Ah, honey, I'm sorry." She reached across the table and touched Michaela's arm. "I remember how hard it was for me, falling head over heels in love with Caleb, but not knowing if he felt the same. I couldn't leave until I was convinced he didn't love me."

"But when you tried to go, he showed up at the airport to stop you, but the flight had already taken off. It was weird the way it had to turn around and take you back. And Caleb was waiting for you to disembark, almost like he'd had something to do with it." Michaela chuckled and shook off the crazy thought. "Look at you now though, living in a fairytale castle with the love of your life. And a newborn baby to boot."

"Yeah. Every morning I wake up and want to pinch myself. I still can't believe how blessed I am." As they finished their meal, Arianna motioned for the check. "Well, you know you're welcome to stay with us as long as you want. I love having you close, Mick. I only wish you lived here."

The check arrived and both of the women reached for it. "I've got this. My treat," Arianna said, counting out several colorful euro notes. "Guess you just have to decide if you want to risk your heart, honey. I don't know Liam very well, and I have to admit that what I do know concerns me. He's a bit of a wild card, a womanizer, I've heard. Of course, that doesn't mean he isn't capable of committing to one woman if he found the right one."

They gathered their things to leave. "I don't know. All this insane hallucinating I've been doing has me pretty freaked out. Maybe I need a good psychological work-up."

Arianna nodded. "I'm worried about you, too. You have no idea how much. Just think this thing through before you leave, because you don't want to live the rest of your life wondering if he was the one." Getting to her feet, Arianna hooked her purse over one shoulder. "You'll make the right decision, sweetie. You always do."

## *Chapter Eleven*

Back at the castle, Michaela retreated to her room for a little down time. With a sea breeze blowing through the window, her feet on an ottoman, she was engrossed in the third book of an Irish trilogy by a new paranormal romance author when there was a knock on the door.

"Come in."

Liam walked into the room and Michaela's heart began to thud dangerously. *Yep, dangerous.* That was the word that described him best. Because the man was definitely a danger. To her sense of peace. To her heart. Maybe even to her life.

She set her book down on the table beside her. "Hey, how'd your meetings go?"

"Very well, thanks." He grabbed a seat on the chair next to hers and picked up her book. "Dark Awakening." He looked up at her, his lips quirked in a rare and sexy smile. "How was lunch?"

"Amazing. We went to the Falls Hotel."

"Mmm." He laid the book back on the table. "I want to talk to you about something, Michaela. Earlier, you mentioned going back to the States, but I'd really rather you didn't."

A crease on her brow, Michaela waited for more.

He sighed. "Truth is, little one, I fancy you. I'd like you to stay a wee while longer."

Michaela didn't let him suffer long. "Truth is, I fancy you too. And, if not for this crazy head injury, or whatever this thing is, I would stay. Originally, I'd planned to be here a month or more. But it's already been a week since my accident and I still keep having these meltdowns. I really need to find out what's going on."

"Agreed. That's why I was going to suggest you see a mate of mine, a psychologist from the University of Ireland. He's coming down here for a visit tomorrow, and I can set you up an appointment, if you like."

Michaela pressed her lips together. "Couldn't hurt to meet him, I guess. Only thing is, I'm beginning to feel like coming back here to the castle was a huge mistake. The idea of a lengthy stay was to help with the new baby, but the visions, the levitating bottle…." Michaela shuddered. "Arianna doesn't trust me alone with him—and who could blame her? At this point, my presence here is doing more harm than good."

Liam got to his feet. "I've an idea. You were doing fairly well whilst away from the castle for a few days. I've business back in Kerry on Monday, so I'll have to be leaving for home. What d'you reckon you meet with MacDara for the psychological work up tomorrow, then return to Sneem with me on Sunday?"

"After the *close encounter* with your ex yesterday, you chose to bring me back here—presumably to dump me on Caleb and Arianna. I'm not sure what you hope to accomplish by my returning to your home." Michaela tried to keep the pout out of her voice, but was unsuccessful.

"I brought you back for your own protection," Liam clarified. "I fear Aideen is mentally unstable. A menace. Truth be told, I can't fathom letting you go now, never seeing you again. So, if you're willing to be patient whilst I finish dealing with that daft woman I made the mistake of dating for a few weeks, I really would like having you stay with me for a while."

Michaela stood up and looked into those electric blue eyes. She heard his intake of breath as she placed her hands lightly on his chest. He grasped her hands and bent his head, taking her mouth in a fiery kiss. She melted against him.

Liam slid his index finger beneath her chin and raised her eyes to meet his. "For me, this is a rare attraction, wee one. If you're after feeling the same, we deserve some time together to sort this thing out."

Her heart filled to overflowing with an uncommon emotion that made her weak and breathless and strong and invincible all at the same time. Michaela stretched onto her toes and touched her lips to his. "Let's go home on Sunday, then."

*Why not? Might as well admit it, girlfriend, you're already in love with the guy, so why not go all in.*

Still, Michaela hoped to God that she wasn't making a huge mistake by moving so fast. There was something different about Liam. Something extraordinary. And she was convinced she would never find anyone else—no other man in the world—who would ever measure up to him. Which meant that, if this thing didn't work out once they had been intimate, the heartache of losing him would probably haunt her for the rest of her life.

'Twas bloody mental, Liam thought, the feeling of relief descending over him the moment the wee pixie had agreed to stay. He'd like to have blamed his reaction on the fact that she might be the One called to bring about resolution of the *Geis.* Truth was, however, that it hadn't a bleeding thing to do with the salvation of mankind—and *everything* to do with his increasing fondness for the girl.

He'd left the castle the previous evening and gone off with friends, arriving back late, after everyone had gone to bed. Now, he was heading downstairs to meet with Caleb and MacDara before Michaela's scheduled assessment.

As he entered the family solar, he discovered that Caleb's wife attended the group. "There's coffee, tea and scones on the table beneath the window," she said. "Help yourself."

"Thanks." Pouring himself a cup of tea, Liam joined the others in one of the chairs scattered about the room.

Arianna continued the conversation she had been having with MacDara when Liam had arrived. "As I was saying, I want your assurances that you're not going to do some…magic thing to mess with her head."

MacDara gave her an indulgent smile. "I've to determine if the visions are organic, or if someone else is 'messing with her head', as you so eloquently stated. You needn't be fearing for your friend, as I'll do nothing without her permission."

"And *you*." This to Liam. "I worry about how you got her to agree to stay. I don't want you leading her on. She's a good girl. Loyal. Very sensitive. I won't have you hurting her."

The ferocity of the woman's defense of her friend impressed Liam. "Noted."

"Where shall we set up?" MacDara asked.

"Here in the study," Caleb said. "We'll leave the room. Give you your privacy."

After Arianna had gone to fetch Michaela, Liam got up and topped off his cup of tea. "Sure, your wife's like a mama bear protecting her cub."

"She is, indeed. And with good cause, I fear. If it turns out that her friend's the Woman of Promise…." Caleb let the thought trail off and shook his head.

Why a sense of doom descended over Liam at his words was anyone's guess.

A few minutes later, the two women entered the room. The men rose to their feet. "Mick, meet MacDara," Arianna said.

"Nice to see you, Michaela. Sorry it isn't under better circumstances."

She shrugged. “Me too. But, hopefully, we’ll get some idea of what’s going on.”

Leaning over, Liam kissed the top of her head, pointedly ignoring the looks directed at him by the other Council members. “We’ll be leaving you to it. You’ll be fine, so.”

As the men filed out of the room, Michaela looked less than convinced.

About an hour later, MacDara sent a telepathic message to Liam requesting that he return to the study. Caleb and Arianna met him in the hall and they walked in together, a somber assembly.

They found Michaela sitting quietly on the sofa, eyes closed, hands in her lap.

“I thought it best if you were all here when I brought her back,” MacDara said.

“What did you do, hypnotize her?” A sharp note of concern sounded in Arianna’s voice.

“I asked her permission to put her under,” MacDara explained. “She’ll believe she’s been in a hypnotic trance, when in reality I’ve put her in my thrall.”

Anger stirred in Liam’s breast. “For over an hour? Bloody hell! Is that not excessive, dangerous for a mere mortal?” His voice elevated, hands formed into fists, he concentrated on his clenched fingers, forcing them to relax.

Three heads spun to look at him, surprise at the outburst etched on their faces. Not usually temper-prone, Liam had to admit that his reaction had been out of the ordinary. “It’s been no more than fifteen minutes.” MacDara spoke quietly, the picture of patience. “We spoke for a wee while, then I did a psychological work-up. When all was well in that regard, I suggested hypnosis.”

Properly chastened, Liam gave a short sigh. "What did you discover, so?"

"Not a thing. I was after coming against a psychic block. Like slamming into a stone wall, so it was. Sorry to say, but that lends credence to the possibility that her mind is being manipulated by an outside source. Possibly a minion."

Her face pale, Arianna sank onto the sofa beside her friend. "Oh, God."

"It's your impression, then, that the visions she's experiencing are the result of something more sinister than the aftereffects of being thrown from her horse," Caleb reiterated.

"I fear so."

Liam gazed down at the little mortal, the feisty, outspoken, complicated woman who had so promptly altered his life. Although the bruises on her body were fading, those beneath her eyes were growing more prominent. Her clothes appeared looser, so she was after losing weight as well.

"What do we tell her?" Arianna asked in a stage whisper. "How can we keep her safe?"

Liam began to pace. "Until this thing is sorted, she mustn't be permitted to leave Ireland."

"We have to let her know that she's in danger," Arianna insisted. When Caleb cut her a look, she put her hand up. "I know I can't tell her about the curse specifically, but when we were at lunch, she suggested that her visions might be the result of a haunting here at the castle. I'll go with that, let her know that something inexplicable—something *supernatural*—is going on here. If she understands that she could be at risk, she'll be more careful."

"I agree with Arianna," Liam said. "Should this all be a result of her being called into a quest for the artifact, we've to decide how best to further that along. Likely, the visions are leading her in the direction of the item, so once it's located and turned over to me, she'll be free of them." *And I'll be free of these uncomfortable feelings of attachment.* "Perhaps, if she were to keep a log—write down the contents of each vision—that record would help us decipher their meaning."

MacDara stood to his feet. "Then we've a plan."

༺༻

Feeling rested and alert, Michaela awoke to a semi-circle of gloomy faces. "What? Why so glum? Do I have a brain tumor or something?" Still groggy from the hypnosis, she grew concerned when no one answered her question. "What the heck? Why are you all looking at me like I've just been sentenced to death?"

Arianna reached down and grabbed her hand. "Come with me, babe. We're going down to your room to talk."

As the two women left the solar, Michaela noticed that the men were gathering into a circle. "What's going on, Arianna? I get the distinct impression that something really bad is happening."

"Not necessarily." Arianna gave a frustrated sigh. "I just have to figure out how to explain this to you."

Back in Michaela's suite, the two friends curled up in overstuffed chairs that were arranged side by side. "Remember when you said you thought that all this weirdness you've been experiencing might have something to do with a haunting?"

Michaela's mouth dropped open. "You don't really think that's true?"

"Look, unlike Tara, we both know that there are things on this earth that defy a natural explanation."

"True, but how does that affect me?"

"I believe that something…not of this world…has attached itself to you. I believe that's what's bringing on the nightmares, causing the problems you've been having."

"A ghost, you mean."

"A demon, more like."

Michaela felt the color drain from her face. "Demon? Are you for real?"

"I'm afraid so."

"Crap. I need to get on the next plane out of here."

"Doesn't work that way, sweetie. Whatever it is will just follow you home."

"How do you know that? What do I do?" Michaela paused. "I can't believe we're having this conversation."

"Yeah. Pretty creepy, huh?"

"Look, I've never been…psychic…or anything spooky like that. So, why now, all of a sudden?"

"I can't say exactly. Maybe it has something to do with being in Ireland. You know, where the fairies live."

Flabbergasted, Michaela's mouth fell open. "Fairies? Seriously, Arianna?"

Her friend shrugged. "Most Irish people believe in their existence."

Michaela shuddered. "Ghosts, fairies, demons…. Geez, I feel like I've been dropped into the middle of a horror movie."

Arianna blew out a breath. "I know the feeling," she commiserated softly.

"Okay, so what do I do now? You know Liam wants me to go back with him to Sneem."

"Yep. That worries me, too."

"You? I think I'm falling head over heels in love with the guy." With that confession, Michaela got to her feet and went to the window, then looked back over her shoulder at her friend. "He's the first man I've ever known who's capable of hurting me, Arianna."

"You have no idea, sweetie." Arianna shook her head. "You have no idea."

## *Chapter Twelve*

Apparently, not to be deterred from her campaign to get her son and his ex back together again, Liam's mother had left several messages on his voicemail whilst he'd been in Clare. Oblivious to the fact that the world would likely cease to exist beyond this year, she was on and on about Aideen's willingness to bear his heir. Because childbirth was so excruciatingly painful for women of the *Túatha de Danann*, many of their women refused to procreate. And as birth control was left to the will of the female, it was considered important to the future of their race for a man to choose a wife who would agree to give him a child.

Whether or not the world survived the approaching apocalypse, Liam had no interest in siring a child on Aideen. Neither had he any interest in increasing the vast number of people already crowding this planet. Having had enough of his mother's incessant harping on the topic, he'd chosen not to return her calls. Instead, he rang his sister requesting that she intervene with the inevitable fallout from his mother for bringing the wee yank with him back to Sneem. The two siblings had agreed to meet at the pub for a pint and a chat when he took Michaela into town later that day to do some personal shopping.

Sitting across the table from him, Catriona smiled and took a sip of Guinness. "So, brother of mine, what's the *craic* with the pretty little mortal you keep bringing home with you?"

Liam sighed. "Ah, sure, it's complicated."

His sister reached up and played with a strand of her spiked, platinum blonde hair. "Relationships usually are. With mere mortals, they're powder kegs, to be sure. And you'd best beware of an explosion with this particular one, because the sparks flying between ye are actually visible to the naked eye."

He shrugged. "And therein lies the problem."

Her manicured nails painted their signature black, Catriona ran one finger around the rim of her glass. "I know Council business is highly classified, so you're not free to discuss specifics. But, as children, we're all raised aware of the *Geis* and the restrictions of confidentiality it places upon us. We all know that time is running out, that there are but a few months remaining before everything will be resolved. Or not. I suppose, what I'm asking is, since there's no longer any danger to her of birth poisoning, have the two of you been intimate?"

Accustomed to such frank conversations with his only sibling, he shook his head. "First, she was all banjaxed from the fall off her horse. Then…I don't know…." He sighed. "The thing is, I've never felt an…attachment…like this to anyone before."

His sister huffed out a laugh. "Thanks."

Liam smirked. "You know what I mean. I'm referring to the bonding that couples experience. Like you and Cian."

"I know what you're saying, big brother, I'm just winding you up is all. In all seriousness, though, that attachment you're referring to normally comes only after physical intimacy. The bonding Cian and myself enjoy is the result of consummation of the marriage vow."

"Exactly."

Catriona pondered the information for a few seconds, then looked up at Liam, her eyes huge. "You're not thinking she's the Woman…em…that she has some connection to the…you know… to the *Geis*?"

"You know I'm not at liberty to discuss that."

Before the conversation could go any further, one of the pub's double wooden doors swung open. And in walked Liam's current nightmare in the flesh. "Shite, Aideen," he cursed, under his breath. "How in God's name did she know I'd be here?"

Catriona bit her lip. "I might have mentioned it to Mam when we were after speaking earlier."

"For feck's sake, Catriona."

"Well, you asked me to ring her. And you didn't say your whereabouts were to remain a secret from our mother."

As Aideen approached their table in the corner, admiring glances followed her across the room. The glimmer of magic she wrapped around herself like a royal robe drew the attention of mere mortal males like flies to a pile of manure. Liam found the analogy appropriate, given that what he had once found sexually arousing now left a stench in his nostrils.

"I'm going to the loo." Her chair scraped across the wooden floor as his sister promptly fled the inevitable confrontation.

"Coward." With a frustrated glance at the retreating back of her, he pushed his chair away from the table and stood up.

"Liam—." Aideen touched his arm.

Seething, he shook off the woman's grasp. "Are you daft? What in bloody hell is wrong with you?" he demanded. "Have you no dignity, no self respect? What part of 'I don't fancy you' do you not understand?"

The perfect bow-shaped mouth dropped open, lavender eyes blazing. The sortilege firing her soul raised the small hairs at the base of Liam's neck, a challenge that brought his own innate powers winging to the surface. Before things could go any farther, however, his peripheral vision caught the bemused stares of the pub's patrons. It was only then that he noticed the rattle of the glasses on the shelves, the shudder of the rafters overhead, and the trembling sway of the floorboards beneath their feet.

He glanced toward the restrooms and discovered that his sister had stopped the moment she had felt magic fire the air. Concern on her face, she met Liam's gaze. Immediately, he swept the pub's patrons with a suggestion that they were merely experiencing a minor earth tremor.

He spun back to Aideen, grasped hold of her arm and gave it a shake. "Do *not*," he hissed in a threatening undertone. "We'll take this outside, where we can be private."

He planned to usher her out the front door, but as he turned that direction, his icy gaze crashed headlong into one of melted chocolate. Standing at the entrance of the pub, the wee woman he'd brought home with him from Clare had walked in on the scene—and clearly misinterpreted what she was seeing. Confusion in her eyes, her gaze moved to his hand on Aideen's arm, then back up to search his face. Her features clouded with hurt, she backed out the door she had just entered.

"Bollocks! Michaela, no. It's not.... *Wait*!"

"Trouble in paradise, is it?" Aideen purred, her lips parted in a smug half-smile.

Liam inhaled a deep breath through his nose and fought for self-control. "This ends here, now, Aideen. *Full stop.* And stay away from me mother. Believe me when I tell you, woman, you'll not fare well in a challenge with the likes of me." Without waiting for a response, he turned his back on her and dashed outside.

Backing out of the pub's front door, Michaela felt shaky, her insides quivering. Thankfully, the minute she was clear of the building the earth stopped spinning beneath her feet. What the hell had she walked in on in there, anyway? While she wasn't happy to have found Liam in a heated encounter with his ex-girlfriend, that was not what had caused her to leave the pub so abruptly.

No, it had been something else entirely. Passing through that front door had been like stepping into another dimension. The floor had begun to sway beneath her feet as a dreamlike mist fogged her vision. A weird kind of static electricity had seemed to emanate from both Liam and the woman, whose sparkling skin reminded Michaela of the effect of sunlight effect on the vampires in the movie *Twilight*. Obviously, getting away from Clare and whatever hitchhiking ghost she had picked up at the castle hadn't put a halt to the strange episodes. Her only hope was that there was a logical explanation for the earth shaking beneath her feet. Was there any record of earthquakes occurring here in Ireland?

Not a second after her grand departure, however, Michaela realized she had nowhere else to go. She had arrived here in Liam's car, was staying at his home. She grabbed her phone from her purse, but before she could punch in Arianna's number, Liam chased out the door after her.

"Michaela, please." He reached for her hand, but she pulled it away. "Please, don't. At least let me explain before you make that call."

Catriona followed him out the door. "Listen to him," she mouthed, her eyes imploring Michaela to give her brother a chance.

Catching her bottom lip between her teeth, Michaela looked from brother to sister and back again. The intensity in the blue eyes looking down at her melted her heart and she gave a short nod.

"Do you mind if we get out of here, away from that bloody demented…?" Liam asked, his voice trailing off.

"Good idea."

His sister gave him a peck on the cheek. "I'll ring you later." She turned to Michaela and raised her brows meaningfully. "It's yourself he wants. I was there, Michaela. This really wasn't his fault."

As he pulled out onto the road, Liam floored the Veyron, the G-force slamming her back against the seat as he took the curves at breakneck speed. Mulling over his sister's comments, Michaela stole a glance at the magnificent specimen sitting beside her. Just like the million-dollar piece of machinery he mastered with such ease, the man was just too much. Too rich, too talented, too sexy and irresistible. Just too damned mysterious for her own good. Michaela looked at his hands, one resting strategically on the gearshift, the other wrapped around the steering wheel. She couldn't imagine what it would be like having those long, slender fingers on her flesh, coaxing her to the point of no return, commanding her response, possessing her body and soul.

He glanced over at her, ash-blonde hair draping his face, his lips curved in a cocky grin. "I can scarce wait to get my hands on you, little vixen." He spoke the words softly, his voice barely audible above the engine's roar.

*What the hell?* Had she said any of that *out loud*?

Embarrassed, Michaela bit her lip and turned to stare out the passenger window.

With the car in fourth gear, he reached over and squeezed her knee. "Now, as far as that scene with Aideen, sure, I want you to know I had nothing to do with her showing up there."

Michaela shrugged. "You don't owe me an explanation. You're a free agent, Liam. We're not sleeping together—or even dating, exactly. As a matter of fact, I don't know what we're even doing here."

"Well, then, I reckon it's about time we got that sorted."

"What…what do you mean?"

"I've a feeling we're going to be very good together, Michaela. Very compatible."

It was all foreplay, every word he spoke in that deep, lilting accent, the way those pale blue eyes touched the depths of her woman's soul. God, she wanted this man—wanted him bad. And yet, at the same time, she was afraid of him, frightened to lose herself in him. Because if she did, and he ever went away, she feared she might never find herself again.

"I'm sorry, Liam, but I need more time before.... There's just so much going on."

"There's no rush here, no pressure, little one. I just want you to know that I told Aideen *again* that she and I were through. I'll do my best to keep her from interfering with our time together in future."

"I appreciate that, but I don't think you understand. Running into you and that woman together wasn't the only thing that upset me when I stepped into the pub."

Liam looked at her, an eyebrow raised.

"It was like experiencing an earthquake, but the ground was only shaking *inside* the pub. Glasses were rattling. I could feel the floor moving, buckling beneath my feet. Just when I think I'm getting over whatever it is that's plaguing me, something weird like this happens again."

Liam ran his fingers through his hair, pushing it back from his face. A waste of time, Michaela noted, as the messy strands only fell forward again in a silken frame. "I'm sorry, luv."

As they sped the last few miles to Liam's property, Michaela sank back into the seat and watched the beauty that was Ireland flash past her window. She was happy that they were having this conversation, a real talk about the two of them, about where their relationship may be going. Still, with all the weird stuff going on around her, she couldn't help feeling uncertain.

I mean, just what the heck had she gotten herself into here, anyway?

ꕥ

Liam awoke to the muted sound of blood-curdling screams and raced to Michaela's room at the top of the stairs. Flinging the door open, he found her sitting up in the queen-size sleigh bed, knees drawn to her chest, hunched against the mahogany headboard. Eyes blind to reality, she was seeing something so horrific, so terrifying, that she wept openly, screaming, begging to be released from whatever tormented her, whatever monster that was holding her captive.

"Michaela, wake up!" Liam ordered sharply. Massaging her shoulders, he tried to take her into his arms, to hold her, but she resisted his comforting gestures.

Both arms flailing, she batted him away. "Nooooooo! God, let me go."

"*Mo chroí,* it's me, Liam. Wake up, my love. 'Tis only another dream."

As the tiny sprite went limp in his arms, Liam wrapped himself around her. Inside his chest was the stirring of some alien emotion, an uncomfortable fullness as if his heart had suddenly swollen to five times its original size. His mind unsettled by the experience, he encouraged her with soft-spoken Gaelic endearments. With those words of magic in the language of his people, he drew her slowly out of the dream-state and back to himself.

"Oh God, Liam, it was horrible. The earth was exploding, bits and pieces flying off into space." She trembled against him, sobbing quietly. "What's happening to me? I don't understand."

'Twas a strange array of feelings that overcame him then, a man not particularly known for his emotional depth, of a race of people not originally of this earth. He felt helpless, hopeless, concerned, and frustrated all at the same time. But as the wee Yank settled in his arms, another, even more disturbing, sensation poured over him. Possessiveness. A fierce will to defend and protect this woman caught him by surprise.

"Please, stay here with me tonight. I need you to touch me. Here, now." Her voice a whisper, she took his hand and held it to one small, pert breast.

At the touch of the erect nipple beneath his fingertips, his nude body leapt immediately to attention. Rejoicing at her invitation, it demanded he take her here, now, hard and fast, that he relieve himself of the bloody frustration he'd been after suffering since the night they'd first met. But, for all the fire smoldering in his loins, he managed to take her mouth gently. As he kissed her eyes, her cheeks, that soft place where her neck and shoulder met, her low moans encouraged him to go further. The delicate scent of her skin, all warm and musky from sleeping, pushed him almost beyond the point of no return.

"I want you to hold me, Liam, to make love to me." Weeping softly, she nibbled his earlobe. "Please, make me feel something real."

He sipped the tears from her cheeks, the moisture on his lips somehow extinguishing the raging inferno burning within. He felt off-balanced. This holding back was an experience to which he was unaccustomed. Amongst his people, sexual intimacy was enjoyed freely, shared without the strings of attachment so prevalent amongst those in the mere mortal community.

Why then this bloody hesitancy to indulge himself?

"I want you, *a ghrá geal*, my bright love, but just earlier today you said you weren't ready for this. Right now, you're sad and troubled. If we do this tonight, I fear you'll regret it in the morning."

Michaela huffed a disappointed breath and flipped onto her side. The view of her slender back curving down into a tiny waist, flaring into a womanly hip, gave him second thoughts about this daft, self-imposed celibacy.

*Shite.* He reached out and gathered the long, black hair that draped over her shoulders. Wrapping it around his hand, he bent and whispered in her ear. "We'll have our time together, little one. 'Tis inevitable, so it is. Just let me hold you and ward off the night terrors whilst you sleep tonight."

As he pulled her into his arms, she melted against him, her breathing becoming slow and steady in sleep. Whilst he, on the other hand, was hard and hot, his body giving him a royal bollocking for continuing to ignore its demands. As he lay in the darkness, watching her breathe, sleep evaded him, his mind racing with possibilities he'd never before cared to consider. 'Twasn't 'til dawn kissed the room with shades of mauve and gray that he slipped quietly from her side.

At the door, he turned to look back at the tiny imp and shook his head. "Jesus, Mary and Joseph, what are you doing to me, woman?" A frown creasing his brow, he let himself quietly out of the room before his true nature could get the better of him.

# Chapter Thirteen

Michaela sighed and curled into a fetal position. A light rain beating against the window kept the room at half-light. The events of the previous evening played through her mind and left her feeling disorientated, confused and...embarrassed. Liam had awakened her from another terrible nightmare and she had all but thrown herself at him, practically begging him to make love to her.

And he had turned her down. *Again.*

What the hell? She was a smart, attractive, sexually desirable woman to whom men had always been drawn. But now, when she may have finally met 'the one', a man who mesmerized her, made her blood sizzle and her heart sing, he wanted no part of her. What the hell, indeed.

Huffing out another heavy breath, Michaela rolled out of bed and took a quick shower. She didn't wash her hair, so it took only a few minutes to throw on a pair of faded blue jeans, a white and gray, long-sleeved Tommy T-shirt, and apply a little makeup. At the door to the bedroom, she hesitated, hand on the doorknob. She felt uncomfortable after last night, not sure how to behave when she saw Liam.

Deciding just to play it by ear, she headed downstairs and found him working at his computer. "Good morning."

He looked up at her. "Mornin'. I'd ask how you slept, but I already know that you had another bad night."

"Oh, yeah."

He seemed distant this morning, quiet and introspective. His normal attitude, which could best be described as amused arrogance, was nowhere in sight. Was he sorry he brought her back here with him? Did he feel pressured into taking care of her? Michaela had always been an independent woman and hated feeling handicapped. Needy.

"I was up early and already had me breakfast. But the cook's in this morning, so just tell her what you'd like and she'll make it for you."

"Thanks, but I'm not hungry. I'll just grab a cup of coffee and sit on the porch. Read for a while."

Liam nodded and turned back to the computer.

In the kitchen, the buxom woman who managed Liam's meals a few days a week greeted Michaela. "Good mornin', miss. My name's Assumpta."

"Hi, nice to meet you. I'm Michaela."

"Shall I make you something to eat?" the pleasant woman asked. "A full Irish, like?"

"No, thanks. Just a cup of coffee, please." The woman grabbed a mug from the cabinet. "While you're doing that, I'm going to run back upstairs and get a book. It's rainy and dark outside, the perfect day to do a little reading."

Coffee mug and book in hand, Michaela made her way to the glassed-in porch outside the kitchen that overlooked the organic vegetable garden. As she stretched out on a plush chaise lounge in the corner, she saw a doe with two of her babies prancing around outside the fenced enclosure.

Smiling, Michaela sipped her coffee, then set it down on the white bamboo table to the right of the lounge. She sank back into the cushions, book in her lap, and closed her eyes. As she began to doze, the patter of rain against the glass surrounding her seemed to keep pace with the strumming of her heart. Nonsensical daydreams flitted through her mind, visions of tiny fairies playing with the woodland creatures that lived in the forest and beyond.

*All at once, the magical beings romping through the dark woods began to transform, growing to human size. Michaela recognized her best friend, Arianna, dancing round and round holding her newborn baby to her breast. Caleb was there, as well. And Liam. And several others whom she had met during her stay at the castle in County Clare. As the frolicking group laughed and played, a creeping fog began to encroach on the happy scene from beyond the wooded vale. She recognized it instinctively. It was Death. Death to all. To her horror, she realized then that no one but her could see it coming. Michaela leapt to her feet and tried to call out a warning. But the words fell from her mouth all garbled, a distressed inner groan that only she could hear.*

*As her heart clenched in panic, she looked to her left. Wind Spirit stood there, his eyes rolling in trepidation. Shaking his head, he blew and nickered, his giant front hoof pawing the ground. As he galloped toward her, she tried to call out again to her friends, but to no avail. Wind Spirit drew near to her, and she prepared for the mount. The stallion was over sixteen hands tall and bareback. But as he arrived at her side, he slowed for her. Michaela grabbed a handful of his flowing mane, jumped up and with her belly across his back, swung her leg over his body.*

*The great beast flew. She tried to slow his gait, to redirect him toward her friends, so that she could warn them. He had always been so obedient, so responsive, but today he had a mind of his own. It occurred to her then that he seemed to be on a rescue mission, all right. But it wasn't her friends he was intent on saving.*

*It was Michaela, herself.*

Loud, angry voices jolted Michaela from the dreamy state. Not certain how long—or whether—she had actually slept, she felt disoriented and tried to tune out the drama ensuing from inside the house. Still, snippets of conversation reached her ears, then more as the troupe seemed to be walking through the house. Now they stepped into the kitchen, in full view of Michaela sitting on the porch on the chaise lounge. *Awkward.* Liam nodded permission to the cook to make her escape. Feeling trapped where she sat, Michaela raised her book and stared at the page, as if reading.

"I demand that you stop seeing that woman," a female voice was screeching. "I'll not be fecking replaced by a common mere mortal."

"Now calm yourself, Aideen. Your spewing poison is not helping your case here," Liam's mother scolded.

"And you, Mother, how dare you bring this woman into my home."

Michaela shivered at his tone, as cold and dangerous as black ice.

"I heard about the scene you made at the pub in Sneem," his mother defended herself. "Thought it best that the two of ye talk things out here in private."

"There's bloody nothing left to discuss," Liam said. "Herself and meself are through, mother. Not because I've met another woman, but because she's mental. And I can't tolerate the sight of her."

For a moment, everyone went silent. Then the door leading out to the porch exploded open. "You!"

Michaela looked up calmly from her book. Head tipped to one side, she stared into the strange colored eyes blazing down at her. "Are you speaking to me?"

"You dare to address me with such…such arrogance?" Aideen stepped in closer, hovering.

The sickly sweet scent of some exotic perfume the woman was wearing affected her like an opiate, dulling her senses. Michaela shook her head to clear it, as she detected another odor: a scent like the ozone in the air left behind after a lightning strike.

"Poor, common little mortal." Aideen seemed to preen, purring like a cat. "You've obviously no idea who—or *what*—it is you're dealing with here."

"Aideen?" Liam spoke her name as if in warning and stepped in front of her.

Michaela rose to her feet, straightened to all of her slightly less than five feet in height. "I can take care of myself," she assured Liam, then shifted her attention to the other woman, a smug smile on her face. "But are you really trying to instigate a physical altercation over a man? That's so low class, so…common. Isn't that the word you used?"

Just as Michaela had planned, her last comment pushed Liam's tall, willowy ex right over the edge. Aideen lost it. Totally. Teeth bared, eyes glowing red as if she were possessed of the devil, she began ranting and raving, saying things that led Michaela to wonder if the woman weren't completely insane.

"You think this is what he fancies?" she screamed at Michaela, spittle flying from her lush, red lips. "A weak, frail mere mortal? A woman forbidden to himself by the *Geis?* When he has a woman of the *Túatha de Danann* willing to provide him an heir. A thing you can never do, without being taken by the birthing death."

"Enough!" Liam bellowed.

And for the first time since all this had begun, Michaela was genuinely afraid. Of Liam. Of Aideen. Of being caught up in something alien, something she didn't understand. Even Liam's mother looked horrified at the altercation between her son and his former paramour. It seemed her meddling had gotten her in way over her head.

Aideen, on the other hand, seemed to be vibrating, her body held in place by some invisible power that prevented her from jumping all over her rival for Liam's affections.

The room was fraught with tension. A strange energy, like waves of electricity, had Michaela's ears buzzing, her teeth clenching. That force seemed to reverberate from Aideen's body in a rich, sky-blue glow, like argon gas excited by the electrical current. But as that power arced and reached for Michaela, it was readily absorbed by Liam and converted into the very force field that seemed to be holding the demented woman at bay.

Liam slowly turned his head and looked at Michaela. A herd of elephants stampeding through her chest, she was frozen to the spot, unable to look away from the sparking blue eyes holding her captive. As her knees gave out beneath her, she had one last chilling thought.

Liam's mother wasn't the *only* one here who had gotten in way over her head.

❧

With Aideen paralyzed by Liam's power, he moved toward Michaela at the speed of light, barely managing to scoop the tiny elf into his arms before her body touched the floor. He lowered her gently onto a cushioned settee near the door and placed a throw pillow beneath her head.

Once he'd assured himself that the wee Yank was truly unconscious, he turned his attention back to Aideen. His hand raised, he pointed a finger in her direction and drew a symbol in the air.

Just like that, the evil faerie woman disappeared from sight.

Lips tight, brows drawn together, he locked eyes with his mother. "Why could you not just leave it alone? Since when has my sex life been your business?"

His mother, Helena, sniffed. "You're my son and I was only trying to help."

"You've helped alright. Now, I've to clean up the mess."

If the wee woman at his home was the long-awaited Chosen

One, her knowledge of the *Túatha de Danann* and the existence of the *Geis* had disqualified her unequivocally from the quest. The game was over, the planet and its inhabitants already doomed.

"You know yerself, you've done Aideen no favors here, Mother."

"What've you done with her, so?"

"Vanished her. Sent her to a holding chamber in an underground portion of the house."

"Can she not…escape?"

"She's going nowhere. The room is soundproof, and I've set a magical safeguard around its perimeter." His tone was cold, eyes lifeless. "She'll be dealt with by the Council, according to Brehon Law."

His mother frowned. "Will she be tried for treason?"

"That's none of your concern. Sure, you know I can't discuss Council business with you. But, suffice it to say, 'twill not go well with her."

Helena moved to a lounge chair. Back stiff, head held at a haughty angle, she sat. She looked at Michaela, who appeared to be sleeping peacefully on the chaise. "And herself?"

"I put her in thrall, to mitigate the circumstances. I'll plant a suggestion, wipe her mind clean of any memory of the magical row, before I awaken her."

His mother sighed. "This is why it's never smart to be messin' with a mere mortal."

"I had everything perfectly under control, until yourself and Aideen showed up. Now, if you'll excuse me…."

He leaned over, ran his fingers gently over Michaela's face, and whispered to her in an ancient language known only to the *Tuátha de Danann*. The wee woman frowned, sniffled, but he sensed no release.

"Bollocks," Liam cursed under his breath.

"What is it?" his mother asked.

"Aideen wasn't flinging our magic around just now. 'Twas black magic she was using. Forbidden because it imprints events and words—those *particular* words—indelibly on a mere mortal's mind, making the task of wiping the memories next to impossible."

Liam pulled a chair up beside Michaela and took her hand in his. Beginning again, he spoke to her, entreating her softly for several minutes, until he felt a certain tension begin to flow out of her innermost being.

Her eyelids fluttered, then slowly opened. She pushed herself up to a sitting position, eyes filled with fearful disbelief. "Just what the frig are you people? Aliens? Irish fairies or something?"

When he only stared at her, she looked at Liam's mother, who averted her gaze. "*Okay…?*" Michaela chewed on her lower lip. "Tell you what. I'll get my things and you can take me to the airport. I'm going home."

"I'm sorry, luv, but I fear I can't allow that to happen."

Michaela sputtered and her mouth dropped open. "Did you just tell me that you're not going to let me leave? That you're holding me prisoner here? Are you kidding me?"

൭൴

Liam sighed and said nothing. He stood to his feet and paced away from her.

Still feeling wobbly, Michaela got up off the chaise. "You can't keep me here," she repeated, then turned on her heel and stomped off to her room to call Arianna. She locked the door behind her and dragged her cell phone out of her purse. For the first time, there was no signal.

*I'll use the home phone then.*

No dial tone.

Really? Just how far did this dude's evil 'powers' go?

Geared up for a good knockdown, drag-out, she went to the

door and unlocked it. Grabbing the doorknob, she turned and pulled. But the door wouldn't budge.

What the hell? She had thought he was bluffing about holding her here. Could this really be happening?

Back at Castle MacNamara, Arianna stood looking at her husband, eyes wide. "Liam has Michaela locked in her room? Has the man lost his freaking mind?"

"C'mere to me, *banchéile mo chroí*, wife of my heart. Allow me to explain what has happened quickly, so I can notify the Council."

Arianna sat beside her husband on the sofa in the solar. As he spoke, she could feel her shoulders growing taut, the fury hardening her features. "So, Liam believes it might have been that woman, that… Aideen…causing the visions haunting Michaela. He thinks she's been illegally using black magic?"

"He only said 'twas possible. After the supernatural activity Michaela witnessed, she retired to her bedroom voluntarily. Liam's after placing an abjuration, a protective barrier, around the room to deflect any more attacks. To block anything demonic from reaching her."

Arianna felt the blood drain from her face. "My God, she must be terrified! I have to call her." She pounded out the number to her friend's mobile, but the force field Liam had erected wouldn't let the call go through. Fire in her eyes, she spun back to Caleb. "Get Liam back on the phone. I will have access to Michaela. *Now.*"

Her husband nodded and dialed. "My wife wants to speak with her friend. She's demanding you release the line to her." A pause. "I understand, but she's right, O'Neill. Michaela's already aware that something otherworldly's going on. Sure, Arianna's the only one she'll be willing to trust at present."

He pushed the button to end the call. "You'll be able get through now."

Arianna huffed and hit redial. This time it rang.

"Hello? Oh God, oh God, Arianna. Thank God you called." Michaela's voice was high-pitched, bordering on hysterical. "Something crazy's going on here. It's spooky, creepy. I believe—and don't think I'm having another vision or something, this really happened—I think Liam and the whole freaking crowd here are space aliens or something."

"I know, babe. I know."

"You know?" An unbelieving pause. "No, you're just saying that, humoring me. You think I've finally lost my mind."

"That's not true, honey. What you saw is real." Arianna hesitated. She well understood the apocalyptic consequences of what they were facing, the danger inherent in saying too much. She knew she had to keep her friend in the dark. Having grown proficient in her inherited fey abilities, she could have easily manipulated Michaela mentally. But she just didn't feel right about using magic on someone she loved, someone who had to be feeling desperately alone right now, and afraid. "Look, Mick, there's too much to explain over the phone. And some things I'm not at liberty to tell you at all. Just know that Caleb and I are flying out there now to see you."

"You're coming here?"

"Yes. And please, honey, stay in your room until I get there."

"Don't have much choice, do I?" she muttered.

"Trust me on this, Mick. You're much safer that way."

"Safer? What…?" She let out a breath. "Okay, then."

"Don't worry, we'll figure this whole thing out together when I get there."

"Yeah, right." She didn't sound convinced. "Arianna? What about Liam?" Her voice was low, child-like. "He locked me in my room."

"I know he did, sweetie. But it was only to protect you. He's one of the good guys, babe."

With those feeble assurances, Arianna bade her best friend farewell.

Not an hour had passed since her conversation with Arianna, when the door to Michaela's room burst open. Heart in her throat, she jumped to her feet as her friend rushed in. The concern on Arianna's face was apparent. Michaela had a mirror; she knew she looked like hell. Her usual tawny complexion had gone pale and she continued to lose weight.

She fell into Arianna's arms. "What's going on? What's happening to me here?" she wailed. "I don't even know what's real anymore."

Arianna blew out a breath. She had a strange look on her face. They had been friends for a long time, and Michaela knew that look. It was guilt. "Let's sit down, honey. We have to talk."

# *Chapter Fourteen*

Insomnia was an unusual ailment for Tara, who usually slept like the dead she studied. But tonight—with her calls to Ireland going unanswered for most of the day—concern had her feeling wide awake, her mind racing. When sleep continued to evade her, she threw in the towel on trying to get any rest and returned to the dig site, figuring she would log in a few of the artifacts her team had unearthed that afternoon.

It was late, very late, by the time Arianna called her back. The longer the two women spoke, the more reticent her friend had become. Feeling frustrated, Tara finally said goodbye and hung up the phone, more concerned about Michaela at the end of the conversation than she had been at the beginning. Setting her cell on one of the worktables, she moved around the dusty, enclosed space, her mind continuing to work the puzzle of her two friends' unusual behavior. She mentally counted the number of times she had tried to call Michaela that day, only to have each attempt go directly into voicemail as if her phone was shut off.

Worried, she had begun to reach out to Arianna, but it was several hours and multiple voice and text messages later before her calls were finally returned. Not that she had learned anything, though, because extracting information from her had been akin to pulling an impacted wisdom tooth. And forget getting Michaela on the phone either. Arianna had said she was sleeping, but Tara knew the girl far too well. She had been bald-faced lying, plain and simple. When Arianna finally figured out that Tara wasn't letting it go, she admitted that Michaela had been out of town, staying with the Brad Pitt lookalike Tara had met at the castle during her recent visit. Why was she surprised? With that rugged chains and black leather, rebellious James Dean kind of look, the guy was just Michaela's type. But running off with him so soon after meeting him?

*Smart, Michaela. Real smart.*

Before they hung up, Arianna had told her that she and Caleb had flown down to Sneem to be with Michaela because she was still having 'episodes'. When Tara went off on her for not encouraging their little friend to return to the States for a full medical work up, Arianna's voice had sounded strained. Temper brewing, she had vehemently defended herself, reporting that Michaela had not only had a full battery of medical tests, but also a psychological evaluation while in County Clare. Supposedly, she had been given a clean bill of health.

Bottom line was that, speaking with Arianna had done nothing to alleviate her concerns. The girl was hiding something—and it was something a lot more serious than Michaela's latest fling.

As Tara carefully brushed the dust off a circa two-thousand-year-old woman's brooch uncovered earlier that morning, she fought the effects of exhaustion from the insomnia plaguing her. She swore that if she weren't in the middle of one of the most important digs of her career, she would turn the project over to her second-in-command and fly back to Ireland first thing in the morning.

But, state approval for Tara and her team to come to Naples to explore the site of the AD 79 eruption of Mount Vesuvius had required months of paperwork and hours of communication between her company and the Italian government. When permission was finally granted, the consent was considered quite a coup among her peers within the archeological community.

Although over a thousand bodies had been discovered from the dig site since excavations began in the late 1700s, only about a hundred of the former citizens of Pompeii had been preserved in caste form at the moment of death. Although costly and intricate, Tara's team used resin casting to preserve any relevant finds. Unlike plaster alone, which preserved the bodies' general shapes, this technique created more perfect replicas, including details like teeth, hairpins, and the ornate piece of jewelry she held now in her hand.

As much as Tara had looked forward to this project, the trip to Pompeii couldn't have come at a worse time. With Michaela in Ireland, suffering what Tara believed—despite the so-called medical reports—to be symptoms of a traumatic brain injury, she had been distracted, sleeping fitfully, and worrying about her friend. While the two of them were very different people and bickered incessantly, she loved that girl like the little sister she had never had, and would have protected her with her last breath.

Without her usual sharp, left-brained focus, Tara knew she wasn't on top of her game. Not a good thing for a site director, the one upon whom the excavators relied for direction. Still, her people were a cohesive group, well experienced in the Harris matrix and single context recording they were using. The exhibition supervisor, Assistant Professor Mary Voss—a former site director herself—was smart, accomplished, and recognized in her field. Reassuring was the knowledge that Mary could well have proceeded with the dig on her own should Tara ever have been unable to continue.

Hence the reason she was torn about remaining in Pompeii.

The artificial lighting filtered through the room and created a smoky haze over the ash and pumice coating its contents as she examined the never-before-catalogued caste bodies the team had discovered earlier that afternoon. Their faces frozen into death masks reflecting the trauma of their passing, these former living, breathing human beings were forever trapped in their poses at the time of death.

It was weird. Tonight, for the first time in her career, the dead bodies in the room seemed to unnerve her. Though the site was below ground, and did not open directly to the outside, a strange, dank breeze wafted over her. A cold chill skated up and down her spine, raising the tiny hairs on the nape of her neck.

Shaking off the sensation as the result of too much caffeine and too little sleep, she reached for her tape recorder. As she was speaking into the tiny instrument, she heard what sounded like a low, growling moan and switched off the recorder. Listening, she heard it again, a menacing sound that she couldn't identify as either human or animal. Her heartbeat and respiration increased dramatically. Moisture beaded on her forehead. Tara shouldn't have been at the site alone; it violated every rule in the book. Swallowing the huge lump in her throat, she let her eyes wander around the stuffy, earthen room, for the first time finding it eerie. The lifelike bodies of the dead seemed to be holding their collective breath, she thought, before realizing that it was she, herself, who wasn't breathing. The unreasonable fear gripped her throat in a stranglehold. Tara straightened her spine, centered herself and inhaled deeply.

A noise, like something hitting the floor, echoed through the chamber. She jumped. "Hello? Mary? James? Is that you?" Her voice shaky, her question was absorbed by the silence.

Tara huffed, mocking her own reaction to the strange phenomena. Grabbing up her backpack, she stuffed her cell phone inside, and tossed it over one shoulder. She glanced at her watch. Half past three a.m., the hour very late—or very early—depending on how one might choose to look at it. Either way, she figured it left her time to attempt a couple of winks before heading back down here for work in the morning.

❧

It was after nine by the time Tara dragged her tired, aching butt back to the dig site. She had always been the first one there in the morning, the last to leave. So, the look Mary gave her as she walked through the entrance came as no surprise.

"I was just about to come check on you," the woman said. "Thought you might be sick."

Mary's salt and pepper hair framed her face in a wispy bob. Attractive at slightly over five feet tall, she was always impeccably dressed, her crisp white shirt and green cargo pants spotless. Although her job kept her digging in the dirt, in caves and caverns beneath the earth, she didn't use that as an excuse to dress slovenly–unlike Tara, who tended to go without makeup, pull her hair back into a pony tail and not worry so much about the soil stains that the last wash had failed to remove from her beige shorts.

"Nah. Couldn't get to sleep until dawn, and when I finally did, I overslept."

"Of course." Mary laughed. "I thought you might have had a late night. Gone out to see the sites with that hot Italian guy you were spending time with yesterday."

"Antonio?" The black-haired, olive-skinned hunk of a man was their government liaison. "No, thank you very much. The man is far more in love with himself than any woman could ever be with him. Anyway, you know the idiom: Don't crap where you work. The last thing I need is a casual fling with one of these Italian Romeos."

But Mary wasn't listening. With her superior intellect and a mind like greased lightning, the woman had already moved on to the next topic. "I noticed you'd been down here after we closed the site yesterday. Following up on anything important?" She left unspoken the fact that Tara shouldn't have been down here working alone.

"Decided to come down and record some of my thoughts while they were still fresh in my mind. Um…Mary? Do you know if James had to be down here for anything last night?"

Mary looked up from her notepad, concern etched on her face. "No, we went out on the town. Dinner. Sightseeing. Why? You didn't hear anyone messing around while you here working?"

"I don't know what I heard. A low growling sound, like an animal maybe. And something falling onto the floor."

"Hmm. Maybe a stray cat got in before we locked things up."

"Yeah, maybe. No biggie." Tara brushed the experience off as adeptly as she brushed the dust off a priceless artifact. "Did the volunteers from the university show up today?"

"Yep. James is supervising them in the next grid. He's having to teach them single context recording. Sad to say, the American exchange students have only had experience doing excavations in squares or trenches."

Tara grimaced. "Too bad, but that's the way it's often done when there's not enough funding."

"Should just leave it alone, then. Leave the ground untouched. If you can't do something right…."

"Yeah, just don't do it at all," Tara agreed.

Mary gathered up her tools and bustled away, headed to join her husband at grid two. Tara turned back to the resin casting she had been working on the evening before and refocused her energies on the permanent preservation of the fallen residents of Pompeii.

Back in her hotel room that evening, Tara tried to reach Michaela again. And again, the call went straight into voicemail. So, that's how they want to play it, huh? Instead of wasting her time trying to contact Arianna, she searched for flights to Ireland. She would give it a day, two at most. If she didn't hear back from Michaela, or find out exactly what was going by then, she would leave things here in Mary's capable hands and go investigate the situation for herself.

# *Chapter Fifteen*

Council members had begun to arrive at Liam's place in Sneem long before sunrise. He dismissed the cook as soon as breakfast was prepared, leaving members free to speak openly. The collective mood melancholy, they gathered in the kitchen, conversing in low tones.

Liam watched Arianna prepare a breakfast tray with scrambled eggs, sliced tomatoes and buttered toast, then pour a huge mug of coffee to take upstairs to her friend. He nodded to her as she left the kitchen, tray in hands, mumbling a few words to release the magical safeguard he had set on the room. He could picture how Michaela would look this morning, sitting up in bed, her long, gypsy-black hair hanging down both sides of her face in tangles.

Having always enjoyed peace in his home, he disliked the chaos, the drama, the intrusion of others. He looked forward to a time when this situation might be resolved, so that he could have back the privacy of his home, and, with any luck a'tall, the wee Yank to himself.

ꕥ

As the door swung open, Michaela jumped off the bed. Arianna proceeded across the massive room and set the tray on a coffee table. "Thank God you're still here." Michaela spoke in a rush. "I had a horrible night and Liam hasn't checked on me even once since he locked me up here."

Her friend took her into her arms and rocked her back and forth. "He did check on you, sweetheart—we both did—every half hour or so all night. He's downstairs meeting with the others right now. And, FYI, he's looking every bit as rough as you do. Now, come on. Let's get some caffeine and food into you. In that order," she added with a small smile.

Feeling the world begin to stabilize at her friend's presence, Michaela took a seat on the small settee in front of the table. She took a long sip of coffee and groaned with pleasure.

Arianna sat down facing her, one knee propped on the seat cushion. "I told you yesterday there's something going on here that I can't discuss. It's something with such far reaching consequences, you can't even begin to imagine the magnitude of the situation."

Michaela's eyes fixed on her best friend, she bit into a piece of toast and nodded. "And so…this involves me how?"

"We're not even sure yet that it does. I just need you to cooperate with me, to trust me 'til we figure it out."

"My trust in you is the only reason I agreed to stay penned up in this room for the past twenty-four hours." Michaela chewed and swallowed, her voice slightly raised. "If not for that, I'd have kicked that damned door down and escaped."

"I know you would have, babe. And I appreciate you working with me on this."

"I just wish you would tell me what the hell's going on here."

"I wish I could. And I will one day. Promise. I think I mentioned that certain people would be arriving here today to try to help us with this."

"Yeah? So, what happens next?"

"Remember the psychologist, MacDara?"

Her face set in a permanent pout, Michaela gave a single nod.

"Well, he'll be here. There'll also be seven others you haven't met."

"Great." Michaela sighed. "This is some weird crap, Arianna. You know that, right?"

"Totally." Arianna bit her lip. "I just don't know what else to do, what to tell you. Except that, one day, you'll understand everything. For now—and I know I sound like a broken record—I just need you to trust me. Can you do that?"

"Always have," Michaela said unflinchingly. "Always will."

Arianna frowned and looked at Michaela's tray. "You didn't eat much. You finished?"

"Yep. Not hungry." Her lips thinned. "Can't imagine why."

Standing to her feet, Arianna gave her a hug. "I know, honey. Now, just go hop in the shower and get ready. I'll be back up in a little while to get you."

"That's it, then." Michaela stood up.

Arianna lowered her eyes. "For now."

"Okay," Michaela said with a sigh. "I'll get ready."

As Arianna left the room, Michaela would have sworn she heard her friend mumble several words in a foreign language, just before the snick of a tumbler signified that the lock on the door to her room had engaged. So, it seemed that even her best friend was intent on keeping her prisoner here. With that gloomy thought foremost in her mind, she grabbed some clothes out of her suitcase and headed into the bathroom to shower.

❧

About an hour later, Liam climbed the stairs to Michaela's room. Why 'twas important to him that he be the one to introduce her to the Council he'd no idea. As he stood outside the locked door, his heart picked up a beat in anticipation of seeing her. Dread he'd never experienced before gripped him now. Fear that she wouldn't accept him…that he would never see that pixie grin on her face again. That he would never hear that lusty catch in her breath when he kissed her. Never feel the soft cool texture of her supple skin beneath his fingertips.

Before he came upstairs, Arianna had released the hold she placed on the door. He straightened his shoulders and knocked.

"Come in."

Michaela sat in a chair facing the door, as if waiting. Obviously expecting her friend to arrive, her eyebrows raised in surprise at seeing him. He didn't need access to her mind to know what she was thinking. He could read the emotions flitting across her face. First, there was pleasure at seeing him, and then immediate disdain as she recalled that he had held her here against her will. That recollection brought on a look of fear, and then overwhelming sadness.

A sadness he felt to the depths of his very own being.

"I've come to bring you downstairs to meet the others." His voice was soft and imploring.

"Oh, so it's okay for me to be released from my prison cell now?" The verbal slap caught him by surprise. Liam couldn't help but admire the woman's tenacity. Even in this untenable situation, her shoulders were straight, head held high.

"Michaela, I am so, so very sorry for what's happened here. I swear to you, it's not what it seems. I've only been trying to keep you from harm, so."

Just the sight of her filled an empty place inside of Liam; some lonely, vacuous cavern he hadn't known existed until now. The fresh, clean scent of her shampoo reached his nostrils as he drew closer to her. Her thick, black hair hung long and lush past her shoulders, her ethnic appearance, coupled with that stoic posture, bringing to mind an ancient Egyptian queen. Her clothing–a blouse with black and navy geodesic patterns tucked into a pair of faded jeans–however, defeated the analogy.

"Okay. And I suppose, like Arianna, you're 'not at liberty' to explain what's going on?"

Liam shook his head. "I am not. I don't know what else to say, except that I truly care about what happens to you."

Though her eyes were still wary, he could see her features soften.

She let out a breath. "Thank you for that, Liam. I guess that's gotta be enough for now then, doesn't it? So, what do you say we go downstairs and get on with…whatever this is."

Liam took her hand in his and accompanied her down to the study, not missing the raised-brow looks greeting them as they entered the room hand-in-hand. After seating Michaela in a brown leather recliner in the center of a circular array of chairs, he proceeded to introduce her to those members she hadn't met. He found it strange, the unwarranted feeling of hostility boiling inside him at the admiring glances of several of the men.

Arianna went to stand beside her friend as MacDara stepped forward. "Hey, there. It's good to see you again. Sorry it has to be under such unusual circumstances."

She cleared her throat. "Me, too."

Arianna looked at Caleb. "If I may address the group?"

The extraordinary request by a non-Council member brought surprised glances in Caleb's direction. The Chief Brehon–Arianna's husband—gave his consent.

"I know that you've all been kept up to date about what's been going on with my friend here. And, while she understands that something out of the ordinary, something…supernatural even… is going on here, she's accepted the fact that the matter is highly classified, like a top secret government mission. Also, that she might unknowingly be somehow involved. She's agreed, therefore, to cooperate fully with this inquiry, to answer questions about her visions, as well as her recent interactions with Aideen."

Michaela spoke up. "I have something to say." All eyes in the room fixed on her. "I feel very uncomfortable with all this, like I'm on trial or something, although I didn't do anything wrong. I also suspect that I'd have been prevented from leaving if I hadn't agreed to this meeting. So, if you people determine that—whatever's going on here—that it has nothing to do with me, I want to know that I'll be free to leave immediately, to return home to my life in the States."

The thought of her going away, of never seeing her again, stabbed Liam in the heart with a deep, unexpected sense of loss. "You will, o'course," he responded softly.

"And if I am somehow involved? What then?"

The men in the room squirmed in their seats and exchanged telling glances. When no one spoke, she raised troubled eyes to Liam, who had not moved from her side. He looked at Arianna before speaking. "If it's discovered that you're destined to be a part of this, 'twill be unsafe for you to go off on your own." Liam paused, then reached down to touch a lock of her hair. "Just know, luv, that until all this is after being sorted, I'll protect you from harm." He kneeled down, cupped her chin in his hand and looked her square in the eyes. "Sure, with my life, if it comes to it."

Michaela inhaled a deep breath. "Well, let's get this over with then."

A strained silence ensued as the men in the room looked to Caleb, whose place it was to request that his wife leave the room.

Arianna's chin raised stubbornly. "Even an accused murderer is entitled to legal counsel," she protested, addressing her husband. "Michaela will be more at ease if I'm here for moral support."

Again, the highly irregular request caught the other members by surprise.

Liam swallowed a chuckle as Caleb glanced around the room for objections. Apparently, he'd learned to pick his battles with his feisty new wife.

"She's a point," Liam conceded. "I'm sure Michaela will be a lot more comfortable with her friend in attendance."

With the world only weeks away from possible annihilation, nothing was as it had been. Under the circumstances, no one felt the need to raise an objection.

Seamus, the group's scribe and gentle giant called the meeting to order.

Caleb addressed the group. "As you all know, this gathering is for the sole purpose of discovering whether the problems Michaela's having has anything whatsoever to do with…the issue at hand."

MacDara spoke up. "As you all know, I've had the privilege of spending time with herself in Clare, when some of the dreams and visions first began. With your permission," he said, directing the comment toward Michaela, "we can decrease the number of questions, if you'll allow me to review for the members some of the notes I took during our session."

A look of relief crossed Michaela's features and she nodded her agreement.

"This entire way of proceeding is completely out of the ordinary," Brian Rafferty protested. At eighty-two and silver-haired, he was the oldest member of the Council. And the most set in his ways. "We're required to use caution in disclosing anything that would put the…the matter at hand here in jeopardy. Though not wishing to appear rude to our guest, I suggest we ask questions in English, but any pertinent discussions be conducted, as usual, in the hermetic tongue."

❧

To say that she was feeling uncomfortable had been an understatement. She felt like Dorothy, waking up this morning in the Land of Oz. Suddenly, she was inhabiting a fantasy kingdom, where nothing was real. The only constant in the chaos, her only anchor to the real world was her friend, Arianna. And her growing trust in Liam—who had locked her in a room in his home for the past twenty-four hours—which was even stranger still.

She supposed MacDara was sharing his impression of her during their initial counseling session when she had first arrived at the castle in County Clare. She had had no idea then what she was getting into, and now no idea what he was saying. The language he and the others were speaking sounded nothing like Gaelic. She held back a hysterical giggle as she realized it sounded more like the language spoken by the Na'vi in the hit movie, Avatar.

Michaela looked around the room, taking in the model-perfect, almost too-handsome array of Stepford men. Even the oldest of the group attractive in his own deep, dark and forbidding way, each possessed a carnal sexuality that was almost palpable. And then, of course, there was Liam: aloof, rebellious, and devil-may-care. By comparison, all of the other men in the room were trolls. Just looking at the man made it hard for her to breathe.

Michaela was flanked by Arianna on one side, Liam on the other. As if the two were closing ranks, standing guard over her. She felt Arianna's hand upon her shoulder. While her friend seemed not to understand the language the men were speaking, she seemed to be picking up the general gist of the conversation, shooting looks of disapproval or agreement her husband's direction, based upon whatever was being said.

A question was directed to Michaela. "Excuse me?"

The youngest member, Sean O'Casey, if she remembered his name correctly, repeated his question. "Did you originally believe that what you were experiencing was only a dream? Or did you suspect it might have been a vision?"

Michaela cleared her throat. "The first time it happened was during the night, so I tried to convince myself that it was a nightmare. I have to admit that, even then, it seemed too real to be a dream."

"'Twas the first night at the castle," Liam offered to the group. "I heard her screams and went to investigate. I entered her room to find her huddled in the shower, soaking wet, sobbing that the place was on fire."

Michaela nodded. "The second episode was also at the castle, but during the day. It happened in the den. I was wide-awake at the time, so there was no question. I wasn't dreaming. It was a hallucination, pure and simple."

"The concern originally was that she'd suffered a possible brain injury from her fall off her horse during the show in Dublin," MacDara reminded everyone. He looked at Michaela. "I took the liberty of describing the various incidences to the others, so that you'd not have to be reliving them here."

Michaela sent him a grateful smile. "Thanks for that."

Sitting in one of the overstuffed armchairs set up in a circular pattern around Michaela, the priest, Father Conneely, leaned forward. "So, the…incidents…took place mostly at the castle?"

"At first. Arianna and I discussed the possibility that I was picking up some vibe from the past, some…haunting, given the history of a medieval castle. But then Liam invited me to come here to Sneem, to spend some time at his home while I healed from the fall off my horse. It seemed like the dreams…or visions, or whatever they are…lessened. But then I ran into that woman… Aideen in town, and strange things began to happen again."

Throughout the questioning, Michaela was sensitive to Liam's supportive presence, aware of his occasional reassuring touch—the squeeze of a shoulder, a light rub on the back of her neck. From time to time, Liam would shoot a hard look at Caleb, who would then censor, or rephrase, whatever question Michaela was being asked.

The attention made her feel safe and protected, at least until the conversation turned to the subject of Aideen. Then, she sensed a menacing side of the man in whose home she was staying, a scary part of him that she had never encountered before. An almost visible darkness seemed to settle over the others, as well.

After about an hour of the grueling Q&A, Liam demanded

the interrogation be brought to an end. "If no one has any further questions, I'd like for Michaela to be excused. She's been through enough for one day and seems to be growing weary."

Grateful for the intervention, she looked up at him, into the deepest, bluest, most expressive eyes she had ever seen on a man. Her heart skipped a beat at what she found there. It was something intense, something that looked a lot like love.

Swallowing the boulder-sized lump in her throat, she asked a question in a small, quiet voice that only he and Arianna could hear. "And are you going to lock me in my room again?"

"I'll put a different kind of safeguard around your room," he replied softly. "Still, I'd appreciate your remaining there, where you'll be safe, until we've adjourned our meeting."

"Come on," Arianna said. "I'll go with you and we can catch up."

With a thoughtful look in his eyes, Liam watched the two women depart the room.

❧

Council members discussed what they had learned from Michaela and agreed that something extraordinary was indeed happening where she was concerned. "And yet, we were mistaken last year when we thought my wife might be the Woman of Promise," Caleb reminded them. "At the time, we hadn't all the facts and believed Arianna to be a mere mortal, a requirement under the terms of the *Geis* for its dissolution."

"Michaela's a mere mortal, sure," Liam interjected. "She's discussed both her parents with me, and they're clearly of this world."

Caleb agreed with the assessment. "My wife's known her mother and father for most of her life, and can vouch for that fact as well."

MacDara rose from his seat and went to the teacart to refill his cup. "Sure, we've ascertained here today that there's another explanation for the nightmares and visions, one that has no connection to the *Geis* a'tall. Everything that's happened might be only the result of Aideen's jealous tirades."

As MacDara walked back to his chair, Brian stretched both of his legs out in front of him with a low groan. "Either way, Aideen's actions are very concerning. Whether she's acting as a Minion of the Beast in an attempt to thwart the dissolution of the *Geis*, or just using black magic for the sheer dark thrill of it, she's clearly crossed forbidden lines."

From the moment Michaela had left the room, Liam had said little. Now, at the mention of his infamous former lover, he felt his anger stir again. "The woman's pure evil, so she is, and I want her out of here," he spit out. "As you know, I've restrained her in an underground chamber of the house pending her disposition at the conclusion of this meeting."

"I've a request, Liam," Caleb said. "In advance of bringing Aideen up here to attend a hearing to determine formal charges, will you advise the others of her behavior, specific to her interaction with Michaela, both here at the house, as well as previously at the pub?"

"I'll start with the pub, as that was the most public display of magic. In short, the woman's been driving me bloody demented, phoning and stalking me since we stopped seeing one another right after the Dublin Horse Show. 'Twas there that Michaela's horse threw her, where all this *craic* seemed to begin." He paused thoughtfully. "Now that I think of it, the accident happened the morning after I made the wee Yank's acquaintance." Liam detailed the incident at the Brazen Head Pub, where Aideen purposely jostled Michaela's arm, causing her pint to spill down her shirt. "'Twould not be unreasonable to consider that Aideen may have caused the horse to stumble, the strap on the saddle to snap."

Until this moment, thirty-six year old Paddy McClellan, one of the newest members of the Council, had been silent. "Jealousy can be a powerful emotion. Especially for women of the *sidhe*."

The men exchanged knowing glances. "Well, there you are, so," Seamus said. "Michaela's a lovely woman; Aideen's quite clearly on the dark side of daft. Sure, 'twas your attentiveness to the wee Yank that likely started her nefarious plan in motion."

Liam went on to explain how Caleb and Arianna had asked him to pick Michaela up at the hospital and fly her to them in Clare. "We'd a huge row over that, Aideen and meself," he went on. "I told the woman I didn't want to see her again."

He continued with details about Aideen's confrontation with Michaela at the pub in Sneem, as well as the incident that had brought everyone together today. The information he provided reinforced the group's suspicion that the dreams and visions plaguing Michaela might have naught to do with the *Geis* a'tall, being simply the result of Aideen's ongoing black magic assault.

While, on the other hand…the fairie woman's jealousy, coupled with her mental instability and frequent consorting with the devil, would make her the ideal candidate for possession by the Minion of the Beast in the effort to interfere with the Woman of Promise.

"I believe we all agree that we've no way, at present, to make a final decision as to whether Michaela is the One we're seeking." This from Caleb.

Brian Rafferty cocked his head to one side and gave Liam an imploring look. "You seem to have taken the American under yer wing, sure. Have you anything else to add, any feelings on the subject of Michaela's potential involvement in the dissolution of the *Geis*?"

*Bollocks.* Because of his relationship with Michaela, Liam had half-expected the meeting to take this turn, with the other members reaching out to him for answers. And now, when he'd never wanted anything to do with the bloody *Geis* a'tall, he was being drawn into this cosmic drama quite clearly against his will.

"No." While his one-word answer was short and succinct, leaving no room for discussion, the others remained silent, waiting for him to go on. "Look, I know what it is you're asking. And the answer is 'no'. I feel no special bond with the woman, no attachment, no compulsion to be after championing her. I feel nothing for her a'tall."

*And you're a fecking bloody liar,* Liam thought to himself.

Caleb looked at him, a knowing look. After all, hadn't the man been down this road himself, and not a year before? But it was different where Caleb and Arianna were concerned, as it had turned out that his wife was one of them. There had been the likes of waking dreams and such between themselves before they'd ever met in the physical realm. That she turned out to be Caleb's *anam cara* wasn't surprising in the least. But not so with Michaela. There had been nothing of the sort. No ethereal connection had drawn them together. Which was all the more reason that these inexplicable feelings he was having for the little black-haired vixen made no sense a'tall.

Unless....

Caleb got to his feet. "I believe it's time to bring Aideen up from down below, to face the reading of the charges against her. She's clearly violated our laws, revealing herself, not only with her antics at the pub in Sneem, but also to Michaela, who may possibly be this millennium's Woman of Promise. Further, she discussed the prohibition against cross-mating between our people and the mere mortals as set out in the *Geis*. In doing so, she's made herself a danger, not only to our people, but to the future of mankind, and must be dealt with accordingly."

With the indictment drawn up, Seamus applied the seal of the Council of Brehons to the legal paperwork. The charges were serious and carried an ultimate penalty of death. Once the document was officially presented to her, she would be removed to a holding cell at the Council's manse on the Isle of Skye. After being secured in Scotland, she would be permitted to obtain legal counsel. The trial would be scheduled to begin posthaste.

Liam and Sean O'Casey left the room to bring Aideen up to face the Council members. A few minutes passed with the others chatting quietly amongst themselves, before the two men returned to the room—alone.

"She's gone," Liam said simply.

"Gone? How's that possible?" Caleb asked.

"I've not a clue," Liam replied. "The door's still securely locked. Apparently, her frequent practice of the dark arts has increased her powers more than I was after anticipating. She somehow managed to bypass the hex that should well have prevented her escape. I'd even put a lock-down on her ability to transform to fey, which would have allowed her to blink herself through a portal into the realm of the *sidhe.*"

Father Conneely's expression became grave. "'Tis a reckless thing she was doing, moving back and forth between the dimensions that kinda way. Makes no surprise a'tall that she's fallen so far from grace."

Just as mere mortal parents counseled their teenagers against drinking and drugs, parents of the *Túatha* warned their children to avoid the transformation between purely physical beings and the *sidhe,* as each metamorphosis placed them more and more at risk of losing their mortal souls. Many were the tales of those who, attracted to the power and beauty of the other realm, chose to remain permanently in that other dimension.

Sorrow etched on his face, the priest shook his head. "Likely 'twas that which has opened her up to manipulation by demonic forces in the first place."

His expression morose, Liam felt suddenly sick to his stomach, anxious, as if his whole world had suddenly been turned upside down. “In the Realm of Faerie, she’s even more of a threat to Michaela than she is in the flesh.”

“Who now shall step forward as her champion?” Caleb asked.

Liam spoke up without hesitation. “I’ll take her away, so I will. I’ve a place I recently purchased that no one knows anything about, a place where I can keep her hidden. Safe, until Aideen can be found and dealt with appropriately.”

“Sure, now, we’ve only to go upstairs and convince both of the girls ‘tis in Michaela’s best interest for you to be spiriting her away to some secret destination.” And even with the seriousness of the situation, Liam didn’t miss the twinkle of amusement in Caleb’s eyes.

## *Chapter Sixteen*

The chopper danced above the small island off the coast of Kerry. As Liam set it down upon the brown pebbled beach, the whipping winds seemed determined to topple the aircraft. Only recently had he closed the deal on the purchase of the property, so no one, including his family, was aware of its existence in his portfolio. Because of that, he reasoned, 'twould be the perfect hidey-hole for the wee woman he'd taken into his care until the others could track Aideen down and take her into custody.

The sun had already begun to set by the time the council meeting ended. Believing it best that they travel under cover of darkness, Liam had encouraged Michaela to collect her things so that they might leave straight away. As they were departing the castle, he watched Michaela and her friend hold one another for a long moment, the display of affection stirring that place inside him that had lain tolerably empty for so long.

"You take care of her." With the fierceness of a mother bear protecting her cub, MacNamara's wife had charged him with the responsibility for her friend's well being. "Just know, you'll answer to me if anything bad happens to her."

With an apologetic dip of his head, Caleb had wrapped an arm around his wife. The couple stood gazing up into the evening sky until the helicopter rose so high they were no more than specks of sand on the ground.

Now, having safely landed, Liam turned his attention to the woman whose fate had been so deftly placed in his care. The stresses of the previous weeks seemed to have changed her. No longer the flirty, laughing picture of self-confidence he had met in Dublin such a short time ago, she carried an aura of sadness now. It was as if a sinister darkness had wrapped itself around her, determined to strangle the very light from her soul.

He removed his headset and reached out to assist with hers. She jumped, startled by his touch. "Calm, *a mhuirnín*," he murmured, the Gaelic endearment rolling easily off his tongue. "'Twill all be well. You'll see."

The distress in her eyes told him she wasn't at all convinced. "Where are we, anyway? There doesn't seem to be a lot going on around here."

"'Tis a private island, so it is. One of the Blaskets. You recall the day we drove into Killarney for me to sign the papers at my solicitor's office?"

Michaela nodded. "You said you were buying an island. I thought you were kidding," she added dryly.

"I was not. At any rate, I reckon you'll be quite safe here since no one, outside of my solicitor, is aware of the purchase."

"If Aideen's so dangerous that you and I have to hide out here, what's to stop her from using her hocus-pocus to find us?"

"I know her limitations." Liam reached behind the cockpit seats and collected their bags. "Now, just sit tight here for a minute." He climbed out of the helicopter and went around to the passenger side to help her out. As he pulled her rolling case out of the aircraft, she took it from him. Asserting her independence, she dragged it along behind her as they hiked the overgrown path.

The evening was dark and bitter cold, unseasonably so for this time of year. Whether due to the dreary weather, or the emotional turmoil of the past several days, the woman trudging along beside him was trembling. As an icy gust of wind bit through their clothing, Liam relieved her of the carryon and slung an arm around her shoulders. "C'mere to me," he said, pulling her close. "Let me keep you warm. The house isn't far away."

She glanced up with a slight smile. "Well, there's a relief. When I heard we were coming to a deserted island, I had visions of *Survivor*. Hoped we wouldn't be roughing it in a tent."

He chuckled. "Not a'tall. While the island's deserted now, 'twas once the hideout of an infamous member of the IRA. Ole Colin Murphy had the house built in the late 20th century. It's been updated since, though, so I'm sure you'll find it quite comfortable. The place is lovely during the day, well known for its seabird colonies and indigenous red deer."

Michaela shivered again.

Liam looked down at her and frowned. "We're almost there, little one. I'll start a fire directly to warm you up."

"It's not so much the weather bothering me, as the dank and desolate surroundings. Reminds me of the night I told you about, when my friends and I were kidnapped and drugged off the coast of Inishmore. We were restrained and left on the boat that night, so I never really set foot on the island. Still, these places give me the creeps."

Liam gave her shoulders a light massage. "The dismal circumstances surrounding our arrival tonight aren't helping matters either, to be sure."

Michaela gave a weak grin. "True. After this, I'll probably never want to see another island, ever again."

"I'm sorry, luv. We should have never let yourself get dragged into this."

"Oh, well. We wanted to spend some time together, getting to know each other. Guess this is our chance."

Impressed by her tendency to make light of a bad situation, Liam gazed down at her and gave her shoulder a thoughtful squeeze. "So it is, little one. So it is."

Silent and introspective, they hiked the short distance up the rocky path, before stumbling upon a massive wood and stone structure. Renovated in the 1960's, it employed a wind-powered weather station to provide electricity long before solar energy was considered *en vogue*.

Michaela appeared grateful that, with the flick of a switch, electric lights chased away the brooding darkness. Although a central heat and air unit had also been installed, Liam knew 'twould take a while for the large place to warm up. He escorted Michaela to the wife's quarters adjoining the master suite, and squatted down in front of the giant fireplace, piling applewood logs and chunks of peat onto the grate. Catching himself just in the nick of time, he refrained from his routine use of magic, substituting a more conventional approach to getting the fire started.

That done, he looked over his shoulder and caught her watching him. Like a lost little waif, he thought, while his heart did that strange clenching thing that was so foreign to him. 'Twas a reaction he'd no wish to further contemplate.

Instead, he turned to the topic of dinner, a simple meal he'd had the cook prepare for them for this evening since supplies weren't due to be delivered until the following morning. "Are you hungry, Michaela?"

"I'm always hungry. You should know that by now." She forced a laugh. "First though, I'd like a few minutes to freshen up a bit."

Liam admired the woman's strength and stoicism. Her ability to exercise blind faith in her friend, Arianna, whilst confronting issues she couldn't understand—including matters beyond this natural world—made him respect her all the more. 'Twas that blind trust he realized he wanted her to have in him. More, he wanted to earn it, to deserve it. To be the one she leaned on for comfort, looked to for protection. Worse, he wanted to be inside this woman more than he'd ever wanted anything before in his life. "Take all the time you need," he said stiffly, heading toward the door. "I'll be down in the kitchen setting out our meal."

Jaw set, he pulled the door closed behind him. *Bloody hell!* What in the name of all that was holy was happening to him?

Michaela dug a pair of navy jogging pants and a pale blue hoody out of her carryon and slipped them on. In the adjoining bathroom, she splashed water on her face, touched up her makeup and dragged a brush through her wind-tangled hair. She took a good look at herself in the mirror. And sighed. Forlorn, pale, with dark circles under her eyes, she hardly recognized herself anymore. And nothing in this world seemed real.

She couldn't understand the intense feelings of attraction for someone she hardly knew. Someone she was beginning to fear may be way out of her league, just as Arianna had warned. Liam was the only one she had ever met who could make her heart skip a beat just by walking into the room. The first man, whose intelligence and daring intrigued her, whose personality didn't bore her to tears after just a few hours. He was the first man she could see herself loving forever.

The first man with the power to break her heart.

But only if she let him.

So, whatever this…this craziness was, this…looking glass that she had inadvertently fallen through, Michaela felt like she had to hang in there. For the greater good, according to Arianna. Whatever the hell that was supposed to mean.

But inasmuch as Liam was concerned, she had to raise some boundaries, not to protect her from him, but from herself. Not only was dude smoking hot, but there was a sensitive part of him that called to her, drew her in emotionally. The smart, self-reliant woman that she was, she couldn't allow things to go any further, not when there hadn't been so much as a mention of exclusivity. She wouldn't let herself become a passing fling for a man with far too much sexual appeal and, she suspected, far too little concept of fidelity. A man she could even see herself falling in love with. Add the bonding endorphins fired up by such ultimate intimacy to the mix, and she doubted she would survive the inevitable crash and burn of their relationship in one identifiable piece. Michaela knew herself too well, recognized that she was too sensitive, felt things too deeply. Which meant it was better to keep things light, to walk away with her dignity—and the rest of herself—intact when the time came.

Staging a loud protest about the recent lack of food, her empty stomach was demanding immediate attention. With one last look in the mirror, she declared the situation hopeless and headed downstairs to get something to eat.

As she walked into the kitchen, she found the table set for two. The mouthwatering aroma of the hot stew in a large bowl in the center of the table smelled so good it almost made her want to cry. Liam was on the other side of the room with his back to her, building another fire. He was busy tossing logs into a stone fireplace so large it took up one complete wall. As she was about to speak to him, she noticed him writing a symbol in the air that resembled sign language. She sucked in a breath as, to her utter amazement, the entire stack of dry logs burst into flames.

*No freaking way.* "Wow. Some day, you'll have to teach me how you do that." She hoped the dry tone helped mask some of the shock she felt.

Liam's head snapped around and she heard him groan. "You weren't supposed to see that."

"Yeah, I know the drill." Michaela was all too aware of her situation: Alone on a deserted island with a man she had only recently met, with no cell phone service and no way to reach the outside world. Rather like a heroine in one of her paranormal romances, she thought, her mind racing with possible scenarios that would explain the origin of her magic man. "No worries, though. Long as you don't go locking me up again, I'm cool with it. But, I was thinking, if we really want to take this time to try to get to know each other, shouldn't we get past all that? So, what do you say, you just be yourself, and I'll do the same."

"Fair enough." The look he gave her was one of relief, appreciation and…yes, there it was…respect.

A most important component in the scheme of things where Michaela was concerned. Because, as much as she wanted to take things slowly, every word he spoke in that deep, lilting voice of his, every casual touch of his hand managed to drain the blood from her brain and send it rushing south.

"Looks like we're ready to eat," she said, her voice a breathless whisper. "I'm starving."

"As am I." From the look on his face, dude was clearly *not* talking about food.

*Damn.*

"Sit." He waved her over to the large table in the kitchen alcove and sat beside her. "Whilst we eat," he said, buttering a scone and passing it to her, "I'll explain as much about myself as I'm able. And you'll tell me about your life in the States."

"That sounds nice." *Normal.* Michaela ladled a hearty helping of Irish stew into a large bowl and passed it to Liam, before helping herself to a serving of creamy mashed potatoes and adding a few of the crudités included with their meal to her plate.

"Lord knows, you deserve some answers." Speaking almost to himself, he dipped his scone into the stew and took a bite. "You see, I have certain…abilities…that one might consider out of the ordinary."

"Do tell."

He rewarded the ironic quip with a sexy grin that curled her toes. "Right, so. I do want you to know that I can keep you safe here."

"Good to know."

"And that I'm committed to do so."

"Why is that, exactly?"

Again, ice blue eyes turned guarded. "What d'you mean?"

"Why are you promising to keep me safe? Do you feel some obligation connected to…whatever is going on? Or is there some other reason?"

The man looked like any normal human male who was being prevailed upon to explain himself to a woman. "Here's the thing. Yes, I may have a responsibility to act as your protector, your champion. That has yet to be determined. But, there's more to it than that for me. If it turns out that you've no connection to…the matter at hand, I've found that I still fancy being the one looking out for you, seeing that you come to no harm."

"That's good to hear, Liam, because I want to take care of you too."

He looked at her as if she were speaking a foreign language.

"I suppose, in your…culture…the men are all macho and stuff. But I feel like two people who care for one another should…*care* for one another. That it's not always on the man."

"I see," he said, although she quite doubted that he did. "Interesting. Now tell me a bit about yourself and your family."

As they shared their meal, Michaela told him about her life as the daughter of a movie star and a famous Hollywood producer. "Fortunately—and in defiance of my mother's vehement protests to the contrary—my father chose to make our home on the East Coast, rather than in L.A. That made it possible for me to grow up in a relatively normal, albeit an obscenely wealthy, household. Since my parents spent a lot of time traveling the world, I was raised by servants much of the time."

Liam scooped up another serving of mashed potatoes, adding it to her bowl before replenishing his own. "That must have been difficult."

"It was lonely sometimes. I guess that's why I'm so close to Arianna," she added thoughtfully. "She's the sibling I never had."

"And your other friend...what's her name...the archaeologist?" Liam reached for another roll.

It irked Michaela—just the teeniest little bit—that he would ask about her. "Tara. Yeah, we're like family too, but our relationship has always been a little weird."

"Weird? How?"

"I don't know how to explain it. We love each other, don't get me wrong. I'd do anything for her, and I know she feels the same. Still, we've never been really compatible, never seem to see eye-to-eye on anything."

Liam chuckled. "I have mates like that." He went on to describe boyhood antics with his best friend, Cian, who was now happily married to Liam's sister. "Thought it best to keep it in the family."

As they finished their meal, a sense of wellbeing poured over Michaela, like warm oil drizzled on one's body in a pricey spa. Liam had made no vows or promises, spoken no words of love, and made no long-term commitment. But he had been honest and real, wasn't playing games—which scored huge points on Michaela's new relationship-ometer. She couldn't help but hold his assurance of looking out for her close to her heart. Who could say, but that when all the insanity that had initiated their connection finally ended, they may find that a solid foundation had been laid? That there might yet remain hope for a future together.

Sated by the hot, filling meal, Michaela could feel the warmth of the room begin to envelope her, to leach the last bit of energy from her bone-weary body. She was blinking, fighting to keep her eyes open.

Observant, as always, Liam touched her hand. "You've had an incredibly stressful day, luv. What d'you say we go to bed early tonight? You've your own room, o'course, but I'd feel safer if you were after sharing my bed, lying beside me at night."

Michaela bit her lip. "I don't think we should...."

"Sleep, that's all. I agree that this isn't the time for anything else. I do nothing by half measures, *a chuisle*. When I finally take you—and take you I will, have no doubt of that—I want you to be fully present, fully there with me."

His words brought heat to her core. "I want that too, when the time is right. I just want you to know that I'm not a tease, Liam. I just need to know if this is going anywhere, if there's anything real...anything lasting between us, before we take things to the next level."

"Understood."

"I've never been afraid of anything...anything in this mortal world. But dealing with all this...paranormal activity...these horrific dreams and visions, well, I have to admit it's taken a toll on me. I really would feel much safer sleeping beside you."

"It's decided, then. Go on to bed, whilst I do the washing up. I'll join you in a wee while."

---

Michaela was curled up against Liam's back, sound asleep, when a scratching noise drew her from an exhausted slumber. Scrubbing at her eyes, her gaze went immediately to the foot of the bed, where Aideen was standing, looking down at them. But before she could panic about Liam's crazy ex invading their bedroom, a sickening realization settled over her. That the woman wasn't *standing* at the foot of the bed at all. She was hovering, her form diaphanous, like a ghostly apparition. Michaela's first thought was that the awful woman had died and now come back to haunt them. Or maybe, this was just a dream, another nightmare.

But when she found herself beginning to hyperventilate,

the craving for oxygen was proof enough that she was awake. Cringing away from the spirit floating in mid-air, she tried to push back against the headboard. Grabbing Liam's arm, she gave it a hard shake. "Wake up! She's here. Oh God, Liam! Aideen's here. Please wake up." He didn't stir, just kept sleeping like he had been drugged.

The phantom floating a foot or more above the floor howled in laughter. The eerie sound sent chills skating down Michaela's spine. "He'll not be helping you. No one will." The woman's taunts rang from her lips like tinkling chimes troubled by a winter wind. "I've placed your lover under a sleep spell. No matter how you try, you'll not be able to awaken him."

The ghost-like entity floated to the ceiling above the bed, eyes glowing red. Frozen in horror, Michaela pressed further back against the pillows. "What are you at now, you insipid mortal? How dare you contend with the likes of me! You've not a clue what you're dealing with here. Or with whom. Like meself, the man lying spent beside you is of the *Túatha de Danann.* And he's breaking the prohibitions of our people by getting the leg over with you. He's mine, so he is. Do you hear me? Stay away from him. Or I vow, if the *Geis* doesn't kill you, I'll be doing the job meself."

A tapping on the window behind Aideen drew her attention. The woman glanced over her shoulder, then turned back, a malignant grin like vermin crawling across her face. "They've come for you." As the angry specter dissolved into a shimmery gray mist, her triumphant announcement faded into an echo.

Now, Michaela had watched enough spooky movies to know that she shouldn't go anywhere near that window. But, just like the hapless characters in those late-night movies, she felt compelled to slide from beneath the thick duvet, leaving the warmth of Liam's sleeping body behind. She was shivering violently, more likely from sheer terror than from the cold. Defenseless against the force drawing her ever closer to that window, she continued barefoot, step by halting step.

A scratching sound, like that which had originally awakened her, came from behind the curtain on that window. Trembling so violently that she could hardly grasp the fabric, she yanked the curtain aside. In a blink, in a flash, she was somehow transported to the other side of the glass. Looking back through the filth-covered portal, she could see Liam still sound asleep on the bed where she had left him.

"Liam! Oh, God. Liam, help me!" Screaming at the top of her lungs, she banged on the window with both fists. But she might as well have been in a vacuum, because every sound she made was absorbed by her surroundings.

She blinked once, twice. The third time she opened her eyes, she discovered, to her great horror, that she had been transported somewhere far beneath the earth. Standing on the cold, stone floor of a crypt, she let out a shriek as a pair of scaly hands grasped one of her ankles. She could smell the rotting flesh that peeled off the cadaverous paw as it dragged her, kicking and screaming, to the broken edge of the floor. Flames of red and orange, blue and white roared from the base of eternal damnation, as hundreds of fiery fingers reached for her, the brush of those burning digits raising huge blisters with every contact.

Scraping the skin from her knees and knuckles, she fought to get away, letting out one blood-curdling scream after another.

"No!" There it was. Liam's voice, traveling through the pages of time, flying toward her from galaxies and universes away. Deep and commanding, it seized her where she stood, extinguishing the sizzling torment, drawing her slowly away from the edge of the hellish precipice.

Strong, warm hands were shaking her awake, muscled arms

enfolding her as she blubbered to him in hiccuping sobs. "Aideen was here. A ghost, floating. Haunting me. I couldn't wake you up. Then everything changed. The room. Everything. And there was something behind the window. Drawing me against my will. On the other side of the window, a monster grabbed my ankle, tried to pull me through a crack in the floor. If you hadn't woken up, it would have dragged me away. To hell, burning forever and ever."

"'Twasn't real, little one. Just another dream." Liam murmured the assurances again and again, each time dropping small kisses on her forehead, eyelids, her cheeks. "Nothing can harm you here. Do you hear me? *Nothing.*"

Michaela curled into him, wrapped her legs around his body, shivering, soaking up his warmth, his heat. With the proof of his desire for her hard against her belly, her hands moved wildly over his back, his arms, touching, further igniting his passion, and making frantic demands. "I need you, Liam," she whispered, biting his ear. "I need you now. Please, make all the darkness go away."

She heard a masculine groan and then he was kissing her, his hands molding, owning, making her his own. An empty chasm opened inside her, the depths of which she knew only he could fill. His kiss went deep and sure, the magic of his touch healing the blistered flesh she could still feel burning, banishing all thought of the phantasm tainting her soul. When she was whole again, his hands took possession of her deepest desires as he transported her to a new and glorious place that she had never been before.

His chest heaving with every breath, he pulled back to look down at her. Electric blue eyes warmed the dark, cold places inside her, made her yearn for every secret of his beautiful being, for his essence to fill her to overflowing. His head bent and he whispered in her ear. Words she didn't understand filled her heart with joy and a tender love unlike any she had ever known. "Liam, I love…."

He placed a gentle finger on her lips. "Sshh, *a ghrá.* Sleep now."

And she did.

# *Chapter Seventeen*

Michaela came from great wealth. But even from her perspective, the word 'opulent' didn't begin to describe the luxury of the island estate she awoke to the following morning. Looking out the bedroom window, she smiled as she decided that only sortilege could have formed the wood and stone structure that fit so perfectly in these fairytale surroundings. Frustrated to have awakened alone yet again, she padded barefoot to her own room and slipped into the shower, scrubbing off the layers of stress piled on her by the turmoil of the past twenty-four hours.

Feeling her old self again, she came down the winding staircase, admiring the special designer touches, like the oil paintings gracing the walls and the antique candelabras. Through the decorative glass on a side door, she could see chieftain chairs placed strategically on an open terrace overlooking the sea. She could picture Liam sitting there with her at dusk, the two of them watching a red deer tiptoe through the lush green woodland, nibbling a final meal before darkness fell across the island.

The smell of coffee brewing in the rustic kitchen elicited a pleasured sigh. Oh, thank God. Tea-drinking Liam had remembered her caffeine addiction and packed accordingly. Yep, she thought, smiling, her mystery man was definitely a keeper.

As she filled the mug he had left for her on the counter, she felt a twinge of disappointment over finding the kitchen empty. Deciding she would sit out on the terrace and enjoy the morning breeze, Michaela sank into one of the chieftain chairs she had spotted on her way downstairs.

In the light of a new day, in this idyllic setting, the troubling events of the day before seemed to fade into a distant dream that was more fiction than reality.

The glass door opened behind her. *Liam.*

"So, how's the *craic* this fine morning?" While his lips turned into that adorable half-smile she had come to love, she could detect the concern lurking behind those ice-blue eyes.

"It's a new day. A better day."

"You do seem more you're old self."

She removed her sunglasses and smiled up at him. "And what do you really know about my 'old self'?"

"Not as much as I'd like." He playfully tapped her nose. "Nor as much as I intend."

*Wow. A woman could definitely get used to living with that sexy Irish accent. Not to mention that there's something just plain hot about a dude with supernatural powers.*

She slipped her glasses back on. "Speaking of getting to know one another, I'm a little confused about last night."

"Confused, you say? And how's that?"

"Well, you woke me up from that horrible dream…."

"Aye, I did."

"And…we…we were…."

With his usual arrogant amusement, he watched her struggle, but refused to bail her out.

"I guess, what I'm asking is…. Well, did we…make love?"

"Ah, you wound me, *a mhuirnín.* How can you not remember such torrid passion?"

Michaela could feel her cheeks flame red, which, with her olive complexion, had to be a feat in itself. He didn't let her suffer for long, though, before laughing aloud. How sweet and precious was the rare sound of his boyish laughter.

"I kissed you, little one, touched you and brought you release.

But we'd both agreed to wait for the *piece de resistance* until we've concluded this…business we're about."

"So we did," she replied, using his own Irishism. Then adding, "*Brat!*" she stuck her tongue out at him.

He smiled down at her. "Now, on a random note, what d'ya say we get out of here for a wee hike. Might do you good spending the day exploring the caves and cliffs around the island."

"That sounds amazing. Do we have anything in the kitchen to make sandwiches?"

"We do."

"Then I'll go whip us up a picnic lunch and we can take off."

"Brilliant."

Less than an hour later, they were making their way across a rope bridge that stretched between two mountain peaks. A bit of an adrenaline junky herself, Michaela's juices were pumping at full throttle as they hung onto the railing swinging hundreds of feet above the crashing sea.

They spent the daylight hours laughing and playing like kids without a care in the world. After settling down in a secluded spot to eat their lunch, they went on to explore more of the island paradise, including ancient ruins that were almost lost amongst the indigenous flora.

❧

They hiked the rustic road that wrapped around the sheer rise of the outer cliffs, where a single misstep would have proved fatal. Cheeks flushed from the fresh air and exercise, Michaela looked over the edge at the death-defying drop to the coast below. "Loving this," she said, grinning up at Liam.

He smiled back and gave her long braid a tug.

The setting sun found the two of them on the northern most section of the island perched atop the highest cliff. Though 'twas late in the day, Liam knew that the darkness crawling across the landscape wasn't natural. "Something's happening," he warned, his voice low. "Best we collect our things now and head towards the house."

But as they rolled their blanket and stuffed it into Liam's backpack, a bouncing silvery ball appeared on the horizon. "Don't move." Liam shoved Michaela behind him. "Stay there, *a chuisle,* and let me take care of this."

Michaela moved in close and lay her forehead against his spine. Liam reached back and tugged her arms around his waist, his heart uncomfortably full. As the strange light drew nearer, it began to take on human shape and form. Just as he'd suspected, the figure of Aideen bled out of the ether.

"Gotcha!" She leaned to the right and pointed one long finger at Michaela. "Thought I warned you to stay away from me man."

"Shut your eyes, Michaela," Liam hissed. "Whatever you do, do *not* look at her."

"*Do not look at her.*" Repeating his words in a mocking tone, Aideen began to levitate.

Liam made a slicing motion with his hand to interrupt her assent. She did an airborne somersault and landed deftly on both feet.

Cackling in great amusement, the woman slowly clapped her hands. "Bravo, lover. Sure, and let the games begin."

With that pronouncement, she threw one hand skyward and thunder roared. Gale-force winds began to whip and howl, as if intent on tearing the couple from one another's arms.

"Oh God," Michaela whimpered and clutched at Liam's shirt. With one hand, he held her arms locked around his waist, preventing her from being blown over the edge of the treacherous cliff, as the violent gusts blew her feet out from under her, her legs flapping like a flag in the wind.

With his free hand, he drew a protective circle around the two of them. Within its circumference, the winds died instantly; everything became deathly still. He could feel the fire in his eyes as he raised his hand toward the heavens and, with a swooping motion, drew down a bolt of lightning, carving a smoking crevasse in the rocky earth that effectively separated Aideen from themselves.

Liam's voice took on the authority of the Council of Brehons, upon which he served. "You've been indicted on serious charges against our people," he thundered. "'Twill go better with you, should you turn yourself in."

"Ach, Liam. What a bleedin' bore you've become," Aideen whinged, stomping one foot. "Can't imagine that I'd ever fancied a life with the likes of you."

With that, she smiled, raised her hands above her head and transformed into a spirit being. Her form shimmering, the color of amethyst doused in the noonday sun, she murmured an incantation in the native tongue of the *sidhe*. The musical sound fell from her lips like chiming silver bells.

In a measure of time that was incalculable, she transported herself over the cavernous crater and sidled up beside Michaela. She called to the mere mortal, her voice a heavenly note that enticed her to open her eyes, despite Liam's explicit instructions. With just that one glance, the faerie woman glamoured her, thus enthralling the wee mortal to follow her toward a vine-covered mound tucked into a hillock behind them.

Thus enchanted, Michaela seemed to dissolve from Liam's grasp and was swept up into the air. An opening formed in the side of the fairie fort and swallowed the two women in an instant, in the twinkling of an eye.

Liam dashed toward the clump of earth that had returned to a solid mass. Alone, he stood on the craggy hillside, the wind tearing at his hair and clothes, the maniacal sound of a mad woman's laughter reverberating off the valleys and peaks.

For a moment, everything went black. A sense of moving at great velocity made Michaela feel light-headed and motion sick. Before she could question what was happening to her, she landed on her feet on solid ground. Eyes wide, body shaking, her breathing labored, she turned in a semi-circle, her stance in the defensive mode she had been trained for as she took in her surroundings. All around her, weeping willow trees dripped with lichen. Flowering plants swayed and danced, flowing together into one living, breathing entity that expelled a celestial fragrance, while painting the world with the vibrancy of an uber-spring.

Had she died and gone to heaven? she wondered. "Or is this just another vision?" But even as she asked the question, she recognized that this experience was the polar opposite of all the others. No monstrous creatures clawed at her. There was no putrid stench or slimy walls. On the contrary, the scents of honeysuckle, pine, and flowering plants were an extraordinary delight to her olfactory senses. It was an overwhelmingly pleasant encounter, probably like being high on a hallucinogen. *Magic* mushrooms, she thought, giggling to herself as she spotted a strange sight several hundred yards ahead of her. Oh, yeah, definitely tripping. Either that, or she really was seeing those chair-size toadstools occupied by human-like beings of mist and light.

*Alice in Wonderland*, she thought, as another giggle spilled from her lips. Spellbound, she watched the sound her laughter made floating from her mouth in musical notes that smelled like chocolate and tasted like a peppermint patty.

All the while, the wicked witch who had predicated this

phantasm was nowhere in sight. Instead, Michaela was being ushered along by tiny luminous entities the size of butterflies, who buzzed around her, traveling from her head to her feet in a dizzying swirl. It must have taken a few minutes—although time seemed to have stopped, to have no meaning here—before Michaela realized that she was being led down the winding, overgrown path directly toward the beings of light in the distance.

It was then that she realized she was no longer wearing her jeans and T-shirt, but was clothed in a silken gown in a shimmering color that she couldn't identify. The fabric, which seemed a mixture of colors blended into one, of blues and rose and gold, draped her body in a sensuous wrap that accentuated every curve.

As the butterfly creatures delivered her to the toadstool banquet table in the distance, she began to put things together. Before this, she had been in Ireland with a group of magical people. And now, she was in a moonstruck land. The Realm of Fairy, she determined, and giggled again like a child on a ride at Disney World. The scent of roses floated by in the shape of petals and she inhaled them, along with other heavenly smells, like that of lavender and jasmine, fragrances that only paled in the physical realm as compared to that which she was encountering here.

Music spilled over her, the notes like a river current, mesmeric, dream-like and addictive. The closer she drew to the banquet table, the greater the volume. Draped in ethereal robes of finest silk, the entities danced and laughed and played instruments decorated with rubies, diamonds and jade, their bases constructed of purest gold.

Michaela looked to the head of the table and, just like that, lost whatever sanity she had still possessed. There sat a man, whose gilded beauty, sparkling eyes, pale skin and long, golden hair defied description. Attired in a tunic of shimmering gemstones reflecting every color in the rainbow, there were simply no words in the English language that would do him justice.

Aideen folded herself out of mid-air. Michaela felt no fear or trepidation at her appearing, but rather an intense appreciation for introducing her to this garden paradise. The woman bowed and, in sonorous tones, addressed the regal male. "I gift this mortal to you, oh Prince of the *Sidhe*."

The man smiled at Michaela and she sighed audibly at his great beauty. He tipped his head and then, in deep and dulcet tones that warmed all of the cold, lonely places within her, he spoke a single word. "Welcome."

He turned to acknowledge Aideen. "I accept yer gift. Now, go. Prepare her for me."

# Chapter Eighteen

Within seconds, Liam called Caleb to alert him to the dire situation. "She's gone, man. Michaela's gone. Ripped right out of my arms. Aideen's bewitched her, taken her away to the middle earth."

"*Bollocks!* Hold on." Caleb called out to his wife, a sense of urgency in his tone. "Arianna, give the baby to Granny. We've to go. *Now!*"

"What's wrong, Caleb? What's wrong?"

"Aideen's abducted Michaela."

The woman cried out in despair. "No, *no*! Oh, my God, what have we done?"

Caleb returned to the phone. "Hang in there, mate. I'll contact the other members and be there straight away."

Liam worked feverishly to retrieve Michaela as he waited for the others to converge on the island, her last known location within the mortal world. Devastated, he had never known such abject sorrow. Somehow, only God knew how, Aideen had managed to find Michaela and himself. Right in front of his face, she'd succeeded in calling her perceived rival into a faerie fort. He'd clearly underestimated her power. And though he'd tried every incantation he knew to unlock the barrier, 'twas all to no avail.

Hours had passed since the other men arrived and now midnight beckoned. Spotlights from various ground vehicles remaining on the island continued to crisscross those from air and sea. Though 'twas unlikely the woman would be found still inhabiting the mortal plane, *Túatha* search teams canvassed every nook and cranny, every sea cave and hidden cove, until the break of dawn lightened the charcoal sky with streaks of pink.

The men, along with MacNamara's wife, Arianna, gathered themselves around the kitchen table. Worry and exhaustion carved lines on every face as they planned a daring rescue, a risky mission–even in their world: To recapture a mere mortal from the faerie realm. Leading Michaela back through the maze of the Otherworld and into the physical dimension seemed impossible, at best. At worst, it could be deadly. Not only for Michaela, but for the others involved in the effort, as well.

By daybreak, everyone except Liam, Caleb, and Arianna had left the island, defeat etched on every face. Caleb and his wife had finally lain down in one of the guestrooms for a short rest. His stomach churning, his heart filled with grief, Liam again hiked the winding path where the ways of magic had stolen from him the only woman for whom he'd ever truly cared.

In the middle of the overgrown path, a spirit entity shimmered into existence before his eyes. 'Twas Aideen, come to gloat. "The cheek of you, looking as if someone's died," she said, her voice the chilling sound of a winter wind. "And herself, a woman you barely know. Well, I'm after capturing her to the Realm of the *Sidhe*, and offering the wee morsel as a gift to the Prince. Never fear, she's being well entertained, to be sure. Once a woman's been touched by the hands of the Prince of Faerie, she'll never again be desiring anything a flesh and blood man has to offer." A wicked smile curved those cold, cruel lips. "Sure, isn't that a thing I've discovered for meself?"

"I don't believe that about her," Liam retorted. "Not unless I hear it from her own lips."

The evil smile grew wider. "You fancy hearing her denounce you, *lover*? Tell you she prefers to open her legs to our illustrious Prince? To remain with the *sidhe* for a thousand years or more? Ah, sure, can that not be arranged quite easily enough."

Aideen swished her hands back and forth, unlocking the gate between the two worlds. As the entrance to the faerie rath became transparent, Michaela moved, trance-like, from within its depths.

*Faerie charmed.* Liam's heart clenched in his chest.

"Now, tell him." Aideen glided over to Michaela, teeth bared in the grimace of a smile, eyes glowing red as hot coals. "Tell him you don't fancy him anymore, that 'tis our Prince you wish to lie with forevermore. Tell him you're through with him, and the likes of this tedious physical existence as well." When Michaela made no sound, just stood silently staring straight ahead, the other woman gave her hair a hard yank. "Go on, mortal, *speak*!"

But Michaela remained frozen, her mind like an overloaded computer, unable to process the onslaught of strange data it was receiving.

Spinning around, Aideen glared at Liam. "Did you ever tell her that we're people of myth and magic? That all you're after wanting from her is to use her? To get the leg over, whilst discovering whether she'll be of help in dissolving the *Geis*?"

A moment passed before Aideen seemed to notice the cold smile on Liam's face. The woman faltered, looking suddenly unsure of herself. Liam marked the moment she realized that, though her lips had formed the word "*Geis*", no sound had come forth from her mouth, which, in their world, could mean only one thing. That a magical compulsion had prevented the utterance.

Nonetheless, Aideen's flagrant attempt to speak the forbidden word in front of a mere mortal—ensorcelled though that mere mortal was—brought additional weight to the Council's indictment on charges of treason. The ambush had worked.

Like a horde of worker bees, Council members swarmed from behind rocks and off ledges, and from the ruins of the antiquated monastery inland of the rath. Unbeknownst to Aideen, after making a big production of leaving the island earlier, they had teleported back secretly to lay in wait for her.

As Aideen realized the trap into which she'd fallen, she returned Liam's smile and snapped a triumphant finger over her head. But her plan to disappear right under their noses failed. In preparation for their enchanted 'sting' operation, Council members had set in place a magic damper of sorts, a ten-man rune that had absorbed her powers much as a bad alternator might drain a car battery.

"You're going nowhere, woman." Liam drew a ring of fire around her with his index finger, a flaming barrier that boxed her in, preventing her from fleeing. Waving both hands in the air, he created crackling bands of energy, binding cords that wrapped themselves around the woman, even as she fought like a she-devil against the restraints. But her efforts were futile, succeeding only in strengthening the snares that bound her, rather like wet leather straps tightening as they dry in the sun.

Her attempt to spit out yet another sorcerer's spell also met with failure, as her former lover's machinations had caused her to fall completely mute.

Caleb stepped forward, flanked by several of the other members. "Go, mind your woman," he said to Liam. "We'll take over from here."

While all this transpired, Arianna slipped from the shadows and gathered her tiny friend into her arms. Speaking softly in her ear, she worked on drawing her best friend back to reality. Her stricken face told the story as she accepted that it wasn't working.

After the Council removed Aideen from the scene, Liam walked over to join the other two women. "I need time alone with her." He directed the quiet request toward Arianna.

Caleb pulled his wife gently aside. "You know he's right, *a ghrá.* You've to let him help your friend. We'll go back to the house now and wait for them up there."

Understandably conflicted about leaving Michaela's side, the woman seemed to accept that, under these unique circumstances, her presence was a distraction. "Bring her back to us, Liam," she said, a catch in her voice. "Do you hear me?"

With a solemn nod, he enfolded the enchanted woman into his arms. The physical contact with him began to awaken her from the dream-like stupor and, for a moment, she looked around in confusion, only to slip back again into the soporific state, staring off into space.

After the others had left with Aideen, Brian Rafferty had hung back to have a word with Liam. "Have a care, O'Neill. You know yerself 'tis best that you try wiping the mortal. "

*Wipe her?* Liam's response was colored with annoyance. "The *mortal* has a name. Besides, Michaela's heard nothing of importance today. Am I not after seeing to that?"

Clearing someone's memories was not an exact science and carried the risk of moving a person too far back in time, rewinding their experiences beyond the moment desired. By wiping Michaela, he risked losing some of their time together, returning her feelings for him to the neutral zone, as if they'd only just met. 'Twas strange how the thought of that should sting so.

"Nonetheless, 'tisn't good that she's been to the other side, worse if she's after remembering any of it."

His usually mild temper beginning to flare, Liam dismissed the man outright. "This is my watch, Rafferty. My responsibility. Best you head on back with the others now, help them sort the legal processing of Aideen. Just mind she doesn't escape again."

If he could only get everyone out of here, get Michaela the feck alone, Liam had no doubt he could bring her fully back to herself with no harm done.

Brian gave a shrug, not bothering to hide his skepticism. "As you wish."

Alone with his woman at last, Liam took her hand in his and led her slowly down the rocky mountain footpath. As he'd anticipated, the farther they traveled from the scene of the faerie magic, the less was its pull on her psyche.

As he led her, step by halting step, toward the house, dusk fell around them, turning the trees and foliage a deep hunter green. Liam stopped from time to time, spoke softly in Michaela's ear, encouraging her to come back to him with promises he'd never made to any other woman.

An hour passed before he'd brought her fully back to herself, at which point she gazed up at him, eyes wide with wonder. "Did that really just happen?" At his censoring look, she sighed. "I know, I know. Don't ask, don't tell."

"Indeed." He wrapped his large hand around her much smaller one and led her up the path that would take them to the island property's front door.

After an exhausting meeting with Liam, Caleb and Arianna, Michaela retreated upstairs to the peace and quiet of her own room. After a lot of conversation, she had finally managed to convince her best friend to go home to her newborn child. She assured Arianna that she was well. That she remained unaffected by the adventure's of the day.

A blatant lie.

She stepped into the shower, groaning with pleasure as the hot, steamy water poured down her body. Still she was unable to escape the vignettes of the fairy kingdom playing through her head. The pounding stream beat down on her, massaging her aching muscles and relieving the tension that had her tied into knots. She could no longer separate reality from…from what? A different reality? Had she really entered an alternate universe? Could it be that, what she had originally believed to be dreams, visions, or a hyperactive imagination, had actually been encounters with the supernatural realm? Here in Ireland, she had already encountered a strange new society, a people with esoteric powers. At this point, she knew only that nothing was as it seemed, as she had always believed.

Her body slick from the coconut-scented body wash, she ran her hands over her breasts, moaning at the simple pleasure of her own touch. Her nipples puckered as she closed her eyes and imagined Liam's hands in place of hers, his muscular frame pressed against her back as he nuzzled her neck. But then, completely against her will, images of the magnificent sexual being she had encountered in the ethereal world intruded upon her private thoughts. Suddenly it was his hands she felt, his body pressing against hers.

Michaela's eyes flew open. She felt violated. The breathtaking beauty of that creature aside, it was Liam she wanted. Liam she would have. Until now, insecurity had kept her flip-flopping, going back and forth in her decision to make love to Liam, to take things to the next level. But not any more, she determined. Life was short and—as her time in Ireland had taught her well—completely unpredictable. No one knew what tomorrow would bring.

Her approach to life had always been one of 'seize the day'. *Carpe diem.* So, why not now?

Besides, the experiences of the day had left her feeling particularly hot and edgy, particularly brazen. She was a woman, with a woman's needs, after all. And all this time spent with a man whose every gesture set her body on fire had worn down her defenses.

Michaela stepped out of the shower, her olive complexion rosy from the heat. As she rubbed herself dry with a fluffy, white towel she heard the shower in Liam's room turn off. Letting her hair fall free of the clip she had used to keep it dry, she wrapped the towel around her. Smiling to herself, she tiptoed out into the hallway and padded barefoot to Liam's room.

She felt naughty, very naughty indeed, as she turned the doorknob and sneaked inside. Moonlight spilled through the floor-to-ceiling windows, casting a silvery shadow across the massive room. The size of a football field, it had been decorated with large, mahogany pieces. Very masculine. Very Liam. The heavy drapes, charcoal grays interspersed with sperm-shaped streaks of gray, matched the duvet spread across the king-size bed. A giant fireplace carved of onyx took pride of place on the far wall.

She could hear Liam brushing his teeth and wondered what he was thinking. They had been through so much together in such a short space of time. The struggles they had shared, his intensity in promising to look out for her, made her feel safe, close to him, as if she had known him forever. It was funny, the way she trusted him. While Michaela had always enjoyed a man's company, loved to flirt and laugh and generally have a good time, she had never been even close to falling in love.

Not until now.

For all her professed boldness, however, her knees were weak, her heart palpitating wildly as she dropped her towel and slid beneath the cool, crisp Irish linen sheets. As she lay waiting for him, she began to have second thoughts about her plan to seduce this powerfully virile male. Liam was different—quite literally. And there were things about him—magical, otherworldly things—that she still didn't understand. How would those attributes translate in the bedroom? Was he incapable of being gentle, tender? Was that why he had turned away from her every attempt at seduction to this day? Well, she was just about to find out. She could no longer picture her life without him in it. Stupid, because she could be setting herself up for a whole world of hurt. Because, notwithstanding the passionate way he had cared for her during these confusing days together, there was an arrogance about him, a bad-boy distance he kept that intrigued her even as it made her fear his ability to commit to her, to love her the way she wanted…no, the way she *needed* to be loved.

The bathroom door opened and he emerged amidst a cloud of steam, a black towel slung low around lean male hips. Unaware of her presence in his room, he turned and saw her lying in his bed, the duvet pulled up so that one bronze, pink-nippled breast peeked out at him.

"I was beginning to think you were going to stay in there all night." She purred in her best seductive tone, but he offered no sexy *repartee* in response. He only turned and looked at her with a steady regard, that way he had of studying her that made her feel vulnerable and exposed. And so deliciously turned on she considered jumping up and climbing him like a tree.

Without a word, he released the towel from around his waist. As it dropped to the floor, she bit her lip. Clearly, he was as aroused as she was. His tanned skin shone porcelain smooth as he walked toward the bed, drops of water from his shower beading his muscled chest. This was actually going to happen, she thought, her doubts and insecurities skyrocketing. Here she was alone with a man she hardly knew, and one who admittedly possessed some kind of paranormal ability. What was he anyway? she wondered. The hungry look on his face brought a werewolf to mind. So many secrets and questions, so few answers. And now, she was going to open herself to this man, take him inside her body, give him the gift of the most intimate part of herself.

She had said that she trusted him, but did she trust him enough for that? He had been there for her, non-judgmental...*present*... during some of the most difficult days of her life. Disturbing, scary times, when she had needed a strong shoulder to lean on, a powerful touch to push away the fears.

The answer to her question was, yes, she trusted this man. More than almost anyone she had ever known, and with all her heart.

At the side of the bed, Liam reached out and threw back the duvet. She sucked in a breath, suddenly shy to be lying naked before him. As his eyes roved over her body, she tried to swallow, but discovered that her mouth had gone dry as dust. She wanted desperately to cover herself with her hands, but forced them to remain at her side as he looked his fill. Finally, he reached out and slid his index finger thoughtfully over her lips, then down her chin, her neck, circled one nipple, then continued down over one hip, to her thighs. And stopped.

She was trembling, a combination of fear and desire.

He met her eyes, his head tipped to one side. "Your heart is beating so loudly I can hear it, *a mhuirnín,*" he commented softly.

"You think?" Although she was trying to keep things light, the breathlessness in her voice gave her away.

"I think…I've wanted you since the moment we first met," he responded. "I *know*…I need to be inside you now."

"Then come lie with me." Her voice barely a whisper, she held her arms out to him in welcome.

Liam slid into the bed beside her and pulled her close, the hair on his legs tickling her own smoothly shaven limbs. Michaela could feel him, hot and heavy, throbbing against her hip as he kissed her forehead, her nose, brushed his lips across hers. "You sure about this?" he asked, his blue eyes deep as an ocean. "Having any flashbacks or other repercussions from the events of the day?"

She didn't mention the experience in the shower, the sensation of being taken over by the princely male being. "No. Actually, it was all quite beautiful, surreal."

"Something's troubling you, so. Are you afraid of me, little one?"

She reversed their positions and rolled on top of him, straddling him. "This is me trusting you, Liam," she whispered, nibbling his ear, her long hair trailing over his chest. "Now, no more talk."

# Chapter Nineteen

Far beneath the green hills and the shimmering blue lakes of Eireann existed the timeless realm in which the faeries reigned. Frivolous beings they were, ever frolicking and dancing to the endless strains of the uilleann pipes, the golden harp and the magic fiddle. 'Twasn't that they'd not heard the prophecies of impending doom soon to be unleashed on humankind. But, unlike their foolish cousins, who had chosen to coexist with mere mortals within the physical world, those inhabitants of the Land of *Sidhe* gave neither a care nor a thought to such trivial matters, for they paid no mind to those things occurring outside their own experience.

Their joyous habitation untouched by human world events, they continued as they had always done since time immemorial, their preference to remain all but invisible to the mortal world. Their contact with the mortals who populated the vile and tainted upper earth had always been limited to those who tempted fate by intruding upon their private domain. And this, usually by walking through an enchanted woodland on *Samhain* eve, or such other folly as disturbing a faerie fort or rath.

As in everything that existed, there were, of course, exceptions to the rule. Due to a genetic predisposition toward birth defects, most *sidheogs,* or faerie children, were born disfigured, disabled or otherwise deformed. Because these children weren't aesthetically pleasing, a most important asset amongst the *sidhe*, their mothers would often kidnap a perfect human infant from its cradle, leaving their own child, a changeling, in its place.

In other instances, a mischievous imp was sometimes known to lure an innocent maiden from the human world. And once enchanted by their magic, exposed to the lush smells and tastes and colors of their majestic kingdom, she remained with them voluntary, having neither a wish nor a care ever to return to her former life.

Now 'twas a serious affair, a criminal offence against their people, for one to attempt to steal back such a mortal from their possession. A damning, impossible feat, so it was. And so it had ever been…at least, until today.

The woman brought to them by the *Túatha* cousin, Aideen, had been formally presented as a gift to Orindahl, the Prince of the *Sidhe*, making the infraction plotted against them all the more egregious. Thus the thwarted Prince, his appetite whetted now for a tempting taste of mortal strange, sent forth a decree that she be returned to his dominion—to his bed, in fact—forthwith.

Glad to be home again, Arianna finished feeding Kieran and tucked the sweet smelling infant into his crib for the night. It was late and she was exhausted from dealing with the trauma of Michaela's abduction. Thank God, her friend was safe now in Liam's care. And, with that stone cold bitch in the Council's legal custody, Arianna felt like she could finally let her guard down and rest for a while, without worrying about what other sinister traps the woman might set.

Caleb was in bed when she walked into their room. He looked up from his laptop and gave her that smile that still managed to turn her insides to mush. With a nod of her head, her clothes fell away from her body and floated to the floor around her. Proud of her growing proficiency in the ways of faerie magic, she returned a pixie grin to her one and only.

"Oh, whilst you were with Kieran, I heard the message alert go off on your phone. You might want to check yer texts." At her look of alarm, he assured her that all was well. "I'm just after receiving a Council update from Seamus. Aideen's not being left alone for a minute, *mo chroí,* so you needn't fret. Sure, she'll not be escaping ourselves again."

Arianna grabbed her phone off the bedside table and slipped naked into bed beside her husband. Propping the pillow up behind her, she settled back to read her text. "Oh, crap. We so don't need this right now."

At the raised-brow look Caleb sent her way, she explained. "It's a message from Tara. She's upset that she hasn't been able to get in touch with Michaela for several days, so she's booked a flight here. She'll be arriving at Shannon first thing in the morning."

"What are you going to do?"

She bit her lip. "I'll have to call and try to dissuade her from coming. I'll tell her Michaela's traveling with Liam and phone service is sketchy on the island where she is." Well, it wasn't a total lie, Arianna insisted to herself, trying not to feel so guilty about the half-truth.

After a most unpleasant—and extremely convoluted—conversation with her highly educated and super-intelligent friend, Arianna finally convinced her to put off her trip to Ireland until Michaela returned. Still, she had been like a dog with a bone. She knew damn well that something was up, and it had taken the better part of an hour for Arianna to get her off the phone. Tara was worried about their mutual friend—and rightfully so, as it turned out. But, unlike Michaela, who had, in blind faith, accepted Arianna's account that something supernatural was going on, the pragmatic Dr. Tara Price was the very last person on earth to whom one would wish to offer up such a conclusion. In fact, she would be convinced that Arianna and Michaela had both lost their ever-loving minds and be on the next flight out to Ireland to micro-manage a treatment plan.

Another potential catastrophe averted, another fire put out, Arianna replaced the phone in the charger on the bedside table. Caleb was snoring lightly as she turned onto her side, spooning him, snaking her knee between his legs. And yet, as worn out as she was, sleep continued to evade her. She lay awake into the wee hours of the morning struggling with things that, as recently as a year ago, she would never have believed herself.

Hot lust stirred his juices as Liam's eyes fixed on the little vixen who had so deftly mounted him, like the stallion she controlled with those tautly muscled thighs. But, unlike the horse she'd mastered, there'd be no reigning Liam in tonight. Her cuts and bruises had faded, and he no longer feared hurting her with his sexual prowess. The woman didn't flinch as he tangled his fingers in all that long, black hair cascading onto his chest and tugged, pulling her mouth down to his. His tongue invaded the dark sweetness the access offered him, whilst he cupped a handful of her well-toned arse.

He flipped her onto her back, smiling at the soft gasp that escaped her lips as he took control. God knows he wanted this woman, had fantasized this moment since the day they met. By this time, he was near obsessed with the desire to touch her, taste her, bury himself deep inside the very heart of those delectable charms. Only one thing troubled him, sure. She was after being enthralled—abducted to the Land of Faerie, for feck's sake—an experience akin to the ingesting of a hallucinogen to a mere mortal. Liam wanted her sober, fully present for their first time together. He'd no bloody intention of having it tainted by the remnants of a heady fairie charm.

He framed her face with his hands. "Before we go any further,

I give you one last chance to stop this, *a chuisle.* 'Tisn't my nature to restrain my carnal appetites this kind of way. I've been patient, considerate, taking my time with you. But that ends tonight. After what you went through today, I've to be sure that your mind is clear, that you're not still under the influence of faerie magic."

"I know exactly what I'm doing," Michaela told him, brushing the hair back from his face. "Exactly what I want." Whilst her words were bold, he recognized the look of befuddled awe in the long-lashed, chocolate eyes staring up at him.

He'd admit it, so. That reckless part of him wanting her to acknowledge the precarious power with which she'd been trifling all along. "I've no practice with romance, wee one, nor do I claim to be a gentle lover. When I'm finished with you tonight, I'll have ruthlessly marked you as my own. With my hands and lips and teeth, with my body, sure, I'll ruin you for any mere mortal man."

He saw her throat constrict as she swallowed hard. Her small, pink tongue darted out and licked her lower lip. Liam held back a groan.

"Promises, promises." With that breathless whisper, she stretched to kiss his neck, his shoulder, chest just below one flat brown nipple.

Aye, the time for talking was over, Liam thought, hard as a fecking standing stone. He'd not be denying himself, nor denying this woman, any longer. His eyes locked on hers, he cupped her breast in his hand, pleased by the way her breath caught in her throat. He bent his head and swirled his tongue around one pert nipple until it stood erect, then moved slowly down her body, kissing and sucking, tasting the musky essence of that which he'd denied himself for so long.

Contrary to popular opinion, Liam had never taken a mere mortal as a lover. Aside from the obvious issues with the *Geis,* 'twould have been too much drama, too many complications for a man who preferred keeping things simple. Also, there was an innocence about this woman that made no logical sense a'tall. During the time he'd come to know the wee Yank, her behavior had been bold and brazen, to be sure. She'd attempted an overt seduction on several occasions, not shy about asking plainly for what she wanted. Now, however, when their mating was imminent, he sensed a reticence in her touch. She seemed timid, awkward, generally unsure of herself.

He supposed the fact that he'd only his experiences with the voracious appetites of a *Túatha* woman for comparison. And, one of his own would just as soon copulate hanging upside down from a ceiling's rafters as lying sprawled out in a bed. Attributing her apparent nervousness to the differences between the two races, Liam positioned himself between her well-toned thighs and slowly rubbed himself against her garden of delight. At the intimate touch, he heard her muffled moan, felt her hesitance as she withdrew her hips a mere centimeter from his.

He stopped and grasped her chin, forcing her to meet his gaze. "Michaela? Do you want me to stop?"

She chewed on her lip. "No. No. I'm just…." She sighed "I…."

Since she was having a problem expressing whatever was troubling her, he slipped into her mind. What he saw there truly shocked him—and he a man not easily surprised. Why had he not recognized this before now? "You've not been with a man before." 'Twas a statement, not a question. "Why did you not tell me this?"

"It's not a big deal, really. I...I didn't want it to be a…an issue between us. I didn't want you to think that it changed anything, that I expected anything…you know, any long term commitment or vows of love, or promises of forever. I just want to make love to you, to…to give myself to you. I want you to be my first, Liam. No expectations. No strings attached. "

He stared down at her, a frown wrinkling his brow as he tried to understand the wee woman he held naked in his arms. He'd always been led to believe that a mere mortal woman looked for commitment in a man, romance, monogamy. Ultimately marriage. "So…you don't wish to have a relationship with me? You want…." *How did they say it in the mortal world? Oh, aye.* "'Tis only casual sex you're after then?"

"God, no." The vehement protest came quickly, so quickly, in fact, that it seemed to embarrass her. "What I mean is…what I'm trying to say is that I would love for things to progress between us. I care for you, Liam, or I wouldn't be lying here with you like this. I guess I've always thought virginity was generally overrated. That it shouldn't be the thing that decides whether what happens here between us tonight is a one-night-stand, or the beginning of something special."

He comprehended now why her touch had seemed so tentative, so unsure. But the revelation of her innocence raised more questions for him than it answered. Should he mate with her now? Or stop, leave her untouched for a man willing to offer something more than a reckless night's passion? And why did the mere thought of another man possessing her provoke this murderous rage, when he was usually quite adept at harnessing the turbulent nature of his people?

His unruly member throbbed against her moist heat, demanding that he accept her sweet offering, that he feast at the table she'd so deliciously spread before him. Jaw set, his decision made, he rolled off her and pulled her into the crook of his arm. "We'll sleep now," he dictated, without preamble.

She propped herself up on one elbow and looked down at him, brown eyes flashing. "See? You're making a big deal out of it. That's why I hesitated saying anything in the first place."

"Michaela…?" The tone of his voice rose at the last syllable, a note of warning.

"Don't even think about trying to protect me from myself, Liam. That would be insulting. I've been taking care of myself my whole life. You want me, I know you do." Not to be denied, the bold brat wrapped her hand around his swollen rod and pumped once for emphasis. "Tell me you don't want this and I'll stop," she said, throwing his own words back in his face.

His eyes glazed over. He could hear the sound in his head, the resounding snap as he lost all self-control. "So, you fancy a ride on the wild side, do you now? You wish to learn of the erotic arts at the hand of a master, no strings attached? And this, after I've warned you, given you every opportunity to rethink this reckless passion." Even while she tortured him with her wanton touch, driving him fecking mental with the need to fill her up, to have her in every possible way a man could conceive of taking a woman…until he'd purged himself of this madness, of this bloody need for her. This fiery obsession. "Oh, aye, I'll have you now, little one, so I will. I'll give you everything those big brown eyes of yours have been demanding…sure, and more than you could ever have imagined."

At his intensity, at her first unveiled glimpse of the *Túatha de Danann* male she dared to toy with, the wee woman again looked uncertain. As if she'd only just realized that she may have bitten off more than she could chew. But Liam was no saint, God knows. All those acquainted with him would be gladly attesting to that. 'Twas best she accepted now that this little scenario she'd been playing at would conclude exactly as she'd intended.

He bent his head and took her mouth in a ravishing kiss. His hands moved deftly over her body, touching her, stroking her to a fever point, even as he slipped inside her mind, revealing mental images of the things he planned to do to her.

Clay in his hands for the molding, she was moaning, thrusting mindlessly against him as she sought that which continued to evade her. "Oh God, Liam. I need you now."

By this time, he was beyond thought, beyond reasoning. His mouth covering hers, his tongue invading the moist dark recesses, he dipped one finger, two into the pot of honey she offered him, stretching her, preparing her to receive him. Moving down her writhing body, he sipped, licked, tasted her sweetness, her low moan of surrender edging him on, pushing him harder. Faster.

She was whimpering, pleading, begging him to take her. Poised above her, he breathed words in Gaelic, words he knew she didn't understand. Prepared to thrust, to make her his own for now and all of eternity, he gazed down into her eyes.

The sudden terror he encountered in those chocolate depths stopped him cold, like ice water tossed in his face. "Michaela? What…?"

She started struggling against him, frantically pushing him away. "No, no, no, no, no. Oh God, no. Don't touch me. Why have you come for me? Leave me alone."

Gobsmacked by the abrupt about-face, Liam untangled their bodies and pulled away from her. But she grabbed for his arm blindly, hysterically screaming for him to hold her. "Don't let him have me," she begged, tears streaming down her face. "Don't let them take me away again."

Liam whispered a few words and her body went limp under the glamour. He immediately shifted his conscience to that of the *sidhe.* Understanding of Michaela's reaction plunged him into a primordial sea of ice, even as fury set a conflagration of hellfire in his soul.

"Orindahl." As he spit out the name of the Prince of Faerie, he turned to tug the sheet over Michaela, covering her nakedness.

Standing before Liam in all of his otherworldly splendor, the Prince tipped his head and, in dulcimer tones, stated his business there. "The mortal is mine. A gift from one of yer own."

"That one had no authority to offer such a gift," Liam asserted, the calm in his manner a lie. In truth, his hands were balled into fists, his temper coiled like a white-hot snake inside him. His all-consuming rage was a violent maelstrom of emotion for which he had no understanding, no point of reference. "The mortal is under my protection."

The prince tipped his head again, a cocky smile alighting on his glimmering face. "Protection? Is that what you call the things you were doing to her?"

"And you," Liam countered. "Attempting to insert yourself between the woman and myself, to taste her through my lips, touch her breasts with my hands, fence with her, using my sword." He shook his head and tsk-tsked, a devise he knew would further infuriate the magical being.

Eyes glittering with malice, the Prince's lips twisted into a cruel scowl and the deceptive cloak of beauty wavered. The air crackled with his annoyance. "You intruded upon my domain this day, *Cousin*."

"As you intrude upon mine now," Liam reminded him lightly.

"I will have her," Orindahl insisted.

"Perhaps. But not tonight."

One beat, two. "No, not tonight." With a sulky pout, the shimmering being conceded the point.

The cardinal rules governing the relationship between the mortal and immortal sides of their legendary race had served them well throughout the millennia. It decreed that neither party may restrain or remove a person or thing from the other's possession until they'd quite finished with it…or them. And while Orindahl accused Liam of taking the woman from his domain, in truth, 'twas Aideen who had taken her in and called her back out again. Therefore, the Prince's true grievance was with Aideen, not Liam.

"Well played, Liam O'Neill," Orindahl said with a begrudging nod. "Well played." And with an elegant flick of his wrist, he vanished in a diamond-studded puff of smoke, the colorful entourage who'd accompanied him to the physical realm trailing behind him.

The confrontation left Liam in a definitive bad humor, for it threatened a plethora of far-reaching complications, not the least of which was that the overall threat to Michaela might now have been increased exponentially. For Liam would have to champion her, not only against the waking Beast and his demonic minions, but against the unwanted amorous intentions of the Prince of the *Sidhe* as well. Her abduction to the Realm had broken two cardinal rules governing a mere mortal's interaction with the Kingdom. The first was simple: avoid attracting their attention. The second, even more importantly, was to avoid causing offense.

And if things weren't difficult enough, there now stood a challenge between himself and the arrogant Prince of Faerie…and over a woman, no less.

*Brilliant*, Liam thought. *Just bleedin' brilliant.*

'Twas unlikely after three thousand years that the Woman of Promise would be revealed. Nonetheless, he'd no choice but to play this thing out if there was even a single chance that Michaela was the mere mortal ordained to light the path of deliverance from the *Geis,* the wicked tool of revenge exacted against his race for an ancient battle lost. And a single misstep on Liam's part could rip the torch from her grasp, thus plunging the whole of bloody humanity into interminable darkness.

Now that Liam was again thinking with the head on top of his shoulders, rather than the one further south, he decided that the Prince's interruption might have been fortunate, after all. Pulling the wee woman into his arms, he trailed a finger down the side of her face as he drew her gently out of the enthrallment. With her curled up beside him and sleeping like a swaddled babe, he was having no luck making sense of the strange flood of emotions he was experiencing. And, while his people knew nothing of that daft sentiment mere mortals were after referring to as romantic love, he'd to admit to an ever-growing fondness for the woman lying beside him.

After resetting the magical safeguards around his property, Liam drifted into a tumultuous sleep disturbed by the faerie music playing in his head. 'Twas Orindahl's way of taunting him, of letting him know that whilst Liam might have won the battle this time, sure, he'd not won the war. The capricious creature hadn't finished with Michaela yet. No, he'd not finished with her a'tall. And one fine day, the Prince of Fairie would be after returning for his prize.

And Liam would be here waiting for him.

## Chapter Twenty

*Fado, fado....*

The *marcra sidhe* escorted their Prince back to the shadowy realm in another dimension of time and space, existing down below, over and around, through and beyond the crystal veil. A whispering hush descended over those awaiting the faerie cavalcade at their illustrious ruler's empty-handed return. A harbinger of things to come, an unusual silence fell amongst the playful sprites, whose chief occupation was feasting, dancing, playing music, and making love. Orindahl's original plan had been to share but a timeless hour's dalliance with the black-haired mortal before moving on to his infinite other interests. But the woman's wrongful removal and retention from him, and the *Túatha* cousin's stubborn refusal to return her, had shifted his mindset. Now, once he reacquired the woman, he'd not be done with her. Ever.

He gathered his subjects around his throne for the grand announcement. "'Tis time," said he, "that I took a wife." As a roar of delight broke out amongst the masses, he raised a hand. "She, whom I've chosen, is the maiden who was gifted to me by the one called Aideen, part of our family from the upper earth."

Such a marriage had been a common enough practice amongst the men of the *sheagh sidhe* in the past, as the faerie hosts were well known for stealing away beautiful mortal virgins to be their brides. The practice had slowed of late, however, because an untouched woman of marriageable age was increasingly more difficult to find. During his recent visit to the upper earth, he'd discovered that the mortal female with the ebony locks nicely fulfilled that requirement.

The information cemented Orindahl's resolve to have the woman as his own.

During their confrontation, the cousin had spoken correctly of the laws set in place forever ago, one of which forbade each from invading the other's domain and taking that which he coveted. Marriage was the only sacrament that could not be violated in either direction. And once the royal wedding took place, the black-haired mortal would be lost to his cousin forever.

At the announcement of the impending nuptials, the sound of laughter rolled through the kingdom like tinkling bells. The whimsical creatures clapped their hands and resumed their merriment, singing and dancing to the wild strains of unearthly music that the enchanted lyre played upon itself.

Duties were chosen and given. The halls of the hewn timber palace were decorated with resplendent hues of color and magic. Joy filled the air, for upon his marriage, the Prince would become King, and his bride Queen of the Realm. At long, long last, the royal fortress would hear the laughter of faerie children, a rare and wondrous happening in their present reality.

And this mortal chosen to be Queen of the *Sidhe* would never again experience sadness, pain, or suffering. For neither would she know, nor would she remember, the things of her former life on the upper earth.

In this idyllic land would she live happily ever after. Forever and ever.

Forevermore.

## *Chapter Twenty-One*

Tara's flight left the Naples International Airport shortly after eight a.m. After a brief layover in Dublin, she was off again, landing at Shannon in the West of Ireland around lunchtime. She hadn't given Arianna or Michaela any notice of her pending arrival. She wasn't giving either of them another opportunity to dance around whatever was going on there.

After all that had happened to the three of them last Thanksgiving, Tara couldn't help but feel ill at ease. She wasn't stupid, after all; she knew her friends were keeping something from her. Probably an ill-conceived, though well-meaning attempt to avoid interfering with her job. Still, she was damned tired of being circle-talked and put off, and had decided to do what she did best, which was to confront the issue head-on. Once she knew what was going on, what trouble her wild-child little friend had gotten herself into this time, she would be in a better position to figure out a solution to the problem. A problem that Tara strongly suspected somehow involved the incredibly attractive man she had met on her last visit to the castle.

After renting a compact car at the airport, she threw her carry-on into the back seat and headed straight for Ennistymon. Less than a half-hour later, the tiny 4-cylinder engine was straining up the steep, winding road leading to her friend's extraordinary home. She still couldn't get over all the changes in Arianna's life within the past year. She had relocated to Ireland, gotten married, and borne a child. Not to mention the fact that the girl was now living in a flipping *castle*, for God's sake, she thought, unable to prevent a fleeting smile.

The property's steward—what was his name again? Oh, yeah, Mr. Flanagan—answered her knock on the door.

"I'm here to see Arianna. She's not expecting me."

The slight man blustered for a moment, seeming taken aback by the inappropriate nature of her surprise visit. *Well, that was just too damn bad!* "If you'll wait here a moment, Miss, I'll see if the lady can attend you now."

Tara grumbled under her breath as the gigantic front door shut in her face. "Oh, she'll *attend* me alright."

A few minutes passed before the door swung open wide. "What the heck…."

"Yeah, same to you," Tara shot back. The shock on Arianna's face was priceless.

"I thought you were going to put off coming until Michaela got back from the island."

Tara glanced at her friend sideways. "Yeah, right. The island." A pause. "Well, are you going to invite me in, or what?"

"Oh, yeah, yeah. Of course. It's just that you caught me off guard."

"The point, exactly. Now, what do you say we go upstairs so you can fill me in on what's going on with our dear little air-headed friend."

Arianna puffed her cheeks and blew out a breath, the expression on her face like she had just been sentenced to death by firing squad. "You're not going to want to hear it," she warned, in a singsong voice.

"Try me," Tara countered. "Now, come on. Let's go sit down. How 'bout the kitchen? I didn't have time for breakfast, and I'm starving."

A robust woman was bustling around as they walked in. Arianna made the introductions. "Maeve, I'd like you to meet Tara, one of my best friends from the States. Tara, Maeve here is Flanagan's daughter, the castle chef."

"Ach, chef, now is it?" The woman beamed good-naturedly. "Just call me 'Cook', like everyone else round here," she said to Tara. "Now, can I get you a bite of lunch, luveen? I've a lamb stew on the cooker, a roasted chicken in the oven."

Tara smiled back at her. "Either one. Whatever you're cooking smells so good my stomach's growling."

"Well, sure, won't I just fix you a nice bowl of stew and some fresh baked bread for a start?"

"That sounds great."

"Let's sit over by the window," Arianna suggested. "It's away from the all the lunchtime hubbub. Give us a little privacy."

As they pulled chairs out and sat down, Tara jumped right on the subject at hand. No one could ever accuse her of beating around the bush. "So where's our girl?"

"Yes, I'm doing well. The baby's healthy. And my marriage is darn near perfect. Thanks for asking."

"I *know* how you're doing. What I don't know is what the hell is going on with Michaela. So, where is she? Really."

"So, here's the deal. She's still having nightmares and the occasional meltdown." As Tara opened her mouth, Arianna held up her hand. "And, *yes*, she has been thoroughly checked out, poked and prodded, with pictures taken of every part of her body, inside and out. On top of that, she's seen a psychologist, a friend of ours, MacDara Darmody, to make sure she's not suffering some kind of mental breakdown."

"And?"

"And all the tests…*everything* checks out perfectly. There's absolutely no *logical* explanation for what's been happening."

Tara didn't miss the emphasis on the word 'logical'. *Surely, she's not going to start harping on all that psychic crap….*

"That's exactly what I'm going to do," Arianna said plainly.

Tara did a double-take. *Okay, coincidence.*

As Maeve placed steaming bowls of stew in front of the two women, Tara took the opportunity to shovel a spoonful into her mouth. "Oh, my God. This is heaven."

Arianna grinned. "Yep, Maeve here's a gem. We stole her from one of the Michelin-starred restaurants in Dublin. We're very fortunate to have her."

"You think?" Tara shoved up another huge bite. "Wow."

"Glad you're enjoying it." Arianna took a small taste of her stew, then pushed the bowl aside.

"Yeah. Okay. Now while I chow down, you can fill me in on whatever stupidity is going on with our mutual friend…sans all the hocus-pocus commentary, please. Just tell me that she hasn't gone and gotten herself preggers."

"No, of course not." Arianna leaned closer and lowered her voice. "Look, Tara, she's really into this guy. I think she may even be in love with him. This is the first time she's ever felt this way about anyone."

Eyes squinted, Tara stared at Arianna. "What? The first time? I think Mick's 'first time' had to be when she was like twelve years old."

Arianna shook her head. "We've been mistaken about her… sexual escapades, Tara. The truth is—and I'm not telling tales out of school. I'm sure she'll eventually tell you this herself. But, the truth is, our Michaela has never been with a man."

"Never been with a *man*?"

Arianna instantly got what Tara was asking. "No, she likes guys, T. She's just never met anyone who did it for her like this before."

"What the f—"

"Exactly."

"So, what was all that about, her acting all sexually liberated, like she was out there, doing every good looking male on the eastern seaboard?"

"I don't know, honey. You know the kind of screwed up childhood she had. Maybe it has something to do with that. All I can tell you is she admitted that this is the first man—"

"So, she *has* slept with the guy."

"No.... I don't know. The last time we talked about it, they hadn't done anything. He's been holding back. You know, because of her injuries and stuff."

"Well, that impresses me," she grudgingly admitted as she buttered a large chunk of Irish soda bread and dipped it into her stew.

"Yep. Granted, the guy's so hot he just looks like trouble. But I do really believe he cares for her in his own way."

"So what's the problem then? Why all the cloak and dagger nonsense? I don't get it."

"Yeah, well, that's the part you're not going to want to hear," Arianna repeated. "In fact, you might want to think about getting on the next flight back to Naples. Just leave this alone."

"I'm not going anywhere until I see Michaela with my own eyes. Where is she, anyway?"

"I told you. She's on an island with the love of her life."

"An island, huh? So, what do I do? Book a flight? I still can't handle getting onto a boat."

"There are no commercial flights there. It's a private island, Tara. Liam owns it."

"Whoa. Well, this just keeps getting better and better, doesn't it? So, let me see. What you're telling me is that our sweet, clueless little friend is alone on a deserted island with a man she's only just met. Good grief, Arianna! What the hell!"

"Look. I've known the guy for quite a while now. Caleb's known him for years. He's not the problem here."

"So, you admit it. There *is* a problem. And, if it's not him, then what exactly is it?"

"His ex." Arianna raised her brows and looked Tara dead in the face.

"Don't tell me. There's some kind of Fatal Attraction thing going on."

"Worse."

"Worse, how?"

"This woman is…God, how do I tell you this?" Arianna paused, chewed her bottom lip in that way she did whenever she was nervous. "Okay, the thing is, the woman has magical powers. We believe she's tormenting Michaela, the one causing all the terrible nightmares, visions and stuff."

"You're kidding, right? What you really mean is that this ex-girlfriend is nuts. That she *believes* she's got magical powers and has figured a way to stalk Michaela, to set things up to eff with her head."

"No, that's *not* what I mean, Tara. What I'm trying to tell you is…well, maybe Shakespeare said it best. 'There are more things in heaven and earth, than are dreamt of in your philosophy'."

"Seriously, Arianna? The Bard?" Tara set her spoon down in her empty bowl. "C'mon."

"I'm serious here, T. Liam's jealous ex is causing real problems for our girl. Real problems."

"Okay, I'm fed and full. You have any suggestions on how I can charter a private flight to this island Michaela's on? There's no way I'm going back to Naples 'til I've seen her for myself."

Arianna let out a defeated sigh. "We'll fly you over in the helicopter."

Tara shrugged. "Works for me. How soon can we get out of here?"

## Chapter Twenty-Two

Michaela woke up the following morning lost in a cloud of confusion. Over the past couple of weeks, her life had become a surreal adventure where she could no longer differentiate between dream and reality. Although her memories of the events of yesterday were rapidly fading, she seemed to recall something about Aideen spiriting her away to another dimension. Michaela had suspected it was just another vision…that is, until she demanded answers from Liam. Although he was non-committal, his one-word reply confirmed that she had actually been the victim of a fairy abduction. A *fairy* abduction, for God's sake!

Speaking of Liam, she was mortified for falling asleep on him last night. Quite literally, falling *asleep*. They had been kissing and touching, just about to make love, when she basically passed out on him. *Awkward.*

And now, with everything else that was going on, Tara was due to arrive on the island any minute—a complication she just didn't need right now. As she stood beside Liam at the helipad waiting for Caleb to land, he reiterated the importance of not revealing anything to her friend about the crazy supernatural goings on.

"Are you kidding me?" Michaela scoffed. "She doesn't believe that stuff. If I told her what's been happening here, she'd throw me in a burlap sack and drag me back to the States to have my head examined."

Arm in arm, Liam and Michaela stood looking to the sky as the chopper landed. The sea winds tugging at her hair and clothes, Tara ducked beneath its rotating blades. After greeting Liam, she grabbed Michaela in a bear hug, before pushing her away at arm's length to take a good look at her. "You okay, Mick?"

"I'm good." At the dubious look on her friend's face, Michaela added, "Really, Tara. I've never been better."

Back at the house, the men escaped to the study while Michaela led the way to the kitchen and poured each of the girls a glass of Riesling. "Let's go grab a chair on the porch and catch up. View's awesome from there."

Settling in for a long chat, the three life-long friends caught up on the recent happenings in their lives. Tara spoke about the Vesuvius dig, Arianna, about being a new mother. Michaela, of course, gushed about the new man in her life.

"So, why have you been so impossible to get hold of?" Tara asked. "You've only been here on the island for what, a couple of days?"

Michaela cleared her throat. "Cell phone reception here is nil. At Liam's house in Kerry, it's off and on."

"Arianna said you're still having problems with nightmares and stuff."

"Yeah, some. Luckily, the knot on my head's all healed up, so I don't think it has anything to do with that."

"Hmm.... So, I hear you had a run-in with one of Liam's exes."

*Damn.* It was like Tara had a checklist in her head, and was popping off the questions one by one. "Yeah. Liam dumped her and she's jealous that he's with me. Normal break-up BS."

"Really. Well, according to Arianna, there's more to it than that. Something about her stalking you with her evil powers." This she said tongue-in-cheek.

Michaela shot Arianna a raised-brow look. "Really? You told her that?" At her friend's shrug, she turned to Tara. "Look, T. You really don't want to go there. Trust me on that."

"So, entertain me."

Michaela sighed. "I don't know what you want me to say. Yes, I believe there's something weird, something otherworldly, going on here. But you don't believe in that stuff, so what's the point of discussing it?"

"Just trying to get a handle on how messed up you are in the head, Mick. How important it is for me to get you the hell out of here. Get you back home, back to the status quo."

Michaela shook her head. "Not happening, girlfriend. I'm not going anywhere. Granted, Liam and I haven't known each other for very long, but I really believe he may be 'the one'. So, I'm not leaving here until I know one way or the other. End of discussion."

"Look, Tara," Arianna finally chimed in. "You've seen for yourself that Michaela's fine. We'll all just have to agree to disagree about what's causing these dreams and visions. But don't forget that I met Caleb in my dreams before I ever got to Ireland."

Tara snorted. "Yep, got my own theory about that, too."

Arianna pursed her lips wryly. "Of course you do."

Tara ignored the surly comment. "It's simple. You admitted to knowing him as a small child. Your mind grew him up, simply filled in the blanks when the two of you finally met."

"Doesn't explain why he dreamed of me."

"Same explanation," Tara insisted.

Arianna laughed. "You're impossible."

"And *you* have been living in the land of fairies for far too long," Tara added, with a twinkle in her eyes.

"Okay, so you're a scientist. I get that. But have you ever considered what world-renowned physicists have to say about multiple universes and alternate realities? You can't just write off everything in this world that doesn't have a logical explanation."

Michaela watched the exchange between her two best friends, both of whom were only looking out for her best interests. She may not have much of a family, but she had been very, very blessed in life with her choice of friends. She didn't want either of them to get hurt, or part ways with a disagreement hanging over their heads.

"Look guys," she interrupted. "All philosophical differences aside, this is my life, my decision. I love you both but, at this point, your opinion is moot. As I said before, I'm not going anywhere, not right now. I've never met anyone like Liam before, and I know I never will again. Simply put, I'm staying right where I am until I've seen this thing through."

"Have you two been intimate?" Tara asked without hesitation.

Michaela snickered. "Been trying my damn level best to get him to do the nasty, but the man insists on acting like a gentleman."

Tara nodded. "Hmm…."

"Exactly. Since I'm not currently riding an orgasmic oxytocin high, you don't have anything to worry about."

Obviously smart enough to know when she had been beaten, Tara threw in the towel. "So, that's it, I guess. Might as well get on back to digging up old bones."

"Don't go yet," Michaela said. "I really would like for you to get to know Liam a little better. What do you say we all have dinner together before you take off?"

As the sun was setting, Liam and Michaela threw together a quick meal from the supplies that had arrived on the island earlier that day. As the group sat around the table eating, Michaela couldn't help but feel a twinge of jealousy at Liam's obvious interest in Tara. A man would have to be a eunuch not to notice her long, slender legs, her lithe blonde beauty, which was almost unfair considering that she could eat like a pack mule. With an IQ that was virtually off the charts, her escapades around the world led to a lively dinner conversation. The tiny pitchfork-wielding imp on Michaela's left shoulder kept pointing out the appreciative glint in Tara's eyes each time she looked at Liam, as well. Of course, the girl would have had to be blind not to notice that muscled body, the full sensual lips and the square jaw lightly furred with a five o'clock shadow. Not to mention that mesmerizing ice-blue gaze capable of making a woman feel like she was the only one in the world.

The group collectively decided that Caleb and Arianna would stay the night. So rather than fly Tara all the way back to Shannon for her connecting flight to Dublin, she changed her departure to Kerry. As soon as Caleb and Tara had left in the chopper, the other three retreated to the comfy screened-in porch to relax.

When Michaela excused herself to go to the bathroom, Liam took the opportunity to fill Arianna in on the Prince of Faerie's blatant intrusion on the couple the night before. "Until now, we've only had to be guarding your friend against a jealous *Túatha* woman involved with demonic entities from the underworld—a gargantuan task, to be sure. But Michaela's abduction to the middle earth has reset the parameters for an entirely different set of dangers and problems."

"I thought there were laws," Arianna sputtered. "Rules governing that sort of thing."

Liam shrugged. "So there are. He left once I reminded him of that."

"I don't like this. I don't like it at all."

"No, 'tis not a good thing. You know yourself, she's already been abducted once. What's to stop it from happening a second time?"

"God!"

Liam felt awkward, not only sitting here alone with a colleague's wife, but upsetting her into the bargain. "Ah, sure, as you've pointed out though, there are laws governing the interaction between the two sides of our family."

"You don't really think he'll come back here, do you? Try to take her away again?"

Liam considered the question for a moment. "Aideen was after presenting her as a gift to the Prince, so wasn't he quite miffed to have had her returned to the mortal realm. Whilst I'm sure he considers her removal a grave offense committed against him, in actuality, no laws were broken. Aideen, who had delivered her there, simply called her back to the surface. In essence, Michaela left the realm of her own free will."

"Yeah, right. As if any faerie-charmed human being has a free will."

Giving a shrug, Liam raised the snifter of Jameson to his lips and sipped.

"Michaela hasn't mentioned anything about this. Does she even know the intrusion happened?"

Liam sighed. "We were…distracted…when he appeared. I put her in thrall to protect her whilst dealing with him. She'll be remembering bits and bobs of her time spent in the middle earth, but most of the memories will fade over time."

Arianna looked away, her fingers tapping on the arm of her chair. Liam could see her brain working. "So, will you please explain these…laws to me?"

"It's fairly simple, really. We avoid trespassing upon one another's domains. For example, though the Prince may call to Michaela through the use of *pishogues* or faerie spells, though he may seduce her, attempt to draw her to himself, he's prohibited from physically removing her from this dimension."

"So, if she succumbs to his…seduction, what then?"

"Then, she's chosen that existence of her own free will. The only protection for a maiden, on either side, is marriage. The *sheagh sidhe* are prohibited from so much as calling to a married woman, mere mortal or otherwise. Neither may we attempt to call such a one back from that realm once she's wed one of them."

Caleb's wife gave Liam a direct stare that left him squirming. "Well?"

Liam shook his head. "Sure, I'm enamored of your wee American friend, but a discussion of marriage between ourselves is a bit premature, wouldn't you say?" When that response failed to satisfy the woman, he added, "Do you truly believe that Michaela would agree to marry me, having known me for such a short while?"

He saw his colleague's wife wilt right before his eyes. "No. She wouldn't. And she likes you—she really cares about you, Liam. She's closer to you than I've ever seen her with any other man. But I know she considers marriage a sacred vow, a life-long commitment, far too important to be entered into lightly or with someone she hardly knows."

As Michaela opened the door to rejoin them, Arianna lowered her voice and repeated the question he'd been dreading answering. "So, do you believe Orindahl is gone for good?"

A frown crowding his brow, Liam shook his head. "Most assuredly not," he answered, keeping his voice low. "I fear the Prince of Faerie isn't finished with Michaela yet. And, sure, he's tricks up his sleeve we can't even begin to imagine."

# *Chapter Twenty-Three*

Michaela felt like the direction of her life had been plucked right out of her hands. Like a rock skipped across a lake, it was spinning out of her control. When Caleb had returned from dropping Tara off at the airport the previous evening, the two couples talked late into the night. Like a double date with her best friend and her new husband, the visit had felt almost normal.

Though guarded, the interaction between the two alpha males had been interesting to witness, defined by an underlying tension between the two of them. Since the point of staying on Liam's private island had been to hide Michaela away from the witchy woman—a moot point at present—it had been decided that they would all return to the castle together the following morning.

Again, Michaela had slept in Liam's arms. Again, untouched. While she had felt safe with him, warm and protected, gone were his amorous advances of the night before. No doubt a result of her confession of being a virgin, she surmised, which could mean only one thing: He didn't want to be her first. Beneath all the bad-boy symbols of rebellion, the chains and black leather, jets and helicopters, the high performance, million-dollar vehicles, Liam was an honorable man. And he refused to deflower a virgin unless he planned to make a commitment to her.

Whenever they had stayed at the castle before, they each had their own private rooms. This time, however, Arianna put them together in the bedroom Michaela had used during previous visits. Liam took off immediately to find Caleb. After spending some quality time with her precious godchild, little Kieran, Michaela had gone back to her room and changed into her riding boots. She and Wind Spirit needed a little quality time together of their own. She was looking forward to spending a few hours with him exploring the picturesque castle grounds.

She had expected to run into Liam and Caleb at the stables, but the men were nowhere to be found. After checking in with the groom, she went to find her equine best friend. She smiled as he snorted a greeting, bumping his head against her. "I've missed you too, buddy. What do you say we spend the day together?" He nuzzled her arm, seeking the apple she had snagged from the fruit bowl before leaving the castle. She held it up and he plucked it from her fingers.

She saddled him up and mounted him. Feeling the weight of his long-time friend on his back, his skin quivered with pleasure. Since Michaela wasn't familiar with the terrain or the layout of the property, she kept him at a leisurely trot as they picked their way across the verdant landscape. How peaceful it was here. With the billowy wind tearing at her hair and the sound of waves crashing against the distant shore below, she could feel the tension ooze from her body. As she road the castle grounds, she sucked in a deep breath of the salty sea air, pleasantly sweetened by the flora of the region. She soaked in all of nature's vivid hues: the vibrant blues of the gentians, pale mauves of the foxgloves and the ponticum; the riotous crimsons and purples of the fuchsia, and the gorse bushes' lemony yellows. As she passed a hawthorn hedgerow and leaned down to pluck a handful of blackberries from one of the branches, she could have sworn she heard a giggle. She turned her head and, for a moment, thought she had seen a colorful winged creature fluttering in the brush. She snapped her head in that direction, but nothing was there.

*No way. Had she just seen a fairy?* A huge grin broke across her face as she considered how that seemed to be happening a lot of late. "Wow, how cool is that? You know, I can understand now why Arianna was so taken with this place that she decided to move here," she told Wind Spirit, reaching down to pat his withers as he snuffled in response. "Yep, you're right, boy. It wasn't Ireland that kept her here. It was all about Caleb."

A stubbornly independent and strong-willed woman herself, Michaela got that now. With her increasing feelings for Liam, she could understand perfectly how a woman would be willing to pack up and move to the other side of the world—to enter a brand new reality if it came to that—just for the opportunity of building a life with the one she loved.

"What am I going to do, boy?" she asked her friend as they traversed the western boundary of the property nearest the cliffs. "There are still so many secrets, so much I don't understand."

Spotting a long stretch of meadow ahead, she decided it looked safe enough to give Wind Spirit his head. At a gentle nudge to his flanks with her booted heels, he leaned happily into a three beat gait.

God, this was exhilarating. Exactly what she had been needing, she thought, as he cantered past a maize of trees to the right. With her hand on the reins, her thighs controlling the movement of the magnificent beast beneath her, she could actually feel the brain fog lifting, clarity replacing the growing confusion of her experiences over the past couple of weeks. She pondered the recent turn of events. There were the nightmares, of course, which were like being trapped in a freaking horror movie. But what concerned her most were the blackout periods, those times when she would suddenly pass out, or fall asleep, and then wake with no recollection of anything that had happened to her. It wasn't only the bad dreams that were dragging her down, however, but the incomprehensible images dancing around in her head while she was awake. For the life of her, she couldn't seem to shake the image of Aideen hovering in the air, immersed in a shimmering light. And the recollection of a radiant male creature in a magical land that defied all earthly description was firmly implanted in her brain. Not a dream or vision, she stressed to herself, but the memory of an actual event, something that had really happened to her.

Clearly, if she were to remain here, she required answers. But just how much of the dark magic that seemed to be Liam's life—that had somehow ensnared her in its own net of intrigue—would he be willing…or able…to share with her? And when?

Noting that the sun was sinking low in the sky, Michaela dug the cell phone out of her back pocket and checked the time. Good grief, she had been out riding for almost five hours. Having forgotten to turn her ringer back on when she woke up this morning, she had logged at least a half dozen missed calls from both Arianna and Liam.

She dialed Liam and he answered on the first ring. "Where are you? Everyone's worried sick. Sure, we were about to send out a search party to look for you."

"Sorry about that. I was out on the property riding. Guess I got lost in paradise."

She could hear his audible sigh. "I'll let the others know you're well and on your way back."

"Thanks. See you in a few."

As she brushed Wind Spirit down, watered and fed him an extra treat, Michaela grumbled under her breath. "Okay, so it's nice to be missed, to have people care about me. Still, I'm not going to start making excuses about where I go or how I spend my time. I've been coming and going as I damn well please for a very long time now." She gave the stallion a final pat on his neck. "And that's not about to change now, is it, boy?"

"She was on her way back over an hour ago and it's getting dark."

As the minutes ticked by, a cloud of doom descended over Liam.

He, Caleb, and Arianna had decided to forego having dinner with the thirty or more staff members gathered in the great hall and dined privately at the kitchen table. But the gorgeous meal the cook had set out for them remained virtually untouched.

"I know how she likes to spoil Wind Spirit." Arianna placed a miniscule serving of the organic bangers and mash on her plate, and then passed the bowl to Caleb. "She's probably giving him a good brush-down and an extra portion of hay."

Caleb's wife was trying to assuage his concerns, but Liam could read the worry in her eyes. "I've a bad feeling about this," he said, getting to his feet. "If you'll excuse me, I'm taking a hike down to the stables to escort her back."

When Liam arrived at the paddock, he found it empty. The stables housed about a dozen of Caleb's prized bloodstock. He located Michaela's stallion in one of the stalls, but no sign of the woman herself. "There you are, boy," he said, giving his head a scrub. "So, where's your friend got off to?"

The great beast shook his head and rolled his eyes. Spooked, Liam realized, his heart sinking like a chunk of Connemara marble in his chest. Shifting his perception into that of the *sidhe*, he sensed lingering traces of metaphysical energy. He sniffed at the air and detected the sweet bouquet of an otherworldly fragrance. And riding upon the light ocean breeze was an unearthly melody like the voices of angels.

Gobsmacked, Liam acknowledged that Orindahl had done his worst, and moving much more quickly than he had credited him. Using every otherworldly arrow in his magical quiver, the fey prince had managed to charm Michaela, had called her to himself.

Thoroughly sick to his stomach, Liam identified the curious emotion as one of grief mixed with tinges of something indefinable:

An inner rage spawned by mental images of his woman lying naked in the other man's arms. Was this unsettling feeling the thing that mere mortals referred to as jealousy? How very odd, he thought, whilst his well-honed sixth sense continued to nag at him about something else. He closed his eyes and listened closely, straining to make out the telling whispers in the wind. As much as he was after rejecting the notion that the wee Yank might have some ethereal connection to the resolution of the *Geis*—to Liam himself—he'd now to accept the fact that he'd been feeling something unique about her all along. 'Twas like a subtle warmth embedded in an icy winter gust identifying the first hint of spring, when the increase in temperature was so fleeting as to be mistaken for naught but an illusion of the longing for it.

Yes, just like spring. In the cycle of nature, 'twas a time of awakening, of warmth and light and rebirth. Was it that breath of hope, the bright light of deliverance, he'd been sensing in Michaela all along? Was it possible that she really was the Chosen One prophesied by the ancient scrolls, the Woman of Promise for this final millennium? Had she been drawn here by the Fates, destined to save all of humankind from the cataclysmic evil soon to come? And, in so doing, would she breathe life back into his people who, like Liam himself, were after growing colder with each passing generation? Perhaps, he thought, that was why even the land itself had seemed to groan at her coming. All that aside, the foremost question in Liam's mind was whether she could survive such a mission, whether she could triumph in a battle against the ultimate evil and come out unscathed.

His head swirled with air-spun memories of the two of them together, the way those chocolate eyes of hers would gaze into his. Eyes filled with awe and trust, even when the world around her—*his* world—had ceased to make any logical sense to her a'tall. His body grew hard as he remembered the way she'd submitted to him, opening like the delicate petals of a flower, her soft feminine sighs encouraging him to fill her, to possess her, to make her his very own.

What was it about her that seemed to center him, to soothe the restless spirit that had always been his curse? She was like a soft ocean breeze to his senses, like a gentle summer rain. Just the thought of her brought the scents of heather and wildflowers to his nostrils.

He realized he was overcome by the simple need to touch her, to reacquaint himself with the shape of her face, the texture of her flawless skin. An ironic chuckle left his lips as he admitted to himself that she was, indeed, his *anam cara*. It had taken losing her to Orindahl for Liam to finally recognize that she owned his heart, his soul. For, truth be told, he could no longer imagine his life without her.

With this sudden wealth of insight, he closed his eyes and summoned Caleb to the stables. Here, at the scene of the crime, they would develop yet another rescue plan, one whose execution would effect her safe return to the mortal realm. To himself.

❧

It was the best, most delicious, most incredibly awesome dream Michaela had ever had. Her fondest wish was never to awaken from it, but rather to spend eternity laughing and dancing along the floral paths lined by weeping willows and twisted oak trees. To forever play hide and seek with the fluttering creatures, who cavorted around the thorny hedges of the living hillsides of this somnambulant fairytale world.

But as she played and giggled like a small child, she couldn't escape the ache she felt deep down inside of her. It was as if she had lost something dear to her, as if someone she loved with all her heart had died. Try as she might, however, she could remember nothing that had been her life before today. And today was so amazing, so magnificent, so overwhelmingly joyful, it was hard to concentrate, to try to remember—or even to care—about what might have gone before.

All of the playful games finally drew Michaela through the grand entrance of a royal fortress, a palace constructed of hewn timber, resplendent with fabrics of spun gold and priceless silk tied back with silver threads. As she entered through the door, several tiny nymphs with long, golden curls greeted her. Giggling behind their hands, they led her down a shimmering hallway and into a private room, all the while referring to her as 'her majesty' this and that. Once there, they guided her to a bath the size of an entire room, where they nimbly stripped off her clothes. Strange, but she felt no shyness or ill of ease as they washed her body with scented oils and rinsed her hair in the fragrant water. As she stepped out of the bath, she was dry instantly. After leading her up the steps to a dressing room, her entourage curled her hair into long, black ringlets. They remarked over its dark shade, as everyone who lived on this magical isle, it seemed, was blonde and fair.

All polished and pampered, buffed and perfumed with fragrances that were a delight to the senses, she was assisted into a long, white gown made of ivory and diamonds and other precious gems and materials that Michaela couldn't identify.

Finally, she understood the reason for the joyous celebration: it seemed that this was her wedding day. But the smile faded from her face as she pondered just who, on earth, could possibly be her groom?

"How the hell did this happen?" Arianna looked pale and spent. This was taking a terrible toll on all of them.

"You know yourself, no mortal woman can stand against the

whispers of a faerie charm," Liam muttered. "I knew he'd be back for her. I should have forbidden her to go off on her own."

"Yeah. Woulda, coulda, shoulda." Arianna snapped at him and her husband reached out to touch her hand. He gave his head a slight shake, a sign for her to back off. "Sorry, Liam. I know there's no way that you could have prevented this. I'm just overwhelmed is all."

"Understood."

"And you might as well forget about 'forbidding' Michaela anything. That would have only made her more determined to dig in her heels, to do what she wanted."

"I've noticed that." Liam's dry reply camouflaged the devastation he was feeling.

"We just have to figure a way to get her back." Arianna turned to Caleb. "So, what the hell do we do now? How does all this *calling* someone work?"

They had already searched the entire area surrounding the stables together, and then Liam and Caleb went out on horseback, surveying every part of the property for traces of supernatural activity, that certain energy that would have been left behind during an abduction. The trail revealed that, after finishing with the stallion, Michaela had been drawn out onto the grounds toward the maze. 'Twas the faerie rath there that proved to be her last point of contact above earth.

Liam's spirits were growing darker by the minute. Although he told himself that he would get her back, the faeries were whimsical, capricious creatures and, with every passing hour, hope of her recovery grew slimmer.

Hands on his hips, Caleb spoke thoughtfully, almost to himself. "We've to sort a way of drawing her out to the upper earth without physically invading Orandahl's domain."

"Orindahl can just bloody well feck off." Though Liam hadn't raised his voice, his tone was deadly. "The Prince has crossed a line this time, sure, taken what's mine."

At that possessive assertion, Arianna spun a look at him. "Yours?"

"Aye. And I'll have her back, so I will. By force or no."

At that, Caleb's head snapped in his direction. "You'd be willing to start a war with the *sidhe* over this?"

"She's mine," was Liam's only response.

"Maybe it won't come to that," Arianna said, her bottom lip caught between her teeth. "Now, c'mere to me, gentlemen. I believe I have a plan."

## *Chapter Twenty-Four*

With a smile lighting her features, Michaela continued to dream of the fairies….

She awoke to two female forms shimmering into existence before her eyes, each holding the other's hand. How she knew these things, she couldn't say, but she identified one of the women as a water sprite, while the other looked achingly familiar. "Michaela, listen to me," that second one said. "The Prince will never let you go. He'll marry you just to spite Liam, to trap you here forever. Whatever you do, don't accept the golden scepter."

Still locked in a dream state, Michaela felt her heart warm at the sound of that name on the woman's lips. *Liam.* Was this the man she had anticipated meeting in the throne room? The one for whom she longed, the one who owned her heart?

The water sprite turned to the other woman. "Remember child, we may not compel her to return with us. She must choose to do so voluntarily."

The familiar one from the conscious world turned to her. "Come with us now, honey. Please. The Prince put up safeguards to keep Liam out, but he's waiting for you up above. If you don't come back to him, he'll invade this realm and all will be destroyed."

"I hear the others returning," the faerie woman warned, her voice low and melodious. "Hurry, daughter. We must go now."

As the door to the bedchamber swung open, the two female forms faded into the ether. Michaela could hear her friend's whisper lingering in the air. "Listen for Liam's call, sweetheart, and follow the sound of his voice. Mick, just follow the sound of his voice…."

In an atmosphere of welcome and mirth, the perpetual grin on her face had left her cheeks aching, her eyes feeling all squinty and out of focus. Of their own accord, her feet tapped to the lively music of the magic lyre until she feared she might surely dance them both off. She sighed, her heart filled to overflowing with the incredible wonder of it all. The remarkable creatures, vibrant colors, and unsurpassed beauty of her surroundings were almost more than a mortal mind could bear.

And yet, with all the joy and splendor in her midst, a miniscule ache in her heart gave her pause and, again, the sense that something important was missing.

Four butterfly creatures with lovely human faces and long, gold-spun hair arrived in her chamber. Buzzing around her, they encouraged her to follow them down a winding corridor decorated in a vivid array of rainbow colors. As the troupe approached a picturesque pair of double doors at the other end of the hall, Michaela could hear the lyrical notes of a wedding march. Fanciful beings of every construction, young and old, small and large, lined the hallway on both sides, their cheering deafening as she continued toward what she somehow understood was to become her final destiny. Michaela pictured the love of her heart, the muscular build, ash-blonde hair, and ice-blue eyes of the man to whom she was soon to pledge herself for all time.

At her approach, the imposing double doors swung slowly open. Michaela's smile widened at the splendor of the gem-encrusted throne on the other side of a mile-wide room draped in silken fabrics in a vast selection of colors, of scarlets, purples and blue greens. In a crimson robe sewn with threads of solid silver, the illustrious prince rose to his feet and extended his hand, offering to Michaela a golden scepter. She remembered how the familiar figure had admonished her not to accept it. Somehow, in the dream world she inhabited, Michaela understood that this was a royal pledge of marriage, an offer to make her his fairy princess for all time. She had only to reach out, to accept his gift, and the ceremony would continue.

As she drew closer to him, the hazy mist swirling around his face suddenly parted. Her tremulous steps halted as confusion clouded her gaze. Something here was definitely amiss, she thought. The pale blonde man holding his hand out to her, while magnificently radiant and beautiful beyond belief, was not at all the one she had been expecting.

*Surely, this is not my groom*, she thought, the sadness in her heart increasing a thousand-fold. *Where, oh where, is my one true love?*

As a frown crossed her brow the enchanted façade of her surroundings faded and all of the vibrant colors bursting forth in the room began to bleed into various shades of black and white. Instantly, she recognized the stubborn selfishness, the underlying cruelty, and the cold-hearted arrogance of the male being seated on the majestic throne. As he recognized her change of heart, anger flooded his features. A frightened hush rolled throughout the multitudes in attendance as his subjects sank slowly to their knees, heads bowed in humble obeisance to their illustrious and fearsome prince. For a moment, the underlying music that had seemed to be the very foundation of the realm's existence became a cacophony and then ceased abruptly. Michaela's hands covered her ears, which ached at the vacuum created by the sudden silence.

Michaela blinked and, without pomp or circumstance, found herself transported instantly back to her chamber. Alone. Relieved to have been returned here, she knew intuitively that she had not escaped the prince's wrath. He would marry her this day, and not because he cared for her—or even knew her for that matter. No, he would have her to wife for one reason, and one reason only: Simply because he wished it.

Caleb leaned against the trunk of an ancient white thorn tree as Liam paced back and forth along the borders of the maze. Because of the increased existential energy, he was quite certain that this area, where spiked thistles and ferns surrounded a slight protuberance in the earth, marked the exact point of Michaela's departure from the physical plane. Caleb's wife was an intelligent woman, he reasoned, and her plan had been a sound one. That she would contact her mother, a water sprite and one of the *sidhe*, and have her 'abduct' Arianna into the land of Faerie to meet with Michaela, to *wake her up*, so to speak. In so doing, no alarms would be set off, as the comings and goings of the *sheagh sidhe*, the members of the faerie host, would, of course, be deemed unremarkable.

Still, Liam was a man who preferred, not only immediate action, but also to handle his own affairs himself. As such, he'd been quite looking forward to transforming physically and descending into the lower earth to confront the flagrant Orindahl face-to-face. He'd scoffed at the charm the Prince had set in place to prevent his entry, convinced that counteracting it would have proved no challenge a'tall. But after Caleb's wife had suggested that her cunning plan stood more chance of success than an open contest with Orindahl, Liam called upon every ounce of the ancient magic flowing through his veins to resist the overwhelming urge to take matters into his own hands. Sure, 'twas a testament to his sheer strength of will that he'd been able to do so.

Shortly before dawn, Arianna and her mother shimmered into their earthly forms beside him. Caleb grabbed his wife's hand and pulled her into his arms. "Thank God you're safe, *a mhuirnín.*" He turned to her mother. "And thank *you. Again.*"

The petite sea nymph had long blonde hair and skin so pale it shone bluish white from her life beneath the waves. She tipped her head in acknowledgement of her son-in-law. Then with a smile and a knowing wink, she gave a flick of her wrist and vanished from sight.

"You look ashen," Caleb scolded his wife, rubbing her wrists. "You're chilled to the bone, as well."

"It was one wild ride," Arianna confessed, visibly shaken and fatigued. "But we found her."

Liam let out the breath he'd been holding. "What happened, so? Did you speak with her? How's she faring?"

Arianna bit her lip. "She seems to be holding up okay, but she looks dazed, like she's been drugged."

"She believes she's dreaming." Liam voiced his conclusion aloud.

"I think so too. But things are much worse than we thought, Liam."

"Worse? How so?"

"My mother said that the buzz throughout the realm was that the Prince had planned to marry Michaela, but during the wedding she did something to displease him. Whatever it was brought the entire ceremony to an abrupt halt."

Liam frowned at the news. Orindahl was wasting no time in invoking the protection of the marriage rites. "Thanks be to God that the marriage was interrupted. Still, 'tisn't good for a mortal to anger the Prince of Faerie. Did she say anything to you about that?"

"No. I think she wasn't able to form words, to speak. You know, like in a dream."

"What exactly did you tell her?"

"As you instructed me, I told her not to accept the golden scepter. And to listen for your call. I also told her that you were prepared to invade the *sidhe*, bring war between the two worlds, if necessary, to get her back."

Resolve turned Liam's face to stone. "I'll do whatever it takes."

While she had heard enough to disqualify her from dissolving the *Geis,* Michaela might still very well be the prophesied Woman of Promise. For that reason alone, Liam knew the Council would be forced to back him in any extraction attempt. Wedding or no. "Perhaps it won't come to that," Caleb muttered, looking troubled.

"Perhaps not." Liam agreed in a tone that communicated his complete disregard of the long-standing laws governing the two realms of existence.

"And now, I'll have my wife back," Caleb said firmly. "'Tis nearly morning and she's been at this ordeal all night. She's after requiring a bite to eat and a bit of a lie in."

"I'll stay here and continue calling to Michaela," Liam said.

Caleb nodded. "We'll send one of the servants with food and supplies."

*"Go raibh mile maith agat."* Liam expressed his gratitude to them both.

"No worries. Call to me when you've made contact with herself, and I'll return here to help." With that, Caleb slipped an arm around his wife's waist and they departed down the path leading toward the keep.

Not a half-hour later, Caleb's wife was coming back down the path. "Hey," she said as she joined him.

Liam turned to her, brows raised, head tilted. "Hiya."

"I finally convinced Caleb that I'm not going to be able to sleep, so thought I'd help and brought us some stuff." She set down the basket she was carrying and opened it, revealing several sandwiches, fruit and drinks. "Here, take this," she said, offering the blanket she had brought with her. "We could be here a while."

"Thank you." He spread the blanket out on the ground for the two of them to sit on.

"How long…? I mean, do you have any idea what it will take for her to be able to hear you?"

"I've to confess I've never dealt with a situation quite like this one before." Liam let out a long sigh. "I'll keep on trying for a wee while, but then I'm going after her. If Orindahl succeeds in marrying her, she'll no longer hear my calls a'tall. We'll be forced to invade the Realm to rescue her."

"I was thinking, since you're the man she loves and I'm her best friend in the world, maybe, if we close ranks and try calling her together, that might speed things up."

Understanding that the woman needed to feel as if she were doing something to help her friend, Liam gave a slight smile. "Aye. Worth a chance, sure."

Arianna swallowed. "When I was in college, I took a class in Ancient Legends and Folklore. There's a poem I learned by Alfred Perceval Graves."

Liam thought for a moment, then smiled again. "Little Sister."

Caleb's wife nodded and returned his smile. "That's the one. Anyway, I thought that maybe I could try calling her, using that piece of ancient Irish poetry."

Liam looked at her in wonder, unable to fathom the kind of care and devotion that Michaela commanded from her friends. This woman, raised in the mortal world with no former knowledge of the *Túatha de Danann*, had contacted her mother, a fabled water sprite. Arianna was then after traveling to the middle earth with a faerie, leaving hearth and home behind, including her husband and newborn babe. And all of this in the slim hope of rescuing her best friend. "You begin, whilst I stand watch," he said finally.

Arianna cleared her throat and, in a voice sweet and low, repeated the verse from memory:

Little sister, whom the Fey
    Hides away within his dun,
Deep below yon seeding fern,
    Oh, list and learn my magic tune.
Long ago, when snared like thee
    By the *sidhe*, my harp and I,
O'er them move the slumber spell,
    Warbling well its lullaby.
'Til with dreamy smiles they sank,
    Rank on rank, before the strain,
And I rose from out the rath,
    And found my path to earth again.
Little sister, to my woe,
    Hid below among the *sidhe*,
List and learn the magic tune,
    That it full soon will succor thee.

Through the long hours before the dawning, the two of them nibbled on sandwiches and took turns with the calling. Whilst Liam chanted in his native tongue, faerie tale promises to make all her dreams come true, Caleb's wife recited her verse like a mantra, again and again. And, with every repetition, he felt more at ease, more comforted, ever more certain that the tiny wee elf held captive in the land beneath the blue lakes and green hills would hear their calls and follow the sound of their voices.

Suddenly, from beneath their feet came a rumbling sound. The earth quivered and quaked, before the ground split apart and, as if giving birth, pushed forth the object of Liam's desire. For an instant, the transformation seemed to be struggling, however, shifting back and forth from an ethereal form to that of solid flesh.

Liam scrambled to her point of entry, with Arianna close at his side. "That's it, c'mere to me, *a ghrá*," he encouraged his dark-haired girl. "Return to me now."

At the sound of his voice, Michaela's flesh seemed to solidify. Eyes glazed over, she looked blankly at Liam, then Arianna, and, without a word, collapsed into a heap on a pile of dried leaves.

Liam fell to his knees on one side of her, her friend on the other. Caleb's wife looked panicked and afraid. "Mick. *Mick!* You have to wake up. You're safe now. You're back with us."

When she failed to respond, Liam scooped the wee thing into his arms and rose to his feet. "Let's get her out of here now. Orindahl's taking this thing with Michaela as a challenge to his authority. Sure, he'll be around as soon as he realizes she's gone missing."

Arianna gathered up the blanket and picnic basket and hurried after Liam. "How are we going to keep him away from her?"

Liam glanced over his shoulder at Caleb's wife. "There'll be a wedding, o'course."

"A wedding? You're really going to propose?"

"Won't the ceremony brand her as me own?" He noted the concerned look on the woman's face. "You know yourself 'tis the only way to keep her safe from the Prince."

Arianna touched his arm. "Do you love her, Liam?"

At first baffled by the question, he then remembered that Caleb's wife had been raised as a mere mortal. "Love? Surely you know by now that isn't a sentiment shared by our people."

"That's a copout, Liam," she replied, her chin set in a stubborn display. "Actually, the longer I'm married to my husband, the more certain I am that he loves me. Romantic love is a divine gift available to all living beings."

*Bollocks.* A man of relative wisdom, he'd no wish to get into a row with the wife of a colleague and chose to hold his tongue instead, letting the philosophical debate end there.

He refused to acknowledge the strange fluttering in the region of his heart each time he glanced upon the woman in his arms, just as he chose to ignore his body's physical reaction to her abduction. The weakness in his knees had reminded him of the spindly-legged newborn fawns born on his property. And the sickening panic that had soured his stomach and set his heart to racing as if he were dying had been predicated by fear alone, the dread that she might be lost to him forever.

No, he insisted to himself, he would never love the wee imp the way Caleb's wife had suggested. For he possessed neither the understanding of that silly, mortal emotion, nor the capacity to seek it out. But in taking the woman to wife, he would honor and protect her...worship her body with his own. And he'd be faithful, he vowed, his commitment to her as unwavering as the one she'd be required to make in choosing to live in his world, where she would never quite fit in, and with a people she could never fully understand.

Dark clouds covered the noonday sun as they approached the front door of the keep. Arianna had to have sent word ahead to her husband, as a flood of people poured down the giant stone steps and closed a protective circle around them.

"We've prepared yer room with the appropriate safeguards," Caleb said.

With a nod, Liam gave up the carefree life he'd been living, changed now forever.

## Chapter Twenty-Five

Michaela lay locked in a deep, enchanted sleep for the rest of that day and all throughout the night. When she'd yet to stir by mid-morning of the following day, Liam began to imagine the worst. "Have you a local doctor you can recommend?" he asked Arianna when she came to the bedroom to relieve him for a wee while. "Preferably one familiar with faerie spells."

"That's a good idea." Concern etched on her face, she leaned over and gently smoothed Michaela's hair from her brow. "Ask Caleb when you go downstairs to get a bite to eat."

Caleb was presently meeting with council members who'd begun to arrive at the castle early that morning. "How are you holding up, mate?" he asked as Liam joined the group, his hair still wet from a quick shower.

"Not too bad a'tall. And yourself?"

"Knackered. But happy to have me wife back from the Middle Earth in one piece. 'Tis been very hard on her, between caring for the baby and this thing with her friend."

Liam nodded in agreement. "She's sitting with Michaela right now, whilst I grabbed a shower and a bite to eat. If the wee Yank doesn't wake up soon, though, I'm thinking to have her examined by one of our doctors."

Father James, who was sitting with the others, chimed in. "Being a priest, I've some experience with this sort of thing. I've seen it take as long as several days for a mere mortal to return fully to consciousness."

"You've dealt with *pishogues*, so?" Liam asked.

"Faerie charms. I have, yes." He gave a wry chuckle. "We may be distant cousins, the faeries and meself, but haven't they given me a wide berth ever since me ordination. And aren't they known for avoiding a man of the cloth, for tending to flee from a priest rather than confronting him." At the troubled look on Liam's face, he added, "Now don't you be fretting yourself about it all now, my friend. I'll be staying here as long as I'm needed alright, as long as I can be of help."

"*Go raibh mile maith agat*," Liam said, thanking his fellow council member for the offer of support. Feeling slightly better about things, he walked over to the teacart and poured himself a cuppa, before joining the others.

The group's scribe, Seamus O'Donnell, yawned and stretched his long legs out in front of him. "Whilst we have to concern ourselves with Orindahl's antics, sure, we mustn't allow ourselves to become distracted from the real source of danger to the woman."

*"An Garda Geis,* the Guardian of the Enchantment," Father James said, referring to the demonic entity.

"*If* it turns out that Michaela *is* this...Woman of Promise," Liam corrected. "If not, the threat of Orindahl calling her back to the Land of Faerie still remains very real. 'Tis a danger that can be extinguished only in one of two ways: I've either to marry the girl, or send her on home to America."

Caleb frowned. "And yet we can't allow her to leave, not until we've determined the question of her possible involvement in the *Geis*."

Which left only the one option available to Liam. Marriage. And, as much as he'd come to care for the wee sprite, he was beginning to feel more than a little boxed in. A confirmed bachelor until this point, he'd been quite enjoying living his life as a single man. "I believe for now we should be concerning ourselves with her recovery from the *pishogue,* and any after effects it may have on her long term."

MacDara Darmody, the group's resident psychologist, had been sitting quietly, listening to the conversation. "Will I stop upstairs for a look at her when you go back up?" he asked Liam.

'Twas interesting, Liam thought, the way everyone automatically assumed that the woman's care and protection were in his hands. Which would be the case if it turned out that she was, in fact, the anointed one, and he her champion. Or, in the alternative, if they should wed, an uncomfortable topic already on the agenda for the meeting later today. "That would be grand."

"I gather you'll both be staying here at the castle for the immediate future?" MacDara asked.

"We will," Liam replied, sipping his tea.

Caleb turned to Liam. "That's a wise decision, mate. This is a stone fortification, built for protection against enemy attacks. The cliff drops hundreds of feet to the sea on one side, whilst the bawn secures the property's outer perimeter. With the portcullis lowered and the drawbridge raised, the castle's all but impregnable. You know yerself, your wan may well have two independent supernatural forces coming against her—the faeries from the Middle Earth, as well as minions sent from the Underworld to possess a mortal host. Given those circumstances, I'm pleased you've decided to remain here."

"How secure is the area surrounding the moat?"

"Anyone attempting to gain access to the demesne by swimming across will be making only the slightest dent in the voracious appetites of the alligators guarding it."

Liam gave an amused smile. Even for a member of their clan, Caleb had always been a bit of an extreme character. "You really do keep alligators here, so?"

"They're normally housed in a subterranean iron-gated pen until nightfall, when they're after being released as an extra security measure. But, given the current situation, I've left them free to swim the moat both night and day."

"We'll be taking this thing one day at a time so," Liam said, getting to his feet. "For now, if you'll all excuse me, I'm going back up to check on her."

He glanced at MacDara, who stood up and left the room with him. In the hall, they passed silver-haired Brian Rafferty, arriving early for the meeting. At eighty-two, he was the oldest member of the council.

"Hiya, how's things?" he asked.

"Not too bad. You know we called her back from Faerie." At Liam's comment, Brian nodded his head. "She still hasn't awakened, though. We're going back up to look in on her now. We'll let all of ye know if anything changes."

Caleb's wife stood to her feet as the two men entered the sitting room outside the bedchamber where Michaela lay sleeping. MacDara took a seat on the sofa, whilst Liam went to her side. "Sleeping beauty," he said, in a whisper. Thinking he'd spoken the words only to himself, he glanced up and caught the soft smile on Arianna's face.

She reached out and squeezed his shoulder. "I just wish we could figure out whether she has anything to do with the Enchantment. If she isn't this…Chosen Woman…,she's not your responsibility. This is the third time in a year that she's been abducted while visiting here, first by Caleb's crazy cousin, on our trip to Inishmore, then by Aideen, and then by the freaking faerie prince himself. And he's still out to get her back. It's too much, Liam. This is not a good place for her. And she's not one of us. We need to send her home, get her back to the real world where she belongs, before something irreversible happens to her."

Liam's immediate reaction to the suggestion was puzzling. Sure, he should have been doing an Irish jig at the idea of shedding the burden of responsibility for this woman he hardly knew. Hadn't she proved to be a problem for him since day one? Since the moment they met, hadn't it always been one bloody thing or another with her? A fall off the horse. A head injury. Wicked bad nightmares and strange hallucinations. A hot lust the likes of which he'd never known. And now a possible war with the bloody Realm of Faerie.

With all of that in mind, the words that flew from his mouth managed to shock even himself. "I plan to take her to wife."

Arianna frowned, pressed her lips together, and then sighed. "I'm not going to stand around while you *charm* her into marrying you, Liam. *Romance* her, yes. Use you're powers to manipulate her? Sorry, my friend, but not on my watch."

Maybe because she was a Yank, Liam thought, but MacNamara's wife possessed the singular ability to get straight to the point. "Fair enough."

The woman's expression softened. "She deserves to marry someone capable of loving her, Liam."

Once married, they would be permanently bound together. Until now, Liam would have been the first to acknowledge his own low threshold for boredom, particularly where the fairer sex was concerned. Surprisingly, he'd yet to experience any of that with Michaela, no matter that they'd been together almost constantly since the incident at the horse show in Dublin. It didn't escape him, nor did it plague him to no end, that whilst there were women aplenty, women of his own kind who'd be pleased to heartily welcome him to their beds, he'd not sought any of them out during the past few weeks. And no matter how hot and hard he'd been, how achingly aroused, he'd not bedded the wee Yank, refused to take that which she'd so willingly offered. Wild and wanton, she'd summoned him into her bed, invited him to sink his demanding, unruly member into the fiery heart of her. And yet he'd turned her down. Again and again.

*For her own good.*

Pragmatic recognition of the absurdity of that notion would

normally have pre-empted such foolhardiness. He shook his head. *Jaysus, woman. What are you doing to me?*

Although…the unusual abstinence might explain the sensual hold the wee mortal temptress seemed to have on him. Was it sexual frustration, pure and simple—that and nothing more—responsible for muddling his mind? For causing him to consider the folly of a marriage to a mere mortal, a woman who'd not share the rapacious carnal appetites of his kind? Would he be sentencing himself to a lifetime of sexual mediocrity, forced to harness the wild animal within himself so as not to harm her, to cage the beast clawing and straining at the tethers of such confinement, demanding to be unleashed?

'Twas a quandary, sure, given that his people mated forever, a vow of marriage was a life-long commitment. Perhaps, 'twould be wise to visit one of his former *inamoratas* to clear his head, to provide release to his body, before allowing this talk of marriage to go any further. His mind catalogued a list of potential candidates, a lover to suit his current fancy. Hmm…she'd have to be small and dainty, o'course, but athletic…with long silken strands of moon-kissed hair curving around high, full breasts of a perfect size to fill a man's hand. Her face had to be delicate, her sun-toned skin as soft as rose petals…her berry-tinted lips forming just the hint of an insolent smirk as she challenged him to spar. And the color of her eyes…oh, yes, her eyes…those would have to be the color of hot fudge melting over a scoop of vanilla ice cream….

A wise man, Liam quickly became aware of the wrinkle in his plan.

For him, desire had but one face: that of the lithesome nymph whose eyes warmed him like a turf fire on an icy winter day. Passion had one sylph-like, sensual body crowned by an ebony cascade of finest silk. The thought of joining himself with any woman, other than the one lying in a faerie charmed sleep before him, left him dispossessed of desire.

Obscenely cold as death.

*Bloody hell.*

He'd been bewitched, intrigued by her feminine mystique, which was like a burst of sunshine on a cold, misty day. That impish grin of hers seemed to possess an almost magical power over him, able to lighten his mood, put a smile on his face no matter his humor at the minute.

Sure, 'twas a rare and delicate flower she appeared to be, a slender bloom, all fragrant and petal-soft. Still, throughout the traumas she'd endured, he'd witnessed another side of her. She possessed the inner strength of the winter honeysuckle, a plant able to withstand the freezing cold, while the beauty of its fragile blossom and lemony fragrance promised to brighten the long, dark months ahead.

As he considered these things, Michaela's breathing began to deepen, her eyelids to flutter. As he bent his head to whisper encouragement in her ear, his gaze collided with that of Michaela's friend, echoing the relief he saw there. "Wake up, little one," he said softly, picking up her hand and molding it with his.

Slowly, Michaela opened her eyes and focused on his face. "Hey," she said dreamily, her voice all scratchy from the deep sleep.

"Hey yourself, sleepy head." He caressed her cheek. "How do you feel? You've been out a long time."

"Mmm. You wouldn't believe the dreams I had."

Liam's eyes met Arianna's. "Would you ask MacDara to join us now that she's awake?"

Only then realizing that Arianna was in the room, Michaela glanced at her, confused. "What's going on? The psychologist dude is here?"

"Yep," her friend replied. "I'd like him to have another look at you, if you don't mind."

"Why? Is something wrong? What's going on?" Disheveled and mussed, she pushed onto one elbow, looking from Liam to Arianna.

Liam answered. "We'll talk more about that in a wee while, sure."

"Okay…I guess." She fiddled with her hair, tried to smooth it. "But I need to get up first, get dressed. I feel like a mess."

"You're lovely, Michaela," Liam assured her, his voice deep and low. "As always."

"Nonetheless, if you'll excuse us for a few minutes…" Arianna began, a twinkle in her eyes.

Liam shrugged and nodded, then turned and left the room. A few minutes later, Arianna came to the door and invited him and MacDara to join them.

Michaela was sitting in an overstuffed armchair, her black hair brushed and plaited into one long braid that fell down her back. She gave a faint smile as the two men entered the room.

"How's things?" MacDara asked.

"I really don't know," she answered truthfully. "I have no idea what's going on around here."

It had been decided that Michaela would be told everything about the faerie abduction, everything except specific information on the existence of the *Túatha de Danann* and the problem of the ancient curse. "You were called to the Land of Faerie by the Prince, Orindahl," MacDara explained. "Liam and your friend, Arianna, called you back. And here you are."

An incredulous look came over Michaela's face. "The 'Land of *Fairy*?'"

Arianna stepped up to the chair. "What do you remember?"

"I thought I was dreaming…a sweet dream, filled with music and dancing and a world I could have lived in forever."

Liam felt his heart sink at her declaration. "'Twas faerie charmed, you were," he informed her gruffly. "The Prince was trying to lure you into marriage."

"Oh, yeah. I remember…something. But most of it's a blur." She gave him a weak smile. "Beautiful as it all was, I'm relieved to be back here. I remember thinking of you while I was there, Liam. That's when the wedding ceremony stopped. Just like that."

Liam could see them in her eyes, questions he'd no right to answer. And yet he had to make her understand. "Your marrying him is the only thing that would have made it impossible for me to call you back to this world, Michaela."

Alarm replaced the question in her eyes. "You mean I'd have been trapped there? Forever?"

"Maybe not forever," Liam told her, then, in a tone that was stone cold grim, he added, "Just a few thousand years or more."

Michaela's eyes grew large and she snapped a frightened look at Arianna, who took a deep breath. And said nothing. "I've gotta go home."

"I agree." The quiet words were Arianna's.

"You can't leave here," Liam insisted. "Not yet. Not until we know…."

"Know what?"

"I wish I could tell you that, wee one. But I cannot."

"So, I'm just supposed to sit here and risk getting abducted to the freaking fairy kingdom again? I think not."

"That's not going to happen."

"It's happened once…or twice—God, I don't even know how many times." Her voice raised in frustration. "How can you guarantee that it won't happen again?"

"Simple. You'll marry me, be my wife. Then he won't be able to touch you."

Michaela's chin dropped. "*Marry* you? We hardly know each other. And that's your idea of the way to propose to a woman? Seriously?"

Liam felt like she had just kicked his feet out from under him. "I…em…."

"Sorry, Liam. I really, really, *really* care about you, might even love you. I just don't think we're there yet. There's been too much craziness going on for us to even spend quality time together, let alone get to know each other like normal people. As much as I love being with you, there's just no way we're ready to consider spending our lives together."

Caught off-guard by the rejection, Liam saw the glimmer of amusement in MacDara's eyes as he watched from near the door. Like Aideen, every *Túatha* woman Liam had ever dated had made it clear they'd have welcomed such a proposal. "You're turning me down, so?"

"I have to, Liam. When—*if*—I ever decide to marry a man, it's going to because he loves me, because he can't stand the thought of living without me. It won't be for some kind of weird protection spell, or whatever this is you're *'proposing'*."

Michaela turned to Arianna, who was perched up on the edge of the bed listening to the exchange. "It's time for me to head back to the States," she said simply. "I'm going to see if I can get a flight out later today."

Liam's first inclination was to fight her on this decision, to force his will on her until she agreed to marry him. But no purpose would be served in confusing the issue further by dancing around a discussion of his heritage, his inability to love her the way she wanted to be loved. And, as far as the distant possibility that she may be the Woman of Promise, sure, she either was, or she was not. The ultimate test would be in breaking things off between them. If she were the Chosen One—and everything she had heard from Aideen had not violated the terms of the *Geis*—then Fate would simply have to intervene, to draw her back to her task here before the appointed time. And if she were not this One, she'd simply return to her life in the States free of any further threat from the Beast or the Prince of Faerie.

Or, ultimately, from Liam himself.

# *Chapter Twenty-Six*

Though Michaela had come off as strong and unaffected by her decision to return home, it had all been an act. In reality, she would have given anything to spend her life married to Liam. But she couldn't ignore the fact that she had gotten herself in way too deep where this unique and amazing man was concerned, which was the reason his coldhearted 'proposal' had cut her to the quick. She had hoped that his feelings for her had grown deeper in the time they had been together, but the nonchalant way he had suggested marriage proved her wrong. It was time to go home, get back to the real world, back to reality. Yeah…reality, a concept she seemed to have lost her grip on in the short time she had been away.

As the plane taxied down the runway, she choked back tears. Her heart was broken; she felt bereft, empty inside. Changed forever. She returned home a different woman from the fun-loving free spirit who had arrived in Dublin just a few short weeks ago. Which begged the question: Had she fallen in love with Liam—or simply fallen under his spell? And, speaking of spells, what the hell was all that airy-fairy nonsense she had been privy to the entire time she was there? Who could say? But even Arianna seemed to have been part of the conspiracy—an insider, while Michaela had remained an outsider, lost in a fog of confusion during her entire stay.

The real pity of it was that she and Liam had been good together, compatible, enjoyed the same things, like a good martial arts sparring match, the adrenaline rush of a fast car, or the heart-pounding panic of a jet plunging from the sky. If they had met under other, more normal, circumstances, they would have probably stood a good chance of making it work. But, from the moment they had stumbled across one another at the pub in Dublin, absolutely nothing about any of it had been normal. While Michaela had always been open to the possibility of the existence of other worlds, other dimensions, she still had a hard time wrapping her head around all the talk of Irish fairies. Not to mention her supposed kidnapping by a frigging fairy prince. If Arianna hadn't been there to confirm everything she was experiencing, Michaela would have totally believed she had lost her mind.

The eight-and-a-half hour flight from Shannon to JFK gave her the time she needed to acclimate to the real world. By the time her plane landed, her experiences in Ireland had begun to feel like a long, convoluted dream. But the soul-crushing anguish of leaving the only man she had ever loved behind made it all too real.

Fingers linked behind his head, Liam glanced at the clock on his bedside table for the millionth time. God Almighty, he'd not be surviving another day like this one. Back in his own bed after days away—both on the island and bouncing back and forth from the castle in Clare—he should have been sleeping like the dead. Instead, he lay staring at the ceiling as the endless hours ticked by. The time alone had given him the opportunity to take a good, hard look at himself, however. What he was after discovering was that, without the wee sprite at his side, his once fun-loving existence had become cold and lifeless, a kaleidoscope totally devoid of color.

His lips curved at the echoing memory of her giggles as the two of them had sparred in the workout room like a pair of gamboling puppies. Guileless as children so they'd been, he thought, as the smile on his face slowly faded. 'Twas all a hopeless façade. There was no real joy, no innocence in his life. Certainly no time for child's play or foolishness, not in this pre-apocalyptic window of time. Only with herself gone did he come to recognize just how truly bleak and empty was his dismal existence. 'Twas a desolation he'd never have identified had it not been for its dramatic contrast to the life he'd shared with Michaela these past weeks, his world suddenly brightened by the radiant light in a pair of chocolate eyes, the golden sunshine emanating from that quirky smile.

The woman confused him, sure. Hadn't he come up with the perfect solution to their problem, a way to keep her by his side and under his protection? 'Twas quite simple, really, although he'd have had to be walking a fine line, telling her enough so she'd take seriously the evil plotting against her, without violating the terms of the *Geis,* in the event that she truly proved to be this long-awaited savior. And somehow, no matter how remote the possibility, Aideen's blathering on about things prohibited by the *Geis* hadn't stolen away the planet's last chance for survival.

But before she would agree to wed him, the wee mortal required something more than his commitment, his devotion. She demanded the impossible, he thought, huffing out a breath. She wanted him to be 'in love' with her, for feck's sake.

Lying in bed like this, all itchy and nervous with need, not surprising given that he'd not spent his seed in a woman since he and the wee Yank had met—a record for a *Túatha* male—or female, for that matter. Clarity finally found him as he acknowledged the reason he'd not sought out another. 'Twas because his desire belonged to the tiny sprite who, by now, was more than four thousand miles away.

Liam felt his heart sink at what may prove to have been an irreversible error on his part. The emptiness he discovered within himself now was an unnamed thing, something with which he'd no prior experience, something that refused to lend itself to interpretation, to comprehension. 'Twas as if in her leaving she'd removed the sun from the sky, the planets from their orbits, and taken them with her, thereby condemning him forever to a world of utter darkness.

Could this be what a mere mortal defined as "falling in love"?

If so, that meant he'd be able to offer Michaela what she desired most from him, his newfound heart. It occurred to him that he'd made a total cock-up of things too important to have been left to chance. 'Twas a cock-up he planned to rectify straightaway. Rolling out of bed, he stripped off and stepped beneath the hard, driving pulse of the electric shower. Toweling off, he pulled his carryon out of the closet and threw in the few items he'd need for a day or two in the States. 'Twould be a short trip, as he planned to bring the wee woman back with him to Ireland. Not because she may be the Chosen One, nor because her presence here may save all of humankind from the approaching darkness. No, his reason for bringing her home was a purely selfish one. 'Twas because, for him, there was simply no life without this woman, his *anam cara*.

The veritable light of his world.

***

Still sleeping off the effects of the jet lag, Michaela tried to ignore the insistent knocking on the front door of her condo. But whoever was there just wasn't going away. Bleary-eyed, she glanced at the clock on her bedside table. Just after six p.m. She had slept for almost twenty-four hours.

She stumbled groggily toward the front door, muttering curses the whole way. "Who's there?"

"It's me, Liam."

*Liam?* Michaela's heart did a little leap in her chest at the familiar sound of the deep male voice. She pulled her robe around her and opened the door. "What…?"

Ice-blue eyes, glinting with mischief, smiled down at her as he stepped inside, wheeling his carryon into the foyer. As she stood there, staring at him incredulously, he turned and shut the door, then took her into his arms, his mouth finding hers. As Michaela melted into the fiery kiss, she noted that it was different this time, more passionate, more possessive.

Knees weak, she pulled her mouth from his and wriggled away. "What are you doing here?" she breathed.

"Why, I've come to take you home, o'course." He said it simply, as if it were somehow understood that he would show up on her doorstep uninvited and spirit her away.

"I *am* home, Liam," she corrected firmly. "And this is where I intend to stay."

"Ach, *a mhuirnín*. You don't mean that." He sounded wounded, as if her words had stabbed him in the heart.

"I am not going back to Ireland. Not now. Not ever again."

"But—"

Whatever he was about to say, Michaela didn't want to hear. She turned and led the way into the living room, with him trailing behind her. "Okay, sit," she instructed, pointing to the leather sofa.

Eyes wide with surprise at the change in her, he complied with her…request.

She sat down beside him. "Now look, Liam, you need to understand something. Two of the times I visited Ireland, really, *really* bad things have happened to me. On my first trip over, I ended up being kidnapped by some…lunatic. I was drugged almost to an overdose and consider myself lucky to have gotten out of there with my life. This last time I went…. Hell, where do I even begin? First, I fall off my horse—which I have *never* done, not since I was five years old and first learning to ride. Then the hallucinations and nightmares begin, which may, or may not, have been connected to my becoming the target of some black magic attack by your jealous ex-girlfriend. But was that enough? Oh, no. Because then I get abducted to the frigging fairy kingdom—not once, but twice."

"Right," he said.

"Oh, yeah. And what about all the paranormal goings on surrounding you? Even my best friend's not *'at liberty'* to tell me what's up with you guys. I mean, what the hell, Liam? Where's that at?"

"Em.... Do you suppose I might use the facilities?" Liam asked innocently, when she finally stopped to take a breath.

Michaela bit her lip. Damn. Dude had flown practically halfway around the globe to see her and she hadn't even offered him the use of a toilet. "Oh...of course. I...uh...I'm so sorry. I'm jetlagged out of my mind and just not myself. I usually have better manners than this."

"No worries, luv. I should have called first, instead of popping in unexpectedly."

Showing him to the downstairs bathroom, she reached into the linen closet, pulled out a washcloth and towel, and offered them to him. "Here you go, so you can freshen up. Um, can I get you a cup of coffee? Anything?"

"A cuppa tea would be grand."

Michaela put up a pot of coffee for herself and pulled a box of Irish breakfast tea Arianna had kept in the cupboard out for Liam. While a cup of water heated in the microwave, she soaked in the familiar comfort of her kitchen. She loved this place, the island bar in the middle, and the way the sun shining through the window over the sink reflected off the glass-front cabinets. In these everyday surroundings she felt like she could breathe again, like she had located the sanity she feared she had lost. The fog that had hung over her head the entire time she had been in Ireland seemed to have melted away the instant the plane had left Irish airspace.

As she was dropping cookie dough onto a baking sheet, Liam

joined her at the kitchen counter and broke off a piece of raw dough. Playfully slapping at his hand, she stuck the tray in the oven and set the temperature to 350 degrees. "There, grab a seat at the table while these bake." She set his cup of tea in front of him. "Sorry, since I just got back, I don't have any milk. But I do have some non-dairy creamer."

He waved his hand. "Just sugar is fine."

"Don't keep sugar in the house either, sorry. Stevia okay? Are you hungry? I can make you a sandwich? I have a can of tuna in the pantry."

"I was after eating on the flight. Sure, I'll wait for the biscuits," he said, referring to the cookies baking in the oven. "They smell gorgeous."

"Chocolate chip, my favorite." Offering him a big smile, she poured herself a cup of coffee, added the creamer and Stevia, and joined him at the table.

It was strange having him here. Good strange, she clarified, as she absently stirred her coffee. It was like waking up in the morning and finding the man you had been dreaming about was actually real. Kind of like Arianna had done.

"I'm prepared to stay here in Maine until I can convince you to return with me," Liam announced.

"Better rent an apartment then," she muttered under her breath, as she got up from the table. Opening the oven, she reached inside with a potholder, still managing to burn her index finger on the tray. "Ouch."

Liam was at her side in an instant. "Let me see." Examining the red, angry blotch, he slipped her finger into his mouth and sucked on it gently. Instantly the heat left her hand and went straight to her core. *God.*

Drawing her finger from his mouth, he picked up the potholder she had dropped and removed the baking sheet from the oven.

Setting it down on a wire tray on the granite counter, he turned the oven off. "There now."

Michaela glanced down at her finger. Where the skin should have been blistering, it was smooth and even-toned. *Whoa.*

She grabbed a spatula out of the drawer and began to shovel the soft, melty cookies onto a plate. While Liam set the plate on the table, she retrieved a couple of saucers from the cabinet. Sitting down, he bit into a cookie and groaned with pleasure as he blew air around the hot bite. Joining him at the table, Michaela helped herself to a cookie. "Oh, yum."

"Indeed." Liam slurped a sip of tea.

"So. You say you're prepared to stay here until you can change my mind about returning to Ireland?"

"I am."

"And, what if it takes six months? A year?"

"You're my *anam cara,* Michaela, my soul mate. So, unless you tell me you don't feel the same, don't wish to explore that which is obviously between us, I'm committed to staying as long as it takes."

She nodded and took another bite, unable to stifle the wild leaping of her heart at his words. On the flight out of Ireland, she had tried to come to terms with leaving him behind, with the fact that she was losing him forever. It had felt like death. But now here he was, their relationship suddenly resurrected. And, as always, he was being straight up about his intentions. No mind games, no BS.

"I'll find a hotel room," he offered. "We'll…date. Take it from there."

"Nope. No hotel rooms. You made me welcome in your home, Liam. Now, I'll make you welcome in mine."

"That's even better. 'Twill give me more time to charm you," he added, with a teasing twinkle in his eyes.

"Oh, no. I've had enough of that to last a lifetime. We're on my turf now, so there will be no charms, no…fairy spells allowed. We have to be on an even keel, just the two of us, without embellishment. You have to promise me, Liam."

His eyebrows went up at her request. Then he looked down, considered for a moment, and nodded. "We'll do it your way, sure," he said. "Just so you understand what 'tis you're after asking of me."

"Just a level playing field."

"Oh, so much more than that," Liam said. "What you refer to as tricks and charms are actually an integral part of my nature, my heritage. 'Twould be akin to me asking you to change the color of your eyes, or grow an extra two inches in stature."

Michaela bit her lip as she took in his words. She had read enough paranormal romances for her mind to be racing with possible scenarios to explain her magical lover. Still, she had no solid explanation for who…and what…he really was.

"I've been told so little about your background, I had no idea you felt that way," she confessed. "I just have to know that my feelings for you are truly *my* feelings, and not some magical manipulation of my emotions that I can't comprehend. So, tell you what. Let's just be ourselves and see where this thing goes."

"Fair enough, so." Liam smiled that sexy turn of lips that turned her knees to rubber. "I'll not do anything supernatural to affect your perception of me…of ourselves. Agreed?"

"Agreed." Michaela smiled back at him. "Now, go on into the living room and make yourself at home while I jump in the shower. Then we'll get out of here for a bite to eat and I'll show you around the area."

As she disappeared into her bedroom, Michaela heard the television go on, then the sound of channels changing as Liam took over the remote control. Shutting the door behind her, she leaned against it, weak-kneed and breathless at the unexpected turn of events. Heartbroken from the loss of the man she loved, she had been convinced she had no other choice, that returning here to familiar ground was the only way to hold onto the sanity she could feel slipping through her fingers like dry sand on a tropical shore. When she had arrived home the afternoon before, her well-known environment had seemed to comfort her, to steady her.

She had dreamed of him, tossing and turning throughout the night, so waking to his knock this evening had indeed been a dream come true. With him here, everything in her familiar surroundings seemed different somehow, as if an ethereal light had reached into every corner and brightened every inch of every room with a warm, rosy glow. She hadn't expected that he would pursue her, follow her home to the United States like this. If any other man had just shown up unannounced at her doorstep that way, she would have probably considered it stalking behavior. But after all the time she had spent in Liam's company over the past couple of weeks, she knew him better than that. It was one of the things she found most attractive about him—that he was a man who knew what he wanted, and went for it.

All Michaela knew for sure, as she climbed into the shower, was that the sick, empty place in the pit of her stomach had filled and healed instantly at the sight of him. She massaged shampoo into her hair and scalp, then rinsed the sudsy remains down the drain. While the conditioner did its magic, she soaped up with her favorite scented body wash. Eyes closed, she ran her hands down her slick and naked body. She moaned, imagining Liam's hands in place of hers, his body molded against her back, his breath hot, mouth moving on the side of her neck. By the time she had rinsed the conditioner out of her hair, she was ready to invite him into her bedroom, into her life. Here, on her own stomping grounds, she felt well and strong, just like her old self again. She was more than ready now for them to take things to the next level.

Michaela wanted him, not only in her bed and in her body, but in her heart and soul. As she put the finishing touches on her makeup, she made a solemn vow. That before the sun rose in the morning, she would make love with Liam; she would know him in that most intimate of ways. She would finally have from him the thing that she had desired for so long.

## *Chapter Twenty-Seven*

It was almost midnight by the time Liam and Michaela stumbled back through the front door of her condo. Admittedly, she was a little buzzed. They had ordered a couple of drinks before dinner at the new steakhouse that had recently opened on the other side of town near Biddeford Mall. On the way home, they had stopped off at the grocery store to replace the refrigerated items that had expired during the time she was gone. It all felt so down-to-earth, so normal. Like a regular couple, they had held hands as they walked along, talking and joking about silly, everyday things. Michaela had kept stealing glances at him. He was so damned hot in those metal studded jeans, black leather boots and form-fitting tee-shirt that he seemed out of place here. Like a rock-star, with that dirty blonde hair falling all scrunchy on either side of his face. Michaela hadn't missed the way he turned women's heads everywhere they had gone. Not surprising, because every time she looked into those electric blue eyes of his she felt a jolt of pure sexual desire so startling that it took her breath away.

Now that they were home, though, she had to admit to feeling slightly awkward. She had never invited a man into her bedroom to spend the night before, and she wasn't sure about the proper protocol.

Liam shut the door behind them and set the grocery bags he was carrying down on a hall table. He pulled her into his arms, eyes softened as though he understood her uncertainty. Or had read her thoughts.... "There's no rush, no pressure, luveen," he said softly, his mouth beside her ear. "I'll take a quick shower now, will I? Then we can relax on the sofa and watch the telly for a wee while."

*God.* Every deep raspy word in that lilting Irish accent made her go all soft and mushy inside. She swallowed, trying not to betray the excited tremor in her voice. “You’ll find a fresh towel and washcloth in the linen closet. I’ll make us some popcorn while you shower.”

“Brilliant.” He bent and pecked a kiss on her nose, then went to retrieve his rolling suitcase from the corner of the living room.

As he disappeared into her bedroom, Michaela went to prepare their snack. When the popcorn had finished popping she poured it into a large bowl and topped it with melted butter. Then she pulled a bottle of Moscato out of the fridge, uncorked it, and placed it on a silver tray beside two wineglasses. As she delivered the popcorn to the living room, she could feel herself growing more nervous by the minute.

When she went back to the kitchen to get the silver tray, Liam met her at the door and took it from her hands. His fingers brushed against one of her breasts and her heart began to beat so rapidly she figured she would need a defibrillator before the night was over. Feeling unsure of herself, she managed to keep it together as she escorted him back to the living room, where he placed the tray on the coffee table. They sat down together on the brown leather sofa that Michaela and her friends had picked out at Arianna’s antique store downtown. They had furnished the condo almost exclusively from that little shop. Because of that, the space was warm and rich, smelling of leather and lemon-oiled hardwoods from the eclectic combination of pieces representing various periods throughout history.

Michaela picked up the remote and turned on the television as Liam poured each of them a glass of wine. He smiled and clinked her glass with his. “Cheers.”

This was way too perfect, she thought, smiling back at him. It was almost too normal, too real. She kept sliding glances at him, hardly able to believe that he was actually sitting here beside her in her own living room, getting ready to watch TV like a thousand other couples in a thousand other homes across the city.

Liam set his glass on a coaster on the table beside the sofa and slipped his arm around her, pulling her close. They flipped through channels, passing on a couple of sit-coms, a vampire series, and a reality show about millionaires being pitched for various projects, before finally settling in to watch a romantic comedy. As they laughed and kissed and cuddled, the assault of magic she had experienced during her time in Ireland began to fade into a dreamlike memory.

"So, how's it feel, being home again?" he asked, during a commercial.

"It was good being home, but sad, too. It felt like something was missing, like I had left something important back in Ireland." Reaching up, she brushed a lock of hair away from his face. "You."

Liam kissed her. Not one of his long, sensual kisses, with lips and tongue and teeth, but a gentle brush of their mouths. Sweet, simple, affectionate.

"I knew I cared for you, little one," he said. "But when you left, I was totally gutted. Shattered. 'Twas then I realized that your absence in my life would be a long, endless void that could never be filled."

Michaela loved the poetic way he spoke, his sexy Irish accent, and the low, raspy sound of his voice. But what man would reveal himself to a woman like this, would confess such a thing straight up? A man who knew what he wanted and refused to play silly games, perhaps.

"I feel the same way, Liam. It killed me to leave you behind, but with everything going on there, I feared for my sanity. Even my life." She looked down. She couldn't continue to stare into those endless blue eyes. Probing, electric. Magical. She was sure he didn't mean to mesmerize her, but the soulful connection as they gazed into one another's eyes made her feel like she was floating, high on some psychotropic drug.

"So, you've had no…episodes…since you've returned?"

"I only got home yesterday, but no, so far so good. Nothing crazier than my usual insanity, at any rate," she joked.

A serious expression crept over Liam's features and he bent his head, touched his lips to hers. "I want to take you to bed now, Michaela. To…make love to you." He stumbled at the expression, as if it weren't familiar to him.

"Well, it's about damn time," she teased softly. Wrapping her hand around the back of his head, she pulled his mouth down to hers for a fiery kiss, a promise of things to come.

What sounded like a low growl rumbled from Liam's chest as he stood and scooped her into his arms. "I'll have you now then, will I?"

Michaela shivered at his words, her body throbbing, going all soft and moist inside. She wrapped her arms around his neck. "You know the way to the bedroom," she purred, her voice a breathless whisper.

With one arm, he threw back the duvet and lay her in the middle of the bed, then slowly began to undress her. There was something so hot, and yet so scary, about lying there before him completely nude, while he was still fully clothed. Michaela fought the urge to cover herself with her hands.

"Don't ever hide from me," he ordered softly, plucking the thought right from her mind.

She nodded and licked her lips.

As she watched him wide-eyed, he gestured with one hand and his clothes dissolved into a heap on the floor. Michaela choked back a gasp at the sight of that sculpted body, the raging proof of his desire for her. "Liam…"

"Shhh…," he whispered, as he slid into bed beside her. "I'd

never hurt you, love. I remember that you've no experience with a man."

Michaela chewed her bottom lip. How could he possibly not hurt her with that…that—?

"You asked me not to charm you, not to make you feel things that aren't real." He kissed her eyes, her nose, the side of her neck as he reached for her braid, methodically unplaiting the strands of waist-length hair. "Sure, I'll only use my powers to protect you so, to take the discomfort away when the time comes."

At this point, Michaela was way beyond caring about the particulars of who and what Liam was, or what he could do. It was enough that he was a man, the man she loved, the one she desired more than anyone she had ever known in her life. She breathed him in, his fresh, wild scent earthy, like a cool pine forest, a verdant summer woodland. Every time she closed her eyes, she relived the memory of a fairytale land where magic lived and thrived, and impossible dreams came true.

She moaned and pulled him on top of her, stretching her neck to meet his lips. She thrust her hips impatiently against his, matching the exquisite pace of his tongue invading her mouth as the erotic pressure drove her to the very edge of madness.

"Slow, easy," he whispered in her ear, his muscled body taut, breath heaving. "We've all night, love, a lifetime, if you wish it."

It took a moment before the words filtered through the fiery red haze engulfing her. Panting, she looked up at him. "A…a lifetime?"

He looked down at her, his hands framing her face. "Did you not hear me before, woman? You're my *anam cara,* my soul mate. More than anything in this world, I want you by my side, tonight and always, if only you'll have me. But we're very different people, yourself and myself. Very different, indeed. And I've to know you can live with that."

"I've heard everything you've said to me, everything but that you love me. I can live with our differences, Liam. Because I'm truly in love with you, I'm willing to move to Ireland, to uproot my entire life to be with you. But I have to know that you feel the same about me."

And that was the one thing he couldn't promise her, Michaela realized, the lost look on his face engulfing her heart in a glacier-size chunk of ice, cooling the fevered passion. As overwhelming sadness washed over her, she pushed gently against Liam's chest and he rolled off her. Somehow, during their heated encounter, the duvet had ended up on the floor. Feeling suddenly awkward at her nudity, she bit her lip. With his usual discernment—or was it mind-reading capability?—he reached down and pulled it back onto the bed, tugging it over her to cover her nakedness. Michaela pushed into a sitting position, her back bolstered by the bed pillows.

Completely unconcerned about his own lack of clothing, Liam sat on the side of the bed. "I can offer you my loyalty, little one. My faithfulness, my protection. I'll share with you all that's mine. And while I feel an attachment to you so strong that I've never felt it for any other human being, sure, I've no understanding of this thing you refer to as being 'in love'. I'll willingly give you all that is my own to give, *a mhuirnín.* But how can I offer you that which I do not possess?"

He looked so dejected that Michaela's heart went out to him. This man, this *magic* man, could have any damn woman on the planet that he wanted. She remembered how many times she had put herself out there, making it clear that she desired him. She felt a hot rush of embarrassment at how unusually forward she had been in projecting her willingness to take their relationship to the next level.

To take him into her bed, her body. Her life.

He could have taken advantage of her feelings for him then,

could have done so now. He could have manipulated her, told her whatever she wanted to hear, but he hadn't. No, he'd been brutally honest, nothing but honorable in his refusal of what she had so brazenly put on offer, unwilling to breach those boundaries and cross the line into sexual intimacy when he was incapable of reciprocating her feelings.

Now, when asking her to spend her life with him, he had chosen to explain his limitations, trusting her with the very essence of the person he was. There was a lot to be said for this kind of integrity in a man. She loved him, wanted him, could no longer imagine her life without him. So, there was only one question remaining: Could she live with him, love him forever, with no promise of ever receiving that same kind of love in return?

Or, maybe a more relevant question was whether she could live without him.

Her decision made, Michaela reached up and touched his face. He turned his head and kissed her arm. "I guess my love for you will just have to be enough for the both of us," she said, with a sigh.

He looked like he had just received a death row pardon. "You're accepting my proposal, then?"

"Well, I don't recall that you actually proposed," Michaela hedged, in jest.

Liam frowned. "Oh, aye. There is that." Buck-naked and hot as hell, he went to retrieve something from his carryon, then returned and sat beside her. "Sure, I was after planning to do this over a candlelight dinner in a day or two," he said, with a twinkle in his eyes. "I'd not anticipated that we'd both be stripped down and lying naked in your bed at the minute."

A giggle escaped Michaela's lips. "Candlelight? Well, see? You have a whole stream of untapped romance in your soul, my love. You'll get there yet."

"Indeed." The teasing light left his eyes as he reached for her hand. The ring he slipped onto her finger was an exquisite piece of jewelry. The magnificent heart-shaped diamond solitaire set in yellow gold fit her tiny finger perfectly. "Michaela, will you agree to be my wife, my *anam cara*? To stand with me and for me, for as long as we both live?"

Her answer was a mere breath of air. "Yes."

"This ring I offer you now is my promise of fidelity, protection and provision. All that's mine I share with you now, my body, my soul, my worldly possessions. Such is my commitment to you."

As Liam leaned in for a kiss, Michaela could only think that his marriage proposal had sounded more like wedding vows. If not for having attended Arianna and Caleb's formal wedding ceremony, she might have thought this was how people in his society got married, with the words of commitment alone. Funny, but that would have suited her perfectly. She had always believed that marriage should be a commitment between two people, ordained by God and not some government-sponsored piece of paper.

In those expressive blue eyes that had always astounded her, Michaela found home—home and something more. Something that looked a lot like love. "I love you, Liam, with all my heart and soul. And maybe one day I can teach you how to love me too. Until that day, and beyond, I offer you my faithfulness. I promise to share all that I have with you, my body, my soul, all that I am, for now and forever."

## Chapter Twenty-Eight

Their vows spoken, promises given and received, the woman who had so taken Liam's life by storm threw off the duvet she'd been using for shelter, and held her arms out, offering herself to him. "For God's sake, make love to me already. Every time we've started to do this, something interrupts us, stops us cold. I can't wait anymore, Liam. I need you to make me yours."

His body reacted instantly to her words, to her softly angled curves, her lush pink-nippled breasts set off by the olive tone of her complexion. And yet, for the first time since he was a green lad of twelve, he found himself feeling hesitant and unsure. This was not just another sexual liaison, another of the playful dalliances he'd always enjoyed with a willing partner like himself. The woman lying exposed in front of him was his life mate, his wife. Even more concerning for him was that she was a mere mortal…and an innocent, two situations with which he was patently unfamiliar. 'Twas as if a strange metamorphosis was after taking him over now. Being with this untried woman, whom he'd just taken to wife, was making him feel things he'd not experienced before. There was an overwhelming sense of responsibility for her, a certain protectiveness. A deep commitment to keep her safe from all harm—including himself.

The sexual appetite of a *Túatha* man or woman might best described as animalistic, near insatiable. By comparison, a mere mortal woman was fragile—even one as athletic and physically fit as was his *anam cara*. 'Twas one of the reasons Liam had hesitated to bed her in the first place, refusing to touch her whilst she was recovering from her injuries. And now, with these strange new emotions boiling inside him, he didn't trust himself. What if he was after losing himself in her, his profound ardor frightening her, his innate mating prowess even causing her physical harm.

And then, o'course, there was the issue of pregnancy. Whilst the *Geis* held no present threat to herself in that regard—'twould either be resolved before the deadline in a couple of months, or the world wouldn't exist long enough for a child to come to term—she may not wish to conceive a child at the minute. And, unlike the *Túatha* female, who possessed the ability to control conception by her own strength of will, the wee mortal was like to become with child the instant they mated.

Liam felt his heart lurch in his chest as a picture of her abdomen, softly rounded with his child, intruded upon his consciousness. Strangely, for the first time in his life, he realized he wanted that…a family, a home. And didn't the woman welcoming him into her arms, her body, possess all of the maternal qualities so coveted by his people? Mere mortal qualities like infinite patience and unconditional love were after being lost through generations of interbreeding with their own kind. Aye, he thought, 'twas that life he wanted to experience with his wee mortal sprite.

And yet a creeping darkness infringed upon that pleasant thought, a mocking inner voice whispering a chilling reminder that 'twas a foolhardy hope at best, given the current state of affairs.

Slipping into bed beside his woman, Liam gathered her into his arms. "There's something you must know, *a ghrá*. Something I've to tell you now."

She grinned up at him with that teasing light in her eyes that had made him fancy her from the very beginning. 'Twas just that thing that made him wish they might have a lifetime together. "What? You're not already married, are you?"

He didn't smile back. "I am," he said. "To yourself."

She bit her lip and reached out, smoothing the hair back from his face. "What's is it, Liam?" she asked softly.

"If...*when*...we make love," he said, stumbling again over the unfamiliar reference, "You'll likely be conceiving instantly."

A dark shadow crawled across her face and she looked away. "I won't ask why that would be." The soft-spoken declaration was a reference to all of the secrets he'd been forced to keep from her during their time together. "Whatever the reason, however, it's not something that concerns the two of us. I fell off my horse one other time, when I was first learning to ride, and I was injured. I can't have a child, Liam." She licked her lips, looking away. "Maybe I should have told you that before now, in case you wanted a family."

He grasped her chin gently with his thumb and forefinger and turned her head so that her gaze met his again. "*You* are my family now, little one. And don't you ever be fretting over your inability to conceive. If and when we decide the time is right to have a child, I've the gift of healing whatever's wrong."

Michaela looked at him with wonder in her eyes. She raised her hand and traced the contours of his face. "How can I love you so much when there's so much about you that I don't understand? Will you ever be able to tell me who you really are?"

Liam grasped her hand in his and brought it to his mouth, kissing her knuckles. If another were to be identified as the Woman of Promise, he would then be free to reveal himself to her. Either way, however, 'twouldn't be long, as there were less than two months remaining before the *Geis* must be fulfilled. "Soon, *a mhuirnín*, I'll be able to tell you everything. For now, though, before we consummate our union, you must know one more thing. There's no divorce amongst my people, Michaela. Like the wolf, we're after mating forever. Once wed, our mutual desire will always be only for one another. You'll never escape me, *a ghrá,* nor will you ever wish to do so."

And there it was again. The pixie grin that had so promptly transformed Liam's rock hard heart into one of living, beating human flesh. "I can't imagine anything more perfect than being yours forever, my love."

*Forever.* How bittersweet was the sentiment, he thought, considering how short a time that might ultimately prove to be. But those were concerns for another day, another time. "Aye, *go deo, a chuisle mo chroí,*" he agreed softly in her ear. "Forever, my heart's finest treasure."

Such a strange transformation was Liam's physical response to this tiny woman as, for the first time in his life, he paced himself, exploring her mouth with his tongue, and molding her slender form against the sinewy contours of his demanding male body. As he moved on top of her, he couldn't help but thrill at the sound of her faint gasp as the hardness of his member brushed a warning of what was to come against her moist feminine core. He trapped her wrists with his hands and pinned them above her head as he suckled first one ripe breast and then the other. Writhing beneath him, she moaned low in her throat, the erotic sound threatening to push him to the edge of his patience. He was on fire. Not a mere mortal man, the alien part of himself reveled in the thought of taking her hard and fast, encouraging him to immerse her in magic and then pour himself into every part of her, over and over, until he finally succeeded in dousing the conflagration that had been burning inside him these past weeks. After all, the woman was his wife. And when he'd finished with her this night, she would have known more satisfaction in a single encounter than ever would have been known to her, not in a lifetime spent with a weak, pathetic mere mortal husband.

Poised to succumb to the roaring of the animal dwelling within him, to be that which he truly was, that which he'd always been, he heard the soft-spoken hesitance in her voice.

"God, Liam, I want you so much. But I'm afraid I won't know how to please you."

'Twas all it took, the simple sound of her voice, the confession of her insecurities, to calm the ravening beast within him. "I'm your husband, wee one," he whispered, his voice gravelly from pent-up frustration. "Trust me to teach you all you need to know."

Transferring both of her dainty wrists to one of his hands, he reached between their bodies and began to pleasure her, as she writhed and moaned, her dainty whimpers telling him that she was almost ready for him. He released her hands and moved further down her body, using his mouth to bring her closer to the edge. "Mmm, you feel so good, *mo chroí*, so hot and wet. I'm hungry for you, wife."

Her fingers tangled in his hair. "Oh, God, Oh, God. Liam." She thrust her hips against his mouth, screaming as he drove her mercilessly over the edge, again and again, until he felt her body go limp beneath him. "No more, please. I can't take anymore. I want you inside me now, Liam. I need you to fill me up."

In his defense, he'd plan to take more time with her, to coax and cajole, beguile and entice his wee mortal wife gently into the ways of carnal pleasure. But her erotic demands had been petrol to the smoldering flames of his self-control, a fuse lit on his explosive desire.

But then he noticed it, the acrid scent of fear, an intoxicating cocktail when mixed with the musk of her arousal. Though her words had been bold, he'd to remind himself that she was still an innocent and likely terrified of receiving his burgeoning masculinity, both craving and dreading the moment of penetration at the same time. Understanding of her needs drew him back from the precarious edge of insanity and allowed him to reign himself in, to leash the beast-like urges of his nature that were clawing for release. He'd simply not allow the memory of their first time together to be tainted with fear, for her very mortal sensibilities to be haunted by the perception that it had been an act of violence.

"I'll not hurt you, *a ghrá,*" he vowed, and felt her body relax under the spellbinding effect of his voice. His weight supported on his forearms, he positioned himself between those slim, muscular thighs that could only belong to an equestrian, slowly rubbing himself against her moist heat. She lifted her hips, pushing back against him, her body growing more soft and pliant as he kept up the mesmeric rhythm. "There's no hurry, *a mhuirnín.*"

With a crooked grin, she reached up and brushed the hair from his face. Chocolate brown eyes melted as they gazed into his. "Will you stop talking and just take me now?"

"I've to repeat certain words before we join our bodies together, Michaela. In my…culture…'tis considered a binding ritual."

She looked confused for a moment, as if she'd just awakened from a sweet dream. "A…binding ritual?"

"Aye. Once I invoke the binding and we are joined physically, our marriage will be forever. As I've told you, neither of us will ever desire another. So, if you've any reservations, or are unsure in any way, tell me now. 'Tis your last chance to escape me, my love."

Until that moment, he hadn't realized the fear he held inside, that she might reject him, might be unwilling to make so permanent a commitment. But the twinkle in her eyes and that soft, sweet smile poured relief over him, like ice cream melting over a warm brownie.

She touched her finger to his lips to silence him. "When I felt like I had to leave Ireland…when I believed I'd lost you forever, a hole opened up inside me that I knew no one else could ever fill. So go ahead and speak your piece, husband of mine. Say whatever it is you have to say. Because from this day forward, I am yours and you are mine, eternally."

Drowning in the moment, Liam began to recite that which would cause them to become as the swans, that which would mate them for life. "As we consummate our vows this night, one to the other, as we become one in the physical sense, so shall we become one in spirit, *anam cara,* soul mates for all time. Will you invite me inside yourself now, *a banchéile mo chroí,* wife of my heart? And in so doing, will you bind yourself to me, for now and forevermore?"

"For now and for always," she promised softly. "I love you, Liam. I think I've been waiting for you my whole life."

His heart swelling, filling with that emotion that was becoming increasingly familiar to him of late, he smiled down at his wife. With teasing nibbles, he kissed her lips, the sides of her mouth, growing ever more enamored—more bewitched by her—with each passing moment. She reached between their bodies and he felt her hand wrap around his rigid member as she guided him to the place that promised him a kind of magic he'd never known. He'd agreed not to use a faerie charm on her, not to do anything that would alter her feelings for him. But she was so tiny, her frame so petite, the act of mating so new to her, that he feared, even with caution, he might tear her, might injure her with his size. 'Twas a thing he'd be bloody damned to allow when by uttering the merest incantation, all discomfort of their first time together would be erased.

He reminded himself to keep this first encounter grounded, to refrain from scaring her with his usual antics and customs, like teleporting the two of them from room to room.

He kissed her deeply and, with esoteric words whispered in the ancient tongue of his people, he completed the binding, the two separate beings becoming truly one entity. Her low moan of pleasure became an instant cry of release as she clenched around him, her responsiveness surprising even him. Oh, he'd chosen well with this woman, Liam thought. She was, indeed, his *anam cara.*

For hours, Michaela and her enigmatic new husband made

love, intimately exploring one another's bodies, learning the other's rhythms and preferences. As she became surer of herself, more comfortable with him, she would see a twinkle in Liam's eye and then suddenly candles would appear, already lit and burning, on dressers and bedside tables throughout her bedroom. Or, in the alternative, he might simply flick his wrist in the air. And the sweet, haunting strains of some Celtic melody would fill the room with ethereal sound.

Some of the time, her amazing man was soft and tender with her. And then there were those breathtaking other times, when he would offer her a glimpse of the feral sexuality he'd warned her about, the animalistic part of himself inherent in his nature. For Michaela, an adrenaline junky herself, the dangerous edge he displayed proved to be a tantalizing part of their foreplay. And, if she did say so herself, she gave quite as good as she got. Changing their positions, she would trap him between her knees, riding him like the virile fine stallion he was. She laughed aloud as he levitated them both into the air, then spun them around until she was again on the bottom, luxuriating in the masculine weight of a very aroused male body pressing her down into the mattress.

"No fair," she giggled, as the air sparked with magic, making her feel like a real-life fairytale princess.

"Best get used to it, you bold brat." Laser blue eyes locked onto hers, glittering in the darkness.

Her cries of release echoing in her ears, they finally lay sated, spooning together, his legs entangled with hers. As Liam's body curled protectively around her back, the musky scent of their uninhibited lovemaking lingered in the air around them. Michaela kissed the knuckles of the much larger hand wrapped around hers, her heart filled with a depth of happiness that she had been afraid to believe even existed. If only he were free to explain to her who… what he was, life would indeed be perfect.

"So many questions…" she murmured, but just as she was drifting off to sleep her eyes popped open. "Liam?"

Behind her, he nuzzled her neck and grunted sleepily. "Hmm?"

"Just what did Aideen mean when she said you were of the Tua day Danon?" she asked, trying to pronounce the words she had heard the woman say. "And what exactly is a gesh?"

Liam pulled her onto her back and stared down at her, his expression stark. Grasping her chin, he warned her in a low tone. "Those are esoteric secrets, my love. And, from this moment forth, you're not to speak of such things, except between ourselves."

His intensity alarmed her. "Okay. Don't get your boxers in a knot. But I heard it more than once and I think that, since we're married, I have a right to know what it means?"

"What are you saying, you heard it more than once? I know Aideen was after blathering the stuff the day she and my mother were at my house. But where did you ever hear it a second time?"

Michaela rolled onto her side and propped her head on her hand. She played idly with the patch of dark blonde hair on his chest. "You know that night I told you about, at your place, when I dreamed of Aideen and the window in the crypt? She was like, floating in the air, hovering over me. She warned me to stay away from you, said you were some kind of otherworldly creature called a Tua…. Whatever. That's when she threatened me, said that if something called a gesh didn't kill me, then she'd take care of the job herself."

"Hmm…twice," he murmured to himself, then remained silent for several seconds. "Sure, whilst its against our laws for Aideen to've discussed such matters outside of our own community, the damage has already been done. Since the two of us are married now, ask away, *a ghrá.* What d'you fancy knowing?"

"Everything. I want to know everything about you, everything about this supernatural world that I never knew existed."

Liam pulled his new wife into his arms. "Where do I start? Tell me, how much do you know about auld Irish legend?"

"Not a lot. I remember Arianna talking about it some when we were younger."

"Clearly, you know the bit about my people being possessed of certain abilities that would be considered…out of the ordinary… in the natural world."

"Yeah, I get that part. But where do you come from?"

And with that question, he began to relate a story so bizarre, so totally unbelievable, that Michaela had to wonder if she weren't imagining things again.

"My ancestors, the *Túatha de Danann,* resided on a planet millions of light-years away. One day, our scientists discovered that an asteroid was on a collision course with our world. As there were no other planets in our solar system, in our galaxy, that would support life, they began to send out probes, searching for a new home for our people."

Michaela struggled out of his arms and looked down at him in disbelief. "Good God. You're actually telling me you're a space alien?"

"Originally from another world, yes. When this planet—planet earth—was found, we boarded starships and spent countless millennia traveling through the stars, finally arriving at our new home about four thousand years ago in a technologically backward time."

"So, are you…are you *human*? Do you really look like this in your native world, or is your appearance some kind of mesmerizing thing you do to make yourself look more like earthlings?"

Liam chuckled. "Earthlings, Michaela? I fear you've been after watching far too many sci-fi films, my love. But to answer your question, we're *created* beings, homo sapiens like yourself. Also, after arriving here our people began to intermarry with those whose origins were of the earth, causing our DNA to intermingle."

"So, what did Aideen mean about the gesh killing me? And why is it okay all of a sudden for you to explain all this to me?"

"The *Geis* is an enchantment cast against our people about three thousand years ago. For this curse to be broken, a woman whose origin is of the earth must complete a specific task. But she is forbidden any knowledge of our people, or of the existence of the *Geis*, which will disqualify her from the appointment."

Michaela sat up and slid to the edge of the bed. She blew out a breath. "I'm sorry, babe, but I need to get up. This is a lot to take in, a lot to digest. I need a cup of coffee to clear my head."

As she slipped on her robe, Liam pulled on a pair of jeans. "Fair enough. We'll go to the kitchen, will we? I'll have a cuppa tea."

As he headed toward the door of the bedroom, bare-chested, Michaela scooped his tee-shirt off a chair and tossed it at him. "Here, put this on. Having you at the kitchen table half-naked will be far too distracting."

He chuckled again and locked an arm around her neck in a playful chokehold. "Too distracting, is it? Well, we'll just have to see about that."

# *Chapter Twenty-Nine*

Liam sat at the kitchen table while Michaela put up a pot of coffee. While it was brewing, she nuked a cup of water and brewed his usual cup of tea. It was the middle of the night, which made the entire revelation about his origins even more surreal. Okay, so she had known there was something…extraordinary…about this man. But she had been thinking more in terms of psychic phenomena stuff, you know, like precognition, mental telepathy, that sort of thing. This space odyssey confession had come out of left field. And it was OTP, way, *way* over the top.

As they sipped their drinks and talked, Liam continued to answer her questions, to try to explain things to her that were clearly inexplicable.

"One thing I still don't understand," she ventured, then gave a short laugh. "Actually, I don't understand most of what you've just told me. But what I really don't get is why you had to keep all of this stuff secret…until now. What changed, that you can suddenly tell me everything?"

"You remember asking about the *Geis*?"

She nodded. "What is that, exactly?"

"A curse on my people that can ultimately result in a world-wide apocalypse."

Michaela could actually feel herself going pale. "You said something about your beliefs that a woman would come along and save the day?"

"I did."

When he said nothing else, it all began to sink in. "Oh, my God. Don't tell me everyone thought I might be that woman."

"'Twas considered a distinct possibility, yes."

"But how? Why me?"

"Nothing specific, just a feeling everyone had, as well as your relationship with Caleb's wife."

"Arianna? But what could she possibly have to do with all this?"

"Perhaps, I should let her explain that herself."

"Okay, that'll work." Michaela took another sip of her coffee, then got up from the table. She dug around in the fridge and took out a cup of organic vanilla yogurt she had bought that evening at the store. "Want some?"

Liam smiled and shook his head. "Have any more of those biscuits you baked earlier?"

"Sure do." Michaela got the plastic baggie of chocolate chip cookies off the counter and put them in front of Liam. Then she sat back down at the table, with one leg folded beneath her. "Now, let me understand this. The reason the guys in your…group wanted to question me about Aideen was because she wasn't supposed to tell me any of this?"

He tilted his head. "Yer wan committed a grave offence by revealing those forbidden secrets to you, *a mhuirnín.* If you're somehow fated to intervene in this crisis, the things she was after telling you has compromised your ability to do so."

Their wild, abandoned lovemaking had been followed by a conversation that would have had most people heading straight to a psychiatrist's couch. Feeling emotionally vulnerable, mentally scattered, Michaela got up from the table and refilled her coffee mug. "Another cup of tea?" she asked, suddenly aware that she was being a piss poor host to her new…husband? "Can I get you a snack or anything?"

Liam joined her at the counter and massaged her shoulders,

bent and kissed the back of her neck. "No thank you, my love. I'm going to jump into the shower now. Give you a few minutes on your own to sort all this out in your head."

"Wait a minute. What makes everyone think I might be this… this messianic woman, anyway? Why not Arianna? I mean, wouldn't that make more sense since she was born in Ireland."

Liam looked away for a moment, and then returned her steadfast gaze. "As I said before, I believe that's something you should be taking up with your friend."

"I really wish I could talk to her right now, but I don't want to wake her up. It's three o'clock in the morning."

"Not in Ireland, it isn't," Liam reminded her with a wink as he left the kitchen.

"No, not in Ireland," she muttered under her breath as she cleared away the table and rinsed out Liam's cup.

Feet tucked beneath her, she settled on the living room sofa. She hissed as she burned her tongue on a hot sip of coffee. Setting her cup down on a coaster on the antique cherry wood end table beside her, she grabbed up her cell phone and dialed Arianna. "Pick up, pick up, pick up," she chanted as the phone continued to ring.

"Good grief, Michaela. What time is it there?" Arianna asked. "It's gotta to be the middle of the night."

"Yeah, and what about you? How come you sound so wide awake at eight o'clock in the morning?"

"It's called motherhood. Been up with the baby since six. Now, answer the question. What's going on there? You okay? Is Liam there with you?"

"Yes, I'm fine. And yes, he's here. He's in the shower." Michaela paused, and then everything came spilling out. "He asked me to marry him, Arianna. And I said, 'yes'. And I think we're somehow married now."

"I know, honey, it was the same when Caleb proposed to me.

It's the way of their clan, babe. The vows are exchanged when the man and woman agree to marry." Arianna hesitated, then plunged right in. "Have you? I mean, did the two of you consummate your vows?"

"Did I sleep with him? Oh, yeah. Oh, my God, Arianna. Wow. He's amazing. I'm so in love with this man."

"I'm so happy for you, sweetheart. For both of you. So, what are your plans? Are you staying in the States for a while, or coming back here?"

"No, he needs to be in Ireland, what with all the crazy stuff that's going on."

"What stuff?" Arianna hedged.

"It's okay, honey. You don't have to hold anything back anymore. Liam told me everything."

Arianna's gulp was almost audible. "He did?"

"After we made love, I asked him about the gesh, about the… what's it called? Tua day…something or other."

"Whoa, whoa, whoa. You actually asked him about that? What did he tell you?"

"He explained about the curse, about the origins of his people. He told me that everyone thought I might be the woman to bring a solution to the problem. But, after Aideen spilled her guts to me about everything, I'm somehow disqualified from the job."

Arianna blew out a long breath that Michaela could hear clearly over the phone. "God, Mick. Where do I start? Congratulations I guess are in order first. Are you sure about this? Are you happy?"

"I'm sure. And I've never been happier in my life."

"Good. And, as far as all this other stuff goes, I guess you have a bunch of questions. I wish I were there with you right now. It's a lot to take in."

"Yeah, tell me about it."

"Did Liam say anything about…about me?"

"Not in particular, no. When I asked him why they didn't consider that you might have been this…person…I mean, since you're Irish and all, he just told me I should talk to you."

"Well, I hope you're sitting down, girlfriend. Cause what I'm about to tell you is going to knock you off your feet."

"I'm stretched out on the sofa already, so spill."

"What did Liam tell you about his people?"

"I got the feeling that his ancestors were some kind of space aliens from a dying world."

"That about sums it up. Did he mention anything about a connection to Irish legend?"

"He did ask me if I knew much about it. That's about it."

"Okay, so, as you know, he's from a race of people who arrived on this planet from another world. Their natural abilities on their home planet included things we here would consider magical, like the ability to shape-shift, to pass through solid objects, and to fly. While the radiation they experienced during centuries of space travel erased many of those traits from their genetic makeup, other traits, like the power to levitate, to communicate telepathically and to teleport over short distances, became even more refined."

"Damn," Michaela muttered. "I kept feeling like he was reading my mind, but then figured I had to be going wackadoo to even consider such a thing."

"Been there," Arianna commiserated. "Something else you experienced was Liam's power to mesmerize, to put you into a hypnotic thrall."

"*God!* So that's what was going on every time I lost consciousness?"

"Not only that, but we believe Aideen somehow used her powers to snap Wind Spirit's saddle."

"Okay, but what does all that have to do with Irish legend?"

"Well, over the centuries Liam's people were engaged in battles with other tribes. About three thousand years ago they lost a fight to a group of warriors called the Milesians. Those people respected them so much that they offered to share Ireland with them, or to give them for their habitation the entire middle earth. Liam's ancestors divided into two groups, one remaining in the land above, while the others chose to take up residence in the middle earth, otherwise known as the faerie kingdom, where Aideen abducted you."

Michaela felt a cold chill crawl up her spine. "So, you're saying that Liam is actually related to the fairies."

"That's what I'm saying. But there's more. I…you remember how Da moved to the States from Ireland when I was three?"

"Yep."

"When I was growing up he always told me that my mother had died, as you know. Well, when I got to Ireland, I discovered that she was still alive."

"God, Arianna. He lied to you?"

"He only did it because he was afraid for me. Do you still remember the time you were held by the Prince of Faerie, when he was planning to marry you?"

"Vaguely."

"But you do remember me coming to talk to you, to convince you to listen out for Liam's call so that you could escape."

"I thought it was all a dream. But, yes, I remember that. You were with some fairy creature."

"A water sprite," her friend clarified, as if they were discussing something as ordinary as a shopping trip to the mall. After a brief pause, she added, "Mick, that fairy woman was my mother."

Michaela swallowed thickly. She could feel herself going pale at the implications of what her friend had just said. "You don't mean…." She just couldn't seem to put it into words.

"My ancestry is the same as Caleb's. My father was a mere mortal, as was Caleb's mother."

"I'm so confused," Michaela breathed.

"I know you are, honey. It's a lot to wrap your head around right now. Just learning of the existence of a magical race would have been mind-boggling enough. But then there's the issue of the curse as well."

"Liam explained that to me. Listen, I just heard the shower shut off. I'll call you tomorrow, let you know our travel plans."

"Sounds great. And, sweetie? Congratulations again. And while I get that this all sounds really crazy right now, just know that this will be the happiest time of your life."

As Michaela ended the call, Liam walked into the living room with a towel wrapped around his waist, his body flushed from the hot shower. Mesmerized by the fluid movement of muscle and sinew beneath his skin as he moved toward her, she was reminded of a jungle cat, long and lean and ultimately dangerous. Her breath caught in her throat at the sheer male beauty of him, she couldn't help but stare at this man, her new husband. The one she had vowed to bind herself to forever, to spend the rest of her life with.

He sat down on the sofa beside her and pulled her legs across his lap. "A penny for your thoughts?"

"I'm afraid it's going to cost you a lot more than that," she laughed. "Sorry, but the brain's pretty much in meltdown mode at the moment."

"Did you talk to your friend? Did she tell you everything?"

"If you mean, did she tell me she's one of you, yes, she did. But I still have questions—lots of them."

"Course you do, little one. So, please, ask away."

She licked dry lips to moisten them. "Okay, so, I accept the fact that your ancestors arrived on the earth thousands of years ago from an endangered planet. And, at some point, you agreed to share Ireland with another tribe."

Liam massaged the arch of her right foot as he met her gaze. "Right."

"What I still don't understand...what I mean is...look, I'm not religious or anything, but I believe in God, and that He created the earth, created the people who live on it. If your people are magic—"

"We're created beings, as well, *a mhuirnín*." Liam smiled a soft and gentle upturn of his lips. "We believe in the same God Almighty as do the inhabitants of earth. How do I explain this?" He paused, seemed to be choosing his words carefully. "In our world, there was no eating of a forbidden fruit. Our people obeyed the rules the Creator set in place for our existence. Because of that, there was no need for a savior."

"So you don't believe in Jesus?"

"Course I do. He came to save the inhabitants of earth from their sin."

"Sin that your people weren't born with?"

"'Tis a complicated matter, faith in God, the differences in our beginnings. In our world, we were born with innate abilities, pure and powerful, not so very different from the first man and woman on earth. As were they, we were created with elemental magic in our blood, abilities to heal, to move mountains, to teleport from one place to another, to walk on water, if you will. Aptitudes that Christ proposed, during his time on earth, should be the possession of every man and woman of faith today."

Michaela pulled her feet in and shifted her body, snuggling into Liam's arms. "In Dublin, as we were leaving the hospital, you touched my head and the pain stopped."

"Aye."

"Hmm. Sounds like your people are basically good. Then, what happened to your ex? How could she be so evil?" A cold chill settled over her at the question and she moved in closer for warmth.

"Besides the fact that she's been jumping back and forth between the mortal world and the Land of Faerie, we're thinking that Aideen's been messin' with the dark side, so to speak."

"You mean black magic."

"Aye. With the deadline for dissolving of the *Geis* quickly approaching, the powers of evil are running rampant."

"I've been watching the news. Everything seems to be getting more and more crazy. There are more killings, more natural disasters. It's as if people are losing their minds. How much worse can it get?"

Liam sat quietly for a moment. Michaela could feel him shutting down. "That's enough talking for one night, my love. I fancy taking my new wife back to bed and introducing her to some more of those powers we've been speaking of."

His words, spoken in that deep Irish accented voice, made her body clench with need. "Mmm…I like the sound of that," she said, letting out a squeal as he scooped her off the sofa and carried her into the bedroom.

# *Chapter Thirty*

The ardent newlyweds spent most of the next couple of days locked away in their own personal fantasy, while Michaela's fiery new husband made wild, abandoned love to her in ways clearly not of this world. The few moments she managed to tear herself out of his torrid arms, she had spent arranging her affairs for an extended stay outside the country. Since she and her friends owned their home outright, she didn't have to worry about anything there, except keeping up with her share of the condo association fees, so that Tara wouldn't be encumbered with an unexpected financial burden. Deciding it would be best to tell her parents and others that she and Liam had run off and eloped, the couple visited the county courthouse to tie up any legal loose ends. Michaela had to admit that the quick civil ceremony had helped her to affirm her whirlwind newlywed status.

A few days later, they were leaving to return to Ireland, their first class status allowing them to rest most of the way back. The sun was bright and warm over the manor house as they arrived in Sneem late the following morning. As the taxi pulled up in front of their marital home, Michaela's handsome new husband turned to her with a sexy glint in his eyes. "*Fáilte abhaile, bean chéile.*" At her questioning glance, he smiled and kissed her gently on the lips. "Welcome home, wife."

"Home," she said thoughtfully and sighed. "Yes, it is, isn't it? It's all so surreal, Liam. I have to admit to feeling a bit overwhelmed by the speed of everything that's happened."

"When something's right, 'tis right, so what's the point in dragging things out?" He reached over the seat to pay the driver. "Come now, I'll introduce you to the staff."

"I think I've met most of them already."

"Not as 'lady of the house'," he clarified, and then addressed the driver. "I'll send someone out to collect our bags straight away."

As they climbed the steps to the large front door, it opened for them. A rotund man with short dark hair, probably in his mid-forties, greeted them. "Padraig, may I present my wife, Michaela."

To his credit, the spectacled manservant barely blinked in astonishment. "My pleasure, mum. Please let me know how I may be of service."

Although Michaela had been to the property a couple of times, she didn't recognize the man. "Thank you, Padraig. Maybe we can sit down together soon and you can familiarize me with the way things are run around here?"

"At yer convenience, mum."

"Please call me Michaela."

The man smiled. "As you wish."

As Padraig left to retrieve their luggage, Liam touched her face. "You look knackered, *a mhuirnín.* Bewildered," he added with a chuckle. "We'll go into the study and rest whilst the cook prepares us a bite of lunch, will we?"

"Sounds like a plan." In the familiar room, Michaela collapsed onto the sofa, instantly aware of the warm feeling of welcome that was like an embrace. "I'm so glad we decided to keep our homecoming a secret for a couple of days."

Liam sat down beside her and pulled her into his arms. "I thought it best if we'd some time to settle in, just ourselves."

Michaela sighed. "I imagine the others will want to come around soon, to talk to me about what I know and how I came to know it. And I'm just not up to it. Not yet."

Liam twirled the end of her long, black braid around his index finger. "You're not at anyone's beck and call, my love. Things are different now that you're my wife. You'll let me know when you're ready to receive guests and we'll invite them to meet with us here."

Padraig came to the door of the study. "Assumpta has yer meal ready, sir. Will you be eating at the table or taking a tray in here?"

"We'd prefer to eat in here," Liam answered. "Remind Herself that my wife is a vegetarian. No meat or fish on her plate."

A few minutes later, steaming trays were delivered to the study. Michaela's was piled high with mashed potatoes and a lush assortment of mixed vegetables, of broccoli and carrots, corn and green beans, tastily prepared and nicely overcooked. The main dish was accompanied by a thick slice of fresh-baked bread slathered in creamy Irish butter and a hot bowl of soup smelling of fresh spices and herbs. Liam's plate was similarly prepared with the addition of a large chunk of roasted pork.

Liam got to his feet and poured each of them a glass of red wine. He offered one to his wife and clinked their glasses together. "*Slaínte,* my love. Now eat up."

Never one to be shy about stuffing her face, Michaela scarfed down her meal like a starving woman. "Wow, that was delicious."

"Did you have enough?"

"Too much," she laughed.

He moved their trays away from the sofa and reached down to pull her to her feet. "Will we go upstairs and christen the marital suite now, love?" He bent his head and whispered in her ear. "I need to be inside you."

As always, her husband's provocative words both shocked and excited her. She was addicted to his touch. From the very first time they had made love, all she could think about was lying naked in his arms. Would her desire for a purely mortal man have been this intense? she wondered absently. Or was this constant craving for her husband due in large part to his dark passion? His otherworldly allure? She had no idea, and frankly couldn't care less.

Michaela gazed into the ice-blue eyes that had so mesmerized her from the first moment they had met. Would her heart always do that funny little stammer thing every time she looked at him? It was all like a dream, she thought, a dream come true. It was still hard to believe the turn her life had taken, or her good fortune that the man she had fallen so hopelessly in love with had actually wanted her to spend her life with him. And yet there was still so much she had to learn about this new husband of hers...her magic man...so many things she couldn't begin to fathom, things she had to take on faith.

One thing had happened that was most important to her, however. Since the night they had vowed to spend their lives together, she had sensed a subtle difference in him. A kind of softening, a protective warmth, a level of commitment she had once feared he didn't possess.

As he bent and swept her into his arms, she let out a small shriek of surprise. He chuckled as he proceeded out of the study, his footsteps sounding clearly on the deep mahogany floors of the hallway. Up the staircase that curved left to the second floor, he entered the massive master bedroom, then kicked the door shut and tossed her onto the bed.

"Take my clothes off," Michaela purred, rolling onto her knees.

"My pleasure," he murmured.

A crackle of energy raised goosebumps up and down her arms and legs as, with a sweep of his hands, he vanished every stitch of fabric off her body. Naked as the day she was born, Michaela laughed out loud and held her arms out to him.

*Curiouser and curiouser,* she pondered as he joined her on the bed...before her beleaguered brain ceased to function at all.

❧

"What the hell was she thinking, anyway?" Arianna pulled the receiver away from her ear as Tara ranted. "I mean, she's only known the guy for what, three weeks? Maybe four? And then when she calls to tell me she's run off and eloped with him, she leaves me a frigging voicemail. Really?"

Arianna rocked a little faster, the baby nursing at her breast. "I thought you'd be pleased that he's serious about her, T. Happy to know he wasn't just taking advantage of her feelings for him."

That seemed to take some of the billow out of her sails. "Of course, I'm glad he's being real with her. But the two of them getting married so soon is a really bad idea. God, they hardly know each other."

"I've known him for a while, Tara, and he's good people. I believe he'll treat her well. Anyway, he makes her happy. And, at the end of the day, what else really matters?"

A conceding grumble came from the other end of the phone.

"Besides, Caleb and I got married pretty quickly ourselves, didn't we? I guess what I'm saying is that when it's right, it's right. You just wait. You'll fall in love one day, and then you'll understand."

"Good God, keep your curses to yourself," Tara scoffed good-naturedly. "I like my life just the way it is, thank you very much. I don't need some man to complete me."

"Okay, okay." For a woman with an IQ in the one-sixties, her genius friend sure had a lot to learn in the romance department. Of course, Tara's previous relationship experience had pretty much soured her on love. "Anyway, as soon as they get back to Ireland, I'm going down to Sneem to help her get settled in. Maybe when you wrap things up in Italy the three of us can all get together there."

"Yeah, yeah. We'll see. Anyway, I gotta go."

"Now be nice when you talk to her, Tara," Arianna cajoled.

"I'm always nice," she shot back, and then rang off.

Caleb was lounging on the sofa watching the six o'clock news on TG4. "So, you're friend's in a bit of an uproar about Liam and Michaela, is she?"

Arianna lifted Kieran to her shoulder and began to pat his little back. "Come on, sweetie," she cooed. "Burp now." She looked at Caleb. "I swear, there are times I think Tara sees herself more as our mother than our friend. She's always trying to look out for us, fix things, you know? I love her, but she can be a real buzz kill sometimes. Not to mention, seriously OCD."

Arianna realized Caleb wasn't listening to her. His eyes glued to the television, he pointed the remote at the screen and turned up the volume. "Bloody hell," he muttered.

"What's wrong, honey?"

"It's getting worse and worse, *a ghrá*. Wars, disease, famine. Terror attacks and earthquakes around the globe all in the news in a single day. It's already begun, I fear. The Waking Madness that will usher in the end of days."

"How's that possible?" Arianna tucked the baby into his cradle and went to curl up on her husband's lap. "I mean, the deadline isn't until Halloween. So, we still have time, right?"

"A short window, yes. But as the time for the dissolution grows nearer, the Ancient Evil slowly comes to consciousness. And the world will increasingly feel the impact of the Awakening."

At her husband's words, a cold, dark shiver ran down Arianna's spine. "Surely, it won't come to that. Something will happen to make things right. The Woman of Promise will appear and everything will be okay."

Caleb ran his hand down his wife's back. "And what if yer wee American friend was that one, after all, me love? Her knowledge of our people, of the Enchantment itself, has now disqualified her from the quest."

"So, what's up with Aideen, anyway? When Michaela comes back to Ireland, will she be safe?"

"Yer wan's been imprisoned at the Council's manse on the Isle of Skye since the incident on the island. Every rune, every magical compulsion available to us has been employed to assure she'll not be escaping again."

Arianna blew out a breath of air. "Well, whatever happens over the next couple of months, I choose to believe that Michaela is not this Chosen One, that someone else will come along and fulfill that role. I just can't accept the fact that our son will never grow up, or that this wonderful life we have will all be coming to an end."

Caleb chuckled. "*A banchéile mo chroí,* wife of my heart, how is it you always see the best in things?"

Her arm around the back of his neck, Arianna kissed him on the cheek. "I have faith, oh husband of mine. Just plain old, garden variety faith."

Caleb chuckled again, then turned her around on his lap, positioning her so that she was straddling him. "Kieran's fast asleep. I think his da needs some of his mum's attention now."

She gave her hips a suggestive roll. "Mmm…I can tell."

Caleb growled and set her to her feet. Following her up off the sofa, he scooped her into his arms, his mouth fixed to hers. Arianna's delighted giggle echoed through the room as the new parents vanished into the ether.

# Chapter Thirty-One

Michaela called Arianna the following day to let her know that she and Liam were back in Ireland. The two couples made plans to get together that same evening for dinner at the manor house in Sneem. With still so much that Michaela didn't understand about her life with her mysterious new husband, she was counting on a hen party with her old friend to get brought up to date.

While the men gathered in the study for a drink and a hand of cards, Arianna joined Michaela in the kitchen, her new baby asleep on her shoulder. Laying Kieran down in a portable bassinet Caleb had set up for him near the table, she joined her friend at the stove.

"Can you believe this?" Michaela asked. "The two of us married to mutual friends and living in another country, all within the space of a year. Not to mention you with a new baby and all the airy fairy stuff we've become involved with along the way."

"Tell me about it," Arianna beamed. "So, how's married life treating you?"

Michaela grinned over her shoulder. "If you're wanting to know how the sex is, oh my God! Makes me feel sorry for the rest of the women in the world, you know, stuck with a regular earthling guy. Know what I mean?"

"Totally." Arianna gathered up several tomatoes, a head of lettuce, a cucumber and an avocado Michaela had washed and left in a colander. Dumping the vegetables into a salad bowl, she carried them to the island counter, where the chopping board had been set out. "About the *airy fairy* stuff, I don't know what Liam's told you, or what you may still have questions about."

Michaela hummed. "Okay, so I know there's a magical race of people and Liam's a member of that race, as is Caleb. And you said that your mother's connected to them somehow, which makes you....God, I don't know, Arianna. This is so freaking unreal, I feel like I'm being punked or something."

Her friend gave a short laugh. "I get that, kiddo. Believe me. I didn't know anything about my heritage, about any of this before I got here last year."

Michaela was standing at the Viking range, stirring the sauce for some homemade cheese raviolis she had prepared for dinner. "Why don't you just start from the beginning, then. Tell me everything you know."

Arianna chewed on her lip. "This is all still really new to me, too, Mick. I think we should invite the guys to join us in here for this. There's a lot of important stuff about the curse—you know, the gesh—that I don't completely understand myself."

Michaela tipped her head and thought about it for a minute. "Okay. But, just so you know, all this talk of a pending apocalypse is totally freaking me out."

As Arianna reached the kitchen door, she looked back over her shoulder. "Tell me about it. That's why I want the hubbies in here. They'll be able to explain everything a lot more clearly than I can."

She stuck her head out into the hall and shouted for Caleb and Liam. About five minutes later, the men appeared in the kitchen, each with a glass of Jameson in his hands.

Liam walked up behind his wife and kissed her on the back of the neck. "Supper ready?"

"Not long now," Michaela answered with a smile.

"We've been talking about the gesh," Arianna explained to the men. "And I really don't feel like I understand things enough to be able to explain it."

Kieran began to grumble from the bassinet. Arianna gave Michaela an apologetic look and went to pick him up. "I got the salad done. Sorry to abandon you, but the little guy's hungry again."

"I got this," Michaela assured her, as her best friend settled down on a kitchen chair, placed a cloth diaper over her shoulder for modesty and began to nurse her newborn. "Liam, if you'll get the garlic bread out of the oven, I'll serve the raviolis to the table."

Caleb took the bread tray from Liam, then collected the bowl of salad and brought them both to the table. "I whipped up some fresh salad dressing," Michaela told her husband. "Would you get it out of the fridge?"

Liam complied, as Michaela delivered a steaming bowl of raviolis to the table. "Okay, guys, *mangia*."

Everyone made appropriate noises about how delicious everything looked, as Arianna finished nursing and tucked the sleeping infant back in his bassinet.

As they passed the bowls and trays around the table, Michaela glanced at her hot new husband, who was digging into the sumptuous feast. "Surprisingly good, given that there's no animal flesh involved," he teased.

"Just because I choose not to feast on a dead animal carcass, that doesn't mean I won't prepare one for you," she said with a flirty grin.

"Well, thanks be to God for that," Liam replied, only partially in jest.

The lack of conversation, combined with the sound of forks scraping against plates, was all the affirmation Michaela needed that the meal was a success. "Okay, so Arianna and I were talking about the…the gesh thing," she said, meeting her husband's cool blue gaze. *Damn.* As her breath caught in her throat, she wondered if the sight of him would always make her heart skip a beat. "What should I expect with all of this *end of the world* stuff, and how can I help?"

At the dubious look on her husband's face, she held up a hand. "Before you answer that, let me preface this whole thing by telling you that I'm a strong woman, more than capable of fighting your battles alongside you. Granted, I may be small, but size can be deceiving. I'm a second-degree black belt and well able to take care of myself."

"Against another mere mortal, perhaps," Liam said mildly, stuffing another bite of ravioli into his mouth.

"Another…. Okay, I've heard that expression several times since we met. Care to expound on it?"

Her husband dragged a hand through his ash-blonde hair, pushing it back from his face. *Damn, dude was hot. And he was all hers.*

"It means simply that while our people are a race of mortal human beings, sure, we're not *merely* mortal. We possess gifts and traits that those whose origins are of the earth don't naturally have."

Michaela let that soak in for a minute. "Okay. So, you told me about your ancestors' interplanetary trip to earth and all that. But with thousands of years of intermarriage between your people and…earthlings…I take it that your DNA has changed, so that you're only distantly related to that original race of people."

"Not so distantly." Liam gave Michaela a glance of that adorable smirk that she had so quickly come to love. "Because of the *Geis,* most of the breeding between our two races was forced to cease long ago."

Michaela gave Arianna a confused glance. "I thought you said that you and Caleb were only half…mere mortal," she said, struggling with the unfamiliar terminology.

Caleb looked up from the ravioli he was pushing onto his fork with a slice of garlic bread. "The Enchantment only affected mortal women, like my mother, negatively," he explained. "Since Arianna's father was the mortal partner in their relationship, the union caused him no physical harm."

Michaela let that sink in. "Is your mom still alive, Caleb?"

The black miasma that descended over the room at her innocent question was almost visible. "She died in childbirth," he replied. "A result of the *Geis*."

"I'm sorry. So, Granny is…?"

"His mother's mother," Arianna explained. "She helped to raise him. I told you how she took care of me when I was little, before Da moved with me to the States."

"Now, Arianna, you know I've always been open to extraordinary concepts, like the possibility of parallel universes. Things that our finite minds can't comprehend. What I don't understand is why I was thrown into the middle of all that chaos when I got to Dublin? I mean, why me? Why all the insanity with the…freaking fairy prince? And that crazy bitch…Aideen?" A quick study, it took Michaela only a second before the light went on. "It never really sank in before, that your crazy ex belongs to this same magical race. That's how she was messing with me, doing spells to make my horse stumble. To make me see things that weren't there." As she talked things through, she began to piece things together more and more. "So, that's why your mother kept pushing the woman down your throat. Like an Italian mother who wants her daughter to marry another Italian. Or a Jewish mother who doesn't want her son to marry a goy."

Liam gave a slight smile at the Yiddish reference. "A good analogy, me love."

Michaela looked at Caleb and spoke in a hushed tone. "That's how you were able to rescue us that night on Inishmore."

Until now, she and Arianna had had an unspoken agreement not to talk about that frightful time on the island, the night she and her friends had been kidnapped. The night Arianna had been burned at the stake. "That's how Caleb knew we were in trouble, sweetie. My mother called to him. It's how he was able to get to me in time."

Michaela frowned.

"She's a merrow, Mick." As her frown grew deeper, Arianna paused, took a breath, bit her lip. "That's a kind of mermaid. She called to Caleb from the deep that night. He took on his supernatural form in order to come and rescue me."

Michaela shook her head in disbelief. "Seriously? You're telling me that your mother's a mermaid?" As many times as she heard Arianna claim to be a part of this other race, it still would not compute. They had known each other since Michaela was twelve years old. And Tara had known Arianna since she was just out of diapers. There was no way she had ever been anything but…normal. Except for the weird dreams she talked about while growing up, of course, dreams about Caleb as it turned out. It would have been easier to swallow the fact that the two of them had somehow gotten themselves involved with some strange, brainwashing cult. Except that Michaela had seen…had experienced too many inexplicable things to turn back now.

"And you had to keep all of this a secret from me originally because I might have been some God-ordained deliverer? Some chosen prophetess who could save the world from the coming destruction?"

Having finished their meal, the others exchanged glances. "That was the part we couldn't explain to you at the time, babe," Arianna replied. "Bottom line is, we're still not sure that you're not that one. All we know is that, if you are, you were disqualified from your role in this cosmic game as soon as you became aware of the Enchantment's existence."

Michaela sat quietly for a few seconds. "That would mean that all of this could be over, that the whole world could conceivably be coming to an end…when?"

Liam reached out and covered her hand with his. "Unless another comes along…sure, the deadline for resolution of the *Geis* is *Samhain*. Halloween, as you know it in the States."

"But that's only a couple of month's away," she protested weakly, as the ramifications of what he'd just told her became suddenly real. She had finally found the man of her dreams, was more in love than she could ever have imagined, had found more happiness than she'd ever believed was possible—and it could all come crashing down on their heads on October 31st. How unfair!

"We've a Council meeting tomorrow on the Isle of Skye," Liam told her. "We'll continue seeking answers, attempting to locate the Woman spoken of in the ancient scrolls."

Michaela felt like the rug had just been pulled out from under her feet. "You mean you're leaving me here? Now? With everything that's going on?"

"Absolutely not," Liam hurried to assure her. "I'll not be leaving you on your own until we've sorted these things out. You'll travel with me and, if you're up for it, the Council would fancy having you there to testify at Aideen's trial."

"A trial?"

"Aye. We're a society, love, one with its own government, its own laws, separate and apart from those of the lands in which we live. What Aideen did by allowing her jealousy to rule her, by harming you, dragging you into this…situation…is considered treason by our leaders. That she may have rendered the Woman of Promise, if 'tis yourself, to be ineligible to participate in dissolving the *Geis*. A most heinous crime indeed."

Arianna spoke up. "I know it's a lot to take in, sweetie. Just trust me when I tell you that this is an amazing world we've discovered. That there's goodness and magic here, and love that I'd never expected to find. No one on this earth is ever promised tomorrow. So, we just have to have faith that all will be well in the end. And be thankful every day for the joy we've found in our lives right now."

"Okay, so you're part of this…community. Does that mean you can do some of these magic tricks yourself?" Michaela teased in an attempt to lighten the mood.

Instantly, Arianna's face fell. And both of the men looked inordinately displeased by her reference to *magic tricks.*

"What?" she asked, defensively.

"They aren't *tricks* exactly," Arianna explained patiently. "The magic is intuitive to their bloodline, a part of the *Tuátha de Danann* heritage. Like your Cherokee background. It's not meant to be a dog and pony show."

At this point, the cook bustled into the kitchen, unaware she was interrupting a serious conversation. "Will I clear the table now? Do the washing up?"

The tension broken, everyone decided to retire to the study. Standing to his feet, Liam offered his hand to his wife. "I've something to show you, *a mhuirnín.*"

"Okay." Feeling suddenly apprehensive, Michaela slipped her hand into his. And that was all it took—just that one innocent touch—to make her stomach flutter and her knees weak.

Trying not to disturb the sleeping infant, Caleb scooped up the bassinet and followed the other three down the hall to the study. Then he stretched out in an overstuffed chair across from the loveseat that Liam and Michaela were relaxing on. After checking on the baby, Arianna curled up in her husband's lap.

Once both couples were settled in, Liam looked down at his wife. "Now, where would you like to go, love? Where would you like to visit? Think of anyplace in the whole world, anytime, past or present, and the three of us will take you there now."

Confused by his sudden offer of travel plans, Michaela sent an inquisitive glance to her husband. Immediately, she experienced the now familiar ruffling in her consciousness. Those exotic eyes of his drew her in as she felt herself drowning in that glacial pond of purest blue. As understanding of his meaning filtered into her brain, she heard the answer to his query whisper from her mind to his. It had to be the most erotic sensation she had ever experienced, the way he shared his thoughts with her, sipped her own thoughts from her mind. Her body was instantly on fire for him, her inner being yearning again for his possession.

As the sound of the clock tick, tick, ticking on the wall behind them seemed to fade into an echoing distance, a heaviness dragged on her eyelids. The thought came to her that Liam was mesmerizing her. At one time, she would have been alarmed by this, would have fought him with every ounce of power she possessed. But from the moment they had first made love, she had come to trust him with everything in her being. Comforted by the thought, she let herself ride the waves of peace washing over her like breakers on a warm gulf coast shore.

*When Michaela opened her eyes, she was on a hillside near the Sea of Galilee a couple of thousand years ago. Now, her faith had always been a quiet one. Simple and private. She had been raised with no organized religion. No belief system at all. No one knew how she prayed, what she prayed for. Therefore, no one could have known that, if she were to pick a place in all of time to visit, it would have been to sit here on this sacred mount while Christ ministered the love of God to His people.*

*She turned to focus her attention on Him, noting that His form was more rugged, His skin tone slightly more swarthy than the famous paintings and other works of art that depicted this Jewish Messiah as a gentile. But as Michaela stared into His face, she realized that this was exactly the way she had always envisioned Him in her heart.*

*Attired in the very jeans and shirts they had all been wearing at dinner, Michaela, her husband and friends sat amongst people dressed in biblical garb. She might have felt out of place, had she not quickly discovered that, while she and Liam, Arianna and Caleb were all physically there, they were visible only to one another. As she sat on this holiest hill, listening to the sermon that would be quoted throughout the ages, Michaela knew she was truly enamored of this Son of Man. She was in love with Him, a divine love, pure and all consuming, that had endured throughout the millennia. She glanced at Liam, who was reclining beside her on the soft, green grass, his eyes fixed on the Son of God. A slight smile settled on his lips as they listened together to the words she had read in the scriptures so many times before.*

*"Blessed are those…."*

*Although she knew the words had been spoken in Aramaic, she heard them in the language that she understood. As the four of them sat amongst the crowds, Michaela knew they were invisible to all those around them. To all, except for Him….*

*As His quiet baritone rumbled through the countryside with the sound of His authority, He paused and turned to look at her. In that one instant, the love pouring from His eyes reached deep into her wounded soul, healing all of life's hurts.*

*He smiled and the love pouring out of Him filled every empty place in her heart. His next words, which had been passed down for thousand of years and recorded for the faithful multitudes, seemed to be meant for her alone. "Ask, and it will be given to you. Seek, and you will find. Knock, and it will be opened to you." Then in her innermost being she heard him say, "Hearken to my words, my child."*

*She felt Liam's hand encompass hers and, just like that, they were flying, propelled forward through time and space, through history in a dreamy kaleidoscope of candy-scented colors.*

When Michaela opened her eyes again, she was wrapped in Liam's arms. She looked across the room and met Arianna's anxious gaze.

"Are you okay?" asked her closest friend in the world.

Dazed by the experience, Michaela couldn't prevent the awestruck smile that captured her lips. "Wow. God, I don't know what to say. I feel…high. Wonderful."

"Yeah," Arianna agreed, her face split into a grin. "Now, *that's* what I'm talking about."

"Brilliant." Chuckling, Caleb got to his feet and reached for his wife's hand. "Now, I believe we should be saying goodnight to the newlyweds."

"If you need anything—" Liam began.

"We're grand," Caleb said. "We've our things already up in the guestroom. We'll leave for Scotland first thing in the morning."

Caleb collected the bassinet and the new family departed the room.

Michaela grinned up at her husband. "That was amazing, baby. I had no idea that all this woo-woo stuff could be so much fun."

Liam cocked his head to one side. "*Woo-woo stuff?*"

"Yeah, you know, all the hocus-pocus."

Appearing amused, Liam reached out and tugged on the long black braid that spilled down her back. "And I've more *hocus-pocus* waiting for you upstairs tonight," he teased, with a wink and a smoldering grin.

"Counting on it." As Michaela wrapped her arms around her new husband, he vanished both of them from the room.

# *Chapter Thirty-Two*

With the deadline for resolution of the *Geis* fast approaching, the Council of Brehons was gathering on the Isle of Skye for another emergency meeting. Perched high above the rugged Scottish coastline, the 14$^{th}$ century gothic stone fortress had been constructed originally for their annual meetings each year on *Samhain* eve. As the fifty-three-room manse contained a charm-protected holding cell for enemies of the *Tuátha de Danann*, it had always served as the formal site for criminal hearings and other matters of justice for their tribe. Hence, it would be the location for Aideen's formal trial the following day.

The newlyweds landed at one of the property's several helipads. Liam immediately noted his wife's chilled reaction to the bleak, forbidding structure. Dark and abandoned, the old mausoleum projected a sense of doom that seemed to permeate its very foundation, a drastic contrast to the warmth of the bright and sunny day.

At the front entrance, Liam signed an intricate rune into the air and the massive door creaked slowly open. He could sense Michaela's immediate relief at the unexpected sense of warmth and cheer that greeted them as they made their way inside.

Someone had been cooking, and the sumptuous aroma of the grilling meats vied with the slightly musty smell of a centuries-old fortress. They followed the low hum of conversation into an old kitchen the size of a football field. Liam, who spent more time in his wife's head than she would probably ever be comfortable with, noted her surprise to find several of the men preparing the evening meal. He leaned down and whispered in her ear. "As this is a secret meeting, we've no cooks or staff onsite. Besides yourself, Arianna and my sister, only Council members—and those with official business here—are in attendance."

"Catriona's gonna be here, too? Cool," his wife responded in hushed tones. "So, what exactly should I expect when I have to testify? Am I going to have to see that awful woman?"

"Absolutely not. I'll request that you testify *in camera*."

"I guess no one knows whether I was meant to be this…Chosen One?" She bit that full lower lip that was like a juicy strawberry.

Liam fought back the urge to whisk her away to the bedroom they would be sharing, a can of whipped cream and angel food cake in tow. "It's complicated, love, even for those of us who've grown up dealing with the situation. Don't worry your wee head about that now."

As they entered the immense kitchen, they found Seamus, Brian, and Father James working together to prepare a meal, whilst Caleb and Arianna enjoyed a cup of coffee at an old wooden table that would have easily seated sixteen.

"Well, there they are." Getting to her feet, Arianna embraced her little American friend, then offered Liam a peck on the cheek. "Congratulations again, you two. Anything new since last night?"

Michaela gave that sexy wee giggle that warmed Liam all the way to his toes. "Nope. Still living in a fairytale," she teased.

"Oh, no you didn't," Arianna joked back. "So did you guys find your room yet?"

"Just walked in the door," Liam replied.

Michaela glanced around the kitchen. "So, where's my baby boy?"

Arianna smiled. "He's with his great-granny at the castle, getting spoiled rotten, no doubt. I stocked up a supply of breast milk for her to give him while I'm away."

"You're so lucky to have her."

"Yeah, we're pretty blessed."

"Why don't you take Michaela upstairs and help her get settled in?" Caleb suggested to his wife. "I'd like a moment alone with Liam here."

"Don't be long, *bean chéile*," Liam said. "You've not eaten anything yet today."

"Aye, we'll have the meal on the table straight away," Seamus called out, then continued to stir flour into a rich and creamy sauce on the modern, gourmet cooker on the other side of the room. The restaurateur had been aptly placed in charge of the day's menu.

With a smile and a wave of acknowledgement, the two wives bustled out of the room.

"Is everyone here?" Liam asked.

"Still waiting for Sean and Paddy, so," Caleb replied. "They're traveling in together."

"And Aideen?"

"Aye, that's what I'm wanting to speak with you about. Her trial's been set for tomorrow morning. Her solicitor will be arriving at six a.m. for a final meeting with her before the hearing, which is scheduled for nine."

"So, what's the story with her?"

"She's still under twenty-four hour guard in the holding cell. It seems that, between traveling back and forth between here and the *sidhe,* and her dabbling in the black arts, she's after growing very powerful."

The tension in the other man's voice told Liam there was more. "And?"

"She's changed, mate, gone totally mental. There's no humanity left in the woman a'tall, which leaves us little choice in the matter before us."

Liam took a seat at the table, his eyes keen on Caleb.

"You know yerself, we've never favored the use of capital punishment," Caleb continued. "Even in extreme cases, we've ordered permanent banishment to Faerie as punishment for the breaking of our laws. But this is different, Liam. Maybe because of the times and the seasons, with the deadline of the *Geis* so near at hand. I'm convinced the woman's a danger to yourself, to your wife, to all of us. Hasn't yer wan already committed high treason by revealing our secrets to a woman who is very likely the Chosen One? And, if your wife's not that one, then another will soon be revealed. I'm of the belief that Aideen's under the control of the Beast and his minions, that she'll endeavor to corrupt that one as well."

As the two men spoke together privately, Seamus, James, and Brian brought the food to the table. "Call the women now," Father James suggested. "Let's put this matter to rest until the trial tomorrow. There'll be time enough then to make any hard decisions that are required."

"Agreed." Caleb closed his eyes and summoned his wife back to the kitchen, then turned to Liam. "I just wanted you to be aware of the action we'll likely be forced to take."

"Understood." Liam said. "My major concern—my *only* concern—at this point is ensuring my wife's safety."

"And 'tis herself, the one Aideen'll be after going for first," Caleb warned.

Liam felt his heart go dark inside him. "She'll have to die then, will she not?" he responded, his tone as cold and hard as an ancient slab of stone.

ꕥ

The two remaining members of the Council of Brehons had arrived at the old manor house late the previous evening. Early morning now, the members were gathered around the long table in the study, which had been designated as the courtroom for all trials and criminal matters. The men chatted quietly as they awaited the appearance of the accused and her legal counsel, Declan McGuire. Some time had passed since Caleb and Seamus had gone down below to escort them both to the formal hearing.

What Liam witnessed as the four returned to the meeting room both surprised and appalled him. The lovely woman he had known for a short while a couple of months ago had gone. Left in her place, just as a faerie woman might leave a changeling child, was the shimmering shell of a mortal being. As they proceeded into the room, she repeatedly attempted to fade into an ephemeral wisp, then, defeated by the protection charm, would return fully to her fleshly form. As her once lavender eyes settled upon him, he witnessed the madness now lurking in their depths. Her irises now colorless, the whites of her eyes red-veined and bulging, she seemed to be fading away, to be sure. Even her vibrant auburn hair had become heavily streaked with gray. Her hands bound in front of her—both by magic and by physical restraints—once boasted nails that were perfectly pared and manicured, but now curved into talons, swiping at everyone she passed. She emitted a low, bone-chilling growl as she moved like an animal, stealthy and sly, guided by her solicitor to the place reserved for the two of them near the head of the table.

Caleb, who served as the Chief Brehon, called the hearing to order. Though 'twas obvious all members were present, Seamus took an ancillary roll call for the record, then requested that the Defendant stand for a formal reading of the charges. As her solicitor encouraged her to comply, she only laughed and sniveled, making high-pitched noises, like a wild chimpanzee.

"'Tis a serious matter being brought before the Council today," Caleb began. "Not in this century, nor in the last, have we been commissioned to hear a case of this magnitude. The charge of high treason carries with it the irrevocable penalty of banishment from the upper earth, as well as a possible sentence of physical death. Therefore, I adjure each and every member of this Council to consider well the matter at hand and find strictly on behalf of the evidence."

Seated next to his client, the thin, balding solicitor with the wire-rimmed spectacles rose to his feet. "I wish to have it confirmed that I'm in possession of a complete list of those who will be presenting evidence here today."

"You are," Caleb stated.

"Ah sure then, I've to object to this witness, Sirs," he said, gesturing to a name on the list. "As you know, we've no rule of law that allows the Council to consider the testimony of a mere mortal."

Like quicksilver, Liam was on his feet, his temper soaring to its melting point. He looked at the Chief Brehon. "May I speak?"

Caleb nodded. "Councilman O'Neill has the floor."

Fixing his icy gaze on Aideen's solicitor, he carefully measured his words. "First, I wish to inform you that the *mere mortal* you reference is my wife. And 'tis herself who was thought to carry the traits of the prophesied deliverer, which makes her testimony in this matter vital." At the mention of a wife, Aideen snapped her head toward Liam. Her eyes shooting daggers, she spewed curses at her former lover, although the words she spoke were in the language of Faerie, which she used as fluently as though 'twere her mother tongue.

"Please control your client," Caleb admonished her legal counsel, "lest we be forced to remove her from the room."

"No need for that," the woman spit out arrogantly. "Would hate to be after missing this ridiculous farce of a hearing. We know already what you're findings will be."

"May we have a moment?" Mr. McGuire asked, then leaned down to speak with his client in undertones for a few minutes.

With the semblance of a pout on her once attractive features, Aideen finally quieted and settled back in her chair.

The solicitor turned to Liam. "Forgive me, please, if my comment about a mere mortal testifying caused offense. I wished only to point out 'twas irregular."

"We live in irregular times," Liam replied to the man, before again taking his seat. "I do have one request of the Council, however," he continued, again addressing Caleb. "And that is that my wife's testimony be taken *in camera*, as I refuse to have her subjected to this woman's presence."

At Liam's defense of his wife, Aideen burst out in a raucous laughter, then slyly put her right hand over her mouth as if 'twere an accident.

"I fear I must object again," her solicitor stated. "My client is up on serious charges here and has the right to face her accuser. Especially one—and again, please forgive me here," he said, directing the aside to Liam—"but especially one who's not of our *Tuátha*, our tribe."

His temper already at a fever pitch, Liam pushed back his chair and stood to his feet. "She'll not be testifying, then," he threatened, whilst the other Council members began to murmur amongst themselves.

Caleb called for order and asked Liam to take his seat. "As we all agree, these are not ordinary times in which we're living. And *because* the witness is not of our race, and will likely be traumatized by any direct contact with the accused, I grant Mr. O'Neill's request that we waive the rule in this circumstance and allow his wife to testify privately."

While Liam was downstairs attending to Council business, Michaela was in their suite of rooms enjoying a cup of coffee with Arianna and Catriona. "I didn't realize you were going to be here today," Michaela told her.

"Cian and I traveled in early this morning," she explained. "I've been asked to testify at Aideen's trial, as well."

"You have?"

"Aye. About the pub incident, you know, with the likes of all the ground shaking *craic* in front of the mere mortals there."

Michaela sighed. "I just want this all to be over with. Liam and I need to have some time alone to get settled into our marriage."

"You need that," his sister agreed. "Especially with your introduction into a new society. 'Twill take some time before you'll be feeling comfortable with it all."

"She's right, Mick," Arianna chimed in. "Even with my genetic connection to this new life, I was raised with a whole different set of beliefs and values. It took a while before the reality of my situation began to sink in, to feel real."

Michaela took a thoughtful sip of her coffee, then set the cup back on the saucer on the end table beside her chair. "It's still different for me. At least, you're one of them," she pointed out. "Everyday is a chance for you to learn something new, to kind of stretch your muscles with your newly discovered powers. While I, on the other hand.... Well, I'll never quite fit in, now will I?"

"Everyone has already accepted you, babe. Just give them time to get to know you better. They'll come to love you every bit as much as I do."

"Yeah, everyone except *your* mom," Michaela told Catriona with a slight laugh.

"Well, she's a piece of work, to be sure," the woman agreed. "But don't fret about it. She'll be coming round soon enough."

At a knock on the door, the three women turned their heads. "Come in," Michaela called out.

Cian peeked into the room. "Catriona, they're asking for you down below."

With a grimace for the distasteful task ahead of her, she unfolded herself from off the sofa. "I'll see you when I've finished," she said, following her husband out the door.

"I'm so nervous I feel like I'm going to vomit," Michaela complained, her voice laden with anxiety. "I just can't wait until this whole thing is over."

"Me too, sweetie," Arianna said, with a heartfelt sigh and a shake of her head. "Me too."

Catriona had just finished testifying before the Council. As she'd related the public display of magic the woman had performed on the afternoon she and Michaela had been out for lunch, Aideen checked her nails as if bored to tears by the entire spectacle. While Liam's wife would testify to all of the other incidents involving Aideen, the use of witnesses in the *Túatha* judicial process was only a fail-safe. Whereas a mere mortal court was dependent upon the testimony of an eyewitness to ascertain the facts in a case, not so the Council of Brehons. Able to verify the accuracy of all such information by utilizing the Gift of Innate Knowledge, they would simply go back in time and visit the incident in question, in essence, witnessing everything for themselves firsthand. However, because this was a capital case, it was vital to present testimony by actual witnesses, whenever available, for the purpose of cross-examination by defense counsel in order to put the facts into context. Also, it would allow the defense to argue mitigating circumstances during closing arguments.

After Catriona was excused from the room, Liam rose to his feet. "I'll be joining me wife in our chamber." He made the announcement with little care for what the others might have thought of the idea.

He entered their suite with the Council scribe close on his heels. Michaela jumped to her feet, a basket of nerves. "Seamus will set up the Mic and video equipment for the testimony now," he explained to her.

"I'll give you guys your privacy." Arianna gave Michaela a peck on the cheek and left the room.

Michaela turned to her husband. "So, what's going to happen now? Is she…will she be listening to what I say?" Chocolate brown eyes huge, cheeks flushed, his wife asked the question in hushed tones.

"She'll be listening, but you won't have to look at her," he said gently. "Just answer the questions as best you recall what happened. 'Twill all be over soon."

She sat back down in the armchair, fiddling with a string hanging off the hem of her shirt as Seamus pulled a small table up in front of her and set up a laptop with a webcam. "Questions will be posed, both by the Council members and by Aideen's solicitor," he advised, handing her a set of earphones. "You know how a webcam works?"

She bit her lip and blew out a breath. "Of course, I do."

Liam leaned down to speak to her. "Now, you'll be able to see Caleb on the screen, only Caleb."

Liam could see the question in her eyes. "No, *a mhuirnín*, I've already told you, you will not have to look at that woman. I wouldn't allow you to be put through that, my love."

She placed the headphones over her ears. "Okay, okay. I'm ready," she said breathlessly.

Michaela was duly sworn in and the questioning began. After the Council concluded their direct examination, Mr. McGuire began his cross. For a grueling forty-five minutes, she was interrogated, first about her accident at the Dublin Horse Show and the subsequent dreams and visions that followed. Of course, Aideen's solicitor was quick to ask her whether the experience might have been simply the result of a head injury, a temporary symptom of a concussion, and no connection to his client at all. The questions became more intense as she was asked to describe Aideen's abduction of her to the Land of Faerie. She was also questioned about the incident at the pub with Catriona, as well as the confrontation with Aideen at Liam's home the morning the woman had accompanied his mother to the property. Again and again, Michaela was asked to repeat, word-for-word, the threats the woman had made against her with special emphasis placed on any mention of either the *Tuátha de Danann* or the *Geis.*

She looked wrung out, as if every bit of energy had been sucked out of her.

"Enough." With no further fanfare, Liam ended the ordeal by shutting the lid of the laptop. "You'll rest now," he told his wife, "whilst I join the others."

Grateful, she looked up at him. "I think I'll go lie down now."

He nodded, kissed the top of her head, and proceeded out of the room.

~

Liam returned to the hearing room to find Aideen's solicitor protesting the interruption of his cross-examination. "I've a few more questions for the witness, Chief Brehon. As this is a capital case, my client deserves every consideration here. Careless mutterings do not warrant the ultimate punishment. A misunderstanding of the circumstances can occur without an opportunity for a robust examination."

"And a robust examination he's had!" Liam exclaimed, allowing his usually levelheaded temper to get the better of him.

As the words tumbled past his lips, Caleb held up one hand for silence. Liam complied.

"That's true enough, Mr. McGuire, but this court has gone above and beyond in these proceedings to ensure that your client has a fair trial. Every one of us seated on this Council has a moral duty to see that justice is served. Our judgment must be unanimous for a conviction. If any one of us finds in favor of your client, or simply abstains from the vote, she'll be set free."

"I understand that, Chief Brehon. Which is why I wish to explore further whether the witness was indeed experiencing the result of head trauma. To inquire as to whether what she *believes* she heard my client say may have been a result of the nightmares she was suffering."

Caleb shook his head. "During the last fifteen minutes of your examination of the witness, you repeatedly asked the same questions—including this one—in a variety of ways, only to get the exact same response from her every time. What new information do you require of her?"

Defense counsel spit and sputtered for a moment. "I would inquire regarding her understanding of those things she claims my client told her. Without that, I can't really see where there's been any harm done by the alleged disclosures."

Liam sat up straighter in his seat, his ire spilling over on all those around him. But before he could open his mouth and again disrupt the proceedings, the Chief Brehon raised a silencing hand. "That's been asked and answered, Counselor," Caleb said. "Several times. Do you have anything new?"

Sweating profusely from his balding pate, Mr. McGuire sat quietly for a few moments, knowing too well that, with the Council of Brehon's use of the Gift of Innate Knowledge, his client's fate would be sealed. He gave a quick shake of his head. "I do not."

"In that case," Caleb went on, "the Counsel finds that you have had adequate opportunity to impeach the witness, but have failed to do so. Therefore, Michaela O'Neill is hereby formally excused from further testimony in this matter. Now, Counselor, if you'd like to commence closing arguments…."

While speaking his final words on his client's behalf, the defense counsel suggested that the mere mortal could have simply been wiped of her memories, thereby relieving his client of any responsibility for interfering with the *Geis.* And whilst she would still suffer banishment for her airing of the forbidden topics, she would be relieved of the ultimate penalty, that of death.

When the hearing concluded, the solicitor took his seat. Brian Rafferty and Father Conneely stood to their feet, and escorted the accused back to her holding cell.

Upon the return of the two Council members to the drawing room, the ten discussed the testimony given, as well as the incident involving Aideen's abduction of Michaela on the island, which they had witnessed personally. Before the formal voting, the men sat back in their chairs, closed their eyes and visited the scene of the alleged crimes through their special gift. With the woman's guilt proven beyond any shadow of a doubt, they exchanged weighted glances, the severity of the situation resting heavily upon each one.

A few moments later, Caleb requested a vote on the matter before them. "On the charge of treason, how does the Council find, so say you one, so say you all?"

"Guilty," the other nine men replied in unison.

Caleb turned to look at Aideen's solicitor. "Guilty as charged."

With a unanimous verdict, Caleb asked Mr. McGuire to leave the room so that the Council might deliberate on sentencing in private.

With a deep sigh, the man rose to his feet. "Understood."

After the solicitor left the room, Caleb opened the discussion before the Councilmen. "I'd like to address the solicitor's suggestion that wiping Michaela's memory of the incident in question would erase the violation of the terms of the *Geis.* Liam, did you not attempt just that when all of this originally happened?"

"I did."

"And will you please share with the other members the outcome of that attempt?"

"Aye. Because Aideen was after engaging in black magic, in witchcraft, at the time this took place, there was no way of wiping Michaela's memory."

The Council members exchanged troubled glances as Liam spoke again. "And may I add one more thing for consideration."

Caleb nodded.

"Mr. McGuire recommended banishment for his client, which is usually the preferred penalty in a case of this nature. What he neglected to address, however, is that—again due to the woman's meddling with the dark arts—'tis been next to impossible to keep her contained." Liam looked toward the ceiling and sighed, then returned his gaze to the Council. "Look, I take no pleasure in voting for the ultimate punishment. But we all know that if she were permanently banished, she'll only return as she wills. Gentlemen, I fear there's but one conclusion available to us this day."

# Chapter Thirty-Three

A knock on the bedroom door woke Michaela from a restless nap. She climbed down from the bed and found Arianna standing in the hall. "Hey, can I come in?" Her best friend's voice sounded strained.

"Yeah. Yeah, of course. Just woke up and haven't got the blood circulating yet."

Michaela was about to close the door when she spotted Liam's pixie sister approaching, her coal black hair streaked with varying shades of pink and blue. "What's up, girl?" she asked, motioning her to come in and join them.

As Catriona walked into the room, she and Arianna exchanged anxious glances. Michaela felt like she could have cut the tension in the air with a knife. "Okay, really guys. What's up?"

Just then, a resounding clap of thunder made her jump. "What the hell was that?" The words had no sooner left her lips than a blood-curdling scream shook the very foundations of the ancient manse. She sucked in a breath, terror in her eyes. All she could think was that the satanic visions that had haunted her for so long had suddenly come back in full force. "No, no, no," she mumbled under her breath.

"Come sit," Arianna ordered, pushing her toward the sofa in front of the unlit fireplace. Within seconds, the waning daylight was gone and the room plunged into darkness. As Arianna clicked on a table lamp, a musty cold and bitter wind swept through the space around them.

When Michaela began to shiver uncontrollably, her lifelong friend went to the fireplace and made a strange gesture with her hands. *Whoosh!* Flames shot from the empty grate, exploding up the flue like lighter fluid poured onto red-hot coals.

With a look of concern, Catriona sat down beside her, taking Michaela's hands in her own and rubbing them, the friction helping to bring a bit of warmth to her frozen digits. "Liam asked me to come be with you for this."

"For what, exactly?" Icy fingers of fear grabbed hold of her intestines and held on tight.

Arianna sat down on Michaela's other side. "They've reached a verdict. Liam figured that a hex against you might escape the magical charm holding Aideen, so he wanted us here for your protection."

"You know they had to have found her guilty," Catriona said, "Or Liam wouldn't have sent us up here."

"So, what happens next?"

"She'll either be banished to the middle earth or sentenced to death."

Michaela didn't need a mirror to know that her olive complexion had gone sickly white. "Sentenced to death? You mean they could execute her? How? When?"

Her friend's kind blue gaze was steady. "Whatever sentence is handed down will be carried out today."

"How's that possible? I mean, the trial was just this morning. What about an appeal? Is there no due process with you people?"

"It's complicated, honey." Arianna slipped an arm around her shoulders as lightning cracked the sky and the wind wailed outside the windows. The floor trembled violently beneath their feet. "I'm sure Liam will explain everything to you as soon as he can. Whatever decision was made, you can be assured that justice was served here today."

"Oh God. A woman could be dying right now and it's all my fault. I would never have agreed to testify if I'd known they could take her out and shoot her like a rabid dog the minute she was convicted."

"You've to understand that they'd no other choice but to deal with her harshly, Michaela," Catriona said. "She'd become that rabid dog you're after talking about, a danger to all who came within her personal space. An evil being, so she is, a practitioner of black magic, she was after dabbling in all manner of witchery, of sorcery. And for one of us, possessors of such extraordinary power at birth, the practice of the black arts intermingled with our own magic is a deadly combination."

Arianna turned to Michaela. "I have to tell you something, babe. If our husbands were forced into this decision today, they'll be torn to pieces over it. This is the time we'll need to be there for them, the way they're always here for us."

"Be there for them how? I don't know what you're talking about."

The other two women shared a knowing glance.

"We've always been straight up with each other, Mick," her friend began. "So, I'm just going to spell this out for you. Now, I know Liam was your first lover and you have nothing to compare him with. But surely you've noticed there's something different about him, a kind of wild, animalistic quality you didn't expect from his lovemaking."

Michaela raised her eyebrows, a smile flirting with her lips. "Yeah, and it suits me just fine. Still, he seems to worry about losing control and hurting me somehow. He always tries to be gentle with me—too gentle sometimes. But, what's that got to do with this?"

Arianna bit her lip. "Well, the fact is that all of our men can be rough in bed. The women too. Liam's probably been afraid that, because of your recent injuries, he might toss you around too hard and make you bang your head. Break a rib even. Let's face it, sweetie, something like that would make you afraid of him, which could put a real damper on your love-life."

Michaela gave a shrug. "I guess."

"Anyway, what you probably don't understand, Mick, is that sexual release can be a kind of healing balm to our men. If he wasn't married, Liam would just go off and hook up with one of our females, a woman with like appetites. Then he'd spend the next day or two in her bed, only coming out when he's succeeded in erasing the horrific memories that would otherwise haunt him."

Michaela's jaw dropped, her eyes opened wide. "If you're suggesting I give him a free pass to go off and screw the brains out of another woman…."

"Good God, no." Disgust in her voice, Arianna shook her head and exchanged an incredulous glance with Catriona, who looked shocked that Michaela would even think such a thing. "What I'm trying to say is that he needs to lose himself in you, Mick. And he'll hold back, afraid to let himself go, afraid of injuring you somehow. The way we take care of our husbands tonight is by drawing them out sexually, seducing them, taking the lead in giving them what they desperately need to survive this day emotionally."

As the bucketing rain poured down the tall windows, Catriona pointed. "Do you see that, Michaela? 'Tis but three in the afternoon and already it's as dark as midnight out there. Do you remember how the weather was when you got here today? Clear skies and gentle breezes, just as it was forecast? This hellish storm is all Aideen's doing, called down as a last rebellion, a demonstration of her destructive power, of her belief that not even the strongest rune can contain her." Catriona sighed and shook her head. "Nor death itself."

Arianna touched her shoulder. "She has no intention of going gentle into that good night," her friend said, softly quoting one of

Michaela's favorite poets.

Another clash of thunder and the floor beneath them began to buck and roll. A cacophony of voices echoed through the room. Another blood-chilling scream sounded amidst a symphony of animal roars, as if a city zoo had overtaken the entire bottom floor.

She was trembling, her heart pounding so loudly in her chest she was sure the others could hear it. Deathly afraid now, it occurred to her that she had spent far too much time in this condition over the past couple of months. The sick revelation settled into the pit of her stomach, leaving her with heart-wrenching questions. Had she made a huge mistake by marrying into this otherworldly clan? And was she brave enough to be a true wife to her husband tonight, the kind of wife that he needed?

A tormented shriek ricocheted throughout the underground chamber. Tara's hand jerked, and she almost lost her grip on the priceless artifact she had been so painstakingly cleaning. Had to be a myna bird, she told herself, since their calls were known to sound so human. Shaken by the experience, she couldn't understand why Michaela would have come suddenly to mind. Neither could she conceive of why the simple call of a bird would make her feel sick to her stomach, all weak and panicky as her adrenaline kicked her into in a fight or flight reaction.

A sudden drop in blood sugar from skipping both breakfast and lunch, she reasoned. Satisfied with the self-diagnosis, she set the lava-encrusted, centuries-old earring gingerly onto the worktable in front of her, before calling out to her associate working in the next chamber. "Mary, I'm doing a food and supplies run. Can I bring you back anything?"

The woman stuck her head around the corner and grinned. "I brought a sandwich with me this morning for lunch. But if you're going into town, I'd love a couple of shots of that dark Italian espresso you can get on the piazza."

"Got it." Tara brushed at her clothing, but was unsuccessful in wiping away the very fine ash still coating everything so many centuries after the eruption.

Since there was only one small café located within the ruins of the buried Roman city, Tara decided to head to the tourist village set up right outside the gates. Although she understood the need for the revenue generated by the tours to the local archaeological sites, she was irritated by the traffic and concerned about the potential destruction of historically significant discoveries.

Down a side street off the main square, Tara stopped in at Al Gamberone, a simple trattoria that served all of her Italian favorites. Sitting at a table by the window, she ordered a glass of Chablis and the cognac-doused shrimp. Although it was late in the afternoon, the restaurant was hopping with summer travelers, parents and their children laughing and playing as they enjoyed the last couple of weeks before school would begin again.

But even with the sun shining brightly through the window and the carefree celebration going on all around her, Tara felt chilled to the bone. She hoped she wasn't coming down with something like bird flu, or some other foreign virus. Whatever it was, she was definitely feeling off her game.

Of course, all of the recent changes in her life could have something to do with her feelings of melancholy. She was almost thirty-two years old and, for most of her life, Michaela and Arianna had been her closest family. Her adoptive parents had passed away a long time ago. Wonderful people, whom she had loved dearly, they had been in their late fifties when they brought her home from the hospital, the generation of most of her schoolmates' grandparents.

As the handsome, olive-skinned waiter brought her lunch to the table, the outrageous flirt gave her a wink. Pretending not to notice the overture, Tara ordered the espresso Mary had requested, asking that he have it ready for her when he brought the check.

Her stomach growled as she dug into the succulent shrimp dish. She decided that, when she wrapped things up here in Italy, she would talk to the girls about putting the condo on the market. Since her friends would no longer be living there, it wasn't fair for them to have their finances tied up in the property.

As she finished wiping up the last bite of sauce with the crusty Italian bread from a basket on the table, she acknowledged that what had really been eating at her was the fact that her two best friends seemed to be shutting her out of their lives. She wasn't an idiot. She knew there was something going on there that they were keeping from her. And it really hurt to know that she was no longer included in the confidences the three of them had shared since they were kids.

During their last conversation, Arianna had told her that when she fell in love one day, she would understand Michaela's actions. But a long time ago Tara had decided that she didn't require a man in her life. No, she never intended to allow herself to fall into a trap like that again.

After paying the bill, she scooped up the bag containing the double espresso and a takeaway order of tiramisu, and made her way back to the ancient site. With the sun baking the top of her head and a high temperature in the mid-eighties, the ice-cold chill that slithered up her spine as she left the restaurant defied explanation.

⁂

It was a solemn assembly. The ten members of the Council of Brehons sat in a semicircle in the holding chamber, facing the woman they had been forced to condemn to death. Her solicitor sat stoically in a straight-back chair beside her as the verdict was read.

"Hear ye, hear ye," the Brehon scribe began. "On full consideration of the capable defense solicitor's arguments, objections, counter-arguments and other evidence presented this day, the Defendant has been found guilty by a unanimous court."

Only slightly interested in the proceedings, Aideen peered at the Counsel members through the bars of her cell. "So, I've been convicted, is it? And just what will be my punishment, so? Will you banish me to the Land of Faerie, where I'm after choosing to spend most of my time, anyways, in a place far better than this? And from which I'll return however and whenever I wish it?"

Her solicitor leaned over and spoke a few quiet words in her ear. Whatever he said stopped the antagonizing taunts.

"Seamus," Caleb said, "will you continue the reading of the sentence, as requested by the Defendant?"

The large man nodded. "It is judged, adjudicated, and decreed that Aideen Bailey, date of birth 15 May 1981, is hereby sentenced to death pursuant to subsection 3.2a of the Brehon code. Said execution shall be carried out forthwith by way of remote cardiac cessation."

"What?" Fire in her eyes, the woman began to screech in protest. "The Council hasn't put anyone to death in over a hundred years! And you will do this to me? *Bastards*!! Death to the lot of you. *And* to the mere mortal, the subject of my demise. Hail Lucifer, great and mighty one. King of the underworld...."

With an outstretched hand, Caleb silenced the prisoner, her voice muted even as her lips continued to move, mouthing vile blasphemies against the living God.

In frustration, she thrashed against the bars of her prison cell, strengthened beyond the physical steel by the magical restraints that contained her. Static electricity crackled through the chamber, raising her auburn hair to pointed spikes. A foul-smelling wind wafted through the room, even as storm clouds began to form above the roof of the manse. The woman attempted to use whatever nefarious energy she might siphon from the powers of the air in an effort to escape the magical charms that bound her. As she realized her tantrum had managed nothing more than to shake the building's foundations, perhaps stir up a bit of wind, a drop of rain or two, the arrogance she had displayed during the trial for her life vanished like a puff of smoke into the atmosphere. Fear resided there now, evident for all to see by the look in her eyes.

Unimpressed by Aideen's antics and, with the rumble of thunder growing louder overhead, Caleb folded his hands together. "Does the condemned wish to make a final statement before the sentence is carried out?"

Eyes downcast, the woman shook her head.

"It is time," the Chief Brehon declared.

As the ten men closed their eyes and began to concentrate, a fluttering, not unlike the sound of a thousand humming birds, filled the air. Within mere seconds, the condemned woman slumped forward, sent painlessly into unconsciousness by the combined focus of the group. The convergence began to slow her heartbeat. Thump, thump. One beat. Two. A third, then a stutter, a sigh. And with one final exhalation, her life's breath left her lungs, her head bowed in death.

For the first time in a hundred years or more, the Council had been forced to terminate the existence of one of their own.

Father James rose to his feet and broke the silence. "Will ye all leave me now?" he asked. "Although this poor, misguided soul was not after desiring my prayers or the sacraments in this life, I'll sit with her now in silent meditation in the hopes that she might be elevated from purgatory."

Exchanging glances with the others, Caleb rose silently to his feet. "The rest of ourselves will meet in the drawing room." With that declaration, he led the way from the downstairs chamber.

⁂

The relentless storm, pounding walls and windows in an endless tantrum all throughout the afternoon, had begun to subside. While the men continued their meeting on the topic of the *Geis,* the wives went down to the kitchen and prepared a huge pot of beef stew for dinner. They sipped on hot beverages—coffee for Michaela and Arianna, tea for Catriona—and nibbled the raw vegetables they chopped as they braised the beef, before adding the carrots, celery and potatoes to the simmering pot. Although none of them had eaten since that morning, they didn't have much of an appetite.

Catriona set a fourth place at the old wooden table. "Cian will be joining us," she explained.

"Isn't he at the meeting?" Michaela asked.

"Sure, he's not a member of the Council," Catriona replied. "He was just after flying me here today so that I could testify."

After the four of them had finished eating, Cian thanked them for the meal and got up from the table. "We should get back to Sneem," he said to his wife. "Are you ready to leave?"

"Go on up and collect our things," she replied. "I'll help tidy up down here, then we can go."

"We've got this," Michaela said. "You go on now. I'll call you some time next week and we'll all get together."

Catriona flashed her brother's grin. "Didn't realize you Yanks were so bossy," she teased. Then giving each of the other women a quick hug, she left the room with her husband.

After they had finished tidying up the mess, Michaela turned to Arianna. "Should we deliver a bowl of stew to the guys? I don't know if they've taken a break since this morning, and it's after seven o'clock."

"Let me check."

Arianna did that eyes-closing, concentrating thing Michaela had seen her do before. Probably sending some kind of telepathic message to her husband, Michaela thought, finding it hard to believe how such a thing was beginning to feel normal to her.

Arianna hung the dishcloth over the faucet to dry. "Caleb said just to leave the pot on the stove. The meeting's ending soon and the men will have a bite together here in the kitchen before everyone heads for home."

Michaela nodded. "Okay. Well, guess we should head back on up to our rooms and start packing."

In the upstairs hall, the two friends hugged briefly.

"Be careful, sweetie," Arianna warned as they parted.

"Careful?"

Arianna sighed. "Yeah, the death sentence." She stumbled over the words. "Our husbands were not only required to act as judge and jury, but as executioner, as well."

A look of horror crawled across Michaela's face. "Oh my God, Arianna. They actually *killed* her?"

"Think about it, Mick. Isn't that the way it should always be? If those who passed judgement were required to carry out the sentence themselves it would make them more accountable for their decisions, wouldn't it?"

Michaela gave her head a shake, as if to clear it. "I…I don't know. I mean, logically, yes. Like if those who declared war were required to fight in the battle, there would be fewer wars, other methods of resolving disputes. But…to think of having someone's blood literally on your hands….I just couldn't do it."

She paused then, her brow furrowed in thought. "Why did you warn me to be careful? Am I in some kind of danger from him? I'm so confused."

"When he first gets back to you, he'll be dealing with the

fallout from all this and probably won't be himself for a while. He might not have the same level of self-control as usual in the bedroom." She paused, raised her brows. "Just sayin'…."

With that parting message, the girls gave each other another quick embrace and went to their rooms.

# Chapter Thirty-Four

As Michaela was collecting her husband's toiletries from the bathroom, she heard the door to the hall open and he called out to her. "Michaela?"

"In here." Meeting him in the bedroom, she tried to hide her stunned reaction to the change in his appearance. A darkness that was almost palpable seemed to be hovering over him, engulfing him. The seductive light in his cool blue eyes had dimmed, replaced by a stranger's bleak and brooding glare. Michaela swallowed hard and fought back a shiver of dread. "Is she…?"

"She is." His response was cold. Forbidding.

Michaela bit her lip and changed the subject. "Figured you'd be exhausted, so I started packing," she offered lightly. "I'm almost done, so we can leave for home whenever you're ready."

The word 'home' evoked a long sigh. His shoulders seemed to relax slightly. "I fancy getting out of this place as soon as possible."

Michaela slipped the razor and shaving cream she was holding into the leather toiletry bag in the suitcase on the bed. Turning, she moved into his arms. It was a stiff embrace, as if such an overt display of affection was an unfamiliar sentiment, an unknown occurrence in his regular environment, and one that made him uncomfortable. He was locked down, she thought, as if holding his emotions tightly in place lest he fall apart and shatter into a million pieces. "I'm so sorry, baby," she whispered into his ear. "I know you've had a terrible day." She heard him sigh, felt his body loosen as it molded around hers.

He nuzzled her ear. "'Tis over," he said simply, quietly. "Sure, it's time to get back to the estate now, so I can hold you in my arms. I need to be inside of you, wife, to fill you up until our joining is after replacing the madness of this day. I need to get lost in you, bury my hardness in your soft moist heat until it warms the chill of death invading my soul."

As her husband looked down at her, Michaela slowly unbuttoned his shirt, then her own. "There's no need to wait until we get home," she whispered. Her seductive gaze locked with his as the shirt slid from her shoulders onto the floor. Then she reached behind herself and unhooked her bra, letting her breasts fall free of the flimsy black fabric holding them. Sliding her hands up his chest, she wrapped her arms around his neck and pressed her naked breasts against him.

"You dare tempt me now, woman?" He drew a ragged breath. "Have you no concept of the risk you take?"

Whatever had happened downstairs earlier that day had scarred him, she thought. Aching and distraught, he was battling emotions with which he had no prior experience.

She stretched onto her toes and whispered in his ear. "I'm your wife, my love. For better, for worse, in good times and bad. So, I dare do whatever it takes to help ease your pain."

She toed off her ankle boots and unbuttoned her jeans. She drew the zipper down slowly, watching him watching her. Her thumbs hooked into the waistband of the faded denims and her black lace panties, and she slid them down her slender hips. She stepped out of the heap of fabric, then turned him around and pushed him roughly onto the bed. "Now, husband, take me to that place where nothing else in this world really matters."

His excitement at her ministrations obvious, he reclined on his elbows and watched her, his eyes moving languidly over his wife's exposed flesh. Each glittering glance was tactile, a heated touch on her naked body. She sucked in a breath. He looked so serious now. Dark and dangerous. The arrogant glint that had always looked back at her had gone, the familiar replaced by something so alien, so foreign, so devastatingly devoid of humanity, that fear of the unknown set her heart to beating mercilessly against her ribcage.

Master of his emotions, he had always been so contained, so self-controlled, she could only hope that the stresses of the day hadn't pushed her husband beyond his limit. Had she made a mistake here? Should she have risked enticing this man into a wild erotic encounter when his thoughts were still full of foreboding, his blood still boiling like hot lava with otherworldly power?

His heated gaze gone feral now, he tipped his head and considered her. An African lion nipping the scruff of his female's neck, holding her in place as he took her from behind.

Michaela shivered, the involuntary action provoked by a mix of fear and lust in equal measure. She felt the now familiar ruffling in her mind.

"You're afraid of me." The back of his fingers trailed down the side of her face.

Deflecting his observation, Michaela touched her finger to his lips. "Shhh…."

He turned his face into her hand and kissed her palm. "I would never hurt you, *a ghrá.* I'll take care of you. Protect you. *Go deo,* my love. Forever."

And with those sweet words of promise, Michaela knew that he would never let anything bad happen to her. She climbed onto the bed and straddled his thighs. Unbuckling his belt, she unsnapped his jeans and drew the zipper down, freeing his maleness from the constricting denim.

He groaned and, voice hoarse, whispered her name as she kissed her way up his body, over his flat, muscular abs, his lightly furred chest. She nibbled on his neck, breathed words of love and passion into his ear. Each time he would try to take the lead in their lovemaking, she would stop him. "No, baby. Just lie there now and let me give you pleasure."

As he quivered beneath her touch, groaned and cursed under his breath, she realized this was exactly what he had needed. She rose above him and took him deep inside her, sensing the release of his anguish, the unraveling of the knot of inner turmoil as she rode him, slow and deep, into a new reality. She felt a shift, as the air shimmered around them with a kind of metaphysical energy. And, for the first time, the two truly became one being. Remarkably, she could actually sense his feelings, share his thoughts. Such intimacy while in the act of lovemaking was a heady experience, an almost spiritual bond that enabled her to experience the desire he felt for her. She knew exactly how he wanted to be touched, when he wanted her to increase the pace or slow things down. At his weakest moment, this powerful man, her beloved husband, had let down all his guards and opened himself up to her. *Literally*. With a sort of mind meld, he had established this bi-directional telepathic coupling that would allow her to invade his mind, as he would invade hers. Moved beyond belief, she recognized his innate need to take control as he poured himself into her.

"Whatever you need, take it now, baby," she breathed. "Anything you want from me, my precious love, it's yours. All yours."

"I want you to come with me," he said softly, his arctic blue eyes staring up into hers.

Her lips turned up in a slight smile. "I like the sound of that."

When he reversed their positions, tucking her body beneath him, the room began to change, the walls to fall away from around them. And she knew that she had misunderstood his meaning. As if in a sweet dream, the room dissolved into a world of marshmallow clouds and scented breezes. Together they lay in fields of wild heather and purple clover in a place where time had no meaning. Hours passed, maybe days, as he loved her. And later, yes, much later, when they found their release it was mutual, and beautiful, and the most earth-shattering experience Michaela had ever known.

They didn't go home that night. Drained, both physically and emotionally, they fell into an exhausted sleep in one another's arms. Michaela's last thought before slumber overtook her was that her life was perfect. More perfect than she had ever imagined it could be.

How very sad it was that it could all come crashing down around their heads in a few weeks, when their lives together had only just begun.

ঌ৯

"*I'm back….*" Reminiscent of the movie *Poltergeist,* Aideen's singsong taunts whispered through the old Scottish manse. Spooned in Liam's arms, Michaela woke from a deep sleep to find an apparition drifting above their bed. *"Fools! They believe they're after ridding the world of my presence."* Her cackling laughter sent chills down Michaela's spine. The temperature in the room had dropped so low that her breath began to fog the air. *"But as you can see, I'm more powerful now that I've thrown off the flesh than ever I was in life."*

Michaela remembered the first time Aideen had intruded on them while they slept. Since she had used some kind of a sleeping spell on Liam, it was probably a useless endeavor to try to wake him up now. There *was* a difference this time, however. Liam was her husband now and, as she had been led to believe, their marriage offered her certain protections from the crazy goings on. Emboldened by this knowledge, she found her voice. "Really, Aideen? This again? Can't you find anything more interesting to do in the…spirit world, than to waste your time haunting your former lover and his new wife?"

*"Wife!"* The ghostly woman spit out the word. *"Are you not terrified of me? In fear for your life? Of where I might take you?"*

"Not really."

While Liam continued to sleep like the dead himself, Michaela wriggled out of his arms. She punched her pillow and stuffed it behind her back. Leaning against the mahogany headboard, she folded her arms across her chest. "Look, I know that now that we're married no one from the fairy kingdom can abduct me, so I guess I'm safe enough."

The dead woman looked perplexed for a moment, then her pale, shimmering face drew into the semblance of a pout. *"But…I'm a ghost!"*

"Yeah, I can see that. And I'm sorry for the way things turned out for you, Aideen, I truly am. But your behavior was really over the top, way over the top, even for you. And now showing up here tonight? Seriously? Whatever went on between the two of you while you were dating, well, it didn't work out. Liam and I are married now, so you just need to get over it. Get on with your…afterlife, or whatever."

Deflated, the apparition breathed an echoing sigh.

"You have to admit that spooking my horse was pretty messed up." Michaela's lips twisted with the accusation. "You could have gotten me killed, or worse. You could left me in a wheelchair for the rest of my life."

A flickering shoulder shrugged in dismissal. *"Had the notion that you were after stealing me man. Let my temper get the better of me, so I did."*

Michaela couldn't believe how her life had changed. Here she was, having a chat with her husband's ex—who just happened to be a freaking ghost—as if it were the most natural thing in the world. "So, you've just been…floating around the estate here since your…death?"

*"Execution."* The woman uttered the correction in a dismal tone. The more she and Michaela spoke, the more solid her form became. Her feet mere inches above the wooden floor, she floated to an armchair on the side of the bed and settled into it.

"And there was no light to follow, no…angels leading the way to heaven?"

*"Heaven?"* The shivery laugh that followed could have come from a blockbuster horror flick. *"Haven't been down below,"* she said, as if speaking to herself. Michaela assumed she was referring to hell. *"It's very scary, very different than when I was after dabbling in the occult. 'Twas a game I was playing at the minute."*

"So, you think you're going to hell?" Michaela asked in a hushed tone.

*"Aye, but truth be told, in life, I'd fancied meself quite the important personage in the kingdom of darkness. Even expected to be elevated to some high position in Lucifer's government, so I did. But wasn't I deceived? Sure, life's breath had no sooner left me body than he was after sending a couple of his foul-smelling demons to come and collect me, to drag me down to the fiery pit. What he failed to take into account, however, is that he's not dealing with a mere mortal here. And haven't I successfully evaded the bastards for the better part of the day."*

There was no question that Aideen had brought all this upon herself. But, even with that—*and* the fact that she had caused Michaela a ton of torment and grief—she couldn't help but feel a certain level of pity for the plight of the misguided woman. "What are you going to do?"

She sighed dramatically. *"Reckon I'll become one of those tragic ghostly spirits that forever haunts the place of her death."*

But no sooner had the words whispered from her lips than a swirling vortex, like a steel-gray tornado cloud, began to form in the center of the room. Sliding further down in the bed in fear of the sight, Michaela gagged at the noxious smell of rotting flesh as two gargoyle-like monsters began to emerge from the midst of the strange twister. Dumbstruck, she turned her stricken gaze toward Aideen, who was observing the unfolding scenario in disbelieving horror.

As the demonic creatures reached for her, Aideen struck out at them with a wild array of hexes and incantations that had likely served her well in the past. But all the magic she threw at them this time, in her incorporeal form, proved useless as their blood-encrusted talons snared their prey. Just like that, the condemned woman began to dissolve…to melt like hot fudge into a dark, gelatinous ooze, reminding Michaela of the demise of Oz's Wicked Witch of the West.

Frozen in place, Michaela peeked over the edge of the duvet. Her gaze locked on the horror show unfolding in front of her as the puddle that had once been Aideen dripped into a wide, dark abyss opening in the floor beneath her.

As soon as she stopped trembling and could move her frozen muscles and joints, Michaela rolled from under the covers and fell onto her knees beside the bed. Remembering the face of the gentle Son of God during their poignant encounter, the words that she spoke turned prayer into a conversation. "Oh, Lord, you who are loving and kind, have mercy on that poor, poor woman. And, Heavenly Father, please, *please*, don't give up on us down here. You, who are omniscient, all-powerful, the Beginning and the End, I beg You to protect the people of this planet, your own creation. Don't let these godless creatures take possession of your beautiful world. For this, I pray in the name of your Son."

Long after the floor had become solid again, Michaela could still hear the bloodcurdling howls of the damned. A sound that would stay with her forever…if they had that long.

# *Chapter Thirty-Five*

This was getting ridiculous, Tara thought. Between the restless legs and the inability to shut her mind down for sleep, she was lying in bed staring up at the ceiling of her hotel room. *Yet again.* The unseasonable storm pounding against the windows wasn't helping matters either. And, while the deadline for wrapping up the Pompeii expedition was looming, work stress had never affected her sleep patterns before. The only thing she could attribute the insomnia to was watching CNN late at night before going to bed. Images from the onslaught of horrific world events seemed to replay over and over again in her head, affecting her ability to drift off to sleep.

It also didn't help that this dig had proved particularly unsettling, spawning a string of nightmares where ghostly spirits haunted the preserved remains of the bodies she studied during the day. And then there was the issue of the tools and paperwork being constantly rearranged. Tara had worked with Mary and Jim enough in the past to know that the problem didn't lie with them. The occasional growls and groans and inexplicable bumps in the night had become so common Mary had joked that the comedy of errors might be poltergeist activity.

Poltergeist? Not likely.

Whatever was going on, Tara was exhausted and really in need of a break. And while she usually scheduled downtime between expeditions into her calendar, she was in no hurry to return home to an empty apartment. With both of her lifelong friends suddenly married and living halfway around the world, she didn't want to deal with the loneliness of banging around in the empty place all by herself.

Fortunately, an unexpected opportunity had presented itself yesterday, a job that she had turned down months ago due to her prior commitment to Pompeii. The historical society had contacted her again, when health issues forced their current director to resign. That the project was located in Ireland was a definite plus in her decision to accept the position. Besides, it would be a nice change of pace, working with a group of archeological grad students on the interesting study. Having moved into a crannog community a couple of months ago, they had been living in the lake dwellings, as had former residents of three thousand years ago.

She had reported the new assignment to Arianna when her friend called to check in with her that afternoon. Although she would be kept busy, Tara would still have time to spend with the new baby, while acclimatizing to the idea of returning home alone.

Sighing, she climbed out of bed and grabbed the emergency bottle of melatonin she kept in her suitcase for occasional bouts of jetlag. Popping a tablet in her mouth, she downed it with a big swig of bottled water. Getting back under the sheets, she took a book off the nightstand and opened to the page she had bookmarked the night before. The scientific text was dry and boring, even by her standards, but she read it until she felt the telltale signs of drowsiness tugging at her eyelids. Punching her pillow, she turned onto her side, hoping for a good night's sleep sans the recurrent night terrors.

During their flight back to County Kerry the following morning, Michaela had finally told Liam about Aideen's after-death encounter. Why she had hesitated to discuss it with her husband until then, she had no idea. To say that he hadn't been happy about her delay in sharing the information would have been an understatement.

Since neither of them were much into drama, he stewed in silence the rest of the flight back. When she was heading upstairs to unpack their luggage, he disappeared into the study without a word. "Probably on the phone with Caleb, telling him about the spookfest with Aideen," she muttered under her breath, slamming his shirts and jeans into the dresser drawers. "The fact that he would do something like that, before we've even had the chance to work out our own differences on the subject is…is just…." Frankly, it irked the very crap out of her.

She wasn't stupid. She knew all too well that a crisis of cosmic proportions was plummeting toward them, like the freaking meteor suspected to have ended the Jurassic Age. But did *everything* in their married life have to revolve around that problem?

After getting all of their clothes put away, she headed down to the study. As expected, she found Liam at his desk, talking on the phone. Plopping down onto the sofa, she grabbed a magazine off the coffee table and began to flip through the pages. She wasn't eavesdropping, not with her hot new husband speaking in Irish so she couldn't understand a single word.

*How convenient.*

After ending the call, Liam spent a couple of minutes shuffling papers around on the desk before looking up. His cold, hard gaze hit her square in the face, his expression so distant, so totally devoid of feeling, that it made her heart ache in her chest. This was it, the one thing she would never be able to live with. The *only* thing that could eventually mess up this fairytale marriage of theirs would be her husband's uncanny ability to close himself off, to shut her out completely, without so much as a second thought.

"You want to talk about this?" In a pissy mood herself, she was having a hard time taking the high road. "Or are you planning on just pouting about it for the rest of the day?"

His eyes met hers in a level stare.

"Don't do that!" she snapped at him. "If you have something to say to me, then damn well just say it."

Without responding to her gibes, he pushed back from his desk, stood up and headed for the door. Michaela jumped to her feet and blocked his path. Both hands on his chest, she gave him a slight shove. "Don't ignore me when I talk to you!"

The look of surprise on his face was far better than the bland, don't-give-a-damn expression that had previously been there. "Sure, you don't want to do this right now, wife." Eyes sparking with something indefinable, he said the word 'wife' in a low, sexy growl.

Unwilling to allow him to turn their disagreement into makeup sex, she shoved him again, a little harder this time. *Bearding the lion in his den.* "You, me, upstairs," she demanded. "We'll work this out in the dojo."

Before she spun and turned her back on him, she caught a glimmer of respect warming the arctic coldness in his eyes.

She stretched her tense muscles, warming up as she waited for him to follow her upstairs. After a few minutes passed, she was beginning to think he was blowing her off, when the door opened. "Right. Let's do this," he said, pulling his tee-shirt over his head.

No fair, she thought, distracted by the nicely sculpted abs, the contoured pecs and muscular arms. *So, he wants to play dirty.*

Tearing off her own shirt, she tossed it aside and began to circle him, her black lace bra returning the distraction. "No magic," she muttered.

"Aye, and I'll be needing that, like," he shot back, voice dripping with sarcasm.

Accustomed to sharing their workouts, she stepped into him

with a familiar series of kicks and chops, a ballet of karate blows all expertly pulled, which he returned in kind. How long they moved back and forth across the floor in that dance of defiance, she couldn't say. But a drop of sweat rolled into her eyes at the exertion and she glanced away, looking for a towel.

His right leg shot out and tangled with hers, bringing her down to the matted floor. His body slick with perspiration, he rolled on top of her, clearly aroused. Her hands trapped above her head in one of his, he took her mouth in a punishing kiss, while his other hand made short work of the yoga pants she had slipped into for comfort after arriving home.

Delivered of the aforementioned bra and her matching panties, she lay naked beneath her husband, all marital discord immediately forgotten. Raising her head, she nipped at his lips, using the diversion to tug one hand free of his grasp. Then, giving as good as she got, she pushed her hand into his workout shorts, evoking a low moan that she could feel radiating from his chest to hers. She stripped off the fabric that was the final barrier standing between them and wrapped her legs around his hips, the sparring match with this unique specimen of a man all the foreplay a girl could ever need.

But he raised his hips, refusing to take what she offered. "Look at me."

Her heart melted inside her, for written in the depths of that glittering gaze was all the love, the truth, the depth of feeling she had ever dreamed of finding there. "I love you, Liam. And, I'm sorry—"

"Shhh…." His finger moved across her lips. "No, *mo chroí*. 'Tis I, meself, the one should be apologizing. Sure, I've been behaving like a complete horse's arse."

"Yeah." Hands framing his face, she smiled up at him. "You were being a bit of a jackass."

He covered her mouth with his, silencing her teasing, then began to move against her. She gasped and he chuckled. "You were saying?"

"Nothing," she murmured breathlessly. "Just make love to me, husband. We'll finish this conversation later."

"First, let me explain. 'Twas sheer terror after gripping me when I learned of your confrontation with Aideen. I can't countenance the possibility of anything ever happening to you, *a mhuirnín.* You've become a part of me, the very essence of the man I am. My life would be a cold, dark existence without you, sure a journey I'd not be able to bear."

Marking their union with those words of love—words Michaela had never allowed herself to believe she would ever hear—her husband joined their bodies, the two truly becoming one…one beating heart, one breathing soul. Forever.

During the next few weeks, life was idyllic. Wrapped in their own private cocoon of happiness, the newlyweds had adjusted nicely to married life. For Michaela, even the day-to-day displays of hocus-pocus, including the mystical sexcapades in the bedroom, had become almost commonplace.

Oh, yeah, she thought, life with her magical mystery man definitely suited her.

A couple of hours ago, Liam had ridden his motorcycle into town to do some errands. Michaela stretched out on the sofa in the study to watch some TV. The five o'clock news on TG4 was just starting. She grabbed the remote off the coffee table and changed the channel. Avoiding the constant barrage of bad news made it easier not to acknowledge that the rest of the world was falling apart around her. How else could she ignore the fact that the happy little bubble she was living in now was about to burst?

It was like watching the Book of Revelation come to life. The floods, earthquakes, volcanic eruptions and other cataclysmic weather aberrations were increasing planet-wide. With stock markets failing, the global economy continued to plummet at an alarming rate. The economic crisis, plaguing nations around the world for almost a decade now, had become like a massive sinkhole, sucking banks and financial institutions into its depths. Corporations were closing their doors, with the resulting unemployment sending societal problems, such as crime and homelessness, soaring to epidemic proportions.

One of the most serious threats to the future existence of mankind, however, was the proliferation of nuclear weapons in third-world countries…like Iran. With no resolution to the problems in the Middle East and other hotbed areas of the world, the threat of a holocaust rose exponentially. And while governments around the globe had begun holding summits to address possible solutions to the worldwide crises, so far it had all been to no avail.

Like lambs to the slaughter, Michaela mused. It was heartbreaking to watch creation fight for its very survival, a cosmic battle the origins of which they were completely unaware. It was already the first of October, with Halloween, the deadline for resolution of this…gesh…thing, fast approaching. And if Liam's behavior was any indication, no one else, even remotely meeting the criteria for the Woman of Promise, had yet come to the Council's attention.

With every passing day, her hope for deliverance grew slimmer, while she and Liam clung desperately to the fragile joy they had found, only too aware that it could all be over in a matter of weeks.

Michaela's phone rang. Probably Liam calling to see if she needed him to pick up anything from the store on his way home from the bank. "Hello?"

"Hey you," Arianna said.

"Oh, hey, girlfriend. What's up?"

"Not much. Just wanted to let you know I talked to Tara today. You know, Mick, with her parents both gone she's essentially alone in the world. I've been thinking, if things go pear-shaped, I want her here with us. I don't want her going through all that horror by herself."

"Yeah, I've been worried about that too. She's not talking to me much lately, though. Still pissed about me getting married without telling her."

"Yeah, well, it looks like we won't have to be worrying about that anymore."

"Really? How's that?"

"You know she was wrapping things up in Italy and planning to head back home?"

"Yep."

"Well, there's been a change of plans. She got a call about taking over an ongoing gig. Turns out it's here in County Clare."

"No way."

"Yes, way. The project's scheduled to last for several more weeks, which will put her here with us if things do end up going south. Sorry, sweetie. Can you hold on a minute?" Her voice muffled, Arianna called out to someone on her end. "I'm in the bedroom. Yeah, just bring him in here to me." Back on the phone again, she sighed. "Looks like I gotta go, Mick. My little man's hungry again."

"No worries, babe. Give my boy a big kiss from his auntie."

"Will do."

"And, Arianna? Liam and I will come up to the castle when Tara gets in town."

"Perfect. Love you, honey."

"Yeah, love you, too."

Michaela ended the call. As she was setting the phone back on the table, she heard Liam banging through the front door, no doubt loaded down with shopping bags. She couldn't help but consider just how normal their lives seemed. They could have been any happily married couple, in any home, anywhere in the world.

And she was happy, happier than she had ever been in her life, than she had ever believed possible. And she planned to make the most of every minute of that happiness, of whatever time she and Liam had left together, until death—or worse—did them part.

With that grim thought dimming the smile on her face, she headed to the kitchen to help her new husband put the groceries away.

"Hey, baby." She kissed Liam's shoulder as he reached up to place a box of Irish oats into the cabinet.

"Hiya." He gave her long braid a playful tug. "So, any new *craic* since I left this morning?"

"Yeah, I talked to Arianna right before you got home." Michaela took the cauliflower, celery and carrots out of the bag from the green grocers and pulled open the door to the fridge.

"Spoke to Caleb earlier meself. We're discussing the idea of the Council and our family members all moving into the castle, holding down the fort there, so to speak."

"When?"

"Within the week."

With the bags all emptied, Michaela took a big bowl out of the cabinet and set about to make them a little late lunch. She dragged lettuce, tomato, avocado, red onion, cucumber and bell pepper out of the vegetable drawer and began to chop, tear and slice the ingredients for a salad. Noting her husband's expression, she chuckled. "I'm not feeding you 'rabbit food', so don't look so depressed, you big baby. I'll heat up the leftover lamb and mashed potatoes from last night's dinner for you."

As the couple sat at the table eating their lunch, a family of deer frolicked outside the kitchen window. Smiling at their antics, Michaela took a sip of iced tea. "Oh, yeah. Forgot to tell you,

Arianna said that Tara—you know, my tall, *hot,* archaeologist friend you met at the castle?—well, she'll be coming to Clare in a few days to take over some ongoing expedition."

Michaela didn't think anything of her comment, until she noted her husband's strange expression. "What? Why are you looking at me like that?"

"Dunno. Felt a strange chill up me spine, like somebody walking over me grave." At the concern in Michaela's eyes, he deflected the observation. "'Tis nothing, I'm sure."

A thoughtful frown crowded Michaela's brow. "Wait a minute. You said the Council members will be moving into the castle until the…the end?"

He turned to look at her. "Aye?"

Michaela got up and went to the kitchen island to get more of the oil and vinegar for her salad. "Tara will be working in town, so she'll be staying at the castle with Arianna. My friend's a…a mere mortal, Liam."

"So she is."

"You don't think that she…that it's possible…." Before she completed the thought, she negated her own suggestion. "Never mind. Delete that."

Liam raised a questioning brow?

"You don't know her, honey. Believe me, Tara's the most rational, reasonable, analytic—the most *anal*—person I've ever known. She's a scientist. If she can't see it, feel it, touch it, she doesn't believe it. There's no way she'd have anything to with all this supernatural chaos."

Liam sighed. "Your friend's an archaeologist, *a stór.* The dissolution of the *Geis* requires that the Woman of Promise locate an ancient artifact, a ring that's been hidden for three thousand years. 'Twouldn't be so strange a twist of fate should she turn out to be the One."

"Oh, God. No." Michaela's heart sank as she remembered the hell of the paranormal attacks she experienced during her first few days in Ireland. "If that's true, she'll be in terrible danger. She'll believe she's losing her mind."

Getting up from the table, Liam pulled his wife to her feet and held her in his arms. "*If* your friend is the One, *mo chroí*, we'll do all in our power to protect her. But that's a big *if*, is it not? Let's not get ahead of ourselves now, will we? We've still over a month to go. And, while I'm not at liberty to discuss specifics, there's been some mention of another who might fit the perimeters of the Chosen One."

Michaela buried her face in her husband's broad shoulder. "Or, maybe I'm this…woman…everybody's waiting for. And when I found out about everything…." A shuddering sigh left her lungs. "We could be doomed already and not even know it."

The back of her head cupped in his hand, Liam sighed again. "We'll just wait and see, now won't we, *a ghrá*. All will be well in the end, my love. Now come, let's finish eating."

A stricken look on her face, she sat back down. With hopelessness taking up residence in her heart, one question haunted her: What if turned out there was no other redeemer? Would it be worse if Michaela had been meant to be the One? For the world to come crashing to an end with no hope of salvation at all? Or for her precious friend to arrive here in Ireland only to be tag-teamed into a cosmic battle against every demon in hell—including the devil himself?

-- THE END --

## ***THE POET PLEADS WITH THE ELEMENTAL POWERS***

By William Butler Yeats

THE Powers whose name and shape no living creature knows
    Have pulled the Immortal Rose;
And though the Seven Lights bowed in their dance and wept,
    The Polar Dragon slept,
His heavy rings uncoiled from glimmering deep to deep:
    When will he wake from sleep?
Great Powers of falling wave and wind and windy fire,
    With your harmonious choir
Encircle her I love and sing her into peace,
    That my old care may cease;
Unfold your flaming wings and cover out of sight
    The nets of day and night.
Dim powers of drowsy thought, let her no longer be
    Like the pale cup of the sea,
When winds have gathered and sun and moon burned dim
    Above its cloudy rim;
But let a gentle silence wrought with music flow
    Whither her footsteps go.

# *DARK AWAKENING*

## *Chapter One*

*There were giants in the earth in those days; and also after that, when the sons of God came in unto the daughters of man, and they bare children to them, the same became mighty men which were of old, men of renown…*Genesis 6:4

And thus it would be again, thought the Minion chosen for the highest honor in this world's final countdown, as he watched the activity down below with increasing interest. Those not originally of the earth—the ones who had stumbled across the planet in a trip across the galaxies and become enmeshed in the drama of the ages—were scurrying about, running this way and that, aware that time was running out, all the while mistaken about the ultimate outcome. They believed that, without the intervention of the Woman, all life in their world would come to an end. Nothing, however, could have been further from the truth. Though perilous times would descend upon mewling mankind, their fate would be much worse than extinction. They would pray for death and never find it, for in a physical realm the service of physical beings would be required. Creation would forfeit their divine inheritance. It would be ripped from their puny grasp and given to the fallen ones, those deserving of the first fruits of the new earth's existence.

Human males would be tagged and enslaved, simple mules for the work of the new administration. And, just as the sons of God had mated with the daughters of man in the beginning, so it would be again, their glorious offspring born a hybrid race of man and demon, living as giants upon the land.

Even now, all who populated Hades fixed their eyes unflinchingly on the Clock of the Ages. As the hand struck one minute before midnight, an uncharacteristic excitement spun like a whirlwind throughout the nine circles of hell. Even those souls condemned to an eternity in the fiery pit seemed to conceive a flutter of hope. Perhaps they might be granted a special dispensation or, at the very least, a trustee position within the kingdom of darkness.

Selected from amongst the worst of the worst that this heaving netherworld had to offer, the Minion waited impatiently for his commander's call to action. For weeks now, for months, the princes of the air had been moving back and forth across the earth, searching, seeking out that one Mortal being so vile, so devoid of hope and goodness, that he or she would freely sign a death warrant on all of humanity. At the appointed time, the Minion would possess that willing puppet and tug on its strings, forcing it to dance to the mesmeric beat of the Lost Chord of the Ancients, until that sacred melody was no more. Quenched by the death of the Woman, the only One who might save humankind from the coming destruction.

Those inhabitants of the earth who had arrived in ships so long ago were more ignorant than the Minion would have believed, had he ever chosen to consider such irrelevant matters. So stupid were they, in fact, that they deserved to die, their numbers further populating the underworld. To believe that they had any chance of salvation at the hands of a woman, a *mere mortal* woman no less, was sheer idiocy on their part.

And as the ticking of the Clock grew ever louder, the Minion watched....

❧

For the past several months a team of archaeological grad students had been participating in the Crannóg Habitat, a six-week communal living experiment replicating the lifestyles of Neolithic Europe lake dwellers in circa 3500 BC. Tara arrived on the first day of October to take over the ongoing project, filling a position left vacant by the illness, and subsequent death, of the previous director, a man highly regarded by his staff and volunteers. Under these most unfortunate circumstances, Tara anticipated that her first meeting with her team would be difficult, at best.

The project's Assistant Director, Heather Moore, a Canadian at work on her thesis at University of Toronto's Anthropology Department, opened the meeting and introduced Tara to everyone gathered around the long table in the historical society's conference room.

Tara read the faces looking back at her. There was Heather, of course. An attractive young woman. Sullen, moody. Apparently of the belief that she, as the project's second-in-command, should have been promoted to Site Director when the position became available. Definitely not an ally.

Of the seven grad student volunteers actually living in the habitat, she saw a wide range of emotions displayed, keen interest from one or two, complete boredom from all the others. Not unusual, she considered. Their passion was the study itself, not the administrative duties required to assess and document.

As Tara was about to address her staff, the door opened and a tall, handsome man walked quietly into the room. He slid the strap of a worn brown leather satchel off his shoulder and sat down in a chair along the wall. Tara glanced at him and then continued. "As you're all aware, it was requested that I take over this project after your former director, Sean Cahill, was forced to resign his position just prior to his death. And, while I'm sure I'll enjoy working with all of you, may I offer my condolences on your loss and tell you how much I regret the manner in which this opening came about. As scientists, we'll of course see this project through to the end and publish our findings. Might I add that I find this an interesting concept, and I look forward to your input as I get brought up to speed on your progress to date. Now, would each of you be kind enough to introduce yourselves and tell me a little about you?"

The man directly to her right cracked a welcoming smile. Cool, an ally, Tara thought, as he spoke up first. "Me name's James Duffy and I'm studying for me master's in the Forensic Archeology Program at NUIG, National University at Galway." Dark hair, blue eyes. Very cute. And very *young.* "Here in the program, I'm playing the part of the eldest son of a family of four. Also, I'm keeping all the activity logs for our group. Anyway I can help you, just let me know."

When meeting a group of people for the first time, Tara tagged each of them with a single word, phrase or name that would help her associate them with their personalities. This one, *Faithful puppy,* she thought with an inward smile. "Thanks, James. I'd really like to get my hands on those logs before the day's over."

"I'll be back over for a supply run about five. I'll bring them then."

"Perfect."

The introductions continued counter-clockwise around the table: Caoife Blake, age twenty-two, another student at NUIG, specialized in forensic archaeology. Her serious eyeglasses and severely pulled back hair earned her the tag, *Studious monkey.*

The others were all doctorate program students from various colleges and universities, all Irish born, according to their speech patterns. Tara figured the study contained a good sampling of ages, the participants ranging from their early-twenties to retirement age.

Bridget and Flynn were 'green' advocate hippie-types originally from the south of Ireland, where they boasted of designing and residing in their own dome habitat. *Cheech and Chong.*

Aisling Hanrahan looked to be about thirty, very pretty in a bleach-blonde, airheaded sort of way. Lots of luck with the thesis, *Paris Hilton.*

Tara perked up when Maire Adair began to introduce herself. No makeup and short, no nonsense, brown hair, she was an academic and researcher about forty-five years old. *Marie Curie,* Tara thought. Sharp lady, should be a big help.

Then there was Eoin Brady, a local businessman about thirty years old. He was quiet and introspective, didn't say enough for Tara to get a handle on him. And then he reached into his pocket, grabbed a tissue and sneezed several times. Allergies, Tara thought. *Sneezy.*

The last to speak was Donncha Collins, clearly the elder of the group. A retired math professor about sixty years old, he had returned to school late in life, probably to check a PhD off his bucket list. *Grumpy.*

In addition to the seven grad students, a reporter attended the group. In her mid-thirties, Ceara O'Donohue was purportedly writing an article on the experience for some academic journal. *Lois Lane.*

With introductions made, Tara excused the staff, telling them that she would be visiting each of them individually throughout the day to get a handle on the status of the project. As they filed out of the room, talking amongst themselves, the Assistant Director, Heather hung back, shuffling paperwork.

The man who had been observing from the back wall got to his feet and approached them.

"May I help you?" Tara asked him.

"Oh, this is Dr. Darmody," Heather gushed, cheeks flooding with color.

"MacDara," the man corrected.

Tara held her hand out to him. "Tara Price. I'm the new site director."

The man's large, warm hand enfolded hers. "Nice to meet you." The rasp of his voice was dark lilting velvet drawn slowly across sensitized flesh.

Tara shook off the impression.

"Dr. Darmody's a clinical psychologist and an ancient civilizations anthropologist," Heather said, filling in the blanks. Her eyes were too bright, pupils dilated. "He's a professor at NUIG, and was a consultant on the initial planning and set-up of the habitat during the funding stage."

The man was striking. Tall, always a plus for Tara. Topping 5'8", she only came up to his shoulders. His hair was a deep, rich chestnut, long and caught back in a leather thong. His sinfully dark eyes drew her in, that slow, sensual smile turning Heather's incessant chatter into an annoying fly buzzing in the background.

Heather's voice finally broke the spell. "Dr. Price? Um…. Is something wrong?"

*Damn. I was staring.* "Sorry. For a second there, I thought I recognized your name," she backpedaled, directing her reply to the man.

"Perhaps you've read some white paper, or other, that I've authored."

"Maybe." While Tara politely offered an agreement, her eidetic memory told her that wasn't it at all.

"The board was after contacting me about Sean's heart attack," he explained. "They requested that I come over and help you get up to date on the project."

Tara forced her gaze away from that full lower lip. An unhappy affair in her teens had left her pregnant and heartbroken, abandoned to face a miscarriage alone. A cynic when it came to romance, she wasn't a prude. But she was picky, her sexual liaisons rare and based on mutual respect and desire, not phony proclamations of love everlasting.

Nonetheless, she couldn't deny the rare jolt of connection. As if he were the glue that would mend the pieces of her broken heart, someone important to her, missing from her life for far too long.

*Whoa. Where in hell did that come from?* Thankfully, it had taken only one good look at Heather—*Eager Beaver,* she dubbed her now with an inward snicker—salivating all over the man to snatch Tara right back out of fantasyland.

Been there, done that. And never going back again.

She offered the far-too-handsome man a polite smile. "Thank you, Dr. Darmody. I really appreciate your dropping by. But I think I'll take a day or two and review the project to date. If I have any questions, I'll contact you."

※

Nowhere close to getting out of here, it was already quarter past five before Tara stopped to call Arianna. "Hey, it's me."

"So, how's your first day?"

"Crazier than usual. Never taken over for another director before, so I've been trying to get a handle on how well their current procedures are working before I institute some of my own."

"Wow, what a mish-mash."

"Yeah, knew it would be. I think it's gong to be interesting though. A little out of my comfort zone, since everything I've done in the past has involved dig sites."

"I'm sure you'll get up to speed without any problem. So, you heading over here soon?"

"That's why I'm calling. It looks like I'm not getting out of here until late tonight. Can I get a rain check on dinner? I'm really fried and figured I'd just grab some fast-food on my way to your old place."

"No problem. I left the key for you under the mat. Clean sheets are on the bed, towels in the linen closet. Also stocked in a few snacks and coffee for the morning, to hold you until you get a chance to get to the store."

"You're a star, babe. So, little Mama, how's my new nephew doing?"

"He's amazing, of course."

Tara chuckled. "Of course." There was a quick rap on her office door, and it began to open. "Guess I better go. Got someone coming in."

"Okay. Call me. Let me know if you need anything."

"Will do. Love you."

"You too." Setting her phone on the desk, Tara smiled at her visitor. *Faithful puppy.* "Hey, James. What's up?"

"Just bringing over the daily logs you asked for earlier. And a coffee." He held up a Styrofoam cup. "Was going bring you a cuppa tea, but then figured, since yer a Yank…"

"No, this is definitely what I need. Thank you."

He set the cup on her desk and dropped a couple of sugar and creamer packets beside it. "Do you fancy going over any of the paperwork before I head back to the site? We could order in a bite…."

"Thanks, but no. I'm up to my eyeballs here. I'll review the logs and get back to you and your team with any questions."

He looked disappointed, but with a good-natured smile and a wave, left her to her work.

A couple of hours passed, as Tara plowed through the data. She discovered that no observations, qualitative or quantitative, had been recorded on the charts since the previous director had left his post over a week ago. As Assistant Director, Heather should have stepped in and overseen these items in the interim. Slacker.

*Probably too busy flirting with Dr. Mac-Sexy to get anything substantive accomplished.*

Tara pushed back from her desk. Leaning back in her chair, she stretched and massaged her temples to relieve the edges of a stress headache pushing against the back of her eyes. Concluding that she ought to have her vision checked, she decided to wrap things up for the night.

After tidying her workspace, she threw on her backpack, and then pulled the strap of her purse over one shoulder. As she left the temporary offices in Craggaunowen, where the Crannógs had been reconstructed, it was only eight o'clock. She gazed across the lake at the artificial island, where fires built by the project participants stood in stark relief against the darkness of the night. She inhaled a long, deep breath of the smoke-scented air. The climate was moist and crisp, still not bad for October. While she wouldn't bother digging in the luggage she had left in the trunk of the Skoda Superb she had rented at the airport early that morning, she made a mental note to bring a light jacket to work with her in the morning.

She pulled open the door and tossed her purse and backpack into the back seat of the car. As she was pulling out onto the N85, she glanced at the GPS on her satellite phone, confirming that it was the shortest route to Arianna's cottage in Ennistymon, about a fifty-minute drive. She had gotten so used to driving on the left side of the road in many of the countries she had visited, that shifting with her left hand had become almost second nature and she moved through the gears smoothly, hardly giving it a second thought. This was Ireland, where the condition of much of the main route was like a back road in a third world country. With few directional signs and even fewer streetlights, she strained to see the road, happy that at least it wasn't raining. While she liked the privacy of having the little place to herself for the few weeks she was in town, she was afraid she might have to rethink her plans. It would no doubt be easier if she found temporary accommodations in Quin, which was only about a twelve-minute commute from the job site.

Eyes aching and the headache that had been threatening finally kicking in to full gear, she felt grateful to finally be arriving at her destination. As she pulled into Arianna's front yard, her headlights shone bright against the two-story cottage. The building was crisp and white, the shrubbery brushing against the outer walls trimmed and well maintained. So, there was no accounting for the unreasoning fear that suddenly grabbed hold of her, leaving her shaky, her palms sweating, stomach tied into knots. But then it occurred to her that the only other time she had visited the property had been at Thanksgiving, almost a year ago—when she and her friends had all been kidnapped. Funny, how the mind worked, she thought. She had had no idea that she was still harboring emotional trauma from the experience.

Leaving her headlights on, Tara unloaded the car and hauled her luggage to the front door. Unlocking it, she felt around on the wall inside the foyer for a light switch. Failing to locate one, she opened the flashlight app on her smart phone and made her way to a lamp on a small table in the living room. With the light on, the room looked warm and inviting, lightly scented with the floral fragrance of potpourri.

Heading back to the car, Tara reached inside the driver's side and turned off the headlights. Plunged into darkness, she grabbed her phone out of her pocket and again made good use of the flashlight. As she looked down to click the door locks, her peripheral vision picked up a flash of something running past the other side of the car. Heart pounding, she immediately pointed her phone in the direction of the movement, but whatever it had been was now gone.

Usually more aware of her surroundings, she scolded herself to be more careful as she hurried inside and shut the front door. Clearly shaken by the close encounter, she surmised that it had been some kind of wild animal. She might have suspected a bear, but the brown bear had long been extinct here. Besides, whatever had dashed past her hadn't been brown, but white and large. Moving so rapidly on its hind legs, the creature had to have been a biped.

And just what bipedal animal, the size of a large bear, was native to Ireland?

# *A Message From the Author*

**By Kathy Morgan**

I hope you enjoyed the ongoing romp through magical Ireland with Arianna, Michaela and Tara in *Dark Obsession,* the second book in the *Celtic Magic Trilogy*. If so, would you please take a few moments to share your opinion by posting a review on Amazon?

And if the sample chapter of the final book in the trilogy, *Dark Awakening,* intrigues you, please drop me an email requesting to be placed on my mailing list for notification of future releases. You can reach me at www.dreamweaverpublishing.com

Many thanks to all my readers, who make the writing so much fun. I look forward to hearing from you!

Made in the USA
Middletown, DE
16 March 2018